I0768520

Maran
Laden's Way
Siren's Way
Maranee River
Keep
Grand Council Keep
Nerine
Parth
Shale
Marance Falls
Dunnea
Fenik
Banki
Relan
SunSpar
Palandra

Baskan Mountains
Baskan Desert
Darkwood
Marane Desert
Murkwater Swamp
Murkwater Lake
Bandit Camp
Nodon
Helna
Bandit Camp
Helnan Grasslands
Shradan
Flagon
Shradan Mines
N
E
S
W

BOUND

ISBN: 979-8-9907379-0-7 (Hardcover)

ISBN: 979-8-9907379-1-4 (Paperback)

ISBN: 979-8-9907379-2-1 (E-book)

This is a work of fiction. Any references to historical events, real people, or real places are used fictitiously. Names, characters, and places are products of the author's imagination.

Cover design and graphics © Breyanna I.L. Evans
Book design © Breyanna I.L. Evans

AzureStar
First printing edition 2024.

breyannaevansauthor@gmail.com
breyannailevansauthor.weebly.com
@breyannailevans

BREYANNA I.L. EVANS

Also by Breyanna I.L. Evans

YA Fiction and Fantasy
Azure Light (Written under Breyanna I.L. James)
Crimson Darkness
Emerald Shadow
Clairvoyance

Children's Books
What I Do Know
Especially You

Poetry
Accidentally External: A Poetry and Short Story Compilation
(Written under Breyanna I.L. James)

Blog
"Writings" breyannailevansauthor.weebly.com

For Brandon, to whom I am mystically, inexplicably bound.

BOUND

BREYANNA I.L. EVANS

Dark, angry clouds roll rapidly across the moonlit sky above me, faster than they should. A cold wind whips dry leaves, dust, and small bits of rubbish all around me. I stand, curved sword drawn just a few paces away from a tall, sturdy man who does the same. The sword's steady weight is a comfort to me, blade tip hanging just inches above the cobblestone streets of this busy city. I look around calmly, confident, ready for the fight that will soon begin. Curious, concerned, and gossiping onlookers gather; exiting shops and shoving each other in order to get a good, safe vantage point to view the fight from.

I draw in a deep breath and close my eyes briefly, just long enough to center myself. Then I lunge, blade clamoring against blade as my opponent, someone I vaguely recognize, shuffles to bring his sword up to catch mine in the nick of time.

The moment he recovers from the shock of my attack, he's out for blood, and although his swings are sloppy, they're wild – relentless. We dance around each other, my moves graceful, trained, calculated, and his erratic. I watch him as he tires, but someone else joins the fight, swinging another blade in a similar heated manner. I sidestep quickly, dodging his blows at first, only catching one quick swing across the lower part of my shoulder, just below where the shoulder-plate of my golden armor ends. The swipe leaves a long wound on my bicep. I take out that assailant with ease and turn my focus back onto my target, rolling my shoulder to see just how badly the man, now unconscious and bleeding on the street, got me. The cut stings, and I'll likely need stitches, but there's been no damage to the muscle.

My opponent has worn himself out now, and despite the bleeding in my arm, I've barely broken a sweat. In three moves, I have him on the ground with his friend. The first move allows me to sweep around him, tucking my leg beneath his, causing him to lose his balance. With the second move I've disarmed him, and I now wield his sword in my left hand. In the third move, I strike the man with the pommel of his own weapon, and he collapses to the ground with a *thud*. The crowd around me explodes in a cacophony of cheers and gasps.

I smile and roll my wounded shoulder again.

Ah, the thrill of the fight.

Except, I have never been in a fight.

This city looks nothing like my village.

And I have no idea how to use a sword.

I wake up covered in sweat and blood with a searing pain in my shoulder. It's the same thing that's happened nearly every day of my life. I always manage to obtain inexplicable injuries, even in my waking hours, though the moments I procure these injuries in my dreams are the wildest. My dreams are always so intense. Before I venture a look down, I know what I'll find. Sure enough, when I gaze downward, dark red blood trickles down my arm from an open wound just below my shoulder.

I groan, clutch the wound to avoid getting more blood on my bedsheets, and do my best to climb out of bed without waking my sister, who sleeps soundly across the room.

I shuffle quietly into the latrine and close the door, letting out a deep sigh before reaching beneath the sink for my sewing kit, some bandages, and my trusty numbing cream, which I apply generously to the wound even before I've cleaned it.

I'm in the middle of cleaning myself up when the door opens and my nine-year-old sister's head peers in.

"Lane, is your disorder acting up again?" Lilah asks, rare blonde hair just like our mamman's hanging all around her face. Her soft, youthful and carefully manicured hands work to rub the sleep from her eyes.

"Guess so," I mumble, holding the bandage between my chin and collar bone as I begin stitching myself up. This numbing cream is extra potent, and it does wonders to numb the pain. Still, I feel the tugging of the needle as I pull it through, over and over again. The village doctor told me years ago that I bruise and bleed so easily because my skin is abnormally fragile. That explanation has never made any sense to me. There have been times where I've hurt myself and didn't bruise or bleed at all. It's only the injuries without a clear cause that turn out like this. This has happened so often for me throughout my life that when I was young, I was sure some kind of magic was behind it, though any talk of magic was quickly dismissed or shut down by the adults around me. The doctor was convinced that I simply had a rare medical condition, so everyone else was, too.

"Sorry, sis," Lilah says, her voice small. She's concerned, as usual.

I shrug, and the action sends a wave of nauseating pain through my arm. The surface is numb, but the wound is still tender, especially after stitching it.

"I'm fine," I say. Then, "Give me a hand with this?" I gesture with my chin and the bandage tumbles to the floor, unravelling.

"Have you been taking your medicine?" Lilah asks as she kneels on the floor beside me. She scoops up the mess of bandaging and passes it back to me.

"Yes," I lie. I don't want her to worry, but I haven't taken my medicine in quite some time. All the medicine does is make me sick to my stomach all day. It does nothing to prevent these injuries, or even to heal them more quickly. I heal quickly enough as it is, anyway.

Lilah winces as she gets a closer look at the long line of stitches.

"You must have bumped something pretty hard... maybe you should go back to the doctor. Increase your dose, or something..." she trails off as I bite back a small moan. I wrap the wound and tie off the bandage.

"Maybe I'll stop by on my way out of town tomorrow," I assure her, tousling her fine hair. I turn and rummage through my sewing kit until I find a bottle of pain serum. The numbing cream is strong initially, but it wears off quickly, and I'm going to need some rest if I want to make good time tomorrow. I open the bottle and take a swig, gulping down the too sweet liquid before it sits too long on my tongue.

Lilah makes a face.

"Let's get you back to bed, huh? If Mamman and Pappan find out we were out of bed, there will be extra chores for both of us tomorrow, and I don't want to be late."

Lilah scrunches up her nose and nods, heading back into our bedroom. She pauses at the door, though, and turns to embrace me. She takes care to avoid my injured arm and whispers into my nightgown, "I love you, Lane. I'm sorry you hurt so easily."

I take a deep breath and return her embrace. "Love you too, Lilah," I whisper back. I catch a glimpse of us in the mirror, and once again, I'm blown away by the stark contrast in our appearance. Lilah's blonde hair and fair skin practically glows in comparison to my black hair and olive complexion.

When I wake, the heat of the late morning sun caresses my face. I sit up in my bed and peer across the room, where Lilah's bed is already empty and neatly made. I rub at my arm, still sore and tender as the memory of last night and my dream come rushing back to me. The pain serum has worn off, leaving my body achy and tired, but I'll manage. With how frequently I obtain these injuries, I'm used to waking up sore. I get out of bed, carefully get dressed, and slowly slip into my jacket just as Lilah skips into our bedroom, golden pigtails bouncing.

"How's your arm?" she asks, big blue eyes full of concern.

I frown and lean backward, looking through the open bedroom door into the hallway that leads to the kitchen.

"Lilah... why did they let me sleep so late?" I ask. I breathe in slowly and count to ten, doing my best not to lose my temper: She knows I hate to be late. She rolls her eyes and swings her arms, slapping her hands against the skirt of her dress each time they pass her legs.

"Don't worry, Lane. I didn't tell them. Though I don't know why you'd want to keep secrets from them," she says, tone scolding. "I just told them you didn't sleep well. Pappan is still loading up materials in the square, so he said you could sleep a while. He sent me to wake you just now."

I nod as we make our way into the kitchen.

Our home is quiet.

"Where's Mamman?" I ask.

Lilah seats herself at the table and nibbles on a freshly baked roll. She must have been awake for some time now if she's already finished her baking. Around her mouthful of bread, she speaks.

"She's also preparing to leave, but I think you woke just in time to say goodbye. She should be out any minute."

"This early?" I ask. "She's not meant to depart for another two days." What in Maran could Mamman and the Council have to discuss that would require her to go even earlier than usual? I grab a roll myself and tear it apart with my fingers, putting bits of it into my mouth.

"Yes, well, you know we have to be prepared for the unexpected," Mamman says, walking briskly into the kitchen, putting an earring into place. "All village representatives have been summoned to come as quickly as possible. There's been talk of an increase in bandit activity throughout Maran, and we must make haste to find a solution to the problem. They grow in numbers by the day."

Mamman plants a kiss on my head as she passes, attention focused on packing herself a bag of food for her journey. She seems more frantic than usual, and her eyes are glazed, as though her mind is far away. Perhaps she's worried about her travels. With the protection and horses that the Women's Council provides every city's representative, Grand Council Keep is still at least a five day's ride from here.

"This means *you* need to be extra careful out there, and write every chance you get, you understand?" she says.

"Always, Mamman," I tell her.

"I've got to get going now; I'm already late to meet Ezekiel and the crew," she says, pulling Lilah into a tight embrace. Lilah closes her eyes and squeezes Mamman right back.

On her way out of the room, Mamman pauses to hold my face in her hands.

"I wish you safe passage and swift return," she says. Her blue eyes, same as Lilah's, glimmer with tears, as they do every time she has to travel to the Keep.

"I wish a safe passage and swift return for you, as well, Ma'," I tell her, patting her hand with mine.

I was supposed to take my Mamman's place on the Council when I come of age on my eighteenth birthday with the rise of the new year, but when she fell ill with Lilah in her belly when I was eight, Pappan started taking me with him on his deliveries. I quickly found I enjoyed his job much better. I've been training with him since then, and when I turned seventeen this year, he allowed me to fully take over as he moved into a new position.

Lilah, however, is the perfect little lady for the Women's Council, and has even been allowed to sit in on Council meetings from time to time despite her young age.

I snag an apple and another roll from the table before securing my bow and quiver of arrows onto my back, then reach with my good arm to toss the bag I'd packed yesterday over my shoulder. Knowing Pappan, if I delay our delivery schedule any later, I'll never hear the end of it.

Outside, the sky is filled with puckered clouds that threaten rain. I rush through the streets of our village, which is now beginning to bustle with people as shops open and many of our village's forges ignite. The smell of coal, hot steel, soot and sweat mixes with that of the bakery's fresh breads and cakes baked early this morning. In the distance, I hear young children running about the streets, laughing and calling after one another. And of course, there's the ever-present sound of someone hammering two metals together.

As I weave past shops and through alleyways, I hear the typical greetings.

"Another trip, Lane?"

"Have a safe delivery, Lane!"

"Safe travels and swift return."

As I pass the smith whom I always get my arrowheads from, I hear the same, "Bring me back something rare to work with" that I always get.

Although I've never found him anything rare besides some damaged wagon wheels and other scraps of discarded metal, I reply with, "I will!"

I pass through the village square and duck into the storage cabin without invitation. I make my way through the back to, the area where we load our supplies prior to every trip. Here, I know my pappan will be waiting.

As expected, there he is, accompanied by his two consultants and the village chief, Bron. The men are arguing over numbers when I approach them.

"Argus," Chief Bron starts at my pappan. My pappan waves off whatever comment Chief Bron was about to make.

"Good morning, young miss Shrayan," Chief Bron tells me. Despite the many years of friendship shared between Chief Bron and my pappan, he insists on calling me by our surname.

"Ah, there she is!" Pappan sighs, gesturing in my direction, looking ready to scold me. "I thought you'd sleep all day! I was getting ready to send *Damar* in your stead," he says sarcastically.

Although Pappan's comment was clearly a joke, it stings my ego. Not just anybody can lead the team as I do. I've been taking these delivery trips for the greater half of my life. Especially now, since the last year's deliveries have been led by me, my pride for my job has me cringing at the thought of *Damar* of all people leading the team.

Damar, the chief's grandson, and one of my greatest annoyances since childhood, peeks around the cargo he's been loading at the mention of his name. Excitement is spelled plainly across his face. He obviously doesn't understand the jest.

Damar has always been eager and overly positive, a trait I find to be exhausting and obnoxious. In addition to that, because our pappans have been good friends since before we were born, he's taken to following me around my entire life. No matter how many times I tell him to find someone else to bother, he's like a shadow at my heels. My only reprieve from his incessant presence comes with leaving town on these trips. There's no way I would let him come with us.

"Come on, Pappan. Don't get his hopes up," I say, turning to fake an apologetic glance at Damar. It's best to keep my cool in front of his pappan, at least. "Besides, you know I'm the next best option after you. I know our route better than almost anyone."

"Oh, please let me go with you, Lane. I'm strong. I know I'd be of use to you in other villages. If your pappan would allow it, I promise I won't get in the way, Damar begs.

Fates. Despite Damar being my age, he sure can whine like a child.

"Damar, Damar," I say smoothly, already turning back to Pappan and the chief. "It's not that we don't *want* you to come; it's just that you're needed here. You protect the entry point for the entire village. If you came with us, there's no telling what could happen to our homes, our people."

Pappan and chief Bron share a look of raised eyebrows and run their hands through their long, dark, graying beards.

"You know, son," chief Bron says. "She has a valid argument. You were appointed by the Council that position. Leaving it without first training a substitute would be highly irresponsible. There's no time for you to train a substitute before Lane and her team leave for their deliveries today, is there?"

Damar's face falls, and his shoulders slump.

"No, sir."

"It's settled then," I say, trying to hold back the relief I feel. "At least for now, until you can find another *qualified* Guardian to tend to things while you're away, you'll stay here and protect our people. If not you, Damar, I don't know *who* will."

"Sure, Lane," Damar says before skulking away. I feel a twinge of guilt, but it quickly dissipates when the rest of my crew comes in from the carts.

"All loaded up," says Zaid, the newest member of my crew. He brushes ash from his hands onto his worn trousers.

I nod, doing my best not to blush. I've always liked Zaid, but he really grew up over the summer months, and since he was hired onto my team last month, I can't seem to shake him. Zaid's hair is nearly black like mine, like most of us here in Palandra, and he has the same olive skin I do. His eyes are such a dark brown they appear almost black, and having grown so much recently, he's nearly a head taller than me, all sturdy muscle from the various internships he's participated in this summer. He smiles warmly at me.

"Morning, Zaid. Is everyone else ready to go? Horses cared for?" I ask.

"Everyone's good to go except you," he states, reaching out to pat the wild hair I forgot to tame this morning. "Four horses, two carts, and four crew members, minus one," he winks, pointing at me. "Philip and Loren are double checking the cart attachments while they wait for you."

My face begins to burn, and I turn away, pretending to check for the all-clear from Pappan and the others. I work to fix my hair and pull it into a tight braid as they inspect our load and approve our departure.

"That should be everything," Pappan says as chief Bron begins chatting politics with Pappan's men. "Your trip will take about eight days' time. Deliver the listed supplies to their specific destinations, then turn around and come on back."

Pappan passes me the finalized list. Then, he pulls me into an embrace so that only I can hear him.

"If anything happens," he whispers.

"Send a letter. I know, Pa'."

He laughs then lets me go with a firm pat on the back.

"Then you're ready. Have a safe trip, Lane. Fates be with you and the crew."

I check out the carts as I pass them. Everything seems to be in order. I mount my horse at the head of the team, and we roll out to the village gates with stocked carts in tow. As we pass through the exit, I catch Lilah's blonde pigtails in my peripheral vision. As she has every trip since she could walk, Lilah chases after us, waving frantically. I blow her a kiss as I have every departure, and she pretends to catch it, waving her closed fist in the air.

Until next time, little sister, I think, and I turn my gaze to the road ahead.

The village grows smaller as we put distance between it and our carts, and my body relaxes. I don't know if it's because I've taken these trips my entire life – long before Pappan started staying back to focus on things in Palandra and letting me take over – but something about being out here in the world is equal parts calming and thrilling to me. One large part of this job I've always loved is the traveling, getting to see some of Maran's many different landscapes and cultures. One day, I hope to see them all. For now, though, I'm grateful to be able to explore the cities and cultures close to home.

Palandra, the village I've called home my entire life, is located on the southernmost peninsula of Maran, with high walls on every side to protect us from the elements. Thanks to our geographical location, we get all kinds of harsh weather – raging storms from the sea, as well as sand storms from all sides when the wind carries no water.

Inside those walls, though, despite the harsh and sandy wilderness around us, we've built a fortitude. Our village contains the largest smithing enterprise in Maran, and my pappan used our sought-after metalworks to create the most profitable trade route on this side of the Maranee River. What started as a trade in metal goods – weapons, armor, kitchen appliances, and so on – quickly turned into a multi-level shipping company, taking and delivering orders from several places along the route.

As we travel farther away from home and into the wilderness – and as the sun moves across the sky above us – our surroundings contain more and more, green vegetation, starting with small bits of dark green grass, to shrubs, and finally, to lush, tropical trees. I've always loved the trees in this region, with their flowers of orange, yellow and red. Every time the wind picks up and rustles the fronds of these flowering trees, the sweet smell of their blossoms fills the lungs of everyone around. To me, these flowers smell of adventure. Of hope.

For newer members of the crew, this is always the time when excitement takes over and the urge to explore this vivid environment becomes almost too much to bear. Having grown up working this trade route, I've been well schooled in the reasons why we don't leave our designated path and its surrounding areas. Although beautiful, Maran can be a dangerous place.

Mostly, my adventures have always been without incident, though my pappan has warned me often enough of the animals that can pose a threat in these regions.

On one trip when I was ten, my pappan and I came across a family of wild forest cats with deep black spots. Another time, a couple of years later, our caravan was intruded upon by a large black bear who dug through our shipment of fish in the night. Both times, I had the protection of my pappan and the rest of the crew. After that last incident, however, I started training and honing my archery skills, just in case.

I've run into other situations where predators encroached upon our camp or crossed our paths, but thankfully, these incidents have been without injury to anyone on the team.

My crew and I set up camp for the night beneath the canopy of several large-leafed, fruit bearing trees with bright red flowers. Though their fruit is not in season, the smell of it is thick and sweet in the air, and I find myself taking longer, deeper breaths as we settle in for the night.

Zaid approaches me in my tent as I stand at a table and pour over the map of our route and the list of supplies that need to be delivered or picked up in each village and city.

He clears his throat, standing just inside the entrance. Without looking up, I wave him in.

"Checking our routes?" he asks. I nod, chewing my bottom lip.

"We'll reach Dunnen by tomorrow, early afternoon, if the weather is clear," I tell him, drawing my finger along the map from Palandra to Dunnen, the first little town on our route. "We're set do deliver two crates of cookware and pick up a shipment of flatbread, flour, and corn. We'll rest the night there."

Although I don't look up at him directly, I can see Zaid nod in my peripheral vision.

I drag my finger past Dunnen.

"Then we'll head to SunSpar. We should be there late the next day if we travel straight through." I know that Zaid has already seen our route and the accompanying list. I never take the crew anywhere without having everyone aware of where we're going and what we're doing. Still, talking things out helps me keep everything straight, and it's something I'm comfortable talking to Zaid about. If we talked about anything else, I worry I wouldn't know what to say, and I like having him around to talk with.

"Weather permitting, of course," Zaid replies. He eyes the list that sits beside my map.

"Of course," I say. When I look up at him, he's got a little smile on his face. He's been with me on these trips a few times before, and I always seem to forget how funny he thinks it is when I add things like "weather permitting" to my estimates, though I don't think it's amusing in the slightest.

I've been caught in too many storms to *guarantee* on-time delivery.

My stomach flutters as I realize I've just been staring at him. I turn quickly back to focusing on my map and nervously tuck some loose strands of hair behind my ears. Fates, I hate how nervous he makes me.

"SunSpar has requested the wagon of shields, a crate of spearheads, and a crate of fishhooks." I tap SunSpar's order on our list, all too aware of how close my finger is to Zaid's. I clear my throat. "From SunSpar, we'll take four barrels of their Sparrenfish up to Nerine."

Zaid chuckles.

"What?" I ask.

"Nothing like traveling for two days with four barrels of fish," he says.

I titter. "At least their barrels are insulated now. Trust me, it used to be *so much worse*, especially in the summer. We might get some rain now that things are cooling off, but in the summer months, when no rain came to wash the stench of those uninsulated barrels, oh there were times I wished for nothing more than the rain."

"All the more reason to appreciate those storms, then, it seems," Zaid says. He meets my gaze and holds it for a moment, his dark eyes glittering, before he turns back to our list. I blink, focusing on the list as well, though my mind is purely focused on remembering that look on his face. Zaid continues, "Think they need all those spearheads for fishing?"

I've wondered the same thing. I've seen people fishing with spears when I have visited SunSpar in the past, but ordering so many after receiving the same amount with our last shipment does make me question if there might be another reason they might want those spearheads. Not that anyone from SunSpar would ever tell us. SunSpar aligns with the Women's Council rulings and guidelines, and they trade with Palandra, but that's about as involved as they ever get with other parts of Maran.

I frown at my map for some time before looking back at Zaid, who leans against the table, smiling at me. That smile brings the blush back to my cheeks, and I open my mouth to change the subject when Loren bursts into my tent.

"Sorry to disturb you, Lane," he says, green eyes flitting between Zaid and me. "But we have a problem."

His red hair has been pulled into a braid that falls halfway down his back. Loren is from Parth, originally, but he moved to live in Palandra with his parents so his pappan could apprentice with one of our finest blacksmiths when Loren was a boy. He's a year older than I am and towers well over a foot higher than me. Even across the tent, I need to look up to see his face clearly.

I stand up straight as Loren steps closer. He's out of breath, and his forehead is soaked with sweat.

"What is it?" I ask, already turning to reach for my bow and arrows, which are never far from me.

"Cats. We've got two of them tracing the tree line. They're eyeing the horses."

I stride from my tent to get a look for myself. The sun is setting, the sky fading from a bright, vibrant orange at the horizon to a deep, rich blue farther up. The dim lighting makes it difficult to see anything too far from our camp. I squint my eyes against the darkening rays of the setting sun, and sure enough, I catch sight of them.

Two spotted forest cats are weaving their way back and forth through the trees, biding their time until nightfall.

These cats are small, though. Cubs. Typical forest cats can grow to be up to four feet high and over eight feet long, tail and all. Where's their mamman? I scan the tree line, but I see no mamman anywhere.

"Where's Philip?" I ask, keeping my eyes on the trees.

"He's out filling our canteens," Loren tells me, trying to contain the panic in his voice. This is the first time these members of my team have been confronted by cats. Although I've been through this before, I can't deny the pounding of my heart or the sweating in my palms. I'm the leader, now. It is my responsibility to protect the crew.

I click my tongue.

"Loren, I want you to keep your eyes on these cubs. Make sure you watch both of them. And call for me *immediately* if you see any more."

Loren nods nervously.

"Zaid?" I call, but I turn around to see that he's already behind me and ready for orders.

"I've never seen cats like these so far from the heart of the forest, and never this far west. What do you think they're doing out here?" he asks.

I pause, narrowing my eyes, considering his question.

"My guess would be that they're looking for their ma'. I'm not going to wait to find out. Zaid, gather the horses. Tie them up in the center of camp with the carts and Guard them."

Zaid has spent some time training in combat, and I've never been on a trip with him where he wasn't armed with a sword at his hip. He grasps the hilt of his sword now.

"Got it," he replies, determination accentuating the sharp line of his jaw as he clenches his teeth.

I square my shoulders and grip my bow, nocking it with an arrow.

"I'm going to get Philip," I say.

It's a short walk through the trees to the small stream where I sent Philip to refill our water canteens. I'm there within minutes. At first, I don't see him. Then, at the water's edge, I find him, standing still as a statue, eyes locked with those of the cubs' mamman.

She's crouching, the tip of her tail twitching back and forth. Her spots blend into her ever-darkening surroundings, but her eyes glow threateningly.

Slowly, I make my way to Philip's side.

"Fates, Lane, I'm so glad to see you," he says, starting to pull his gaze away.

"Don't break eye contact," I tell him through gritted teeth. "You've got her waiting right now. Don't. Move."

I draw my bowstring back with some effort – the pain in my arm is still present as ever – and I worry I might tear my stitches. I hold steady, though, and aim through the growing darkness. I take a deep breath, center myself, focusing my gaze on the large cat before us. *Don't hurt her, Lane,* I tell myself. *Concentrate.* Then, I let my arrow fly through the air. It imbeds itself in the ground at the mamman cat's front paws, making her jump. She looks from the arrow to me. She crouches yet again, and I take another breath. I work to draw another arrow without ripping my stitches, gritting my teeth against the pain. Then I let it loose. As intended, it lands just beside the other one, and she jumps again and growls deeply before turning tail and bounding into the trees.

Philip lets out the breath he's been holding.

"Fates," he says. I pat him on the back as he brushes sweaty, black curls of hair from his forehead. "I thought I was dead, for sure."

"Not on my watch," I tell him, letting out a huff of breath. "You're too important to this team to go out like that. Let's get back to camp, shall we?"

We hike back toward where we've made our camp, where Zaid and Loren are waiting for us. When we do get back to camp, the cubs are nowhere to be seen.

"Scare them off?" Zaid asks. I smile.

"I'm going to get some sleep before it gets dark," I tell my team. "Philip, go relax a little bit. You deserve it. Loren, take the first watch. Wake me right away if you spot those cats again."

Thank Fates, the cats do not reappear, though their strange behavior in leaving their habitat keeps me up for a while. Something must have driven them out.

3

The remainder of our trip to Dunnen goes smoothly, and as expected, we arrive in the early afternoon.

Dunnen is a small village along the banks of the Maranee River's branch that divides the north-western part of Maran from the south-western. This place is known for their wheat crop, corn-based soups, and flatbreads. Its people have always been kind and welcoming to my Pappan, though they've scolded him for allowing someone as young as I to be traveling on such errands.

Since my pappan shifted leadership to me, I dread coming to Dunnen.

Still, we soldier on. Wheat fields surround the road into Dunnen on either side and sprawl out for miles. The moment we enter the village, we're hit with the smell of flour, freshly baked flatbread, which has a softer, more earthy smell than the loaves baked in Palandra and other towns throughout Maran. Stronger than the bread smell, however, is the savory fragrance of soup, being cooked in several kitchens throughout the village. The dirt streets and the flour mill leave thin layers of dust on everything, and I feel the constant need to blow my nose whenever I'm here.

Although the people of Dunnen are expecting our delivery, we are greeted with grumbles and scowls as we pass through the streets with our carts in tow. This village contains a mix of the dark skin and hair from Palandra and SunSpar and the lighter tones from places like Parth and Nerine. Still, they live under the same hot sun that we do, and their serious way of life has set deep lines in all of their faces. We stop into the market to meet with our "partner" and unload the cookware we've brought, but of course we're greeted by an older woman with a frown on her face.

"Anda," I say, greeting her with as much warmth as I can muster. I reach my hand out to shake hers, even though I know already that she'll refuse.

My crew stands behind me, untying ropes and checking the crates.

As I expected, Anda folds her arms across her chest.

"Lane. When is your Pappan going to be back to doing this? I liked him better."

I suppress a sigh.

"Anda, he's retiring," I say. "He won't be back doing, you know that."

Anda harumphs, and her frown is now accompanied by an angry scowl.

"Irresponsible, letting such youth take over business. You've no experience," she tells me, even though I've been visiting this village with my pappan on his deliveries for years. "I don't like doing business with you young folk. I always have to double check everything so you don't screw it up."

It takes everything in me to keep from rolling my eyes.

It's not just Anda. Almost everyone here in Dunnen shares the same view of us "young folk." Philip steps up behind me, ready to retort, but I put my hand up. Dunnen's crop is the most sought after on the western side of the Maranee River. Without it, we would lose a lot of business. As my pappan would tell me, our delivery business needs ignorant fools like this to keep the flow. Every village and city has something important to offer, so it's best to keep the peace.

"Well, Anda, you are welcome to double check anything you like. My crew has just unloaded the goods you ordered. Boys, go ahead and crack those open. Let our esteemed customer take a closer look."

Anda sneers at me and keeps her distance as she shuffles past me, as if my youth might wear off on her. The brown, loose-fitting clothing she wears drags on the ground, leaving tiny trails in the flour and dirt at her feet.

As she checks her load, then double checks it, other Dunnians can be heard shouting and hollering at each other across the market. She stands up straight, popping her back, and gives me a single, solemn nod.

"Very well. I'll send Jasper out with your payment. Have your *boys* carry these crates into the shop," she says, already walking away. She turns back briefly to shout at my crew. "And be careful with those! I won't pay for anything you break!"

The moment she's disappeared back into her shop, my crew and I exhale a sigh of relief. Anda's husband Jasper isn't a ray of sunshine, either, but he's at least more reserved about his feelings toward anyone under the age of forty.

He grumbles his greetings, takes a quick peek into the crates we've brought, then drops five silver pieces into my hand. I roll them around my palm with my thumb, then give him a look that's half narrowed eyes and half smirk.

"Jasper, we've been over this. The price of two crates of cookware like this is six silvers each, a price we've already cut in half because we're also picking the flatbread, corn, and flour."

Jasper grumbles something under his breath and shuffles his feet. I hold my hand out, palm up, waiting for the other coin.

"Well..." he starts.

"We've given you a more than fair price, considering the cost of the metals we've used, the amount of product you're getting, and the amount of goods we're taking from you. If you'd like to pay full price, I can get the corn and flour directly from the miller and the flatbread from another baker."

Jasper's shoulders slump. We go through this same argument every time, but still, he seems surprised and upset that I'd ask him to pay more than he did.

"Oh, fine," he mutters, reaching a large, calloused hand into the pocket of his trousers. He fishes around in there for a moment before pulling out another silver piece and dropping it with a *clink* into my hand.

"Thank you, Jasper. That's better." I dare to reach out and pat him on the shoulder, which sends him grumbling all the way back into the shop.

"Would you like us to follow him, Lane?" Loren asks.

I nod.

"Yes, go ahead and follow him. Be extra careful with those crates, okay? We don't need to give them any more reason to want us out of here," I tell them.

Zaid smiles at me, but he says nothing. Instead, he reaches down and picks up the smaller of the two crates and carries it into the shop. Loren and Philip each take a side of the larger crate. I make my way to the carts to rearrange things so that the goods the boys bring back out won't shift around too much as we travel. Once we've got everything loaded back up and accounted for, the real task begins: Finding a place to stay.

The sun is only beginning to set, and while I hate wasting travel time, there's no way we would get to SunSpar before having to make camp somewhere, and the desert sands between here and SunSpar are softer, easily shifted and carried away on the wind. There's nowhere we could stake down our tents, and the unrelenting night winds would bother the horses at best and topple our carts at worst.

Unfortunately, finding a place to stay in a village full of people who don't want you there is tricky. We do have one place we can go, but whether or not we'll be allowed to stay there is entirely dependent on who is working the front desk. If it's the owner, forget it. We'll have to backtrack or sleep on the streets. If it's the owner's daughter, however, we'll be lucky enough to get a room as long as we're gone early in the morning.

The Fates are on our side this trip, it seems. When we walk into the inn, we are greeted by a sweet girl, probably twenty years of age, with long, light brown hair, bright green eyes, and freckles covering the entirety of her pale face. She smiles warmly at us, then takes a quick look around.

"Two rooms, Lane?" she whispers. I nod.

"That would be great, thank you, Selena."

"Do you have both carts this time?" she asks, scribbling an alias for each member of my crew into her log.

"That's right."

"Alright. Go ahead and pull them into the back shed, behind the horses. You can keep your carts and horses tied up in there, so long as you have them out before dawn. That's when Pappan will take over."

"Out before dawn. Got it. Thank you as always, Selena. You are a gem amongst coal."

She smiles timidly, looks around once more, and nods us toward the back staircase, sliding two keys across the wooden countertop.

"*Before* dawn. I'll bring some food up to your rooms soon. Is corn chowder okay?"

"Perfect," I say.

The boys wait for the all-clear, then they load our carts and tie up our horses in one of the sheds that are used for storing extra kitchen supplies for the inn. When everything has been secured, and the horses fed and watered, they meet me up in the hallway. Our rooms are beside each other. One room for me, and one room for the three others to share. Before this year, I would share my room with my Pappan, but now that it's just me, I get the luxury of having a room to myself, not that I feel I need the privacy. We spend most of our time together, anyway.

We share a meal in my room, then we all head to bed, even though the sun hasn't fully set yet.

I wake long before the sun has risen. Three knocks on the boy's door has Zaid answering, dark eyes tired and puffy, but he's dressed and ready to go. All three of them are. Perfect.

Selena is nowhere to be found when we take our leave, though I leave a silver piece and both keys for her beneath the lip of the counter, where she's hollowed out a little hiding place, because we don't always have enough time to pay when she gives us our keys.

We wrestle the remaining night winds as we head toward SunSpar. Throughout the day as we travel, we deal with a number of obstacles. Mainly, the sand slows us. It shifts beneath our feet, and the horses don't do very well pulling the carts through, so despite having installed metal plates beneath our wheels for this part of our journey, we have to get off our horses and push the carts often.

The heat of the sun also beats down on us, but being from Palandra, we're accustomed to this obstacle. The only person who has any real trouble with the sun is Loren, who is used to the cooler weather and shade that the city of Parth provides. We pause frequently to allow him water breaks and brief moments to catch his breath and rest his muscles. Traveling through sand can be difficult for those not used to it, and it wears on the body.

Being within the city of SunSpar, however, is a tougher experience altogether.

We're met at the city's borders and escorted through the streets. We get there early evening, so of course we're going to have to find another place to stay in yet another town that merely tolerates us for our services.

SunSpar's people do not dislike us for our youth. They are mistrusting of anyone who lives outside the reaches of their city, and this mistrust is reflected in the silence that ensues and the suspicious glances that people cast anytime we come near anyone.

The city, however, is absolutely beautiful. Every building in the entire city is a mosaic of different colored blue stones, and in the evening sunlight, they sparkle like fish scales. The streets are laid with pearls and glimmering bits of oyster and sea shells. The attention to detail is a reflection of the SunSparian's intelligence and craftmanship, as well as their love for the sea. The city carries the slight scent of fish, but it's masked by the smell of sand and the salt of the ocean.

Nearly everyone in the city has sun darkened skin and long dark hair, much like those native to Palandra. The armor that they wear varies in color depending on the rank of the person wearing it. Foot soldiers and Guards wear silver armor with lapis-colored accents. Higher ranking Guards and commanders wear golden armor with white and azure accents, and city officials wear pearlescent armor with white accents.

We meet with the city Chieftess within a building I can only describe as a lavish palace. We meet with her outside the entrance, as she stands before two tall, long, curved doors that seal in the middle with stained-glass windows reaching up at least ten feet on either side.

The Chieftess is a strong woman who stands with her shoulders back and her chin high. Her black hair is pulled back into long, intricate braids that hang in loops well past the middle of her back. Wrinkles have just begun to decorate her face, and she wears them well.

"Welcome," she says to us, as we finish unloading her order and relinquish our carts and our horses into the hands of her Guards. City custom requires that our carts be searched and held until we are ready to leave. I've always felt this to be an invasion of our privacy, but Pappan has always told me to respect the customs of the places we visit and check to ensure everything is all there before we leave. If ever we come up short when we get our belongings back, we can take the matter to the Council.

"Your stock will be safe while you are within city limits," the Chieftess says.

Despite the kind words, her tone is frigid, formal at best. I meet her formality.

"We thank you, Chieftess, for your kindness."

"You've brought everything on the list we sent, I presume?" she asks, thin eyebrows raised.

I can't help but notice the men behind her. Her Guards, of course, are always around, but today they are mere steps behind their leader, hands ready at their glittering swords. I shift my weight and force my gaze back to meet hers.

"As always," I say, keeping my voice steady. I can tell by the shifting and fidgeting going on behind me that my crew feels just as uneasy as I do. "You are more than welcome to check anything you wish."

"Everything's there, alright," Philip remarks. He's been on our crew just a short while longer than Zaid, and he still has a hard time understanding why everyone feels the need to check our deliveries. "Must have a lot of fishing to do with the number of spearheads you ordered," he comments.

Loren smacks Philip's arm. He knows better than to comment on the orders we deliver.

Although the Chieftess keeps her composure, her eyes narrow and her head jerks in Philip's direction.

One of the Guards behind her moves forward, his mouth set in a thin line, a frown wrinkling his brow. The Chieftess puts her hand up, palm open, and the man stops in his tracks.

"Sean, please check the goods our Palandrian visitors have brought us. Amal, see to it that our guests find their rooms for the night. The orders of fish you placed will not be ready until morning. At that time, Amal here will send for you and escort you to the docks. Goodnight."

Without another word, the Chieftess turns her back to us. Her long white robes trail on the glimmering floor as she makes her way through the door of the palace, leaving us with one of her brawny, straight-faced men as the other makes his way to look through the equipment we brought in for them.

"This way," Amal grunts at us, touching me on the shoulder. I brace myself for the pain, but I've healed quite nicely. I've always healed quickly, and in this moment, I'm grateful for it. I move so that his hand releases me, and I glare at him, but I say nothing. Thankfully, he doesn't try to move me again.

"I am capable of finding my own way, thank you. You lead. We'll follow," I tell him. The boys behind me all step forward, ready to fight if need be. I'm touched by their intentions, but I hope they won't act on their protective urges.

We follow Amal through the palace doors. As a young girl, I always felt honored that the leaders of SunSpar would invite us to stay in their palace. Now, I know the truth: The palace is the most secure building in all of SunSpar, and they want to keep us right where they can see us. It's the same reason that, in all my years delivering here, I haven't taken a single step in SunSpar that wasn't escorted.

We're taken up several flights of intricately carved stairs, the walls of which are painted in lovely fresco paintings all depicting one ocean scene or another. Finally, we're escorted to our room. One room, for all of us, though the "room" we're staying in is a suite that's roughly the size of my entire house back home.

When Amal closes the doors behind us, we hear the door lock. This sound makes my skin crawl. I've always known that the people of SunSpar don't like visitors poking around, but I've never before been locked inside my room before. Philip, Loren, and Zaid – who is usually extremely level headed – all jump at the sound.

"They can't do that, can they?" Philip asks, looking to me for answers.

"We are in their territory. They can do whatever they want, though why they would lock us in here, I'm not sure," Zaid says. He turns and tries the door handle. The door doesn't budge.

"They're offended by your poking at their order, Phil," Loren says, tone sharp. Already, Loren has begun pacing.

Philip throws his hands up. "I didn't say anything wrong! It's not like I was insinuating they're building their own *army!*"

"To be fair, Philip," Zaid chimes in. He strides to the window and peeks outside. We're well above ground – no way to jump out of the window without serious injury, possibly even death. "Even I thought your comment was out of place. With how touchy these people are about Guarding their secrets, I can see how they'd be concerned."

I press two fingers to my forehead and rub it in small circles, trying to drown out their bickering.

"They've got to let us out of here!" Philip raises his voice. "We didn't do anything wrong!"

"Everyone, quiet!" I snap. This gets everyone's attention. Zaid sits on a lush, silky chaise lounge. Loren stops pacing and turns to look at me, and Philip relaxes enough that his shoulders are no longer up by his ears. I take a deep breath. "Listen. It's unusual for them to lock us in here, yes. But my mamman told me the Council is concerned about an increase in dangerous and criminal activity. Perhaps they're being extra cautious. Can you blame them? Look at this place." I gesture around at the luxury of the room surrounding us. "It's not like they've thrown us in a dungeon. The Chieftess said they would send for us in the morning. Let's wait out the night and see what happens. If those doors don't unlock by dawn, then we can panic. Sound good?"

The three boys exchange looks, then they nod.

The sun has now almost completely set, and I'm beat. I make my way to the large latrine with its pearlescent bathtub, close the door, and run myself a bath to wash the grime and sand from our travels off my body. When I'm finished and dressed, I do feel a little bit better having taken a bath, and as my crew members each take their turns in the latrine, I plop myself onto the large bed in the center of the room. The mattress is soft, the comforters and pillows downy.

Despite our agreement to wait until morning to panic, I have a hard time settling in for the night. Although the room is huge and there's plenty of space for everyone, I feel claustrophobic knowing we don't have a reasonable exit. Still, the exhaustion from our trip and the stress of working with people who treat us like outcasts eventually outweigh my anxiety, and I fall asleep.

We wake in the morning to a loud banging on the door. Zaid gets up and opens it to reveal Amal, just as moody and grim as yesterday.

"Get dressed. You are expected at the docks," he says, then turns his back.

The four of us scramble to get ready, then we are escorted through the city to the docks at the water's edge. Our carts have been drawn and await us there. Our horses have been brushed, fed, and harnessed. I assign Philip and Zaid to check our inventory as Loren helps me inspect the barrels of fish that have been prepared before they are sealed. The man working the docks squints at us as though he's staring directly at the sun, despite the fact that there's barely a splash of pink on the horizon. We still have hours before the sun has risen.

When everything looks good, I find myself relaxing a bit. Our load is safe, our order has been filled, and finally, we can put some distance between us and this tense, secretive city. We are escorted again to the city boundaries, and we're watched like mice by a hawk as we turn our backs and head toward Nerine. The more distance we put between us and SunSpar, the better we all can breathe.

On the third day we face a major rainstorm that blows in from the sea to our west. It slows our pace tremendously, not only because we have to stop every now and again to re-cover our load, but because our carts are weighed down by the rain, and the wheels are slow to move in the slick, wet sand. Even our own footsteps are weighted and laborious. Still, we trek onward, working as a team to continue through the storm.

The rain also slows us down because it's flooded the river we need to cross. Thankfully, we're able to find the bridge and slowly cross, but even with the bridge, we still trudge through a good six inches of cold water.

By the end of the third day the rain subsides, and we are able to set up camp, regroup, and get some decent sleep.

On the end of the fourth day, my crew and I reach the village of Nerine. This city sits on cliffs that rest above the sea, and its people have access to sea, desert, and forest, depending on what part of the city they exit from.

As with most cities in Maran, Nerine's farthest borders are speckled with fields and smaller homes. As we travel closer to the center of the city, the buildings are larger and more decadently crafted. Nerine's structures stand tall and straight. They aren't adorned with colorful stones and shells as are those in SunSpar. Instead, they are built from sturdy tan stone, with rooftops the color of deep, red rust. Royal blue flags with the sigil of the Women's Council, a circle of feminine figurines linking arms, hang from most windowsills.

I listen to the sound of horse hooves and cart wheels against the cobblestone streets and take a deep breath, thanking the Fates that we've finally reached a city that will welcome us.

Nerine's streets are filled with people running errands and talking to one another. Most of the residents of Nerine have blond hair, blue eyes, and fair skin, though there are enough travelers and residents that have come from other areas that hardly anyone even spares us a sideways glance. As one of the bigger cities in Maran, Nerine's residents are used to strangers passing through, and I'm glad for it.

I dismount my horse and secure my bow and arrows to her saddle. As it's the last village on our list for this trip, I have Loren and Philip ask about securing us all a room in one of the village's inns and board our horses for the night.

That leaves Zaid and me to unload our final delivery at the back of a storehouse in the center of the marketplace. Nerine is a much larger city than Palandra, and their market reflects that. Even at this time of day, when most shopkeepers are bringing their wares inside, exotic looking fruits and fish still fill some of the stalls.

A heavyset man in an embroidered apron approaches to greet us.

"Afternoon," the man says, sizing up the carts and bags we've brought him, which contain a variety of goods including turnips, potatoes, and miscellaneous metal items. He then turns to the insulated barrels, which all contain the fish we picked up in SunSpar.

"Good afternoon," I reply, setting down a sack of flour and reaching out a hand to shake with him. This is not the man I usually deal with, and I wonder briefly if there's been a complete change in staff.

"No, not *good* afternoon," the man grunts. "It's afternoon. I expected you here by midday. Much of my stock's already put away for the night. Thieves about, you know."

Zaid turns to me, dark eyes wide.

I sigh, eyeing the market. The man's right. Most of the stalls are now empty.

"I apologize for the delay, sir. The road was not quite as smooth as we anticipated," I tell him, recalling the rainstorm. This is why I always add "weather permitting" to my estimates. "We plan on staying the night here, and we can pick up the goods you wish to trade in the morning. You have everything on the list we sent last week, I presume?"

The man nods, brushing something off of his apron.

"Yes, yes. Everything will be there. And you get your sixty copper pieces, for the rest. Don't have any silvers, so I hope you have room to carry the coppers. Long as it's all here, you'll get your money." Again, the man eyes our delivery.

"It's there, all right."

The late afternoon sun catches something shining to my right side, and I turn to see someone extremely familiar ducking through the street. He's gone in an instant, and my curiosity peaks.

"Zaid, set this man's mind at ease, please. Go ahead and do the count and square away this part of the transaction. When he gives you the copper, you know what to do with it."

Zaid nods and turns with the man toward the delivery on the street.

"Let Philip and Loren know that I'll be back," I toss over my shoulder, hardly paying attention. I trust my team to take care of things, and I'm pulled by the urge to find out who this person is, and where I've seen him before.

I turn and make my way into the alley I thought I saw the familiar man go. After winding through the alley for a while, I pause, almost sure I've lost him. I think to turn back, but I catch yet another glint of light. This time, I catch a better view, and the shining armor sends a strange ping of recognition through my mind. I'm unsure if or where I've met this man, but I know I've seen this armor. The man opens a deep blue painted wooden door and walks inside yet another stone building proudly flying the flag of the Women's Council.

Giving it just a few seconds' delay, I follow the man into the building, running my hand along the doorframe as I pass inside. Once inside, I'm immediately hit with the smell of alcohol and sweat, so strong I can taste it. Loud, off-key piano music flutters over the indistinct chattering of drunken men and women.

At first I'm shocked by this scene, but I quickly recover. I've been in taverns before – in smaller villages and in my own – but this one is larger and busier than any I've visited. I clear my throat and, as nonchalantly as possible, I find a table in the far corner where I think I'll get the best view of the room, and I take a seat near the piano. I don't want to draw any attention to myself. Instead, I'd like to find a place where I can blend in and observe this person who I swear I've met before. Just standing around looking for him is bound to get me noticed.

For a moment, I panic. I'm unable to find the man through the crowd of moving bodies, but I locate him right near the bar. He plops down on a stool and strikes up an inaudible conversation with the barkeep, who laughs and provides the young man with a drink. I can't see him so well in the dim lighting, but his blond, shoulder-length hair is tucked behind his ears, and his broad, armored shoulders shake when he laughs at something the barkeep has said.

An older woman whose face is caked in coloure approaches me.

"What'll you have to drink, lovey?" she asks over the discordant music.

"Sorry?" I say, not quite sure what she said. She holds a tray in one hand, and the other sits on her hip. Her red and gray dress is stained and worn, but she stands straight and smiles at me, wearing it gracefully.

"What would you like to drink?" she repeats slowly, louder this time.

"Oh," I say, feeling a blush heat my cheeks. I quickly look around the room, not that it helps me any. The mugs are all filled with dark beer, which I have no interest in trying. "I'll have a water, please."

The woman eyes me suspiciously, so I add, "And a wine. Thanks."

I don't know anything about wine, but it's a drink my parents are fond of, and that gives it a layer of respectability in my eyes.

My answer seems to please the woman well enough. She shrugs and glides over to the bar, where she speaks with the barkeep and the man with the long blond hair. They laugh over some exchange, and then the man turns on his barstool and looks in my direction. I curl my hair behind my ear and pretend to be totally engrossed in the energetic music the pianist has just started to play.

I'm afraid to look up until the woman returns with both of my drinks.

"That'll be three tins, lovey."

"I don't have any tins, I'm afraid," I say apologetically. "You're good to keep this, though.

I reach into the purse at my hip and pull out a copper.

The woman's eyes widen for a moment. I hadn't expected the drinks in this place to be so inexpensive, but I suppose with this many customers they can afford to lower the prices. The copper piece I've given her is worth almost twice the price she stated.

"Let me at least get you another wine, then. I'll be back shortly."

The woman places the coin in a pocket on her skirt and heads back to the bar once again. This time, it takes her a while to return. In the meantime, I down my water. I stare at my wine for a moment, wondering if I even want to try it, but I figure it would be suspicious if she came back and I hadn't had any.

I start sipping the dry, bitter drink, and I do my best to keep myself from making faces as I drink it. I really don't like alcohol, but I'm not sure what to do with myself in a place like this. It warms my belly and eases the tension I feel in this crowded place, and as it does, I find myself relaxing a bit.

I alternate between watching the piano player and looking back to the familiar blond man at the bar, still trying to place where I've seen him and that armor before – silver plated with worn golden embellishments along the shoulder plates, chest piece, and thigh plates.

At some point, the woman returns with my second drink, and this one is much easier to consume. I've almost finished it when I see a big, burly man with a thick, unkempt dark beard approach the bar and shout something unintelligible.

The blond man I've been watching turns and says something to the bearded one, and for a moment they just sit there, staring at one another. They do this for long enough that I turn back to my drink, and then there's a clamor of braking glasses and snapping wood as the blond man is kicked from his now broken stool.

Every voice in the bar seems to fade as the moment unfolds. The blond man stands rapidly and swings, smashing a glass bottle against the side of the bearded man's head. He reels for a moment, but then turns the movement into a punch, but I don't get to see what the younger man does, because pain explodes in my own face, and I have to blink several times to clear the black spots from my vision.

I look around me wildly, searching for my attacker, but everyone seems completely focused on the fight between the two men. I look back to the tussle and watch as the blond man wipes fresh blood from his nose. My own nose begins to trickle steadily, and my eyes go wide with horror.

My chair almost falls over as I stand. I cover my face as I hear the *shing* of metal against leather, but I don't care. My heart is pounding, and my hands are quickly filling with blood. I don't want to draw any attention to myself and the absolutely impossible thing that has just happened to me. More than that, though, with my racing heart and my bloody hands and the pain in my face, I just need to get out of there. The tavern walls feel as though they're closing in and will crush me at any moment.

Air. I need air. If I can just get outside...

Without paying any more mind to the encounter between the two men, I rush from the tavern, leaving the fight and its audience behind me.

6

My heart beats a million times a minute as I stumble through the doorway into the alley. I find myself pacing back and forth, terrified, and trying with everything I have to wrap my mind around what just happened. I didn't see anyone attack me; everyone else seemed as preoccupied by the fight at the bar as I was. But surely, *someone* had to have hit me. I can't get that image of the blond man being punched in the face out of my mind. Over and over again it plays, and I relive the explosive pain that my nose still throbs from.

Either I had the stealthiest attacker in the world, or...

Or what, exactly? The impact from the man's punch clear across the tavern from me somehow had an effect on me, also? There's no way. I don't even have to say that sentence aloud for me to know it sounds crazy.

And yet, I've experienced craziness all my life, waking from dreams with the same exact injuries I dreamt having, even getting strange injuries when I've been awake. Crazy is part of my norm, now.

Could this man somehow be the reason for my inexplicable injuries?

My head is whirring from the wine and the jarring impact, and although my nose bleed has slowed to a tiny trickle, I decide it's best to leave this tavern and find out which inn my crew has set us up in.

I need to get my bags and take something for this pain so I can think straight.

I weave back through the city on my way to the marketplace when the left side of my torso is filled with a blinding, stinging pain. I double over and hold my ribcage, where a deep gash the size of my middle finger has formed and now pools thick, red blood through my fingers.

Judging by the pain and the length of the wound, I'd say I will at least need stitches, and all of my supplies I would need to stitch myself back up are with my crew. I need to get to them, but I doubt I'll have time. Already, blood is spilling through my fingers and dripping out onto the stone streets at my feet. I lose my balance for a moment, and I lean against the cold stone wall of a building for support. I do my best to take a deep breath, though the action sends a new wave of pain through my open wound. The breath steadies me a bit, but I feel myself getting more lightheaded by the second.

Fates. There's no way I'll be able to figure out where my team is in time.

I need a medic, and fast.

I stumble through the streets, hand clutching my side, scanning every sign I can see in what little moonlight shines through the clouds above. I barely register that I have been in the tavern for quite some time, as the sun is now completely set. After what feels like an eternity, I find the medic symbol – a pair of glowing hands – carved into a wooden sign, and I bang on the door with the hand that isn't trying to hold my blood inside my body.

The eyepiece slides open, and aged eyes peer out at me.

"I take it this is an emergency?" a creaky, tired woman's voice asks.

"Sorry for the... late intrusion..." I manage between gasps and swallows. My throat is dry and my vision is blurring at the edges. "But. I don't think... this can wait until..." I stagger backward and move my hand to catch myself against the doorframe, revealing the blood-soaked clothes underneath. The wrinkled eyes widen, and the eyepiece closes once again. Then the door swings open, and a short, skinny old woman rushes out.

"Oh, Fates. What have you gotten yourself into, child?" she mutters, scooping her arm around my back to support my weight and help me through the doorway.

Inside the home is warm and bright. Candles litter every free surface, and a fire blazes brightly in the next room. The home smells of flame and medicinal herbs, and the warmth hits me like an unexpected hug. I breathe deeply, and the wound in my side has me doubling over as the woman leads me to a bench piled with colorful blankets and sits me down.

"Wait there just a minute. I'll fetch my kit and some hot water, and we'll take a look."

The woman smiles softly and turns to leave the room. My eyes flutter closed again, and I focus on my shallow breathing while the wound in my side pulses.

The front door crashes open just as the woman returns to kneel at my side. She scowls and mutters, "What is it now?"

She notices the young man who has entered her home, and her face softens a bit.

"Fates. Of course, it'd be you. Go on and sit over there. I'll get to you when I'm done with her." She waves her hands at a bench across from me, and he stumbles over to it before plopping himself down.

I didn't catch his face earlier, but his blond hair and shining armor confirm that this is the same man I was watching in the tavern.

The man lets out a pained grunt, but when his gaze lands on me, he smiles coolly. Without warning, the medic reaches up and uses both hands to set my nose, which results in a popping sound that shifts the pressure in my head and causes another wave of pain to radiate throughout my face.

The man across from me moans as if empathizing with me. The woman passes me a warm, wet wash cloth to clean the sticky, drying blood from my face.

"All right, dear. Let's see that wound of yours. Can you lift your arm?"

With great effort, I do as she says. Sitting here without moving has made my body stiff. Very slowly, I raise my arm so she can cut away the bottom of my shirt. I send her a silent thank you for not removing the whole thing with this man in the room.

The medic mutters short, unintelligible sentences as she works at cleaning the wound. She pulls a familiar container of numbing cream out of her kit and slathers it on the gash generously, then she gets to stitching.

When she's finished, she sits back on her heels and inspects her work. Then, she nods.

"You stay right there," she says, standing up. "Try not to move too much. I'm going to sterilize my tools and start you some tea so I can work on this fool." She shoots a stern look at the blond man before leaving the room again.

It's only then that I find the courage to venture a good look at him.

His face is smeared with dried blood, and his blond hair, soaked with sweat, dangles around his sturdy face. Now that I'm seeing him up close, I can tell I've at least never had a conversation with him, but he's so familiar I know I must have come across him some other way.

He looks maybe two or three years older than me. Stubble grows in along his jaw and above his upper lip. He catches me looking at him and smiles again as he fights to keep his eyes open.

"What're you in for?" he asks, speech slurring. Despite the pain and ale, his voice has a smooth, almost musical quality to it. A quality, I'm sure by the look of him, he's all too aware of.

I frown at him. Somehow, I'm certain that the pain I've been through tonight is his fault. I don't know if it's the wine I drank, or the pain I'm in, or the fact that I'm thoroughly disturbed by the possibility of everything that has happened tonight, but something makes me brave.

"Spent too much time around idiots tonight," I grumble. This comment makes him laugh, and he sits up a little straighter.

"Fair enough. Love when that happens. Idiots are everywhere, I'm afraid," he says. His eyes find their way to the exposed parts of my abdomen, and I move to readjust, wincing at the pain in my side. I pull the cut-off bottom half of my soiled shirt over my midsection.

I want to ask him what happened, or at the very least find out if he's also experienced strange injuries without explanation, but I can't seem to clear my head enough to find the right words. Instead, I focus on making small talk to keep myself from spiraling.

"What caused that?" I ask, gesturing with my chin toward the side of his body that he's applying pressure to.

The *same side* I've been wounded on.

I'm fairly sure I can piece together what happened well enough. I saw the start of that fight. I heard the metal, presumably the blade that cut him, leave its coverings. I felt the results *on my own body* just moments later.

"Damn Roger brought a knife to a fist fight. Very unbecoming of him," he says, smirking through the pained expression on his face.

I find myself frowning again, as well as I can manage past the pain in my nose. I cross my arms and try, unsuccessfully, to get comfortable. My body is extremely stiff, and I've now begun shivering, the blood loss making my body ice cold.

"You *know him*? The one who did that to you?" I ask.

He nods. His breathing is quick and shallow like mine. He probably shouldn't be talking right now, but he continues to do so anyway. I feel myself growing incredibly tired, but the conversation helps keep me awake.

"Owe him money," he says. "He came in to collect the debt, and I wanted to have a civilized conversation with the man, but, well, you don't know Roger. Quick to anger, that one."

The medic returns again with her tools and kneels before this strange man.

"Hush up, you. Don't bother my customers," she tells him as she helps him remove the plates of armor that caught my attention earlier.

He grunts as he adjusts his body and reaches up to remove his shirt. I avert my eyes.

"I'm a customer too, am I not?" he complains.

The woman scoffs.

"Sure, sure. With how often you're here, you ought to pay me rent." Then to herself she mutters, "Fates, that's strange." She turns to look at me for a moment, but whatever she was going to say, she keeps it to herself.

As she works in silence, I find my thoughts returning to my crew. At this point, they're probably worried sick about me. I ran off pretty abruptly earlier and have not sent any word. There's also little chance I'll be able to locate them at this hour. I close my eyes tightly. What a stupid idea this was. I hope they are able to settle in somewhere for the night, and I take comfort knowing that I will find them when they go to meet our vendors tomorrow morning.

I fade in and out of consciousness despite the tugging, nagging pain in my side until I'm jolted awake by the sound of a teapot whistling.

When I open my eyes, the woman has finished patching up the stranger and stands again, rubbing her lower back. She tells him to come with her to the kitchen. Although he is slow to move and it takes him a moment to gain some balance, he doesn't hesitate to stand and follow her into the next room.

The whistling stops, and I can hear the faint sound of water pouring into a cup.

Then, the old woman whispers loudly, "What have you done to that girl?"

"Charm her?" the man says. There's a slapping sound, and I'm startled with a jolt and a stinging in my face as he speaks again. "Ow! I swear, I've done nothing. I just met her sitting there in your office. What are you insinuating? That *I* hurt her?"

Quiet stretches across a long moment before the woman says with a stone cold voice, "You best keep her out of trouble, you hear me? You leave her out of whatever mess you're getting yourself in."

"Fine," he mumbles. He stumbles back into the room and winks at me. "Sorry, sweetheart. Got to be going now. This old bat wants me out." He points in her direction with his thumb.

The woman, who now carries a cup of tea in one hand, smacks him across the back of his head with the other. My eyes widen in surprise.

"Shoo!" she tells him.

I have so many questions. So much that I need to know about this man, and the chances of me seeing him again are slim if I let him walk out that door. But I'm so tired, and so stunned by everything that it takes me a moment to react.

The man shoots me one last smile and exits the building without another word. Just as he walks through the door, I reach out and call, "Wait!" But I receive no answer. The man is gone.

Now the medic turns to me and places the cup of tea gently in my hands. I can't help but notice how the liquid within shakes as I hold it.

"I want you to stay here tonight, dear, where I can keep an eye on you. Rest up, and I'll let you go in the morning, all right?"

I nod before taking a sip of the tea, and I scrunch my face at the sour, bitter taste. The expression makes the woman laugh.

"I know it tastes like horse piss, but it's the best cure I've got for pain. Lasts a lot longer than that cream I put on you, anyhow. It'll help you tomorrow, too, and I'll send some with you, no extra charge."

"Thank you," I say. I finish the awful tea and lay slowly against the pile of blankets. "Ma'am? I came with some people from out of town. Is there any way I can get word to my crew about where I am?" I ask.

She unfolds a blanket and pulls it up over my body.

"Not at this hour, I'm afraid. But don't you worry about that. Just focus on resting, and I'm sure you'll be able to clear all of this up tomorrow."

Disappointed, I let my eyes close again.

Three thoughts drift through my mind before I fall asleep.

I wonder how I'm going to explain any of this to my team.

I need answers.

And I'd like to see that smile again.

I wake late the next morning to the sound of quiet talking. When I open my eyes, an older man with his hands wrapped is just leaving.

"No more dumb tricks, Don," the woman tells him, patting him on the back. "No matter how many scars you have on your hands, they won't withstand the heat. Use the gloves, or I'll get my cakes elsewhere."

The man nods and mumbles his thanks, and the woman closes the door behind him.

"Damn fools," she mutters, shaking her head. "This whole city's full of them."

When she realizes I'm awake, the woman smiles and leads me to the kitchen for breakfast. I realize then that in all the craziness of last night, even after she potentially saved my life, I didn't ask this woman her name. How embarrassing.

"I'm afraid I didn't ask for your name yesterday," I say, tone apologetic.

"Mathilda," the woman says as she cuts into a steaming fruitcake.

"Mathilda. It's wonderful to meet you," I say. "I'm Lane."

Mathilda nods and keeps busy, scooping a hefty piece of cake onto a plate and sliding it across a small table to me as I sit. She sits across from me, placing another cup of steaming tea in front of me, and setting down two bags of tea beside the cup. I place the tea bags inside my bag.

The two of us eat in silence for a moment, and I think of my crew. I stand and almost lose my balance as the pain from my wound has my vision blurring again. I close my eyes and take a breath, clinging to the back of my chair for support. When I think I'm steady enough, I open my eyes again.

"Thank you for everything," I tell Mathilda, handing her the now empty plate. Then a thought occurs to me. Nerine is a large city. Chances are, there are several medics in the area. It might be good to check. "Are you the only medic here?" I ask.

"In Nerine?" Mathilda asks, raising her thin eyebrows. "Fates, no. There are seven of us."

I nod. With my not showing up last night, my team is probably out searching for me, and healers are likely the first place they're going to check.

"I thought as much." I sigh. "I should get going. I left my team yesterday, and they must be worried sick that I haven't come back yet.

I reach into my purse and hold out a mix of coppers and silvers. I'm not sure how much a medic here would charge for all the service this woman has provided me. To me, her aid has been priceless.

Mathilda holds her hands up, refusing the money.

"First one's on me, dear. Just be careful out there, all right? Don't want to find yourself in the wrong company."

"Are you sure?" I ask. What a strange place.

Mathilda smiles kindly and leads me to the front door as I tuck the bag of herbs she's given me into my purse.

"If you see people around in your travels, tell them I'm happy to treat customers who aren't dumb as rocks. Get me some *varied* clientele, huh?"

I tell her I will, and she sends me on my way.

I hobble through the alleyways in search of my crew, hoping I'll find them in the marketplace where I left them yesterday. I'm doing my best not to jostle my wound so much, but every step hurts, and breathing sends sharp pains through my body. But I'm alive, and thanks to the expert stitching, the bleeding has subsided.

When I've almost reached the market, I hear the stranger's voice from last night through an open doorway, and I'm flooded with a feeling that's equal parts relief and urgency. I need to talk with him, see if I can get any information from him as to why I got the same injuries he did last night, and how far back this connection might go. I find myself leaning against the doorway just out of sight, listening in.

"Come on, Will. I'm up for the job. You hire anyone else to do it, and they'll screw it up. You'll end up with half a Council woman, and I doubt you'll get any reward for that. Besides, you *know* I'll keep her safe. Let me do it, and you'll get the gold her husband promised," the blond stranger says.

Silence follows the remark. Then another man's voice joins the argument.

"I heard you got sliced up pretty good last night. Don't you think you should sit this one out?"

I move to peek in through an open window to get a better view. I see the blond stranger shrug.

"I'm still standing. A little cut's not going to slow me down. Give me the job, Will. If you don't, I'll track her down anyway, and you'll be out the cash."

The man, presumably Will, looks to his partner, who shrugs.

"If the idiot gets himself killed, we'll just hire someone else. No skin off our backs."

Finally, Will nods, and he and the blond shake hands.

My chest fills with white hot panic. Did that man say... this stranger could be *killed*? If he gets hit in the face and I bleed for it, if he gets stabbed and I end up spending the night in a medic's care, then there's no way I'm going to risk him getting me killed.

I turn away from the building and limp as quickly as I can to the market. Already the city is busy with merchants bringing their wares to their market stands. The scent of freshly baked breads fills the streets, and I breathe deeply despite my injuries, relishing in the scent.

When I get back to the market, I'm proud to see that my crew has finished loading up the new supplies and are now standing ready to leave, though dark circles surround all of their eyes, and they look around the market anxiously for me. When they see me, Philip and Zaid come rushing up to me, and Loren waves frantically, holding onto the horses' reins.

"Are you all right, Lane? We were up most the night looking for you." Philip notices the bruises on my face, which still feels swollen and sore and is probably black and blue. "Are you..."

I hold my hand up.

"I'm fine. I got into a bit of an accident, but I'm doing all right," I say.

Philip's shoulders relax, but Zaid seems less convinced. His eyes fall to the cut pieces of my blouse and the bandaging underneath. My cheeks heat, and I move my satchel to cover my exposed stomach.

"Listen, you two," I say, thinking over and over, *I'm going to get killed.* "There's a bit of personal business that's come up, and I think I'm going to have to stay here in Nerine for a little longer." Philip opens his mouth. I know he's to offer delaying our trip back, but I shake my head before he can get a word out. "Like I said, it's personal. There's no need for us to delay your return with the trade goods. Go ahead of me. Leave my things with me, and I'll write when I'm ready to come home.

"Are you sure?" Zaid asks. "I could stay and ride back with you."

"What's she saying?" Loren hollers from where he stands with the horses. I shake my head at Zaid. Then I take slow, pained steps toward him so he can be part of our conversation, but I keep my chin up, hoping they can't tell how tired and worn I am. "Lane, you look awful. Are you okay?"

I wave away his concern, though I'm touched that the three of them care so much.

I place my hand on the cart to steady myself. Standing for so long is starting to make me feel dizzy.

"I appreciate you all, and I'm sorry for worrying you last night. I'm really okay. I met a nice woman who helped me after my accident, and she let me stay with her. I'm going to stay here for a little longer," I tell Loren. "The crew's got to have all of you if you're going to avoid pillagers or other cats on the road. You heard what happened to Dillon's team last month. Bandits are getting brave with the smaller groups."

"That's exactly why you need someone with *you* when you head home," Zaid argues, and Philip and Loren mutter their agreement.

I sigh and take the few laborious steps necessary to close the distance between me and my horse. I pat the bow and arrows that sit against her front flank before throwing them and my satchel over my shoulder.

"I'll be just fine. Phil, you've seen me hunt with this thing. I've got nothing to worry about." I fiddle with the pouch on my horse's saddle and withdraw a parchment and some charcoal. Using the hard leather saddle, I scribble a message for Pappan. Then I take my horse's lead and place it in one of Loren's hands.

"Take my horse back for me. Pappan and the others will need her. And when you get home," I start, folding the parchment up and placing it in Loren's other hand. "Tell Pappan I'm doing well, and I'll be home soon."

"I don't like this," Zaid says, deep frown creasing his smooth features. Philip looks as though he's going to be sick. "First you disappear all night, then you come back bloody telling us you got into an accident, and now you want to stay here for personal reasons and travel all the way back by yourself? I don't like it."

"Yeah," Loren says, shifting his weight.

I clench my jaw. I feel bad – he's right, I am asking a lot from them going back without me, without answers. But if I told them why I want to stay, they'd think I've lost my mind. And maybe I have. All the uncertainty paired with the aching in my face and the sharp pain in my sides has me irritable.

"You don't have to like it. But you're *my* crew, and you'll do as I say for the good of the company." My stern tone causes the three of them to look at me with wide, shocked eyes. I let out a huff and force myself to soften my tone. "How about this? Your journey back will take four days if the weather is good. Give me a week, and I'll be back, too."

Zaid steps forward and puts his hand on my shoulder. I try not to flinch at the pain that springs through my side, but my stomach flips in excitement at his touch.

"One week. If we don't hear from you by then, I'm coming back for you," Zaid promises.

I smile and nod. "Deal. Get going now. You don't want to upset Chief Bron with a late delivery."

Reluctantly, my crew members mount their horses and mutter their goodbyes. I watch them until they're out of sight of the market, then I adjust my bow, arrows, and bag so they're clear of my wound. I chew my lip, worried I might be making a mistake in letting them go without me. I hope they'll be all right, but I *need* to talk to this man. I need to find out what he knows about my condition.

I square my shoulders and turn back in the direction of the argument I witnessed just moments ago.

"Excuse me," I say to the men inside when I reach the building where I just saw the blond stranger. They stop talking and stare at me. I clear my throat. "There was a man in here before. Tall, long blond hair. Could you tell me where he went?"

They look at each other, and the short, stout man laughs bitterly.

"Man. You're funny, girl. If Alec Montrose is in town, there's only one place you'll find him."

And the bitter man was one hundred percent correct. I find the stranger, Alec, back in the tavern in the same spot he was in last night, sitting on a new stool. I find myself feeling nervous at first to approach him, but the nerves quickly fade.

Something about seeing him here in the same spot with a mug of dark, foaming ale to his lips angers me. Here I am spending the night in a medic's care, sending my crew on their way without me because a huge piece of my world just clicked into place for the first time, and he's here drinking like nothing even happened.

His hair is washed, but he looks terrible, and thanks to his fight last night, I do, too. Just seeing the deep blue bruises beneath his eyes makes my face hurt. I stride up to his side.

Doing my best to keep myself calm, I speak.

"Didn't think you'd be allowed back in here after last night," I say, causing him to choke on his drink. He recovers quickly, though, and he smiles when he turns to me. Does his face hurt as badly as mine does?

"Ah, you," Alec says. "Nice to see you again." He brings his drink back to his lips, and I look at the barkeep as I take the empty seat next to him. The barkeep turns to talk to me, but I just shake my head.

He frowns at me, so I say, "A water, please. Thank you."

"Interesting choice," Alec muses.

"This businessman isn't angry with you coming back in here the very next day after causing such a ruckus?" I ask, totally awestruck that the barkeep is just going about his business. Surely, he remembers Alec from last night's tussle.

"How could he? I make his pockets jingle. This tavern would likely be closed without my frequent visitation," Alec booms loud enough for the bartender to hear him. The man shoots up a vulgar hand signal in response. Alec speaks quietly now, directly to me. He shrugs. "Truth be told, I get into a lot of fights, here. It's part of the appeal at this point."

Once again, I'm shocked.

"Charming," I say.

"I certainly think so," Alec replies. He raises his eyebrows at me and takes another drink. The barkeep returns with a cup full of water.

I take a deep breath, grateful to have something to occupy my hands. I run my thumbs up and down the cup as I try to decide how to approach the subject I came to speak to him about. Or rather, the two subjects, if I can figure out how to ask him about our injuries without sounding raving mad.

I let out my breath in a huff. My heart is pounding. How do you tell someone you don't know that they shouldn't take up work, because it's dangerous, and by putting themselves in danger, they are also endangering you?

I start by trying to break the ice.

"I've seen that armor before, or at least something like it. Are you a Guard here in Nerine?"

Alec looks down sadly at his armor, but the frown he wears is gone as quickly as it came. He stretches his arms out wide, showing off his armor, drink still in hand. It swishes inside his mug.

"It would seem that way, wouldn't it?" he asks. "No, I'm a sellsword. I travel all of Maran providing my services!"

"Sellsword, right," I mutter. That makes things so much worse. Sellswords do odd jobs for money, providing services ranging from body Guard, to thief, to soldier, to assassin. The men from earlier were right, he really could die – he's made a job of putting himself in danger. I have got to talk him out of this. "Listen, I'm not sure how to say this, so I'm going to just come out and say it." I take a deep breath and close my eyes.

"Ooh, intrigue," he jests, but I'm too busy fighting the nerves in my stomach to acknowledge what he says.

"I overheard you talking to those men earlier about a job. This may sound strange, but you shouldn't take it."

"Is that so?" he asks, bemused look lighting up his face. He sets his drink down, and I notice that the tavern is much quieter now than it was last night. Why is this man drinking so early in the morning, anyway?

"Yes. It's dangerous, isn't it? You could be hurt?"

The question makes him smile again.

"Likely so. I'll be up against bandits and rogue soldiers for sure, but I've done jobs like this in the past. I'm highly motivated, and well trained. I'll be just fine." He repositions himself on his stool. "It's nice of you to be concerned for me, though. I'll keep that in mind on my *arduous* quest."

I roll my eyes. Fates, he's frustrating.

"Oh, you're hilarious," I say, then lower my voice. How can I say this without sounding completely insane? "If you get hurt, I will, too. Maybe you don't mind it, but I'm not particularly fond of being injured."

Now, Alec just frowns at me.

At least I've got his attention. This makes me feel a little more courageous, so I push on.

"Ugh. Let me try this again. Have you ever gotten injuries you couldn't explain to anyone? Injuries you couldn't remember getting?" I ask.

"Oh, absolutely," he says. My relief is short lived as he raises his mug. "This lovely poison has seen to that many times."

Come on, how can I get the point across? What can I say to explain what I've been experiencing, or that I think he's somehow linked in all of this? How can I show him how serious this could be?

"Okay, but I mean when you're lucid. When you haven't done anything that would get you hurt." My eyes search for a scar

I can remember causing. "I'll bet you've broken your arm. Six years ago. Right here." I roll up my sleeve and show him the part of my forearm just above my wrist where a thick, round scar puckers just above the surrounding skin.

This catches his attention, but he only says, "I don't know what you're talking about."

I continue, though, because the feeling in my gut tells me he's lying.

"You have the same scar in the same place, don't you. I fell off my horse when I was eleven and landed straight on my arm, sending the bone through my skin. At the same time, all the way over here, you must have experienced the same break. I'm sure of it, because my nose was broken yesterday when you were punched, and we both ended up needing stitches in the same spot last night after that man pulled his knife on you."

He stares at me, skeptical, and says after a moment of silence, "You're crazy."

I narrow my eyes at him. Somehow, I have to get him to believe me.

"Fine. You don't believe me? Let's go somewhere people won't see us. I'll *show* you what I mean."

Something sparks in his eyes, and his gaze travels across my body. I stand and cross my arms over my chest. This action hurts my side, and Alec winces, too, adjusting again in his stool.

"That is *not* what I meant, and you know it. You can get that thought out of your mind right now," I say, scowling at him.

"Fates, for someone asking me for a favor, you sure have an attitude about it," he says. He slides carefully off his barstool and begins walking – stumbling, really – away. I sit for a moment longer, stunned by this whole interaction, frustrated that he claims not to believe me, and I grapple with the thought that I should follow him. Maybe I should leave him be, but I have to convince him not to go on that journey before he gets me killed.

I don't have to chase him down, though, because he turns around and beckons me over.

"Are you coming, or what?"

Alec winds through the streets until we reach the side of the city that shares space with the desert. I have to rush to keep up with him, and he never once looks back to see if I'm still following him.

By the time we reach the edge of the city, I am out of breath and sweating from the pain in the injury he caused last night. We slow down and eventually come to a stop. Blue sage brush and tall, olive colored grass surrounds us on all sides, and the city is almost out of view behind the desert hills.

"Private enough for you?" Alec says, and by the grin on his face, I figure he's fighting back a wink.

I do my best not to scowl at him. After all, acting hostile is not going to be the smartest way to make him listen to what I have to say.

Though I do my best to make my tone as friendly as possible, I can't help the biting words that escape my mouth next.

"Quit messing around," I warn him, but I have no *or else* to follow it up with. I need him to listen to me.

Alec raises his arms, and his armor sparkles in the sunlight.

"What? You're the one that wanted a private space. The way I see it, I'm doing you a favor," he says.

I roll my eyes and pull up my sleeves.

"Fine." I eye the dagger that's hung on the belt around his waist. It's got a black leather grip and a set of beautiful round emerald stones surrounded by glimmering gold, just like the sword that sits opposite the dagger on the other side of his waist.

"Are you sure you don't believe me? It would save us both some pain if you just took my word for it."

"Seriously?" he laughs. "I don't know you, and what you're claiming is impossible."

I sigh.

Fates.

I shake my hands out, trying to work up the guts to do what I'm about to do. I'm used to being injured, but I've never hurt myself *on purpose*.

I pull my arm back, let out a deep breath, and swing my hand forward, slapping myself hard. My face stings, and my nose injury from yesterday aches with the jarring impact. This mercenary had better believe me, now.

When my vision clears, I look at Alec, whose eyes are wide for an instant. He shakes his head, and any sign of belief disappears from his face, and he frowns deeply.

"You really are mad," he tells me, rubbing the back of his neck with his hand. "I can't believe you just hit yourself."

"You felt it too, right?" I ask, rubbing the part of my jaw and cheek that stings the most. Alec has a red spot forming on his face, but he doesn't seem to notice it.

"Felt the shock of seeing a woman beat herself up? Sure, I did," he says.

I grunt. This is going to be harder than I thought.

"All right, fine. Can I see your dagger? You can tell me where to cut, and you'll see for yourself."

"No can do," he says, holding the dagger's hilt protectively. "My weapons are for my use only. No one touches my blades. Besides, you just hit yourself in the face. Why would I give you a weapon?"

I let out a frustrated huff and scoop up the sharpest rock I can find.

I hold the rock up so he can see it clearly, then roll up my sleeve so he can see the clean, smooth skin in the center of my right palm. He nods cautiously, clearly still confused. I'm just grateful he's still standing here. I try to slow the pounding of my heart. I don't want to hurt myself again. My face is still stinging. But I need him to understand how serious this is before he gets us both killed.

"Now yours," I say, gesturing with my chin to his own hands. He opens them up, and both his palms are clean. Good.

I take a deep breath and thrust the rock into my skin, deep enough to draw blood, but not deep enough to do any real damage. I watch as Alec gasps and looks down at his own palm, eyes wide, mouth agape.

I drop the rock and hold my hand up for him to inspect. He steps forward to look it over, turning his gaze from his hand to mine. Then, he backs away.

"You're a witch," he says, face more serious than I've seen since I first saw him yesterday.

I scoff.

"Trust me, I would be a completely incompetent witch. Everyone in my village thinks I have a medical disorder, because for as long as I can remember, I've gotten these injuries I couldn't explain. Now, I see that somehow, for whatever reason, we're connected. Each time you get hurt, I get hurt, too."

Alec stands completely still, completely silent.

His amber colored eyes close for a moment, and he takes a deep breath. As I wait for him to compose his thoughts, I do my best not to pace. Finally, I can't take any more of this silence.

"Well?" I ask, throwing my hands to my hips. "Now you see, don't you? You can't take that job. If you get hurt, or *killed*, I will too."

Alec folds his arms, shifts his weight, clenches his jaw.

"Okay... let's say I believe you..." he trails off, and I let out a breath of relief.

"Oh, that's great. So now you see why you can't—"

He puts his fingers to my mouth, and I jump away from his touch.

"But. I'm still going on my quest, and there's nothing you can say that will change my mind. That's that."

My shoulders slump.

"Seriously?" I ask. What could possibly be so important about his job that he'd still risk going even after this world-changing discovery?

"Seriously. Your health doesn't mean anything to me, and as I said, I don't know you. Besides, I doubt you'll die, if that's what you're so worried about. I'm a skilled fighter, and I *do* care about myself. I don't plan on dying anytime soon. So if that's all, I really should prepare for my journey."

9

Alec turns his back on me and heads back to the city. I'm frozen in shock for several seconds, and then I snap out of it and realize my mouth has been open.

When I can get myself out of my frozen state, I race in the direction of the city to follow Alec. By the time I've reached city limits, I've lost him. I wander aimlessly, desperately through the streets until the sun is low in the afternoon sky and long shadows are cast between the buildings in town. I even wander back to the tavern two or three times and stop in to look for him, but it's no use. He's nowhere to be found. I have no idea where to look, and the longer I pace through the streets, the more my side throbs and aches. I have trouble catching my breath and keeping my balance.

I step into an alleyway and pull up my dirty, bloody, ripped shirt to check on my injury. I've bled through the bandage again, and most of this blood is fresh.

I'm at a loss. Frustration boils through me and I let out a shout as I ram my fist into the side of the building beside me. This impulsive action sends pain shooting through my hand. Good. I hope Alec felt that. The pain in my hand is quickly overshadowed by the wound in my side, and I stumble, vision doubling.

I need to get back to the medic. It takes me some time, but eventually, I'm able to find my way back to Mathilda's home and knock on the door.

She opens the door, wrinkled face drooping with a frown, but she smiles when her eyes land on me.

"That side of yours need more attention?" she asks, and I nod weakly.

"Come in," she says and steps aside, reaching out to grasp my elbows when I start to sway.

Once I'm inside, Mathilda leads me to the same bench I slept on last night, and I sit down as carefully as possible before lifting the disgusting cloth that is my shirt so she can change the bandage.

Mathilda winces when she sees the wound again. Thanks to the medicine she applied last night, it's already begun to heal, but it's pink and swollen around the edges, and some of the stitches have come undone. I grip the bench until my knuckles turn white as she sterilizes the wound. The alcohol she dumps on it feels like fire in my open wound. The burning spreads rapidly throughout my body, and I do my best to stop myself from trembling.

"Sorry, dear," she mutters as she snips back the stitches that have come undone. She cleans her needle and stitches me back up again.

"Mathilda," I start once she's finished stitching and begins applying ointment and wrapping me in a new bandage. Of all the people I could talk to right now, Mathilda seems the best person to talk to about the burning questions on my mind, after last night. I know she noticed that Alec's injuries are the same as mine; I saw it in her reaction when he came in last night. I have to speak up. "Can I ask you a... strange question?"

"Don't see why not," she replies, keeping her eyes on her work. "Been asked a lot of strange questions in my day."

I take a deep breath.

"Have you ever treated someone who was... somehow bound to another person?"

Mathilda doesn't miss a beat.

"I separated conjoined twins, once, if that's what you're asking," she says, shrugging one shoulder.

This is going to be a difficult conversation. I've had a lot of those today. Still, this woman treats injuries for a living, so I'm hoping she's seen something like this before.

"Well, not exactly. I mean... someone who gets hurt when someone else does. Have you ever heard of a situation like that?"

Mathilda looks up from her work now and something sparks in her eyes, but she purses her lips and stays silent, as if choosing her next words carefully. When she does speak, her voice is hushed, her eyes shifting like she's worried someone might hear.

"Fates," she says under her breath. "I was hoping you hadn't noticed, or that it was merely a strange coincidence."

"So, you do know, then? About Alec and me?"

Mathilda nods solemnly, pensively.

"How do you know each other?" she asks.

I raise my eyebrows and sit up straighter.

"What?" I ask. "I never met him before in my life, until last night."

Another slow, thoughtful nod. She's silent again for another long moment, until finally I break the silence.

"What is it? Do you have any idea what could have caused this to happen?" I ask.

"Tell me exactly what happened last night," she says.

So, I do. I relay everything I can remember from last night: seeing Alec in the market, finding him in the tavern, the fight that broke out, and the injuries that followed.

Mathilda purses her lips again. She runs a finger over one of her eyebrows.

"Was last night the first time something like this has happened to you?" she asks.

"No. I've experienced this for as long as I can remember, but I never knew these injuries were connected to another person until last night."

Mathilda stands and makes her way to the door. She peeks outside, then closes the door and locks it.

"I'm going to tell you a story, dear, and then we can see what you make of it," she says.

I frown, but I allow her to begin.

"Long ago, when the Women's Council set out on their pilgrimage from the Nameless Country to find a new land, it's said that they came across a witch in the mountains. The witch disguised herself as someone lovely, someone who wanted to help the Council get everything they desired and more – safety, new home, status. She told them of a spell she could perform that would bind these women together, make them stronger, and give them the power they needed for their new start away from the Patriarchy.

"Generations of women went to see the witch to bargain for riches, power, status, or family. As time went on, the women discovered that the witch gave her gifts at a terrible cost. Each woman was called to pay the witch back in one way or another. Those who had asked for status lost their ability to bear children, so they had no way to carry their names or legacies. Those who wished for riches died early, much of their fortune left unenjoyed. Those who wished for healthy children often either lost their lives or their children in some other way. The witch always claimed her debt.

"And most often women would disappear, called by some mysterious force, never to return. As the story goes, the Women's Council settled us so far from the mountains to keep away from her, and they did what they could to stop others from attempting to gain things they weren't meant to have. As the years passed, memory of the witch faded to rumor, then to whispers, and most of us forgot entirely."

"How did you hear about this story?" I ask, leaning forward despite my injury, listening eagerly. Mathilda sits across from me where Alec sat last night.

"You work with people as often as I do, from all walks of life, you learn to listen." Her lips form a thin line on her face, and it seems she's choosing her next words with care.

"Nobody believes in magic anymore. We haven't believed for a long time. They'll look at you like you're nuts if you even mention the idea. But if something bound you and Alec together, I'll bet it has something to do with that witch. And if his mamman's gone missing... it makes me wonder." She reaches forward and cleans my knuckles, wrapping my hand with some fresh gauze.

This last bit gives me pause, and I sit up straight again, flinching at the sharp, pulling pain in my side.

"Wait, how did you know all of this?"

Mathilda smiles mischievously. "I treated both of you last night, remember? There's no way the both of you could have those same exact wounds in the same places on the same night if there wasn't something stranger at play. Others in Maran would shun me or call me an old kook if they heard me talking like this, but I *believe* those old stories."

I recall being hushed and ridiculed as a child when I suggested that my mysterious injuries were the result of some kind of magic. I always thought it was just because I was young, so nobody wanted to listen to me anyway. Now, it seems it was the mention of magic that was the problem.

Even now, after all the time spent wondering in my youth, I still find it difficult to grasp what Mathilda is suggesting.

"Interesting," I mutter as I lean carefully back against the wall. "What's this about his mamman going missing?"

Mathilda shrugs.

"Alec came back to see me earlier today. He left just before you showed up, actually. Said that's his next quest: He's going to get his mamman back."

The old woman gets up and busies herself with something on a table near the door. It looks like she's writing something, but I can't tell from where I sit, and I don't feel right about snooping after everything she's done for me.

Now it's starting to make sense. Alec's mamman going missing is certainly reason enough to still want to take the job before anyone else does. But what I can't quite figure out is why others would want to go get her.

"Mathilda, was Alec's mamman taken?" I ask.

Her eyebrows rise on her forehead, but she continues her scribbling.

"No one knows at this point. She was due at Council three days ago and never showed up – that isn't like Julienne. She isn't responding to any letters, and nobody's seen her. Seems as if she's just vanished. The Council is concerned, as is her husband. They're both offering a reward to anyone who can bring her back safely. The few people who saw Julienne in the days leading up to her disappearance say she acted... strangely. Distracted. Like she was anxious about something."

Carefully, I stand to take my leave. I need to find Alec before it's too late.

"Thank you, Mathilda, again," I say.

Mathilda smiles, and the lines around her eyes deepen. She follows me to the door.

"Alec's going to get himself – um... the both of us – hurt, isn't he?" I ask at the door.

Mathilda's smile returns, and she meets my gaze steadily. She pulls one of my hands into hers and grips it tightly. Her skin is warm, calloused and dry.

"Guaranteed. Good luck to you both." She slides a folded piece of parchment into my hand and waves me out the door.

With that, I nod and leave her home once again, and she closes the door gently behind me. On the street, I unfold the parchment to find a crudely drawn map. Across the top of the parchment is written in shaky handwriting: *To Alec's House.*

The blood in my veins thrums with urgency. I need to find Alec. There's no way I'll be able to dissuade him from finding his mamman, but I can go with him and do what I can to keep him from getting hurt. I've got to try, at least. Thanks to Mathilda, I know just where to look.

I follow the map in what I hope is the right direction, past the tavern, through a handful of markets – I'm surprised by how many shops and stands this one city holds – and to the part of town that stands between rocky cliffs that overlook the crystal blue sea and dense forest.

I squint at the map Mathilda drew.

Okay, those swirls definitely look like waves, and I believe those squiggly lines are trees.

"Here goes nothing," I sigh. I veer right toward the forest and keep walking as the houses grow smaller and more spaced out. Finally, I find a stone hut that stands apart from the others, which is circled on Mathilda's map. My first instinct is to go directly up to the hut and bang on the door until Alec agrees to let me go with him. I even go so far as to stride up the dirt path that leads to the front door, but then my doubts get the best of me. Who's to say I followed this silly drawing correctly? I'd feel awful if I imposed on some poor family getting ready for bed.

Instead, I retreat and plant myself on the ground across the way with my back propped up against another home.

It isn't long before my worries get the best of me, though. I fear he may have already left town, and then I will have waited around for nothing. I slowly get back up, dust myself off, and go right back to the door. I close my eyes and hesitate for the smallest of moments before I knock.

I can hear heavy footsteps on the other side of the door, and I hope this home is indeed Alec's.

Then the door swings open and Alec stands before me.

"What are you doing here?" he asks.

"Oh, good, you're still here. I felt like I was waiting out here forever. Thought you'd already gone," I say.

"Had a lot of things to pack. Not that it's any of your business, stalker. Don't you know it's a pretty stupid idea to wander around at this hour? In this city, you'll get yourself robbed, and that's best-case scenario. Besides, it's not polite to watch people's houses. Makes you seem creepy. How did you even find me?" he asks.

I grit my teeth and look around. The sunlight is quickly fading, leaving streaks of orange light in the ever-deepening indigo sky. Ignoring Alec's comments, I take a deep breath and meet his eyes.

"Listen. I know why you're still going out there, and why I can't stop you. I've made my peace with that." I straighten the belongings that are still draped across my back. "That's why I'm coming with you."

Alec stands up tall and rolls his eyes, already pushing past me in the doorway.

"Yeah, I told you. I've got a job, and I don't care to worry about hurting someone I've never met before. You are *not* coming with me. I don't need a liability, and you're only going to slow me down."

I move fast, stepping around him and blocking his path. This action sends a shockwave of pain through me. Alec raises his eyebrows, but he says nothing.

"You're going for your mamman. I understand that. And—" I say, moving again as he tries to get around me. "I'm not asking. I *am* coming with you, whether you like it or not. Ignore me all you want; I'm going to follow you. I don't need you getting us killed – not if there's anything I can do to prevent it."

Alec pauses and looks me over. Something lights in his eyes, and he smirks, running his hand over his chin.

"Alright. Come if you want to. But if you slow me down, I'm leaving your ass behind. Got it?"

I narrow my eyes at him and reach out my hand.

"Deal," I say, and we shake.

"Fine, then," he says, shrugging. He starts walking again. "Let's get moving."

"Um..." I start. I *just* agreed that I wouldn't slow him down, but I realize now that I really have to use the latrine, and I'm filthy. I'd love to clean up at least a little bit if I'm going to be embarking on a quest so soon.

"What is it?" Alec says, tone exasperated.

I purse my lips.

"Well, I know I said I wouldn't slow you down, but could I possibly use your latrine? I've been wandering around all day, and..." I trail off, gesturing to my clothes, which are covered in grime and crusty with dried blood. Fates, how I must have looked all day.

"You're not serious," Alec says.

I raise my arms, and he scrunches his nose.

Alec scoffs.

"Fine, come inside. You can clean yourself up, use the damn latrine, and *then* we're leaving. I want to get as much time on the road before someone else gets wind of this job and muddles everything up."

Without waiting for my reply, Alec shakes his head and saunters off into the house, leaving the door wide open. I hurry to follow, closing the door behind me.

10

Inside Alec's hut looks even smaller than the outside does. On one side he's got a small bed and a simple wooden dresser. On the other side of the room sits a stove, a sink, and a table with one chair. Tucked back in the corner is a small metal tub and privy with a folding screen that's covered in clothing.

His entire home could fit in the bedroom I share with Lilah back home, but at least he's got his own place.

I look at Alec, and he shrugs.

"You have a canteen?" he asks, and I dig through my satchel and pull out my long-empty water canteen. I toss it to him, and he moves toward the sink.

"I didn't know you had running water out here," I say, making conversation, trying to ignore the awkward feeling of being alone in this stranger's house, knowing that the area I'll be cleaning up in is *right there.*

"Well, yeah. Everyone in Nerine has running water," he replies, turning on the tap. I busy myself placing my belongings on the table. "One of the perks of living so close to the sea, I guess."

"Can I get some of that water? And a cloth, if you've got one?" I ask. "I'd really just like to clean up, and I shouldn't keep you here for long. I'll be fast – I promise."

"Of course, your highness," Alec says with a mocking half-smile on his face. He finishes filling the canteen with water and fills a bowl as well, then he turns off the tap and crosses the room, scooping up what I hope is a clean rag from the countertop on the way. He sets the bowl of water beside the privy and removes the clothing that's hung over the folding screen before tossing it onto his bed. "Why not take a full bath, my lady?" he asks sarcastically. "I know I said I'm in a hurry, but really, I've got all the time in the world."

I roll my eyes. "The rag will do fine, *thank you*," I tell him, snatching up the rag. "I promise I'll be quick."

"Go ahead and hang your clothes over the screen there. I'll try to find you something that might fit." At my look of horror, he chuckles. "Relax. It can get cold out on the road, and no one will trust us if you look like you've just murdered someone. Just leave your clothes on the screen." He gestures to my blood-stained shirt.

"Okay..." I mutter as he steps away.

I scoot the screen and work to straighten it so I can get as much coverage as possible.

On the other side, I hear him mumble, "Women."

I hear Alec shuffling things around on the other side of the screen, and I'm grateful for the noise. I'm mortified to be using the latrine so close to someone else, and I don't know if it would be better if I just make conversation with him...

When I'm finished, I take a deep breath and carefully remove my clothes, but I keep a close eye on the edges of the screen. I don't know this man, and I certainly don't feel comfortable getting dressed in such a small, open space. I hang my clothes carefully over the top of the screen. It wobbles a bit, and my heart pounds as I steady it so it doesn't fall over. Carefully, I let it go, and it stays upright. I sit back and work slowly to unwrap the bandage from around my torso. Although I just had it changed earlier today, it's filthy and already bloody again. I set it down.

"You wouldn't happen to have any spare bandage lying around, would you?" I ask through the screen as I splash water on my face, arms, and wound.

Alec grunts and shuffles around some more.

"Heads up," he calls, and a ginormous roll of bandage comes flying over the top of the screen. I barely manage to catch it before it falls into the privy.

"Wow," I say, marveling at the sheer size of the roll in my hands. "You need this much?"

"I'm a sellsword, remember? Injuries happen. That stuff is vital. If you don't want it, I can always take it back—"

"No, it's great. Thank you. Thank you." I let out a huff and narrow my eyes in his direction. I wrap myself up again and put the bandage on the floor beside me, being careful not to get it wet.

The screen wobbles again as my clothes are removed from the top and new – hopefully cleaner – ones are put in their place. I freeze, but I'm able to relax a moment later, as the screen steadies itself once more.

I grab the clothing and get myself dressed. The shirt and strapped trousers Alec chose for me hang loosely off every part of me. I am, however, grateful to know that they are clean, warm and dry. They'll have to do.

"Fates, you almost done?" he asks impatiently. Guilt spreads through me.

"Yes, sorry. I'm ready," I say.

Moving the screen back to where it was, I scoop up both the clean and dirty bandages and step back into the open space that contains the rest of his home. I hand him the roll of clean bandage, which he stuffs into a bag.

Alec has filled another bag with things and is sitting on the table eating an apple. Around the bite he's just taken, he clicks his tongue.

"You'll want to pull that lever there to wash your waste down to the city's septic system," he tells me, pointing to one of two levers beside the privy. "The one next to it washes bathwater back to the sea."

"Advanced," I say, approaching and then pulling the lever he mentioned.

"Why, do you not have a plumbing system where you come from?" he asks.

I make my way back to the table and hang my bag, my bow, and my quiver of arrows back over my shoulder.

"Well, nothing this fancy, anyway. We have a tunnel that goes underneath our home and leads down through the village. We have someone who comes once a month and flushes it out with water. No levers or extravagant separation system."

Alec shrugs and hops off the table.

"Your loss, then. The fancy stuff is pretty great. Let's get going, huh?"

I gesture toward the door. "Lead the way."

He gives me that strange look again, then opens the door and steps out into the darkness that has now completely fallen over the city. We tread back toward town, and homes come closer together as we pass through the streets. I'm surprised once again by the city's vastness and overall vivacity. Even in the darkness, this place seems to have a buzzing sort of life to it. The tavern and several other businesses are still well lit, and laughter and music flood from many doorways.

We walk through the streets without speaking, and Alec's eyes shift this way and that, as if he's watching out for someone. I wonder if someone will be joining us, but earlier he seemed intent on going alone. Perhaps he's avoiding someone, then.

I open my mouth more than once to ask what he's looking for, but he seems so focused; eyes darting around the city streets, checking the shadows, shoulders and back tense and upright, so I remain silent.

Once we're no longer within city limits and he seems to relax, and I speak up with other questions that have been swirling around my mind.

"Do you know where you're going?" I huff. Alec's legs are much longer than mine, and I have to walk at a brisk pace to keep up with him. I like to think I keep myself fairly fit, but my muscles burn and my body aches for sleep already.

Alec scoffs and rolls his eyes.

"I always know where I'm going. It's my job," he says, lifting his chin, even picking up his pace.

"Okay, so where are we going, then?" I ask, half-jogging to keep up.

Thankfully, Alec slows for a moment, whirling to face me. He sighs and rubs his forehead. His amber eyes meet mine, and he points into the distance.

"A week's trek through the forest in that direction will take us to the city of Parth. I have a contact there that may know who's taken my mamman. That's where we're going, got it?" he snaps.

"Fine, that's where we're going," I say. "Sorry." I chew my lip as we continue walking, but it isn't long before I find myself speaking up again. "What makes you think someone's *taken* your mamman?"

This gets him to stop again, and he glares at me.

"She doesn't just act strange for days and then disappear. She's *always* reliable," he says, tone sharp.

He strides forward again.

"Did you see her acting strangely?" I ask, pressing. I know I shouldn't press him about the issue, but I'm genuinely very curious, and walking in silence with Alec is nothing like walking in silence with my crew. It's so tense.

"No. I just got back from a job to find she'd gone missing," he mumbles. "But even when I'm gone, she always leaves a note at my house when she leaves, and she has *never* missed an appointment with the Council. Not once."

At this point, I'm actually jogging, and my side is throbbing. I do my best to catch my breath and clutch my side. I'm not sure if Alec notices this or not; but thankfully, he slows down again, and this time he stays at a normal pace.

"Mathilda told me about a witch in the mountains," I tell him. I'm not entirely certain why I bring this up. I myself find it sounds crazy, and I believed in magic growing up. But I fail to find any other explanation to whatever connects me to Alec, so I think it might be worth mentioning, at least. What Mathilda said about people disappearing and the witch always collecting her debts rings through my mind like a bell.

Alec merely blinks in my direction. Then, he says, "We're wasting time. We're going to Parth, and that's final." He grunts, then mumbles, "Listening to the healer's nonsense."

"Isn't it at least worth looking into as a reason your mamman might have gone missing? You just said yourself that she never does this. And there's this thing happening with us, I just thought..."

"Fates, woman!" he shouts. "What's with all the talking? How about this: If you want to come, fine. Keep your obnoxious questions and your ridiculous opinions to yourself. Okay? This isn't some fairytale, and you sound like a child bringing up witches and magic and mysteries. If we must travel together, let's at least do it *quietly*."

I stop for a moment, shocked, but I shake it off quickly enough and keep going.

"I'm just trying to be informed, you know! I've never seen anything like this. It's important to learn and hear more than one perspective before deciding you know what's right," I say stubbornly.

"Right," he calls back to me. "Seems like you just decided what's right after hearing Mathilda's little story."

After that, I keep quiet, not because he told me to, but because I don't want to hear his griping about my questions anymore.

The farther from town we venture, the denser the forest around us becomes. The night is quiet, mostly. A large, almost full moon hangs high overhead. A soft breeze blows through the trees, rustling leaves and pine needles. Although the moon provides plenty of light for us to see by, I find no animals in our wake.

Finally, Alec slows further and eyes the forest before setting down his bags.

"This is where we'll rest for tonight," he says.

He bends to rummage through one of his bags, and I can tell this motion hurts the wound in his side, because mine starts to hurt again, as well. I step forward and reach out to offer my help, but he pulls back, bag in hand, narrowing his eyes at me. What's this guy's problem?

From the bag Alec pulls out a couple of thin blankets. I blink with surprise, and reach out, thinking he's going to share one of those blankets with me. But he lays them out on top of each other and tosses his bags on top, and I feel foolish for even thinking he'd share. Of course he wouldn't – we've just met, and it's clear he doesn't like me much.

The space between us is quiet, tense. I wonder if he's still irritated with me from earlier, but I decide it's probably best just to let it go for tonight.

"Well," I start. "I'll go get us some firewood. I'll be back."

"Don't wander off too far," he says as I turn to walk into the forest. "I've got enough problems. Don't need to add rescuing you to the list."

I stop in my tracks and grind my teeth. My fists ball up at my sides, fingernails digging into my palms. I remember that we obtain each other's wounds and dig in, feeling the pinch of my nails against my skin. I wince, but I smile when he doesn't say anything else.

"Don't worry about me," I say snidely. "I can take care of myself."

11

I trek into the woods, listening to the crunch of my shoes against the leaves that litter the forest floor, grateful for the moment alone. Traveling with this man looks like it's going to be much harder than I thought.

I spend a few moments gathering wood, snapping the longer branches against my knees. Before long I've got an armful of them, and I head back to where we're making camp for the night. When I get back, Alec has already started a fire, and he sits with his back propped against a nearby tree. I drop my lumber and glare at him.

Alec simply shrugs, lifts the flask in his hands, and smiles at me before taking a long swig. When he swallows his drink, he says, "You took too long."

"You're an ass," I reply, and he shrugs again.

"You're the one who offered to get wood. It's not like I asked you to do it."

I roll my eyes. Curling my legs beneath my body, I sit beside the fire almost opposite Alec and stare into the flames. The burning wood crackles and sparks, and flames lick at the darkness. From the other side, I hear Alec sigh. He takes a long drink from his flask, and I pull my canteen from my bag and go to take a drink as well, but it's empty, so I set it back down with a grunt.

A moment later, Alec's water canteen lands on the ground beside me, tossing dirt onto my boots. I look up, surprised, but he's still scowling at me.

I take a deep breath and try to let my irritation go. I raise the canteen and unscrew the lid, lifting it to my lips. When it's near my nose, however, the strong scent of spirits hits me like a wall. My face scrunches up, and I quickly twist the cap back on and throw it back to him.

"No, thank you," I grumble. The scent stings my nose.

"You really don't like mead, do you?" he asks, taking another hefty drink, leaning back with the action.

"I *really* don't."

"I bet you'd like wine. Girls like you love a nice, sweet wine," he says.

"What do you mean, girls like me?" I snap defensively.

"Snobs, prisses," he says, matter-of-factly. "Girls who think they're better than everyone else."

His comment makes my face flush, and I clench my fists.

"You don't know anything about me," I say. The words feel like a growl, but when they leave my lips, they're soft around the edges. They hang in the air between us for a while before Alec speaks up again.

"Fine then. So, sweetheart, tell me something about yourself. What's your thing?" Alec asks.

"My *name* isn't sweetheart. It's *Lane*," I say. When he doesn't answer, I follow up with, "What do you mean, my thing?"

Alec nods and turns his gaze back to me. The flames send patterns of light and shadow flickering across his face, and his eyes reflect the golden light of the fire.

"Your thing. What are you about?" he asks.

Still confused, I shake my head.

"I'm not entirely sure, I guess. If you're talking about what I do for work, I'm in trading. I take cargo from village to village. I used to go with my pappan when I was younger. Now I run my own crew. One day, I'll take over the whole business from him."

Alec is quiet for a moment, his face pensive. I find myself running my fingers across the ground beneath me. The dirt is cool and calming against my fingertips.

"Is that what you want to do?" he asks. His question takes me completely by surprise. Nobody has outright asked me what I want to do before.

"Well, sure. It's what I've always done. I get to travel, and I like to draw maps of where I've been. I keep notes about all the places I visit, and I like looking at all the progress I've made. Besides, it's much better than the alternative, I think."

Alec leans in, listening intently.

"What's the alternative?"

I sigh.

"Joining the Women's Council like my mamman."

Alec raises his eyebrows as my stomach growls.

"A stubborn female like yourself?" he asks. "I imagine you'd be all over a position on the Women's Council. Think of all the opportunities you'd have to solicit your opinion."

I snort. This mercenary acts as if he knows me. He doesn't know the first thing about me.

"Not that it's any of your business, but I don't belong in a place like that. My mamman tried training me when I was little, and it didn't go well. I don't... I don't want to sit around all day discussing Maran's problems instead of doing something about them. And besides, it's what everyone expects of me. I hate that."

"Hey, I can understand that," he says.

"So, what's your thing?" I ask. When my stomach growls a second time, I shift my weight uncomfortably, and Alec lets out a single laugh.

"I'm tall and mysterious," he says. Before I can think up a witty response, he's on his feet, brushing off the back pockets of his trousers. "We've got an early morning. Get some sleep." He scoops up his canteen and nods in the direction of one of his bags that sits beside the fire. "There's some bread in that bag over there. Don't eat all of it."

At that, the conversation is over. I get up and shuffle through the bag until I find the bread he's talking about. I break off a piece and eat it slowly, savoring the taste. I dig around some more and find another, larger canteen. I twist the top off and take a cautious sniff. My shoulders relax. Water.

I take a big, refreshing drink before setting the canteen back in the bag. Then I crawl back beside the fire and lie down on the cold ground. I tuck my bow and arrows behind my back and stuff my satchel under my head to serve as my pillow. I fall asleep watching the fire.

12

When I wake the campfire has gone out, and red embers smolder in its place, leaving little light to see by. I peer around through the darkness searching for any trace of sunlight, and I find none. It's still hours before sunrise.

I prop myself up on my elbow and rub my eyes.

It's only then that I'm jolted with a terrible realization: Alec is gone. He's left no trace of his ever being there, aside from the smoldering coals of our fire and a few large-booted footprints.

Fates.

"It's not even dawn," I mutter, jumping up and grabbing my belongings. My side throbs at the movement, and I work to steady myself as my vision blurs. I feel like I haven't slept at all. I shivered through most of the night, and my entire body aches from sleeping on the ground. At least when I travel with my crew, I sleep on a mat.

I cannot believe he just left me. I wonder how long he's been gone. Did he simply wait for me to fall asleep and leave then?

How long have I even been sleeping? I growl as I dig through my satchel to find my map. I lean in close to the smoldering embers to try and see my location. I'm able to get a rough idea of the direction I need to go on my way to Parth, and I hurry to get moving. I hope I'll catch up with Alec soon. At least when the sun comes up I'll be able to check my map again and see if I'm still on course for Parth... *If* he was telling me the truth when he told me Parth is where we were headed. At this point, I really can't be sure.

I half-jog, half-walk for the next hour or so, grumbling to myself all the way, swearing to myself that if I catch up with Alec, I'm going to strangle him. My side hurts with every step I take, and I've got an obnoxious kink in my neck, but I find some comfort in the fact that the mercenary probably feels just as awful.

As I walk, I hear a distant howling and the sound of the wind, much colder now than it was when we made camp, whistling through the trees.

I roll my shoulders in an attempt to loosen some of the tension that's come from sleeping directly on the ground, I turn my attention back to concentrating on keeping to the moonlit path ahead. Through the darkness, I can barely make out the shape of a person. Although it causes more pain in my injury, I pick up my pace, doing my best to be quiet in case it's not Alec.

Sure enough, as I get closer to the figure in the shadows, I discover it to be Alec. For someone who is in such a hurry, I'm surprised I was able to catch up with him so quickly. He sits on a fallen tree with his back to me, and by the looks of it, he's stopped to eat some breakfast. Perhaps he imagined I'd sleep longer.

Filled with an anger that makes my blood hot and my body tense, I scoop up a fistful of dirt and throw it in his direction.

"You left me behind!" I yell at the back of his head. He turns, eyebrows raised, mouth full. A half-eaten apple sits in the palm of his hand.

He recovers from the surprise quickly, though, and he retorts with, "What did you expect? I told you I didn't want you slowing me down. I wanted to keep moving, so that's exactly what I did."

"And what? Just leave me alone in the woods with no food or anything?" I ask, throwing my hands to my hips.

Alec shrugs.

"Not my problem. You said you travel often for work, right? You'd probably be fine. And besides, you're the one who tagged along without any supplies," he argues.

Through gritted teeth, I growl, "Because I'm trying to keep *you* from getting *us* injured! You say it's not your problem, but if you'd like to avoid getting yourself hurt, or at least until we figure out how deep this strange connection goes so you don't starve to death by leaving me out here, I *am* your problem. And unfortunately, you are mine."

Alec chews silently for a moment.

"Whatever. Come, don't come. But if I decide it's time to go and you're not up, I'm leaving you behind," he says.

With that, he turns his back on me, scoops up his bags, and continues walking. Although I'd like nothing more than to turn around and put as much distance between the two of us as possible, I hurry to follow him. Until I learn more about whatever it is that's binding us together, and more importantly, how to sever that bond, I'll need to keep an eye on him.

"Heads up," he says, throwing something in my direction. I catch the item with both hands and immediately move to wipe a cool, sticky liquid off my hands onto my shirt. Apple juice. Alec has thrown me his half-eaten apple.

"What's this?" I ask, raising my voice so he can hear me.

Alec turns so I can see half of his face, which holds a wicked grin.

"You mentioned you were worried about not having any food. Now you won't starve to death," he says.

My jaw drops.

"Are you serious?" I ask.

The smile widens as he turns away. "If you don't want it, don't eat it. Not my problem."

I grip the apple, intent on throwing it right at the back of his head, but more juice leaks out onto my fingers, and my stomach growls. Aside from the bread from last night, I can't remember the last thing I ate. I turn the apple to the side that hasn't been bitten, and I force myself to take a bite.

The apple's sweet, juicy flavor spreads across my tongue, and my tastebuds sing. My hesitation forgotten, I scarf down the rest of the apple. It's gone too soon, but my mood has brightened somewhat. I wonder if our time together might be more bearable – and I might be able to learn more about our connection without fearing he will leave me behind every time I close my eyes – if I try some pleasant conversation.

I take a deep breath and wipe the juice from my face, dropping the apple core onto the ground.

Here goes nothing.

I clear my throat.

"Have you always wanted to be a mercenary?" I ask, catching up so I'm walking beside him. He seems proud of his work, perhaps he'll be willing to talk about it. If I can get him talking, maybe I can sort out what he knows of our situation.

In the darkness, Alec's eyes cloud over.

"No," he says. I think he'll continue, tell me what he wanted to be, but he says nothing more.

"What did you want to be instead?" I ask.

"Does it matter?" Although he sounds like he's joking, there's a hint of bitterness in his tone. "Sellsword is what I am. That's all there is to it. What does it matter if I wanted to be something else once upon a time?"

I resist the urge to roll my eyes.

"We all want to be something when we're young. I think those dreams are largely responsible for who we turn out to be."

"Perhaps that's the case where *you* come from," he says.

In the distance, the faintest light paints the horizon with a deep purple that's barely noticeable through the trees.

I drop the subject for the time being, focusing my attention on watching the sunrise ahead of us. As we walk, the purple lightens and stretches across the sky, inviting beneath it the colors of pink, then orange, and then the forest around us lightens immensely. Slowly, creatures begin to scuttle about, and birds chirp all around me. At least we don't have to walk in silence anymore.

As I watch the sky change, Alec remains quiet with his eyes straight ahead. I wonder if he's always like this. I wonder what his mamman is like. She must have been wonderful to him if he's willing to risk everything to bring her back. Or maybe it is just his job, as he claims. I also wonder how I can learn what's happening to us if he refuses to talk about anything.

I pick at the dirt under my fingernails and try to decide if it's worth trying to make conversation again. It can't hurt to keep talking, I suppose.

"Do you like being a sellsword?" I ask.

Alec shrugs, and his face brightens with a half-smile.

"Sure, I do. What's not to like?"

"Well," I say, giving it some thought. "I don't know. I've never met a mercenary before you. I'm not sure how one gets into the profession, or what exactly it entails aside from fighting people and doing their dirty work. Do you need to be professionally trained? I have no idea what kinds of things would draw someone into a job like yours."

He chuckles dryly, and I watch as he adjusts the bags on his shoulders. Judging by the aching in my side, I bet he's hurting, too. I reach out a hand and offer to carry one, and he slings one over to me. I slide it up onto my good shoulder, doing my best not to show my surprise at how heavy it is.

"Fair enough," Alec says. "There's lots to like about a job like this, and there are many ways to go about being enlisted. It's easy. All a guy has to do is be willing to risk his neck for money. No professional training is actually required, though I'd highly recommend it."

"Were you professionally trained?" I find myself leaning toward him, walking closer to his side to listen as he describes his work. I'm grateful he's actually talking to me. Perhaps if I can get him to open up, if I can keep him talking, he'll be less likely to leave me behind again. At the very least, he seems less annoyed by having me around at the moment.

Another smile stretches across his lips, but it's a wry smile that doesn't reach his eyes.

"I was." Our feet fall in time together, footsteps sounding at the same rhythm as we continue on our path.

"That's fascinating," I say. "We have professional fighters in our village, but I was never allowed to train. Not that I really wanted to, I suppose. I was always intimidated by the idea."

Alec harumphs.

"What about the parts you like?" I continue, gently nudging him to keep talking.

"Oh, there's plenty to enjoy about a job like this. The freedom, the travel, the people. The money's not half bad, either, if you know where to look for the higher paying jobs. And everything is dependent upon you. If you want to work, you work. You want to prolong your stay somewhere new, there's not really anyone you have to ask for permission. Plus, the action's *to die for*."

He winks at me, unashamed, and I shake my head.

"I believe it," I mutter.

The pathway we've been walking since last night merges onto a well-travelled dirt road that leads east in one direction and southwest in the other. We take up the eastern route, and I find myself grateful for the more even footing.

By midday, the air between us seems much lighter, more breathable. We stop for a quick lunch and take a short break to rest our legs. Mine burn from walking so much, and stretching them is the loveliest sensation. I lean against a large boulder and wiggle my toes in my boots.

Suddenly, Alec stands upright, head cocked to one side. He's listening for something, but I hear nothing outside the ordinary.

"What is it?" I whisper. He holds his hand out, index finger extended.

He listens for a moment longer before whispering back, "We've got company."

Something about the way he whispers those words sends shivers down my spine, and my entire body tenses; but before I can react, several men with brown burlap flour sacks over their heads jump out of the surrounding trees.

I pull my bow from my back and reach for an arrow as Alec unsheathes his sword. One man approaches me from my left, and I turn and loose an arrow aimed at his leg as he raises a wooden club high above his head. The arrow sinks deep into his flesh, and he screams, letting the club fall from his grasp as he tumbles to the ground, both hands reaching for his wounded leg. The *thunk* of the arrow hitting his leg teamed with his screams has my stomach roiling, but I have no time to vomit now.

I rush forward and kick the club away from him. My heart beats so fast that my chest aches, and I find myself short of breath. Somewhere behind me, I hear Alec grunting, and the sound of metal against wood. I turn, already reaching back for another arrow, but I'm too slow. Another man has jumped out of the tree line and snuck up behind me. He swings at me with a large branch, and I backtrack, tripping over something behind me. I gasp as I fall backward, landing hard on my backside. The man races closer.

I let out a guttural cry and grip my bow tightly with both hands. When the man is close enough, I swing with all my might, knocking him across the face. He lets out a soft grunt and pauses for a moment, as though he's suddenly confused. Then, lifting a hand to the now bloody bag on his face in an attempt to rub the area I've just hit, he stumbles to his knees and topples forward, unconscious.

I roll away from him and take the opportunity to get back on my feet and look around. As I do, a horrible pain shoots across the left side of my face, and I have to blink several times to clear my vision before I'm able to look around to see who has hit me. The man I shot in the leg is still on the ground, whimpering, and no one else is around, but Alec has run two men clean through with his sword.

I'm startled by the sight of those two men bleeding on the forest floor, but I have no time to process, because Alec fends off three more as I stand there gawking.

"Watch out!" I call to him as his sword catches two of the men's clubs. He struggles against the weight they apply to their weapons as the third man hits him in the back with his club. My vision blurs and pain erupts to the right of my spine. I lose my balance for a moment, but Alec's voice helps keep me on my feet.

"Not helping!" he shouts.

Fighting the pain, I nock an arrow and send it flying toward the third man, but it misses as the four men dance around each other. I send off another arrow, which hits one of the other men in the buttocks. While that man is distracted, Alec pushes the other two off of him and slides his blade across the throat of the man I just shot.

I let out a startled squeak and stumble forward. "Stop!" I yell at Alec.

I scoop up one of the clubs from the men lying on the ground and lunge, swinging it at one of the two remaining fighters. I hit him in the side of the head. He blinks at me through two uneven holes in his flour sack mask and then falls back, landing on the ground with a *thud*.

Meanwhile, Alec finishes off the last man. As I turn to him, Alec uses the sleeve of his shirt to wipe blood from his face. I must look as horrified as I feel, because he stops mid-wipe. The two of us stand there, panting and staring at each other. My heart beats a million times a minute. Behind me, the cries of the man I shot in the leg still ring out into the forest.

"What?" he asks when I raise my eyebrows at him.

"Who are these men?" I frown at him, trying to get my breathing under control. I still feel like I'm going to be sick. Pain radiates in my back and my face, and it's sharp and hot in my side.

Alec finishes wiping the blood from his sword onto his trousers before sheathing it.

"Bandits, is my guess." He pulls the mask off of one of the men he killed and holds it out. "Not very creative ones, either."

I blink at him.

"What?" he asks again. "They were going to rob us, and likely do worse than that to you, I'll wager."

"Did you have to *kill* them?" I ask, bewildered. My body begins to shiver as I look around at all the blood.

"Are you serious?" he asks. He's looking at me like I'm insane. I understand things could have just gotten really bad, but I've never seen so much death in one place. I knew I'd be traveling with a mercenary, but I'm surprised and a little embarrassed to find that I didn't expect to witness any killing. I don't want them following us. You didn't kill any of them?" He drops the mask lazily onto the man's body and makes his way to the one I shot in the leg.

"No!" I say, taken aback. Did he *want* me to kill them? I don't even know them!

When he reaches the man, Alec sighs and moves to pull his sword from its sheath once more. I find myself racing toward him, and my hand catches his sleeve, yanking it backward and away from his sword.

"What are you doing?" he asks. "Let go!"

He waves his arm, trying to shake my grip from his sleeve, but I hold on tightly.

"You've killed enough of them. I'm sure they got the message. Leave the rest of them be."

The man lying at our feet lets out a soft cry and looks up at us, though is mask is now crooked, so only one eye is visible beneath it.

"Do *you* want them tracking us?" Alec growls, still trying to get me to release his shirt. My other hand is now clenched over his wrist. "Fates, you're annoying. Will you *let go?*"

"They won't follow us. They won't!" I shout at him. I look to the man below us. "You won't follow us, will you?"

"N-no. I swear it. You're good as gone already!" the man says, voice quivering.

"See?" I turn back to Alec. "Good as gone."

Alec lets out a frustrated grunt and looks to the sky.

"Fates," he mutters. Then he raises his voice. "Fine! What a pain in the ass."

The man at our feet lets out another soft whimper.

"Promise?" I ask, refusing to let go, eyes pleading. "Promise you'll let the rest of them live?"

"You're a child."

"Promise!" I yell.

"I promise, I promise. Now *let go!*" he shouts back at me.

I do, and he yanks his arm away from me. He turns toward the rest of the men, both dead and alive, and addresses them with a deep, booming voice.

"We're going now. If any of you follow us, you'll meet the same fate as your friends!"

"Thank you," I start, but he's already scooped up our bags and stormed off up the dirt road.

We travel the rest of the week without incident, and we reach the city of Parth a few hours after dark on the final day. This city is teeming with music and laughter and life. It's built on a bridge that covers miles of the narrowest part of the Maranee River, and it's earned a reputation of being the place where people go to celebrate, constantly.

I've visited the city of Parth a handful of times in my life, but it's always been during the day when the markets were bustling. When I used to go with my pappan, he'd always have us out of town before dark, grumbling about the city's outrageously high nightly rates for their inns.

When I started making trips on my own, I kept with the same mentality, always figuring that it would be more convenient to camp out for the night elsewhere or travel through the night to one of the woodland encampments southward.

At night, the city takes on a whole new atmosphere. Twinkling lights of all colors hang from windows, draping across the streets from one stone building to the next. The cool night air comes alive with the sounds of different types of music, and as we wander through the cobbled streets, the various melodies, instruments, and sounds create a cacophonous symphony that makes the blood thrum in my veins. I can't help but smile at how alive the city is. If I thought Nerine was lively at night, this place is a whole other story.

Alec has been quiet for the majority of our trip since our run-in with the bandits. I can't tell if he's irritated with me or simply focused on his quest, but I've left him to his thoughts as much as possible. Now, I speak up.

"Where are we headed?" I ask. He regards me with a sideways glance and shifts his bag from one shoulder to the other. As he does, the now almost-healed wound in my side aches.

"We're going to stay tonight at the Windmill Inn. My contact is meant to meet us there, and he'll hopefully have some more information regarding where my mamman has been taken."

I nod slowly.

My face floods with warmth, and I worry about staying within city limits. I have some money, but not enough to cover a room in a fancy place like Parth.

Alec cocks his head to the side and chuckles, as if he can read my mind.

"The beds at the Windmill aren't luxurious by any stretch, but they're far better than sleeping on the ground, and the room comes with a hot meal," he says.

I keep quiet, running through possible answers to his statement in my mind. A couple walks by us holding hands and leaning on each other. Their laughter echoes off the stone buildings around us.

"Ah, money troubles, eh?" Alec asks as I watch the couple and avoid his question. He slaps a large, calloused hand on my shoulder. I squirm away from him.

"I *have* money, thank you. I just didn't go to Nerine expecting a prolonged journey, let alone one that would require me to stay in costly inns." I kick at a loose rock lying in the street and watch as it rolls away ahead of us.

"Well, there are plenty of things a girl like you could do in a city like this for money," he says, running his eyes up and down my body and waggling his eyebrows. I gasp, wrapping my arms tightly around my torso.

"Not on your life," I say, tone biting. "Not on anyone's."

For some reason, this makes him laugh. He throws his head back and lets out a hearty, throaty sound.

"I suppose that's fair. No worries – *I* started this quest prepared, so I've got you covered. First night's board is on me. After that, you're on your own."

I roll my eyes.

A group of women exit from the building to our right. They giggle and chatter, bumping into one another. Their conversations sound an awful lot like hens clucking to me, and I stifle a laugh of my own, turning my attention back to Alec, who is very obviously watching their behinds with a smirk on his face as they pass.

"I don't need you paying for me," I say.

"Fine then," he says with a careless shrug. "Have it your way. Sleep in the streets. I will tell you, though; you'll want to hide out somewhere. Cities like this are known for their partygoers. After midnight, there's no telling who you'll run into."

I turn around quickly so my entire body faces him, and my black braid whips me in the face. My jaw hangs open and my eyebrows raise high on my forehead, and Alec gives me a strange look.

"What?" I ask.

"Oh, you don't want to sleep in the streets?" Alec asks. "Imagine that. Since I'm *incredibly* generous, and you didn't come prepared to stay in a place like this, I'll cover the first night. You can pay me back later. Then, if you're really set on paying for any future stays, you can come up with the money for it on your own. Deal?"

I take a deep breath and exhale it in a huff.

"Fine," I say. "Just tonight. Any other stays in places like this, and I'll pay my own way. And I will pay you back."

We make a series of left- and right-hand turns, roaming deeper and deeper into the city. The moon has started its steady climb toward the center of the sky by the time we reach the Windmill Inn.

Just as its name suggests, the building is shaped like a functioning windmill. The giant mill sits on the front of the building, twinkling light-covered propelling blades so long they almost touch the doorframe with every swing. I've never seen anything quite like it.

Inside, warmth hits us like a slamming door. Fires burn in the hearth on either side of a large, open room. Nearly every table is full, seating customers who chat giddily and eat heartily. Men and women dressed in uniforms of white shirts with loose, puffy sleeves and thick brown aprons over black trousers weave through tables serving food and drink to their happy patrons. The smell of freshly baked bread, onions, and meat fills the establishment, and I find my mouth watering as I take it all in.

I don't realize I've just been standing here until Alec bumps me with his elbow. I blink several times and meet his gaze, and he winks at me.

"It's just an inn," he says, giving me that half-smile. "Come on, let's get something to eat."

"Where?" I ask, looking around the room for any open spot to sit in.

"Don't worry about it," he replies, already making his way across the room. He addresses a man behind the counter and shakes his hand before putting some coins on the counter's surface. The man scoops them up and nods, laughing at something Alec said. Then they both turn their eyes on me, and I decide I should probably move my feet.

I step forward, shuffling across the crowded dining area. The murmur of people eating and talking helps distract me from my anxiety. I've been in plenty of inns before – I don't know why I feel so strange about this one.

"Hello," I say to the man behind the counter.

"Hello there, little lady," he greets in return, bowing his bald head slightly and giving me a warm, toothy smile. "Got two bowls of stew coming your way. Room'll be ready soon." The man slides a key with a thin, fringed black and brown rope tied to it across the counter. Alec scoops the key up and reaches out with his other hand to shake.

"Pleasure, as always," Alec says to the man. He turns around and smirks at me before inclining his head in the direction of the tables. Alec pushes himself away from the counter, and within seconds, he's found himself a place at one of the crowded tables. I raise my eyebrows and follow, intrigued, as he strikes up a conversation with someone that seems to be in his mid-thirties. Alec goes around to the other side of the table, where a couple of other men have made a little bit of space.

"Is this your contact?" I ask when I catch up with him. The man looks me over and reaches out his hand. I take it and shake it firmly. "I'm Lane," I tell him. "It's nice to meet you."

"Likewise," the gentleman says to me. He grins and scoots over, bumping one of his seatmates to make room for us. Then he makes a gesture with his hand for me to take a seat beside him, and I seize the opportunity before someone else can slide into the spot. "I'm Rodrick," the man says to me.

Alec places his hands on the table, fingers intertwined. "Roddy here was just telling me where his eyes say my mamman is headed. She's gone east, toward Helna."

"Eyes?" I ask, confused frown creasing my brow.

Rodrick gives a low, merry chuckle. "Informants. People who watch the city for me. Got eyes in every major city in Maran."

"Interesting," I say. Alec looks at me like I've just said something stupid, and I feel the heat return to my cheeks and look down at my own hands, noting the dirt beneath my fingernails. I'm covered in grime. I even notice a bit of blood left over on my hands from our interaction with the bandits a few days ago.

The man to my other side laughs loudly, and he leans back into me, catching my bow on his back. I mutter an apology and slowly remove my belongings from my back, placing them between my legs beneath the table. As I move them, I accidentally elbow Rodrick in the stomach, but he simply smiles at me.

Over the next few minutes, I listen intently to Alec and Rodrick make conversation and share theories of where Alec's mamman might be going, hoping they might say something that will answer the burning questions I've had since I met Alec and discovered this strange bond we have. Rodrick says that his "eyes" informed him that Alec's mamman was last seen traveling alone, with a dazed look in her eyes. They said she was covered in filth and looked exhausted, but she wouldn't respond to anyone as she passed through town, and wouldn't stop walking.

Some of the places they mention in their theories are names I've only seen on maps. I like to think of myself as a fairly well-traveled individual, but the truth is, I've never been much farther east than Parth, or farther north than Grand Council Keep, where I went only once on a trip with my mamman. My supply runs have allowed me to see a large fraction of our continent, but I've remained mostly local.

Soon, a nice woman comes along with our food, placing two large steaming bowls of stew in front of us, followed by two hefty round loaves of bread.

"Eat up, you two. Stew's great tonight," the woman says, keeping her eyes trained on Alec. "Can I get you anything to drink?"

I straighten at the sight of food, perking up at the thought of something cold to drink.

"Could I get some water, please?" I ask.

The woman nods and gives me a small smile.

"Sure thing, doll." Her gaze returns to Alec, and her face lights up. "Anything for you, handsome?" she asks.

Alec gives her a beaming grin.

"Ale for me, please. Lots of it," he says.

"You got it," she says, and her eyes linger on him for just another moment before she turns to head back toward the kitchen. At this point, Rodrick has finished his meal. He stands, nodding at both of us.

"That's it for me," he says, patting his stomach, leaving his dishes on the table. "If you're ever in Laden's Way, seek me out. I'd be happy to share my table with the two of you." With that, he takes his leave, and Alec and I are once again surrounded by strangers.

I take the chance at extra elbow room and scoot over, then reach down into my bag and pull out my map. I move my bowl of stew over and spread the map out, tracing my finger up to Laden's Way, quite a bit north of Parth. With my other hand, I shove hurried scoops of stew into my mouth. The meat is tender and melts on my tongue, vegetables accenting its flavor perfectly. I moan at the taste and feel myself relax.

Alec leans forward, embracing his own bowl of soup. He gives me a smug look before breaking into his bread and dipping it into the stew's thick broth.

"What's that?" he asks around a mouthful of food.

I raise my eyebrows at him. "A map? Surely someone who travels as much as you have has seen one of these before," I say sarcastically.

Alec rolls his eyes. "No shit. I mean, that's a map I haven't seen before."

I reach into my satchel, pull out my charcoal, and add some notes. I make a note that Rodrick is from Laden's Way, mark a small x where we ran into those bandits, and add some notes about Parth's night life and Windmill Inn.

"Did you do all this yourself?" Alec asks, leaning across the table to get a better look at my map. I sit up proudly and look over the new additions.

"Yes. I mean, the map is an old one I got from my pappan's office when I was younger. I've been adding to it for a few years now. Everywhere I go, I like to sketch in reminders for myself."

Alec nods, taking another bite of broth-soaked bread.

"Impressive," he says.

I wait for him to follow up with a snide remark, but he leaves it at that.

The woman from before returns with our drinks in hand. She carries a glass full of water for me and a pint of ale for Alec. She sets both drinks down gracefully and bites her lip, eyeing him once again. I have to scoot over as she leans forward, placing her palms against the table. Her cleavage is clearly visible, and I look away.

"How long are you in town for?" she asks him in a voice like silk.

"Just tonight," he says easily. "We're moving on from here first thing in the morning."

The woman gives him a pouty look. "Shame. You're room's all ready. I'd be happy to make your time here worthwhile... since you're moving on so soon." She reaches across the table and runs a finger over the top of his hand.

I find myself trying to look anywhere but at the two of them, but I can't seem to keep my eyes off of them for long.

Alec shoots her a charming smile.

"I appreciate the offer, darling, but I don't think that would be very courteous to my travel companion, here. You see, she's got to sleep in that room, and it'd be quite inconsiderate of me to keep her up all night."

"So thoughtful," she says dreamily before sending me a quick glare.

Oh, please, I think. The woman gives Alec's hand a squeeze and backs away from the table.

"If you change your mind, handsome, I'll be here."

"I'll bear it in mind," he says, giving her one last smile before she scoops up Rodrick's dishes and leaves.

I don't realize I'm staring at Alec until he asks, "What?"

I blink my shock away and return my attention to my food. I shovel a big bite of stew into my mouth and busy myself rolling my map back up and putting it away.

"Nothing at all," I say. "Nothing at all."

He shrugs, but his grin remains.

Alec takes a long swig of his ale before holding his pint out to me. My first reaction is to glare at him, but I soften as I realize, surprisingly, that this is a friendly gesture; he's not mocking me.

"I'm good with my water," I say between bites of stew. "But thank you."

Alec shrugs and takes another drink.

"Still bet you'd like wine."

Silence settles in between us once more. Soon enough, exhaustion creeps in, and I stifle a long yawn.

I scrape the bottom of my bowl for the remainder of my stew and hold out my loaf of bread to him. He takes it and puts it into his bag with the rest of our food.

I fight another yawn and scan the room. It's still plenty crowded, but the chatter has died down to a dull murmur as people have begun to retire to their rooms for the night.

"You look tired," Alec says. He holds out the key to our room, and I take it. The metal is warm in my hand, the rope coarse against my skin. Engraved in the key is our room number.

"Leave the room unlocked for me if you plan to sleep anytime soon," Alec says. "I'm going to have another round, see if that lovely waitress of ours will be here for long."

"You're not going to try giving me the slip again, are you?" I ask, narrowing my eyes at him.

"No," he says. "I paid for the room. I'd at least like to sleep somewhere comfortable tonight. I guess you lucked out this time around."

"Thanks," I say. I stand up, grab my belongings, and head up the stairs that lead to the inn's many bedrooms. Tonight has felt pretty nice, after getting to Parth and recovering from our bandit encounter. I feel hopeful that Alec won't try to leave me behind again, and I think we might just be getting to a place where

I can ask him about our connection again, or at least see if he knows what his mamman has to do with any of this. To me, it all feels related somehow.

14

Our room in the Windmill Inn is nice, not too small, and I relax when I notice that there are two beds. I take the opportunity having the room to myself to bathe and wash out the clothes that Alec let me borrow, hanging them up at the end of one of the beds. I braid my hair, dress in a long, somewhat scratchy robe that the innkeepers leave out for their guests.

Pappan would have refused to wear something like this, claiming it's just another way for the business owners to make more money off their guests.

Even with his voice in my head, I pull the robe closer around my body. At least it's something warm, dry, and clean I can sleep in until my – Alec's – clothes are dry.

The events of the day have worn on me, though, and after tucking my belongings beneath the bed I've picked for myself, I climb into it. The covers are warm and soft – much softer than the ground I've been sleeping on. I melt into them.

I send a quick prayer to the Fates – if they even exist – and ask them to watch over my family and my crew, as well as the bandits that we left alive, and the families of those Alec killed. As I start to fall asleep, I realize I should be waiting up. I have no idea where Alec is, and the last time he was in a tavern at night, he got stabbed, and I ended up spending the night in the medic's office. I'm exhausted, though, and I drift off and begin dreaming of the forest. Instead of the typical forest sounds, however, the one in my dream is filled with laughter and music and the sound of clinking dishes.

Sometime late in the night, I'm jolted awake when the door to the room opens, slamming loudly against the wall.

I sit up, sleep blurring my vision. I grasp for my bow beneath my bed and nock an arrow.

"Shhhh!" someone says from the doorway. The light from the hallway completely blocks their facial features.

I try to steady the shaking of my hands so my aim will hold true.

"Who's there?" I ask. I do my best to make my voice strong, authoritative. I'm not sure how successful I am.

"Quiet," Alec says, addressing himself. Then he giggles. "You're going to wake the girl. She's temperamental, you know."

I let my shoulders relax as I'm flooded first with relief, then disappointment, then anger. I straighten my robe and lower my bow, tucking it back beneath the bed.

"Fates! I could have shot you, you imbecile. Why would you barge in like that? Do you not know how to use a door like a normal person?" I snap at him.

At this point, Alec has made his way into the room, dropping his bags to the floor with a heavy thud. He's left the door wide open.

I let out a heavy sigh and throw the blankets off myself. I get up, stomp over to the door and close it, sliding the chain-lock in place before reeling around to face him. My hands are on my hips, and I can feel my frown making a little crease in the center of my forehead.

"Hey, it's *you!*" Alec says. He approaches me, arms out as if he's expecting a hug.

I put my hand out and it crashes against his firm, solid chest, stopping him from putting his arms around me. I'm surprised by how warm it is.

Using the force of my hand on his chest, I push him backward until his calves press against his bed and he falls backward onto it. I brush off my hands and plop down on my own bed across from him.

"You're drunk, aren't you?" I ask flatly.

"Oh, positively wasted," he replies, grinning from ear to ear as though this is the greatest news he's ever shared. "You've got really pretty feet, you know that?"

I look down abruptly at my bare feet. As quickly as I can manage, I pull them up and tuck them beneath my body.

"Is there anything you're serious about?" I ask him, stifling a yawn. I don't know what time it is, but it feels like I haven't slept at all.

Now that the adrenaline has worn off, I feel more exhausted than ever. I lean against my pillow. Alec grins at me. He kicks off his boots and swings his feet over the side of his bed, back and forth, like a toddler. Seeing him like this is both frustrating and a little amusing. I hate that he's always drinking, but it's nice to see him smile so much.

"Oh, I'm serious about a lot of things," he tells me, eyes wide. In the dark, I can't see their color, but I imagine them sparkling.

"Oh yeah?" I ask. My eyelids are heavy, and I have to fight to keep them open. "Like what?"

Alec lies backward.

"Absolutely. You'll see someday, when you know me better."

"When..." I doze off, leaving my sentence unfinished for a time. "If you'll let me."

Alec doesn't reply, however, except with a soft snore. His feet still dangle off the edge of his bed, but he's out like a light. Knowing that he's in here and that he's not going to run off without me again; knowing that the door is locked, and we've got a safe place to sleep for the night, I let sleep pull me back into my dream world, which has now quieted.

In the morning, I wake early. Alec is still as he fell asleep last night, arms splayed out on either side of him, legs still hanging over the edge of his bed. He snores loudly, and I think he might be there long enough for me to get some things taken care of.

I dig through the bags Alec brought in with him last night – grateful he didn't leave them in the dining area in his drunken state – and find something quick to eat. I get dressed in the clothes Alec let me borrow, happy now that they're at least somewhat clean. Then, I gather my belongings and decide to run some errands. With my charcoal and some blank parchment that I pull from my satchel, I scribble Alec a note.

Went to run some errands while you were asleep.

Please do NOT leave without me.

I know where you're headed.

I hate to leave Alec alone after he ditched me before, but I need to get some clothes that fit me and send a letter to my Pappan. I place the note on his chest and leave the room quietly, closing the door behind me. I make my way back downstairs, past the many people sitting down for breakfast, and out into town.

The city is filled with all kinds of shops, and I wish I had enough time to visit them all. I'd also love to find a library here, so I can sit down and read more about this exciting place and add new details to my maps, but I need to get back to check on Alec as soon as possible. I'm already anxious that he'll use the opportunity my absence presents to sneak away and be rid of me once and for all.

I make a mental note to return here when all is said and done, when I have more money and more time to spend exploring.

I seek out clothing shops, hunting for something my size that I can afford. I end up finding a nice outfit with durable yet soft trousers, a cream-colored shirt with loose sleeves that hang just off my shoulders – a popular style here, the saleswoman tells me – and a form-fitting, maroon vest.

Although I'm now low on money, I'm grateful to have some good, clean clothes to wear. I'll find some way to earn more money while we're traveling, I'm sure of it.

Now, to find a postal service. I ask the woman who sells me my outfit where I might find one, and she points me in the right direction.

The postal service is a small, surprisingly clean building with desks laid out across the front room and neatly organized cages containing all different kinds of birds toward the back.

"Well, hello young lady," an older gentleman greets me as I step up to the desk. "What can I do for you today?"

"I'd like to send a message to Palandra, please."

"Sure, sure." He smiles, setting deep wrinkles around his eyes. "Any particular stationary you'd like to send? We've got quite a variety of—"

"No, thank you. Just your regular stationary will be fine. Can I purchase some extra for the road, as well? I'm running short." I hate to be rude, but I'm itching to get back to the inn.

The man nods, reaches behind his desk, and retrieves a piece of plain white parchment and a inkwell pen. Much fancier than the charcoal I'm used to.

"Regular or expedited delivery?" he asks. "We've got falcons who can get your message there quicker than a fox, if you'd like. That's a figure of speech. We don't actually keep foxes at this facility, anymore. They like to eat the birds," he tells me.

"What's your regular option?" I ask, writing a message to my family.

The man's face falls a little bit; he won't be making the sale he'd like to. I roll up the parchment and return his pen as he passes me some twine to tie the message off with.

"Pigeons," he says.

"A pigeon will do just fine. Thank you."

The man takes my letter and mutters his price, and I reach into my bag and pull out my money. After purchasing the clothes, the parchment, and sending this letter, I don't have much left. Perhaps I can sell one of my maps, or I can find a place that will buy my drawings. I don't have any drawings with me, but I now have plenty of parchment and charcoal, and I don't take long to draw when my mind's set on an image.

"Your message should arrive in three to five days, depending on the weather. Come on back whenever you've got another message you'd like to send!" he says as I head for the door.

"I appreciate the help, sir. Have a lovely day," I call back to him as I leave the building.

When I return to the inn, Alec sits at one of the tables with a large mug in front of him. He's huddled over something on the table, and four men also lean over the same focal point. I approach the table, making sure that my bow doesn't hit anyone. I lean forward to see what they're doing.

"I thought you'd be long gone by now," I tell Alec. "Why are you still here?"

Alec shrugs. "Found this note on my chest this morning promising torture if I left. I believe you'd find me. I just don't want to give you cause to be more obnoxious than you already are," he says.

I narrow my eyes at him as one of the men at the table stifles a laugh in response to his comment.

"Oh, *you*—" I start.

Alec holds out a finger, shutting me up and telling the antsy fellows around him to wait. Alec keeps his eyes on four small, colored wooden dice before him. Strange symbols have been carved into each side of the dice, and Alec narrows his eyes as he runs a finger over the symbols before arranging the dice in a straight line.

On the table before him, he's ordered the dice by an X with two dashes next to it, a squiggly line that looks like a snake of some sort, a swirl, and the number six. Finally, he raises his brown eyes to look at me, and his eyebrows shoot up.

"Well, don't you clean up nicely?" he says, half-smile spreading across his lips. "I thought the cover-alls were a nice fit, but this works, too."

I scoff and feel my face heat, but I refuse to give him the satisfaction that comes with a reply, and he refocuses.

"Aha! Read it, boys. Doesn't get much clearer than that. You, my fine friend," he says, pointing to the man across from him. "Have just been eaten by the swamp serpent on your way back to the city. You owe me a copper and a tin."

The man sighs and reaches into his pockets. Alec rolls once more, once again lining the dice up straight.

"And you two," he says, now turning his attention back to the men on his right. "Got caught in the bog trying to help him. You'll barely make it out alive, but you'll have to leave all your belongings behind. That's five tins a piece. Pay up."

The three men grumble as they lay their money on the table. One man who wasn't addressed laughs as their currency clatters against the table's hardwood surface.

"Guess you should have sided with him after all," the man says, slapping the tabletop with a gloved hand.

"Right," says one of the men to Alec's right. Sweeping long, dirty hair away from his face, he glares at Alec. "'nother round."

"What are you doing?" I ask, gesturing to the dice on the table with a raised eyebrow, wondering what these men could be so upset about.

"This, sweetheart, is called Fates." Alec grins from ear to ear as he scoops the money off of the table. "And you've just witnessed my third go with these fools."

"The man's a magician, I swear it!" the one who sits across from Alec says, smacking his forehead with the palm of his hand. He runs his fingers through his thick, graying beard.

I frown.

"How does it work?" I ask.

The four men look to Alec, who leans back confidently.

"The game is one part storytelling, one part strategy, and the rest," he says, scooping up the dice into his hands and rolling them around in his palm. "Is up to Fate."

"How do you play?" I ask.

"You'll have to play to find out," Alec says with a glint of challenge in his eyes.

Playing this phenomenal game, I feel on top of the world. I lose the rest of my money when the dice roll on my turn. The green die tells that I'm attacked by a creature. The tan die tells that someone helps me out of the situation. The black die says that I perish anyway, and the blue die rolls a six, which means one copper and one tin – exactly the amount of money I have left from this morning's purchases.

Hearing Alec spin the story of my Fate – even though I "die" in the end – I can tell why he is the storyteller, despite the fact that most often the player's money goes to him. He has a way with these stories that just brings them to life before our eyes. The way he describes the symbols on the dice and interprets what they mean captivates *everyone* around us, not just those who are playing. It's only as the matches go on and players start to grumble about how much money they're losing that he begins to shorten the stories.

When Alec suggests that I try being the storyteller, I'm nervous. I don't think I can do it as well as he does, and I'm not sure I will even remember what all the symbols mean. Once I start playing, though, I don't want to stop. Every roll of the dice brings some new story to tell, some new Fate – not all bad – to whoever's turn it is. More and more men want to play when I'm the storyteller, hoping that because I'm new to the game, they'll be able to get their money back somehow. I earn my money back eightfold within an hour, though, and I want to keep playing, but Alec stops me.

"We've got a quest of our own, remember? We've made some coin, now let's get going," he says. As we prepare to leave, I'm still riding the adrenaline rush.

I stand outside the Windmill Inn, leaning against the side of the building, feeling the early afternoon sun heat my face and the cool breeze brush against my skin.

I wait for Alec to gather his things from our room. All my belongings are still with me from this morning.

The giant blades of the windmill look so plain during the day, and they spin lazily, stretching toward the sky before returning to swoop down over the doorway again.

"Something on your mind?" Alec asks when he comes outside. I hand him the clothes I changed out of, and he stuffs them into one of his bags.

I straighten, feeling almost guilty. I shake my head and adjust the strap of my satchel on my shoulder.

"Just thinking about the game, is all. How often do you play it?" I ask.

"Oh, all the time," Alec says, rubbing his neck. "Sellswords only get paid after a job is done, you see, in case they don't come back. Got to make money for provisions somehow along the way. Fates is a great way to do that. If you can learn to tell the stories well, you can facilitate the gameplay, and *that's* where your chances of earning money are the highest. Sure, there's always a chance that even the storyteller gets nothing, but that's the gamble."

I give a big stretch, surprised that my side doesn't hurt at the motion, and push myself off the wall to fall in stride with Alec as we head through the streets of Parth once again.

"Thanks for teaching me how to play," I say.

Alec shrugs.

"My pleasure," he says. "You should play games more often. You'll want to be careful, though: It actually looked for a moment like you're capable of having a good time."

I scoff and Alec laughs, shaking his head.

"For your information," I snap. "I am absolutely capable of having a good time! It's all dependent on the company I keep, so you see, it's not *me* at all."

Alec raises his eyebrows at me.

"So, it's me, huh? Well, it's a pity that you're determined to stick with me then, isn't it? I, on the other hand, can have a grand old time completely by myself," he brags.

I eye the flask hooked to the side of his bag. *Not completely by yourself,* I think.

We weave through crowds of people in the streets who act as if it's totally normal for the city to be this jammed with foot traffic. Some people hang their laundry out to dry on lines that swoop from building to building. Others water plants in front of their homes and shops, and still others shout out about their wares to attract customers to their stands and stores.

I observe Alec gracefully dodging through the streets for several minutes, see the confident lines of his face as he carefully watches the people around us. In the sunlight, I realize just how smooth his face looks. He must have shaved this morning. I wonder how long he must have been awake after I left, and if he really didn't leave me behind this morning because he didn't want me to be obnoxious when I found him again.

We've been treading at a slight incline for the past several minutes when Alec stops. He turns to his right and strides up to a break in some of the buildings, coming to a raised wall about mid-torso in height. It's the edge of the bridge, I realize.

Keeping his bags on his shoulder, he raises his elbows and rests them atop the stone surface.

At first, I'm unsure whether or not I should follow him, but I approach him quietly, raising my own arms to place them as he did. I have to lift mine much higher, as Alec stands about a foot taller than I am. The stone's cool temperature reaches my arms even through the thin material of my sleeves.

I look out onto the river, and I'm awed by its beauty, reverenced by the power of the water rushing below us. Although I know Parth was built over one of the Maranee River's narrowest points, it startles me just how vast even this portion of the river is. The water hurries by dozens of feet below us.

I spare Alec a sidelong glance and wait for him to tell me what's on his mind, if he'll tell me at all.

Alec lets out a long sigh as a flock of green-winged birds flutter past us, high overhead.

"Rodrick stopped into the inn as we were leaving. He doesn't know where she is now." He runs the hand that isn't holding onto the straps of his bags through his hair.

"Your mamman?"

I think he's going to snap at me for asking such a silly question. Of course he's talking about his mamman. Rodrick is the informant we met for information regarding where she went. But Alec doesn't snap. Instead, he takes a deep breath.

I raise my eyebrows and look at him expectantly.

"But he says his eyes tell him that she was spotted in the grasslands nearing Helna, and that if she passed through Helna at all, he's got a guy who will have more information for us. He..." Alec trails off for a moment, trying to decide how much to share with me, probably. "He warned me to be careful if we do find her. Said she was acting strange, not herself, but he couldn't tell me anything else."

"Helna, then." I nod. We were already planning to go that way, so this information doesn't feel new to me. "Was she on her own? If she was acting strangely, was she in danger?"

"He didn't say. Said she seemed distressed, and that she could have been with someone, but that his guys couldn't remember."

"Well, that's a reliable source then, isn't it?" I ask, rolling my eyes.

Alec snaps his attention to me, gaze sharp, brown eyes darkened, daring me to challenge him.

"That's all the information I have to go off of. That's why I have to get to Helna. You can come with me, or you can stay here, but don't you try to stop me when this is the only lead I have."

It's only when he's finished that I realize my mouth hangs open. I close it quickly and throw my hands up, surrendering.

"Hey, Helna sounds great. Maybe we find your mamman. Maybe we get information about where she's been. At the very least, I get to see a place that I've never been to and add to my maps. So, let's go to Helna."

Alec narrows his eyes at me.

"Fine, then. Let's get going." He turns and strides away from the bridge's edge. I give the river one more look, admiring its sparkling surface before it disappears from view as I hurry to keep after him.

16

We stop at one of the smaller restaurants on the way out of town. As we eat, we discuss our travel plans.

"So, how far is Helna from here?" I ask, finishing the last of my crème soup and looking over my map. The distance doesn't look too bad on parchment, but I know well enough that some of these older maps didn't quite get Maran's dimensions right. One day, I hope to correct them.

"This is Parth," Alec says, leaning forward and placing his finger on the large bridge marked on the map, which I've drawn in alongside two flowing pints of ale to signify Parth's affinity for endless celebration.

"Indeed," I say. "Parth, I'm familiar with."

Alec disregards my comment and draws a line with his finger across a wide-open space on the map.

"To get to Helna, we'll have a three-day journey to get out of the woods here, then we've got to cross this area, here."

"What is that?" I ask, squinting at an empty space in the map.

"Grassland. Miles and miles of it. It's a bit more dangerous than the forest because everything's so out in the open. There is very little to hide behind should someone or something come looking for trouble."

Although Alec warns me of the risks we'll be taking going through the grassland like that, his back is straight, his tone light, excitement lighting sparks in his amber eyes.

"How long will we be exposed like that?" I ask.

Alec shrugs.

"About a week and a half, if we play our cards right."

I lean forward, eyes wide.

"A week and a half?" I look at the map again. "Surely, we won't be exposed the entire time, right? This must be a well-traveled route. Wouldn't we be safer if we stick to the main roads?"

Alec leans back in his seat and studies me, eyes amused, almost unnoticeable smile quirking up the edges of his mouth. He folds his hands behind his head.

"That's what most people think. But the more you travel on the main roads, the more people you will come across, and the more likely you are to find yourself in trouble. There are a couple of small villages we might stop in on the way through if we need to, but we want to avoid those roads as much as possible."

"You're sure about this?" I ask.

"Absolutely," he says, tone steady and confident. "I've been that way countless times. I've taken the roads, and I've traveled the fields. Trust me when I say the fields are a much better option."

At my skeptical glance, he smiles.

"Unless, of course, you'd like to chance another run-in like we had with those bandits before. I'm a trained professional; I can't guarantee that there wouldn't be at least *some* killing involved. People mess with me and my quest, they pay the price."

Shocked by his nonchalance about death, I sit back in my chair and frown at him.

I can't believe we're going to be stuck together for another ten or more days. I'm going to need to send another letter to my pappan sometime soon. I hope the message I sent earlier today will suffice until we can reach Helna, or hopefully another postal service along the way. I send a quick prayer to the Fates that my family is okay, and that my pappan's business will be fine in my absence.

I want more than anything to turn around and go back home, let Alec carry out his quest alone, but he's just mentioned running into bandits, and I can't afford another serious injury if I'm to travel home on my own, and if he gets himself killed... I shudder. Who knows if news of my death would get back to my family.

I'm still hoping that I can get him to open up, so I can learn what's binding us together, and hopefully, learn how to *unbind* us. Just the thought of finally being free of my mysterious, inexplicable injuries would be reason enough, but knowing now that I won't have to follow this man around the rest of my life trying to keep him from killing us both adds an extra urge to break this bond. I'd love to spend no time with him unless it's absolutely necessary.

"Fine, we'll try it your way. Shall we get going?" I say.

I don't wait for his reply to stand up. I push my chair back in, leave some coin on the table for the young girl who served us, and write a note for her that says, *Thank you so much for your service. Have a wonderful day!*

Alec raises his eyebrows at me.

"What?" I ask.

He shrugs. "Didn't know you could be so pleasant."

"Oh, please," I say, pushing past him. "There's a lot you don't know about me, Mercenary." Although the words have a bite to them, I can't help but smile, and I do my best to hide it by turning away from him, already starting to walk away. Alec scrambles to his feet and follows my lead, and I try to extinguish the satisfaction I feel that, for once, he's trying to catch up with me.

"Tell me about your life at home," Alec says later that evening, after we've walked for hours and finally decide to set up camp for the night. I'm grateful he suddenly wishes to open up, and I hope I might be able to get some answers about this bond, and what any of this has to do with his mamman.

I look up from the sandwich I'm making to see him pulling off his boots. He sits on a log and, after pulling off his socks, he proceeds to smell them. He makes a sour face and drops them beside the fire.

I look away quickly and wipe the disgusted expression from my face.

"Why?" I ask. I've made a sandwich for Alec as well, and I walk it over to him. He takes it, eyes wide with surprise. I shrug at his reaction; it's no big deal. I would have made an extra sandwich for my sister back home, or my crewmates on the road, so I'm used to making a surplus.

"Because we're stuck out here together, so why not fill the dead air?" He rolls his eyes at me. He pulls apart his sandwich, laying the bread and cheese on his lap, then taking a bite of the salted, dried meat. "Must everything be a question with you?"

He smiles past a mouthful of meat.

I eye the display of food that he's sprawled out on his lap, one eyebrow raised.

"Mm," he starts, gesturing at his food. "It lasts longer this way. You fill up faster, and out here, it's important to make your provisions last."

I nod and settle on the ground before the fire, taking a bite of my own sandwich like a normal human being would do. From the corner of my eye, I see him wave his bread at me.

"Now, quit stalling," Alec says. "You said you're a merchant of sorts, a traveling saleswoman. Where do you hail from?" I adjust so I can look him in the eye.

"I'm not a *saleswoman*," I say. "I deliver goods that people order. I barter prices sometimes for delivery fees, but I don't *sell* anything, let alone my own goods." After a moment of silence, I look back up at him to find him staring at me amusedly. "You really want to know?" I ask.

"Please. It very much beats eating in awkward silence," he replies. The firelight sends sparkles dancing in his eyes.

"Fair enough," I say. "I'm from Palandra."

"Ah," he says, nodding as if this makes perfect sense to him. "The land of smithies."

"And other things, too," I say past my own mouthful of food. I adjust on the forest floor, confused as to why I feel so defensive. That is, after all, what my village is mostly known for. Alec throws his hands up.

"My apologies," Alec says. "I've been there from time to time in my travels, but I never stay long. Your taverns are bit lackluster, I'm afraid."

"Well, I wouldn't know. But if our taverns are lackluster, it's only because we in Palandra understand that there is more to life than ale, obnoxious music, and acting like a fool."

Alec bows his head in acknowledgement, but his face spells a challenge.

"Please, then. Share with this fool the wisdom of your people. As I said, I've never stayed in Palandra for long. What *do* the people of your village enjoy, if not ale and obnoxious music?"

I scoff, but at the moment, my mind draws a blank.

"Well," I say, turning away from his inquisitive gaze. "We enjoy a number of things."

"Like what?" he asks, unrelenting smirk plain as day on his face.

"Like... family, and responsibility, and business ventures. And we've got an excellent training program for fighters and explorers. People from our village have been all over the continent."

"Right," he says. He finishes his food and stands, makes his way to the food I left out, and digs into one of his bags for his flask. "People from all over the continent have been all over the continent, but I suppose that's all well and good. But what do you people like to do for *fun?*"

He takes a seat beside me and opens his drink, taking a long swig. A small drip trickles down the side of his jaw, and he wipes it away with a contented sigh. I'm not sure if it's our bond, or just watching him drink, but I feel a small warmth in my belly.

"Fates," I whisper under my breath. "I don't know, Alec. I'm rarely home. I suppose we have festivals, and my people seem to really enjoy them. I did when I was little, but I haven't been to a festival in quite a long time."

I stare at the flames and grit my teeth.

"I apologize," Alec says softly, leaning forward and trying to catch my eye. I turn my face away. "I didn't realize you spend so much of your time away. What do you like to do for fun when you're on the road? There's got to be something that keeps your spirits up while you're so far away from home."

My cheeks heat. I have no idea how to answer this question. I'm just always so busy, I really don't *know* what I do for fun. Working on my maps excites me, and I enjoy using my bow when I'm only practicing and not using it for hunting. For some reason, I worry that he's going to mock me for having such insignificant interests.

"What about you?" I ask. "What do *you* do for fun?"

Alec beams at me as though I've just asked the most entertaining question in the world.

"Besides this?" he holds up his flask, sloshing the liquid inside. "I do lots of things for fun. In fact, I can think of very few times where I'm *not* having a good time."

"Really," I say, voice deadpan. Of course he has a good time all the time.

"Really. Why live life at all if you're not going to enjoy it? I travel, I drink, I'm a master at Fates – as you've already learned – I fight, and I dance."

I sit back and allow my mouth to drop open. "*You* dance?"

"Is that so surprising?" he asks, taking another drink, smile still plastered on his face.

Laughter bubbles up out of my chest, swirling with the embers that disappear into the night sky. I find myself relaxing a bit – it's so nice to smile.

"I suppose not," I say finally. A moment of silence passes between us. "I'd like to see that, I think," I say before finishing off my own meal.

"Perhaps one day you will," he replies. "So, now that we've covered a few of my many hobbies, stop avoiding the question. What do you like to do when you're not at home?"

I chew the inside of my cheek, really pondering the question.

"Well, I have my maps, and I like to shoot, I suppose."

"With that thing?" he asks, pointing across the campsite, where my bow rests safely.

"Yes, sir, with that. It's cathartic going out first thing in the morning, when it's quiet and still, where I can practice in peace. I really enjoy it."

"So, you enjoy hunting, then?" he asks, leaning back onto his hands.

"I'm a proficient hunter, but that's not the kind of shooting that I'm talking about now. I don't enjoy causing pain or death. But I get by doing what I need to."

"I've never learned to shoot a bow," he says, and I'm grateful he leaves the hunting subject be. "I've always thought it'd be interesting, though."

"Well, perhaps I'll teach you, then," I tell him. "I've never learned how to fight, with a sword or otherwise."

This idea causes his smile to widen.

"Then perhaps I'll teach you to fight," he says.

"Sounds like a deal," I respond.

"What about other sources of entertainment? I've glimpsed your maps. They're impressive." Alec makes a swirling motion with his flask, and the ale it contains makes a gentle swishing sound.

"That's about it. I shoot, I organize. I've drawn out a few maps, but I guess that about sums it up. I'm pretty boring."

Something flashes across Alec's face, some expression I can't quite read, and he says, "Maybe you just haven't experienced enough, yet. It'll come to you."

The fire pops, sending a flare of embers up into the darkness. I take a swig out of my water canteen.

"What about your friends? Lovers?" Alec asks, changing the subject. Water threatens to choke me as I sputter and cough it back up.

"I'm sorry, *lovers?*" I ask. "Who are you?"

This time, Alec grins and shrugs nonchalantly.

"What? A man can be curious; as I'm sure you've been curious about me. Besides, I asked about friends, too. But if you want to jump straight to the subject of romance, by all means." He leans forward, places his elbow on his knee, and puts his chin in his hand. "Any gentlemen callers in your life?"

I fight to find the words to respond to this man's outlandish questions. How can he be so relaxed about discussing such a private topic? But if he's open to discussing this, perhaps he'll tell me what he knows about our bond.

"No lovers," I tell him finally, and I straighten my back, proud of myself for being able to give him an answer to something.

Now Alec frowns, tsking at me.

"Surely a nice girl such as yourself has got to have *some* suitors, no?" he presses.

I press my lips tightly together and stare at the fire, listening to the sounds of the forest around us. I think about Zaid and how he makes me feel. Somewhere nearby, an owl calls out.

"Ah I see. There *is* someone!" Alec exclaims, far too excited for my liking. What kind of game is he playing? What kind of entertainment could he be gaining from this conversation? I want to crawl under a rock and hide from this embarrassing topic. If Alec notices my discomfort, he doesn't acknowledge it. "Well, go on then. What's the fellow like?"

I let out a noise that's somewhere between a sigh and a grunt and put my hands to the side of my face. I pray that the heat I feel there is from the fire, not from the blood rushing to my cheeks. I fear it's most likely the latter.

"Fates, okay! I'll tell you what little there is to tell, if you promise to shut up about it."

Alec corrects his posture and raises a hand into the air. "Of course."

I try to wipe the embarrassment from my face.

"There is someone from my village. His name is Zaid, and he's on my crew. He's incredibly intelligent, and well-schooled. Not just in combat, but in philosophy as well. He's apprenticed in all sorts of trades. He's studying to work with the Women's Council as a trade mediator right now, and I can barely find words when I'm around him. But nothing has ever happened, and nothing ever will. Aside from addressing me for work, he barely knows I exist, and that's just the way it is."

When I finish my description, I suck in a deep breath as I realize I've just said all of that in about two breaths. I frown intensely at the flames before me.

Silence stretches on between us for several moments, and I can't take it.

"Well?" I ask. "That's it? No snide remarks? No witty interjections?"

Alec's eyebrows shoot up on his forehead, and three wrinkles that I haven't noticed before appear above them.

"Hey, you asked me to shut up, I've shut up," he says. He scoots off the log he's sitting on and lies down on his back, stretching out his toes before the fire, folding his hands beneath the back of his head.

I give a single nod. Taking another drink from my canteen, I stand and walk the distance between the fire and the spot where my belongings rest. I lie down and clutch my bow in my hands, staring up at the starlight twinkling through the trees.

"Alec?" I ask, and although I don't look at him right away, I can hear him roll over to face me.

"Hmm?"

"Um... since we're talking..." I trail off for a moment, wondering how best to proceed.

"Yes?" he asks.

I clear my throat.

"Well, I guess I'm just wondering if you've always felt like things were different for you."

Another moment of silence is broken by his question. "What do you mean?"

I finally chance a look at him to find that he's propped himself up on his elbow.

"Well, these strange injuries I've always gotten, injuries I now know have come from you, set me apart from other people in my village."

"Oh?" Alec asks, and I nod.

"Our doctor always claimed that I had a medical disorder," I say. "He even prescribed me medicine for it, but his answer never made sense to me. It was only ever the injuries I couldn't explain that appeared this way. Did you ever have anything like that?"

Alec looks as if he's really considering my question.

"Nobody ever explained the injuries I got that way," Alec tells me. "My mamman fussed over me, and my pappan... well. He always said I got hurt because I was weak. No doctor ever examined me that way, and I started drinking at such a young age I never thought to ask questions."

His answer makes me deeply sad. I wonder how long he's been alone for. Even in the presence of his parents, aside from his mamman fussing, it sounds like he's always been on his own.

I open my mouth to tell him that I'm sorry, but he interrupts before I can.

"Did it work for you?" he asks.

"What?"

"The medicine. Did it stop your injuries? Numb your connection, at least?"

I think about that for a moment.

"No, I don't think so. All it did was make me nauseous."

"Too bad," he replies, and I think he must have been more aware of the connection, or at least of the mysterious nature of some of his injuries, than he's letting on.

"Too bad," I agree. "I've always thought there was more to it than that, and with the medicine not working..." I pause, not sure if I want to share this with him.

"With the medicine not working...?" he prompts me to continue.

"I've always wondered what else it could be. A curse, or some other kind of magic, but everyone has always shut down the idea before I could even really put it into words."

"That's because magic isn't real," he says, rolling onto his back again.

But his words are flat, and I *know* there's more to our connection than some medically inexplainable coincidence. I feel it in my gut.

"Maybe so," I say, more to myself than to him. "Either way, I'm interested to know why we're bound, if there was anything in our childhoods that might have linked us this way. I'm going to figure it out. If something made this connection, there's got to be a way to break it. Then we can *both* enjoy our freedom."

Alec has gone quiet, so I assume he's fallen asleep.

My eyes have just fluttered closed when I'm startled by a blanket landing on my head. When I pull the blanket off my face and give him a startled look, Alec simply shrugs.

"You know, it's ridiculous for you to assume that fellow of yours isn't interested," he says. "Especially if you've never spoken to him about it. We fellows are extremely simple, and chances are, he's at least thought about you that way. Just saying."

Fates.

"*Goodnight, Alec,*" I say flatly, though my heart flutters at the idea of Zaid having thought about me romantically. Alec chuckles from across the campsite, but thankfully, he keeps the remainder of his thoughts to himself. I'm not sure I could take any more of his comments tonight.

17

By late afternoon the following day, we've chosen our next campsite and have unpacked our blankets after another trek through the forest.

I hunch over a pile of wood we've gathered, organizing the pieces into a neat bundle so I can start a fire using the flint I always carry with me on my jobs, when Alec approaches me with his blade drawn.

At first I worry. I eye him warily, confused. Then I recall – he won't hurt me: He can't, not unless he wants to receive the same pain himself. Still, seeing him with his sword out is a bit intimidating. Just seeing it in his hand, I can tell he's an experienced fighter. He wields it as though it's a part of him, and although I've only actually seen him use the sword once – back when we were ambushed by those bandits with the flour-sack masks – there's a comfort, a confidence to him when his sword is in hand that makes the whole image just seem right.

"What are you doing?" I ask.

"We made a deal, remember? I'm ready to use that thing you've always got on your back, and I promised I would teach you how to use this beauty." He tosses the blade from one hand to the other in one fluid motion.

I raise my eyebrows at him.

"You want to do this now?" I ask, peering up at the sky. Its orange edges have begun to mix with the darkening blue.

Alec looks around and shrugs.

"I don't see why not. We've already set up for the night. May as well get in some instruction time before we totally lose the daylight, don't you think?" he asks.

He makes a valid point, I suppose, though I doubt he'll be able to hit any sort of target with an arrow in this fading light.

"A deal's a deal, right?" he asks, as though he can see the doubt written across my face.

"Right," I say. I stand and brush the dirt from my trousers. I put my hands on my hips and stretch my back, then remove my bow from its place on my torso. "Let's get started then, shall we?"

Alec follows me as I walk away from our campsite into the trees – far enough away that we can get some realistic practice, but close enough that we can still keep an eye on our things should someone come across our site. For a moment, the only sound between us is the crunching of leaves and branches below our boots and the wind that whistles through the treetops.

"Alright, then," Alec says. He's sheathed his blade, and now he rolls his shoulders and shakes out his hands. "Show me your moves."

I raise my eyebrows again and hold back a laugh.

"My *moves*?" I ask, but I find myself smiling.

Alec nods.

"How else am I supposed to learn it?" he asks.

I roll my eyes. Alec draws his dagger and approaches a tree, slicing a wide X into the bark.

"Shoot that," he says, the challenge lighting his eyes.

I shrug at his request and draw up my bow. As always, the bow's weight in my hand and the feel of the grip within my palm comforts me, steadies me. Years of practice have ensured that, when this tool is in my grasp, I am capable. I know what to do. I pull an arrow from my quiver and run my fingers ever so gently over the feathers. It hasn't been long since I made these arrows, and the feel of the feathers – still somewhat stiff – reminds me of home. They remind me of Lilah watching me craft my own arrows and asking me a million questions in the process.

I nock the arrow, pulling back until the drawstring is taut and the arrow sits level with my chin. I take in a deep, cleansing breath. The breeze brushes against my cheeks and pulls tendrils of my dark hair from its braid. I take aim at the X Alec has carved. I close my eyes and allow my shoulders to relax. Alec moves to stand behind me, saying nothing.

Then, in the tiniest of moments, I release the string from my grasp. My arrow goes flying with a swish that softly splits the air, and then I hear a *thud* as it embeds itself into the tree.

My eyes flutter open and I turn to catch Alec, peering wide-eyed and open-mouthed, gaze traveling back and forth between the tree and me.

I approach the tree and pull the arrow from where it's planted securely in the bark, right in the middle of that silly X.

It only takes Alec a moment to shake off his shock, then he goes to three more trees, carving more X's, each one smaller than the one before it. Then, he strolls back to me, casual grin spread across his lips.

"Again," he insists, returning his dagger to its holster and crossing his arms.

"All three?" I ask. I know I can do it. I've been shooting for years. My arrow rarely goes anywhere I don't intend it to strike. I have no doubt I can hit a few measly targets, and I appreciate the chance to use my bow for the pleasure of practicing with it, but it feels a little strange to be showing off. Aside from Lilah, I never shoot for an audience. Alec said he wanted to learn how to shoot, and I'm not sure what he's expecting to learn from this.

"If you can't do it, you don't have to," he starts, and my decision is made. With fluid, precise movements, I draw, nock, and loose one, two, three arrows in quick succession.

Thud. Thud. Thud.

"Fates, Lane. Who *are you?*"

I allow a tiny smirk to creep onto my face as I turn back to look at him.

"Same person you knew five minutes ago," I tell him.

"Hardly," he says, his voice raising in pitch. "How did you *do* that?"

"Lots of practice."

I watch as that familiar glint of challenge returns to those amber eyes, and he holds his hand out.

"Let me give it a try," he says.

I hold out my bow, and he takes it.

"Let me gather my arrows before you draw it," I make a wide arc, retrieving all three of the arrows I just shot, then I hold them out to him with one hand. "Take one of these." With my other hand, I hold up one arrow, feathers up. "See this notch? You'll want to place the string in the center. Careful!"

He's taken the arrow in his large, calloused hand, clasping it by the feathers.

"What?" he asks. He looks at me like I'm insane.

"Mind those feathers," I warn. "Or that arrow isn't going anywhere but the ground."

Alec frowns. He straightens the feathers gently with his thumb and forefinger, then he sticks his tongue out as he focuses on nocking the arrow.

"Now take your feet and place them like this," I say, spreading my feet apart. "Keep your hips and shoulders straight and your feet perpendicular to the bow."

He adjusts his body according to my example.

"Okay, good," I say, voice low, encouraging. I move to his side and place my hand gently beneath his elbow. "Now raise your elbow up like this, and draw back." Alec's muscular shoulder raises up near his ear, lifting his elbow too high. I place one hand under his elbow to stabilize it, then tap his shoulder with the other. "You'll want to relax this, here."

I look up to see his pulse beating steadily along the curve of his neck, see his Adam's apple bob as he swallows. He smells like pine, like campfire, and something sweet I can't quite pin down, but it draws me in.

It's only when he turns his head to meet my eyes that I realize just how close we're standing. A soft smile upturns the edges of his lips, and he holds my gaze for a moment before I find myself blushing, and I quickly step away from him.

"Uh, good. Just like that," I say, clearing my throat, hoping he can't hear how my heartbeat has accelerated, hoping my voice doesn't sound as thick to him as it does to me. "Now all you have to do is aim, and then let go."

He moves his fingers and releases the string, but the arrow drops almost straight down, and the string flings with a snap against his forearm. He sucks in a breath, and I let out a gasp at the familiar pain. I roll up my billowing sleeve to see a deep red welt already forming.

"Shit!" Alec hisses. He looks from his arm to mine, then he throws his free hand up to rub the back of his neck.

"Sorry," he mutters, his cheeks turning red.

I can't help it – I start to laugh. My laughter bubbles up from the pit of my stomach, flutters through my chest. I sound hysterical, but I just can't help it.

"Don't..." I start, crouching over, slapping my thighs between bouts of laughter. I work to catch my breath. "Don't worry about it. This happens to everyone."

Alec scoffs.

"It didn't happen to you!" He thrusts his hand in my direction.

"Trust me," I say, finally starting to regain some composure. It's funny to see someone so naturally confident at things struggle like a first timer. "It's happened to me *many* times. It'll stop happening the more you practice, as long as you do it correctly. The biggest thing is to keep your gripping arm back; don't let it swing inward – that's what gets you snapped." I gesture to the welt on his arm.

"Oh, that's where these marks have come from!" he shouts, understanding that he experienced this pain when I was learning to shoot years ago.

At this point the sun has sunk low in the sky, and the dusk light stretches long shadows between the trees.

"We can keep trying, if you like," I say, rubbing the new ache on my own arm. "It might be tough in this light, but you're welcome to go again."

"Oh, yeah," Alec says, clearing his throat as he scoops up the arrow he "shot" from the ground. He lets out a dry laugh. "We should probably wait for some better light. You know, so I can do a better job."

"Makes sense to me," I reply, grinning at him. I put my hands on my hips.

"Fates," Alec mutters. He falls in step beside me, and we make our way back to camp. "You made that look so easy."

"Practice is all it takes," I say, beaming up at him. "It's actually quite nice to see you not instantly good at something."

He pauses as we reach the edge of our campsite and gives me a strange look.

"What?" I ask, raising an eyebrow. We've both stopped walking, now.

The corners of his mouth turn up.

"That smile looks good on you," he says softly, stepping closer. If I reached upward, I would be able to place the palm of my hand on his chest. I swallow, and I wonder if he can hear the sound. My heartbeat kicks up again, and my stomach flutters. "You should do it more often," he says.

The heat returns to my face, and I feel like my entire body might catch fire, but this time I don't move away. We stand there, close enough to touch, just looking at each other. My brain feels foggy, and I realize I haven't responded to his comment. I open my mouth to say something, anything, but Alec suddenly tenses, as he looks behind me. I think I've offended him somehow, and I start to apologize, but I'm interrupted.

"Lane, thank the Fates. I found you!" shouts a familiar voice from our campsite.

18

"Zaid?" I squeak. I feel as if my eyes are going to pop out of my head, or my knees will give out from beneath me, or my heart will beat right out of my chest. "What are you doing here? Shouldn't you be back with the crew? Is... is my family alright? Is everything okay?"

Zaid smiles.

"One question at a time. I promise I'll answer them. The crew is covered. Your pappan had just finished interviewing with the two new crew members he's been considering to help out while you're gone. When I left, I even filed for my leave per his very specific protocol," he says.

All I can do is stare at him. Why is he here, of all places? The only thought that makes sense is that he's here because something is wrong with my family. I keep trying to ask, but I can't get my voice to work past the panic in my chest.

It's only when Alec steps forward and offers Zaid his hand that I realize my mouth has been open, and I snap out of it.

"Zaid, is it?" Alec says confidently, as if he can't feel how thick the air is all of a sudden. I feel as though I might choke on it. "I take it from Lane's recognition that you two know each other. Work together, perhaps?"

Zaid gives a nod and reaches out his own hand, and the two shake stiffly, though Zaid's eyes shift from Alec to me, and he smiles warmly, turning my cheeks an even deeper purple. His eyes flick back again before he answers.

"Lane's pappan hired me on as crewmate just recently. I've been learning the ropes of their business for the last couple of months," he says, matter-of-factly.

"Very nice," Alec says. Although they are no longer shaking hands, Alec remains just as close, and Zaid backs away a bit. I shift my weight. Why are they making small talk? Why am I not saying anything? He hasn't answered my questions.

"Who are you?" Zaid asks, and as Alec says his name, I find my voice.

"What's going on, Zaid?" I ask. "Why are you here?"

Zaid's eyes turn toward Alec.

"Perhaps we should speak in private?" he asks.

I nod, already walking back into the tree line.

We've gone several paces into the forest when Zaid reaches out and gently taps my elbow.

"How did you find me?" I ask him, forehead creasing as I frown. "*Why* did you find me? Is everything alright?" Asking these questions only adds a pounding heartbeat to the tightness in my chest. I push myself to breathe past it. Maybe everything is fine. Maybe he was just worried about me being gone from the crew.

Zaid puts his hand up to stop my list of questions, as if it's obvious just how anxious I feel.

"I've been keeping an eye on your family while you've been away, after we got back, of course. You seemed so rushed when we last saw you, and you had those bruises and all that blood on your clothing. I just wanted to do what I could."

"Oh, well, thank you," I tell him, surprised. Aside from working indirectly with my pappan, he's never had any connection with my family.

Zaid continues as if I've said nothing at all.

"I was visiting your pappan when he mentioned you'd sent a letter, and I asked if I could read it, to make sure you were safe. That's when I learned you were headed from Parth to Helna, and I knew from looking at those incredible maps of yours that the fastest route from Parth to Helna is here. So, I thought I'd see if I could catch up with you."

"How did you get here so fast?" I ask, wrapping my arms around myself, grateful that some of the tightness in my chest has receded. I draw in a deep breath. "And *why* did you come? In my letter, I mentioned that I was safe."

"I brought my horse," he says. "I left her back at your campsite." Zaid gestures through the tree line, and sure enough, his horse is grazing the grass around our camp.

Zaid steps forward. He holds his body with a strange, restless tension I haven't seen in him before. I put my hands on my hips.

"Zaid. Is my family alright?"

He nods curtly, but something heavy rests in his gaze, and now it's his turn to take a deep breath.

"Lane, it's your mamman, Ailene. She's been sent on a mandatory leave from the Council. It's only temporary, so they say, but they haven't said how long her leave will be."

Now my racing heartbeat returns, and I try to focus through the whirlwind of confusion and panic I feel. My mamman is a revered member of the Council, not just the sub-Council branch in my village, but one of the Grand Council that meets at the Keep. I have a hard time believing they would send her on leave without a very serious reason.

Zaid keeps on talking, though, and for a moment, I'm grateful for it. It gives me something to focus on.

"Your pappan said she's been acting strangely for a few weeks now, since just before we left on our last delivery. Apparently, the Council has noticed as well, and they've urged her to rest. That's all I know about that.

"According to your pappan, she's been muttering something about needing to go into the Baskan mountains to repay some debt ever since she came back from her last visit to the Keep. He told me in confidence that she was deeply troubled when she returned, and that she seems so adamant about it that he worries she may actually go, though he has no idea what business she would have in the mountains, nor what debt she could be referring to."

Silence creeps between us as I process the information he's just relayed. What reason *could* my mamman have to go to the mountains? I remember Mathilda's tale of a witch in the mountains who made deals with those who passed through, deals which always turned sour. A witch who demanded her price be paid. The only other time I've ever known my mamman to go anywhere near that far from home is when she went with the Grand Council to negotiate trade with Rohnarok for their steel.

"Strange," I mutter. I stare past Zaid at the ground, lost in a whirlwind of thoughts. I can't seem to make sense of any of it right now, but as soon as we reach Helna, I'll be sure to write Pappan to check in and make sure everything is okay. I should be home with my family; but I feel such a strong pull to be with Alec, to make sure he stays out of trouble, and to figure out where this bond came from and what I can do to sever it. Otherwise, my life will be at stake every time Alec goes out for work, or worse, every time he pisses somebody off. It's true that I've survived up to this point in my life, but now that I know all these injuries have come from him, I need to do something about it.

In the meantime, perhaps I can talk with Alec to see if there's any way for us to speed our passage to Helna along. Zaid mentioned he brought his horse, perhaps I could convince him to let us borrow it, for now.

I force myself to take another deep breath, and this helps a little bit to calm me down. That's what I'll do. I'll get to Helna and send a letter to my pappan to see if my ma' is alright.

"There is something else, though," Zaid says, pulling me out of my thoughts, and I realize I've just been frowning at the ground. I haven't yet responded to him.

"Oh, Fates, there's *more?*" I ask. I shift my weight again and do my best to focus on him.

"Yes. When I read in your letter that you were travelling to Helna with a companion, I... I had to come and find you, Lane. I don't think you should be traveling with this... character."

I blink, startled. "Excuse me?"

Zaid steps forward, reaching out to take my hands in his. Electricity zaps through my body at the unfamiliar action – we've never touched, not like this.

"Lane, I can tell by the look of him that he's... well, he's not good company to be around. I just don't understand why you had to stay in Nerine for him, covered in bruises and blood, or why you had to take this journey out of the blue. Is he holding you hostage? He hasn't hurt you, Lane, has he?"

Not directly, I think. Although the wound in my side has healed now, a phantom pain still lingers there. There's no way I could tell any of that to Zaid, though. I still find it impossible, myself.

I pull my hands from his grip.

"N-no! Not at all. I'm traveling with him because I want to help him, nothing more." I don't mention that I worry Alec could get us both killed. That information wouldn't make any sense to him, not the way I'd intend it to, and it would only worry him further.

Zaid's eyebrows form deep crease on his forehead. "Are you close with him? I've never heard you mention him before."

Now my face heats for a whole new reason, and I ball up my fists.

"Zaid, stop."

"I'm just looking out for you. I care about you, Lane. He's trouble; I can feel it."

"Stop!" I shout, then I look around us and lower my voice. "Sorry. This is all too much. I appreciate you looking out for me and my family, and for bringing me news of my mamman. I'll reach out to her as soon as I am able. But please, just give me a second to catch up."

"Oh," Zaid says. He looks as though I've struck him, but I keep going, holding my hands in fists at my sides.

"You and I have barely spoken about anything but work. We've never even breached the topic of personal relationships, so how would you know who I'm close with? Of course I wouldn't have mentioned him. Besides, I'm flattered that you were worried. I appreciate you looking out for my safety. But whom I travel with is not really your concern."

When I finish, I'm breathing heavily, and Zaid could be made of stone by how still he stands.

He's quiet for a moment, then his eyelids flutter and he stutters, "I apologize. I – I meant no offence. I saw you with him, and I don't know him, and I suppose jealousy and concern got the better of me. Of course, you're right. I'm sorry if I've upset you."

The electricity returns and floods through my body again. Did he just say he was *jealous*?

"Why would you be jealous?" I ask. The word feels foreign on my tongue.

Zaid runs his fingers through his dark hair with a pained expression on his face. He sighs.

"I have feelings for you, Lane. That's one of the reasons I asked your pappan for a job, so I could work closely with you – get to know you better. I just... haven't known how to tell you. You're intimidating," he says.

"*I'm* intimidating?" I ask, bewildered. He nods. "You're not joking?"

"I'm truly not joking," he says. He takes another step toward me, this time more warily, as though he's expecting to be yelled at again. Not that I blame him. I'm so shocked by everything I've just heard that I feel dizzy. He reaches out as if to touch me, and I want nothing more than to let him. Fates know how long I've pined after him, how many times I've imagined him proclaiming that he has feelings for me, too; but I feel so overwhelmed. I think I need just a minute to process all of this.

"Oh. Um, I've got to get back to camp. Thank you, for sharing all that. I'll... I'll need to think, if that's okay. Um. Would you like to stay for dinner?" My words sound so hollow, but I can't help it.

"Of course. Take your time. I just overloaded you with information. Uh... sure. I'll stay for dinner," Zaid says.

I nod and try to give him a smile, but I'm not sure it's convincing. I turn. I feel dazed as I walk back to camp. I don't think I've ever experienced such a wide range of emotions in such a short time frame before.

My mind is still reeling.

I'm worried for my mamman. I'm torn between the feeling that I should be home with her and the urge I feel to stay true to this mission with Alec, especially now that he's started opening up to me. I feel like I'm finally able to get some information about what's happening to us. And on top of all of this, Zaid, of all people, has just declared he has feelings for me. I've wanted this since we were in school together, but especially the last couple of months. I have no idea how many times I've daydreamed about him professing an attraction to me. And yet, now that he's said it, I find it so hard to believe.

I need to stop thinking. I need... I need...

Something.

I don't realize I'm practically jogging until I enter the clearing of our campsite. I must appear as flustered as I feel, for when Alec sees me, his expression turns from curious to concerned, and he stands from where he's been sitting and steps forward. In one hand, he holds one of his many flasks.

I storm over to him.

"I'll take that, thank you," I say, reaching down to snatch the container from his grasp. I take three long gulps, then pull the drink away from my lips. I feel my face twisting at the bitter taste, but I swallow past it. "You, sir... you and I have to talk," I say, wiping my mouth with the back of my hand.

I need to tell him what Zaid said about my mamman acting strangely. There's no way that both of our mammans have been acting the same way by coincidence. And if his mamman went missing, I fear mine will, too. I also feel the need to share with him the other information Zaid dropped on me, since we were just talking about my feelings for him.

Alec's raised eyebrows don't lower, and I watch as the straight line of his jaw relaxes as he says, "Alright, we'll talk."

I give a nod.

"Good. That's settled. For now..." I raise the flask in my hand and drink again.

Although the flask is nearly full, I down its contents, and Alec stares at me as if I've just done the most surprising thing he's ever seen. I hold out the flask, and he takes it without saying a word, staring at me as I wipe the spilled drops from my chin with my sleeve.

"So, dinner, then?" I ask. Alec reaches into his pocket and pulls out another flask, holding it out for me. I take it and drink another long swig.

19

It isn't long before my head is spinning. My cheeks and chin feel extremely warm, and there's a fire in my belly as I work to set out my blanket and secure my belongings, and I'm clumsy doing so. When Zaid makes it back to our campsite, I keep my distance, still unsure how to feel about everything he said.

I feel his eyes on me constantly.

To distract myself from the discomfort of his lingering gaze, I busy myself making conversation with Alec. Who'd have thought that *Alec* would be the one I'm more comfortable with in this moment? But I just don't know how to act around Zaid now that he's told me he has feelings for me. I barely knew how to act around him before all of this.

Once I've gathered my meal – a chunk of bread and some chopped vegetables – I sit next to Alec on a log beside the crackling fire he started while Zaid and I were talking.

"So," Alec starts, corners of his mouth tilting up in a knowing smile. He nods his head in Zaid's direction, and thankfully, he keeps his voice low. "Care to share what that was all about?"

I tear into my bread in response.

He raises his eyebrows at me but keeps silent. I frown and chew the inside of my cheek, not sure how much I want to tell him. It might be good if I could talk some of this through out loud, but my thoughts are muddy.

Thanks to the ale, I feel emboldened as I look across the campsite to where Zaid sits, silently eating his dinner and staring at me with those dark eyes I've imagined losing myself in. I feel that I may have offended him by the way he's keeping his distance, and maybe he feels awkward being here and not knowing Alec, but I appreciate him giving me some space to think about all this.

I wonder if he regrets coming here, or at the very least, sharing his feelings with me. I feel badly about shutting him out as soon as he told me, it was just a lot of information to take in, and I've never been good at handling big emotions well. That's why I enjoyed traveling with my pappan; because he doesn't like discussing these things, either. I realize I've been quiet for too long, trying to make sense of my thoughts.

The world tilts for a moment as I turn – too quickly – back to Alec.

I sigh and do my best to lower my voice, though the fuzzy feeling in my brain makes it hard to hear how loud I'm actually being.

"You know, I've had eyes for Zaid for months now," I try to whisper, though the words come out more loudly than I expected. Have I always whispered this loudly? Even as I say the words, I know I shouldn't be sharing this personal information with Alec, whom I've just recently met and even more recently started speaking to. Still, once I've started, my mouth moves faster than my brain, and the influence of the alcohol in my belly pushes the words from me.

Again, Alec's eyebrows shoot up, and the smile has returned, but he says nothing, so I rush to continue.

"Well, I mean, I fancied him in school a little bit, but I didn't know him that well. It was only when we started spending time working together that I got to... um... *fancy* him, fancy him."

"Indeed," Alec says with a quiet laugh.

"And *now*, when my mamman is acting strangely, he comes out here to tell me that he has *feelings*. For me!" I realize that last bit comes out a little louder than I intended, and I slap my hand over my mouth and giggle. I feel so silly.

To this Alec responds with a click of his tongue and a single nod, as if he knew all along that's what this is all about.

I scoff and turn to get a better look at him, but the motion happens too fast, and the world moves in slow motion around me. I lose my balance and flap my arms to save myself from falling, dropping a storm of breadcrumbs at my feet. This causes the mercenary to laugh, which infuriates me all the more.

"Stop that!" I say, a little too loudly. Or at least, I think I'm being loud. I can't really tell. I lower my voice. "What's so funny?"

Alec shrugs one shoulder.

"I'm afraid I don't see the problem," he says. His silver flask sparkles in the firelight as he presses it to his lips. I find myself wanting another drink. Alec catches me watching him drink, and he turns the flask upside down to show he's emptied it. I frown, disappointed.

I peek over at Zaid, who has finished his meal and now busies himself taking care of his horse.

"The *problem* is that he says he has feelings for me!" I remind him.

"I've gathered that information, thanks. You fancy him, he fancies you. I don't see what you're getting so worked up over. Unless, of course, there's someone *else* who's caught your eye."

Alec bites a chunk out of his bread and smiles as though he hasn't a care in the entire world. He wriggles his eyebrows at me, and my face warms even more, another uncomfortable sensation that comes with alcohol consumption.

"Of course not!" I say, whisper shouting again. I take a large bite of the rest of my bread, as well. Around it, I say, "He finds me in the middle of nowhere to tell me that he's worried, that my mamman is acting strangely, that she's been suspended from the Council for it, and then immediately follows up with, 'Oh, by the way, Lane, I have feelings for you.'"

Alec's expression turns serious. "I thought I heard you correctly before. What did he say about your mamman?"

I grunt.

"He said my pappan is worried because she's been acting off, especially since her last trip to the Keep. I guess that she's been muttering something about running off to the mountains to repay a debt... I don't know," I say, rubbing the center of my forehead. "Nothing makes much sense to me right now. Oh. And he said she's been forced to take a leave of absence from the Council. She's *never* been asked to take time off like that."

Alec clenches his jaw. Across the campsite, I hear Zaid removing his saddle and bags from his horse's back.

"Yes... we should talk about that."

My eyes widen. "That's what I was thinking! Something is strange here. There's no way it's a coincidence that both of our mammans have been acting strangely, and yours went missing, and suddenly mine is talking about going to the Baskan mountains. It's *got* to be connected, somehow."

In my excitement, I wobble again, and Alec catches me.

"Whatever it is, we can talk about it when you're... more present," he says. "We're already heading to Helna for information. We'll see what more we can surmise on the way."

I focus on Alec's face: the straight line of his nose, the deep amber of his eyes, the sharp angle of his jaw. The way his long blond hair falls in wavy strands to frame his face. The dark blond stubble that sparkles ever so slightly in the firelight, and how one side of his mouth seems to lift just a little bit higher in the corner than the other.

"You..." I start, running my eyes across all these features. The rest of the world has blurred, but his face is crystal clear. I shake my head. I should *not* be focusing so intently on this man's face, especially when the person I've had my eyes on for months now stands just across the way, but that thought is a soft, fading echo in my mind.

"I...?" Alec asks, and that corner of his mouth lifts, revealing his straight teeth in a smile. Fates, how is it that he can smile so easily?

I clear my throat.

"You've grown quite a stubble since we left Parth," I tell him, speech slurring.

His forehead creases with a frown, but the smile on his face only grows. He leans back, and the hand that is not holding onto me rubs at the hair on his chin.

"Yes, well, that's what happens when one is on the road. I'll shave it again next chance I get if it bothers you."

"Oh, no! That's not what I meant at all. Actually, I... I think it's nice." Without thinking, I raise my hand and press it somewhat gently to his jaw, run a thumb over the hair on his cheek. His expression softens, and the two of us sit there, not saying anything, faces close enough that I can feel the warm breath from his nose on my chin. I lean forward, eyeing those lips that always have some kind of smile on them.

It isn't until Zaid clears his throat that the trance is broken, and we return to our separate seats. I feel embarrassed, and I wonder how much of that interaction Zaid just witnessed.

"If it's alright with you," Zaid says. His voice sounds strained, his tone flat. "I'll camp here for the night. Don't much want to venture out there in the dark."

I look at Alec, who shrugs.

"Sure, Zaid," I say, finally gaining the courage to look at him. "You can stay here." Then he turns to me. "You should get some sleep, Lane. Long day ahead."

I am exhausted. The last couple of weeks have worn on me, and the spirits I've had tonight have made my eyelids heavy. I suppose I could use some good rest, but I feel bubbly. I don't want to lie down and waste this good energy.

"Oh, I'm going to stay up a little longer, if that's alright," I start. "I feel like dancing. Do you guys feel like dancing? Alec, you told me you can dance. Let's see it. Dance with me!"

"I will, someday," Alec says, mischievous glint in his eyes. The way he says "someday" makes my stomach flutter. "Trust me, that's a memory you'll want to keep. For now, let's get you to bed," Alec says.

"It seems we are in agreement," Zaid says. "Lane, it's probably not the best idea to dance around the fire in your state, anyway."

"Boo," I tell them both, but I relent.

I stand quickly, and blood rushes to my head, pounding in my ears. My vision blurs, and I feel myself start to lose my balance, but Alec reaches up at the same moment that Zaid steps forward and puts out his hands. Alec catches my palm and steadies me before letting go.

I take a deep breath.

"Goodnight, gentlemen," I say decisively, then I wobble my way over to the blanket Alec let me use last night. Since Zaid is closest, he walks between me and the fire with his arms out as if I'll fall at any moment. I stumble onto the blanket and lay down. In my peripheral vision, just as I lie down and close my eyes, I notice Zaid getting comfortable on the ground beside the campfire – right between Alec's resting place and my own.

In the morning, as Alec and I work to pack things up, Zaid approaches me. It seems he feels as awkward about last night as I do, and I feel badly for treating him so harshly, but my pounding headache keeps me from feeling any kind emotions very deeply. Fates, how does Alec handle drinking all the time? This headache alone is enough that in this moment, I want to swear off the stuff for life.

"Hey," Zaid says, eyes apologetic. He rubs the back of his neck nervously. "Can we talk?"

With how I'm feeling right now, I don't want to talk to anyone, but I suppose we do need to have this conversation.

"Sure."

I rub my forehead.

Zaid nods once, and we step away from the bags I've just packed. I adjust my bow across my back and do my best to look him in the eye; a task I find most difficult after our conversation – and my behavior that followed – from last night.

Alec's eyes track us as we step aside to talk.

Once we're out of Alec's earshot, Zaid relaxes a little bit, and I can tell he wants to say something. His mouth opens and then closes, and his eyes flit between me and Alec frequently.

"What is it, Zaid?" I ask through my headache.

"I know you're upset with me for coming, and I'm sorry. I was just... worried about you," he says.

I shift my weight and put my hands on my hips.

"I'm not upset with you for finding me, Zaid. I appreciate you bringing me news of my family. That's important to me. I'm just overwhelmed because I'm so far away, and I can't just go home. I'm frustrated because you insulted my friend, whom you know nothing about."

Truth be told, I'm not sure I would consider Alec and myself to be friends, but in this situation, the word feels right.

I feel dizzy and wobbly. I pinch the bridge of my nose, then bring my fingers up to massage my aching temples.

"But—" Zaid starts.

"And," I continue, sighing heavily. If he truly wants to know why I seem upset, aside from worrying about my mamman, perhaps I should just tell him. "And, I've had feelings for you, too."

His face lights up, and his smile is so wide I wonder how the expression can fit on his face.

"Really?" he laughs. "That... that's great!"

"But."

His expression falls. "But?"

"I've got so much going on here, and this all feels so unexpected. Still, I owe *you* an apology for the way I acted last night. I... I've wanted to hear you say you had feelings for me for a while now. But... the timing just isn't right. Not after everything you told me about the trouble with my mamman. Not out here." I can't help looking in Alec's direction when I say this.

Zaid steps forward eagerly, bringing a hand up as though he intends to touch my shoulder, but he thinks better of it and lets his hand fall to his side.

"Um... Since I'm here, would you allow me to travel with you to Helna?" he asks.

From our campsite, I can hear Alec call out, "Leaving you behind!"

"I suppose you could," I say, watching the birds disappear through the treetops before turning my gaze back to him. "Do you have business in Helna?"

"In a manner of speaking, yes," he says. He gives me a small smile that I'm not sure what to make of.

"What do you mean, in a manner of speaking?"

Now Zaid's expression turns guilty, sheepish. His eyes darken a little bit, and he says, "I'd like to escort you, protect you."

I raise my eyebrows. "*Protect me?*" I ask. "Protect me from what, exactly?"

He says nothing for a moment, but his eyes flick for the briefest of moments in the direction of our campsite.

"I just want to have your back, is all," he says.

"Zaid, I travel for a living, and I'm literally accompanied by a trained mercenary. I'm not sure I need much more than that," I tell him.

"Right," he says. "But you're not a trained fighter. I mean, you're a skilled archer, but you're not trained in hand-to-hand combat, and a bow will only serve you in certain situations. It's nice to have your other circumstances covered. I'd like to assist."

"Right. Well, come with us to Helna if you want to, but you know I can take care of myself. I don't need anyone's protection." Truly, I know that the more people we have in our party, the better. I'm used to traveling with Zaid, and the more trained fighters we have in our group, the safer our travels will be. Still, the stubborn side of me hates that anyone thinks I can't take care of myself.

Zaid smiles. "Of course."

I turn and head back to camp just as Alec's making his exit. I jog to catch up with him while Zaid situates his horse.

"That guy really got under your skin yesterday, didn't he?" Alec asks, gesturing to my flushed face, smiling like he knows everything in the whole world.

"Teach me to fight," I say, trying to rub the headache from my temples, ignoring his comment.

This demand seems to surprise him.

"I beg your pardon?" he asks.

I roll my eyes and stamp my foot in the dirt. I feel like a child, but my head is pounding, so I press on anyway.

"I need to cover all my circumstances. I taught you how to shoot an arrow, now it's your turn. Pay up."

20

It only takes us a few more hours to get out of the forest and into the grasslands. As we travel, we come across some small running streams, which we use to fill our canteens. We also cross paths with some skittish deer with dark brown hair and large white spots along their backs. These deer can also be found in the forest between Nerine and Parth, so they're not a new sight to me, but I'm still mesmerized by their large white antlers and graceful movements.

As we get closer to the grasslands, the creatures we see are much smaller – rabbits and birds, mostly. Alec says we should travel by night and rest in the fields by day to avoid running into any unwelcome company.

Through the line of trees ahead of us, I can see tall grass blowing in the wind, but I'm still on the lookout for other animals, so I don't pay much attention until we walk through the last of the trees. The moment I set my sights on the grasslands my breath is stolen away. I've never been this far east before. I've never seen anything like this in my travels, and the knowledge I gained from the drawings in maps and books I've studied shies in comparison. The grasslands are absolutely gorgeous.

This time of year the grass is a rich golden color that practically glows, reflecting the vivid oranges and reds of the setting sun above. The hip-high sea of grass waves, dancing with the wind that passes through it, and all around us the sound of each stalk rubbing against its neighbors fills the air. That sound reminds me of the sea also, and although I'm awed by this incredible sight, I find myself longing for home.

But the smell draws me back to awe very quickly. Each time the wind blows my lungs are filled with the sweet scent of rain, damp earth, and wild grass.

In spite of myself and the pounding headache that still bothers me, I rush forward, running my hands across the seed heads, breathing in that fresh, beautiful scent. My cheeks flush as they make room for a grin. I don't know how Alec could be so weary of these lands. All there is out here is grass as far as the eye can see.

We rest for a short while, each of us taking turns sleeping or lying about, and it's as I wake from a short nap that Alec tells me he's ready to start training me. Having rested and gotten plenty of water to drink, I'm feeling much better.

Alec and I circle one another in the open field as he begins my fighting lessons. Zaid sits nearby, supposedly studying his *Women's Council: A History*, but I notice his eyes are on us much more than they are on his studies. His horse stands in the grass behind him, munching away at the endless food supply.

Alec notices me eyeing Zaid as he watches us.

"Focus," he says. "Concentrate on how your feet feel beneath you. They should feel steady, strong, sure." Although I've had these feet my entire life, and I'm used to practicing precise footing for my archery, they seem unfamiliar as I focus on them so intently.

"Like this?" I ask. Alec nods.

"Focus on your breathing," he says, voice smooth, once again drawing my attention back to my task, reminding me that, at least for now, I need to quiet my mind. "Feel how your body responds to the air you intake, how it energizes you, makes your blood sing, grounds you. When you're wielding a weapon, it's vital to hold onto that grounded feeling. The more connected you are with your body, with the earth, the harder it will be for your opponent to disarm you. The more aware you are of your surroundings, the less likely you will be to stumble and give your opponent the upper hand."

Although Alec and I are still several feet apart, I'm mesmerized by the strange look in his eyes. It's not exactly a sparkle, more like a glint of passion for the words he speaks. Something in his expression shows just how much he enjoys this type of training. But I can also see a deep veneration, almost a solemness in the set of his jaw, the straight line of his back and neck, the rise of his chin. I'm not sure how he was trained, or why, but something tells me he holds his own training in the highest – if not saddest – regard.

"I feel... different," I say, keeping my gaze on him and doing everything in my power to ignore the fact that Zaid is watching us.

"Good." Alec smiles. "That's what you should feel. It's strange how just a little bit of focus can change one's perspective."

I nod.

"Think I'm ready for a weapon now?" I ask.

"Sure," he says, and my eyebrows shoot up. I thought he would take much more convincing. "I've got just the thing in my pack. Hold on."

As Alec jogs back to our bags and rummages around, I try to keep my concentration on my breathing and my footing, but Zaid stands and closes the distance between us.

"You're close," Zaid says softly, a sweet smile on his face. "Here, adjust your feet like this," he says, placing his feet precicely as an example. I do my best to copy his actions. "There you go. You're a natural. I think you'll be ready to join the Council Guard in no time."

His comment makes me smile, and I raise my chin proudly.

Then Alec returns, and I watch the rise and fall of his chest beneath the slightly sweat stained white cotton shirt he's wearing. My gaze finally returns to his face, and his knowing grin waits for me there.

My cheeks burn, and I turn my eyes downward, only after I catch Alec's eyes flit to Zaid.

I stare at my feet and practice taking the same steps I've been taking to create the circle I was tracing in the grass with Alec, with the addition of Zaid's adjustments. This feels a bit more natural.

"Need something?" Alec asks Zaid, and I can't help but peek up at the two of them.

Zaid stands perfectly still. "Not at all," he says. "Just helping her with her footing. I was professionally trained by the Guard. I thought it would be helpful if she used the proper footing."

"Funny," Alec states, but his tone shows no sign of humor. "I was teaching her the proper footing."

"Don't feel bad. It's a hard thing to get right," Zaid says.

It's then that I notice what Alec is holding in his hand.

"Alec, what is that?" I ask.

This seems to pull his attention from Zaid for a moment, and Alec raises his arm proudly, displaying what he carries. In his hand is a long stick that's been carved to have a flattened, curved resemblance of a blade on one end, sharpened to a point. A leather strap has been wrapped and tied off around the other end to serve as a grip.

"This, sweetheart," Alec says. "Is your sword."

He tosses the "sword" into the air and catches it easily with his other hand. He swings it in a wide arc, and the air splits with a *whoosh*. Then, he holds it out for me to take.

In my peripheral vision, I see Zaid roll his eyes.

"I thought I'd get to use yours," I say, letting the disappointment I feel seep into my words.

"I've told you before. No one touches my blades but me, especially Rhetta. This falchion serves only one master." He pats the scabbard attached to the belt on his waist proudly.

The golden and black leather wrapped hilt glints beautifully in the sunlight, and the round-cut emerald stones within send light sparkling off in every direction.

I frown at him. Falchion. It's interesting to hear the name of this type of sword, especially the name he's given it for himself. I make a mental note to ask him about it later, but I return my thoughts to the argument I'm about to make.

"I let you use *my* bow and *my* arrows."

"Do you want to learn how to fight, or not?" he asks, doing nothing to hide the jovial tone in his voice.

I reach out, snatch the wooden sword from his hand, and glare at him.

"Fine," I grumble. "Train me, then."

Zaid steps in, holding his hand out, palm open. The sunlight sparkles across his dark hair as he moves.

"Lane, I don't mean to interrupt," he says, giving me that sincere smile of his.

"Surely," Alec mutters, but Zaid ignores him.

"But I think you're ready to work with a real sword, not a *toy*. After all, you're not a child. Here, you can use mine. I'd be honored to have you practice with my weapon."

Excitement bubbles up inside me, and I reach out for the sword as Zaid unsheathes it and holds it out.

Alec's blade is out in a moment, leaving his dagger on his belt, and he taps the blade of Zaid's sword with the flat of his own, halting the transaction.

"Not so fast," Alec says. His tone is light, but his eyes are serious. "I'm her trainer, and I say she's not ready. If you wanted to teach her, you should have stayed with her from the beginning, like I have."

"Well," Zaid says, gritting his teeth, but keeping his voice even. "I think you should have a little more faith in her."

"Yeah, Alec," I say, stepping closer to Zaid. "Have a little faith in me, will you? I'm ready. I'll be careful."

"Show me your footing," Alec says to Zaid without acknowledging my comment. He drops the wooden sword on the ground. "Let's see if any of that *proper* training has stuck."

"Are you sure you're up for the challenge?" Zaid replies, eyes narrowing.

The two begin circling one another, gazes locked, jaws set. At first, I take this moment as an opportunity to watch their footing, see what I can mimic for myself, but I soon realize these two aren't just giving me a demonstration.

"Alright, gentlemen, no need to get carried away here," I tell them, putting my hands up.

Their swords clash, and the clang of metal on metal reverberates across the open field. The two continue to duel, feet shuffling through the trampled grass, kicking up dirt as they move this way and that, attacking and parrying each other's moves. It's clear to me that they're both well trained, but their styles are different. Zaid's posture is rigid, all methodical, and Alec's is more relaxed, his movements more fluid. Zaid seems to notice this quickly, and he compensates for Alec's natural movements by sending faster, stronger swings.

I find myself mesmerized by the two of them trading blows. Alec thrusts his blade forward, and Zaid dodges, ducking behind Alec and flicking the blade of his sword backward, drawing his blade intentionally against the back of Alec's leg. My own calf stings, and my eyes widen in horror.

I have to stop this.

Alec looks up at me, his face solemn, his eyes knowing. He gives a single nod in silent agreement: This has gone too far.

Alec steps aside to avoid another glancing thrust from Zaid, and in a moment, Alec swings his leg in a wide roundhouse kick that knocks Zaid flat on his backside. Zaid's facial expression turns from shock to anger, and he rushes to his feet, but I scramble in between them.

"That's enough!" I shout, listening to my voice echo against our surroundings. Zaid looks over my shoulder, eyes dead set on Alec. I don't know when I started breathing so heavily, but I find myself struggling to get my breath under control. "Zaid, stop. Take a walk."

Zaid pauses, turning his eyes to me, and they soften, hurt spelling across them.

"What?" he asks.

Guilt churns in my gut at the thought that I've hurt his feelings, but I don't want him to find out about my bond with Alec. Not this way, at least. Already I can feel the blood trickling down my leg beneath my trousers.

"You heard me," I say, keeping my chin up and my back straight. "Go cool off."

Zaid looks from me to Alec. He opens his mouth as if he'd like to argue, but he closes it again. Finally, he says, "Whatever," and storms off. He scoops up his books and leads his horse away from our camp. I'm not sure where he's going, but for the moment, I let out a breath of relief. That was close.

"Well, that was unnecessary," Alec comments.

I glare at him.

"You started it!"

"You still sided with me," Alec says with that obnoxious half-smile on his face.

"I sided with myself," I snap, though I have a feeling Alec is going to believe what he wants to believe, regardless of what I have to say. "I'm going to get this cleaned up before Zaid comes back," I tell Alec. I walk over to our bags and look around until I find some scrap material from our older clothing and Alec's medical kit. I sit down and pull up the leg of my trousers. The wound isn't too bad – just a scratch, really, but it still stings. I clean up the blood and bandage myself. As I do, my disbelief gnaws at me. Did all of that really just happen? For what?

"All better now?" Alec asks me, and I scoff, shoving the medical kit against his chest.

"Your turn."

When Alec has cleaned himself up, and while Zaid is still far from our vicinity, I snatch up the wooden sword and point it at him.

"Alright, Mercenary. Let's get back to it. I'm ready."

Alec adjusts his stance. I steady myself like I had been, focusing on my breathing, doing my best to shake off the entire interaction. I clutch the wooden sword in both hands and hold it out. Alec clasps his hand across his mouth to quiet his laughter.

He comes closer, and my eyes plead with him.

"I assume I'm doing this wrong, already," I say flatly, trying to adjust to reflect some semblance of what Alec and Zaid were doing.

"Oh, no. If you're planning on fighting the grass there, you've got it just right. But I think that even a strong gust of wind might win with you standing that way."

I roll my eyes and let my shoulders droop a little bit.

"If I'm doing such a bad job, then help me fix it!" I raise my voice, but when Alec doesn't respond, doesn't move, I clear my throat and tack on, "Please."

Before I can register what's happening, Alec stands behind me. He places his arms on my shoulders, pulling them backward and upward so that my back is totally, uncomfortably straight. Then his hands slide down my arms, adjusting first my elbows, then my hands. His palms and fingers are calloused and firm against the bare skin on the back of my hands as he corrects my grip.

"You want to hold it like this," he starts. When he turns his head to look at me, his jaw brushes against my cheek, and his breath is hot against the side of my face as he speaks. "Keep your fingers relaxed. If you hold on too tightly, your opponent will knock your blade from your hands before you know they've even struck."

I swallow and nod, adjusting my grip so that my fingers are somewhat loose.

"Like this?" I ask, voice barely above a whisper. I'm having a hard time finding my voice when all I can feel is Alec's close proximity. I worry for the briefest of moments that Zaid will return, and that seeing us like this will hurt him even more; but as Alec's fingers brush over mine, I find those worries melting away. His hands find the leather grip. He gives the sword a little tug, then he nods."

"Very good," he says. "Now, you'll want to adjust the position of your legs.

His hands now find my hips, and as he works to adjust their angle, my breath hitches.

I croak, "I have a weapon, you know. No funny business, or you'll regret making this stick so sharp."

"Trust me, sweetheart. That stick would be the least of my worries," he says, but he backs away and leaves me to practice my stance. Before he heads back to our belongings to clean up camp, he looks me over and gives me a strange smile, and he leaves me to my racing thoughts.

I still can't believe what I just witnessed with those two. I worry about upsetting Zaid when he's been nothing but kind to me, especially when I can't tell him that he clearly misunderstood my reason for sending him away. Oh well, I suppose. There's not much I can do about that, now.

I think about the way Alec just made me feel, standing so close, running his hands over mine. I shiver.

Until I can figure out what I'm doing, how I feel, I need to be careful about how I act around these two.

At the end of the day Alec and I sit together on the ground surrounded by the tall grass. Zaid is studying several books he brought with him a few yards away. He hasn't said anything to me since I sent him walking earlier, and I can't say I blame him for being upset. I just do my best to give him space and hope he'll cool down enough to talk with me soon.

As Alec and I were training with my wooden sword, he told me I wasn't breathing right, so he was going to teach me how to breathe correctly. Now I feel annoyed and discouraged that apparently, according to this mercenary, I can't even do the most basic human thing correctly, so I have to learn how to breathe all over again. I'm also bothered that I got my hopes up. It appeared as though he was going to teach me how to fight, and I would get to practice, but now we've gone straight back to breathing.

We sit cross legged on the ground with our eyes closed, listening to the grass rustling in the wind all around us. The earth is damp beneath my buttocks, and I know that when I stand up, I'm going to have dark circles on my back pockets.

I open one eye to peek at him, and he raises his eyebrows and tries to hide the smile that lurks on the corners of his lips, as if he knew I would look. I close them tightly again.

"Focus," he says. His voice is as soft as the breeze. I raise my own eyebrows and straighten my back, placing my hands gently on my knees and trying to force myself to relax.

I take one deep breath in and let it out, but I can't help but feel Alec's gaze on me. I open my eyes again and glare at him.

"That's not helping, you know," I lecture him.

"What's not helping?" he asks, feigning innocence.

"You staring at me like that. How am I supposed to concentrate on my breathing when you're just sitting there, looking at me?"

Alec smiles.

"If you want to learn how to fight, you're going to have to keep your focus even when there are things going on that distract you, even make you uncomfortable."

"Of course, you would say that," I reply.

"You've got to learn to loosen up," he says. "Or you'll never be more than a mediocre fighter at best. Here, stand up. I'm going to teach you to use your fists before we get back to using your sword."

"I thought you wanted me to focus on my breathing," I grumble, and my mind goes back to the mud that will surely be all over my trousers when I stand.

"Change in exercise," Alec says. "I'm the instructor; and you're not even focusing like I asked you to, anyway. Now, get up."

I let out a deep sigh and do as he says. When I'm up, I stare at him inquisitively.

"Find your footing, like I showed you before," he says.

I shuffle until my footing resembles that which we practiced earlier.

"Ball your hands up into fists and hold them out like this, keeping your dominant hand closest to your face," Alec orders.

He holds his fists up in front of him, his left hand closer to his face than his right. I do my best to mirror him, so my right hand is closer to my face than my left. At his nod of approval, I feel my face lift and my spirit lighten. Finally, I might actually be getting something.

"Like this?" I ask.

"Perfect," he says. "Now, I want you to take your dominant hand..." He brushes his fingers lightly across the knuckles on my right hand. "And swing it forward, straight out, like this. Keep your thumb outward but curled over your other fingers. You don't want it out straight, and you don't want to clutch it, either." He grabs hold of my right hand as I swing it slowly out, and he pulls a little, loosening my thumb from where I have it tucked against my palm, then laying it so it sits against the outsides of my other fingers.

"Won't that hurt?" I ask, frowning at the new placement of my thumb. It feels unnatural to prepare to strike someone with my thumb like this.

"You? Or your opponent?" he asks, chuckling.

"Me," I reply.

"Nope. Your hands will hurt for the first while anyway, while they grow accustomed to frequent impact. But if you keep your thumb tucked in like it just was, you'll likely break it, and then you'll be in a whole other world of hurt."

"Oh," is all I can say. Thumbs on the outside. I correct my thumbs and bring both hands back up to my face as he demonstrated before.

"Great," Alec says. "Now I want you to swing at me. Give it all you've got."

"You don't want me to practice on something else, first?" I squeak. Why in the world would this maniac want me to hit him? He doesn't even know what I'm capable of, and neither do I. On top of that, if I hit him, I'm only going to end up hurting myself.

"We may move to that, but I'd like to see what we're working with, and there's no better way for me to determine the power of your punches than to experience them myself." He smiles at me then, and I worry – not for the first time – that I might be traveling with a lunatic.

I roll my shoulders to loosen them up a bit as he gets into position in front of me.

"I'm not so sure about this," I tell him, voice thick with anxiety. "If I hit you, I'm going to feel it, too, and not just in my hand."

"Why do you want to learn to fight?" he asks, taking me by surprise.

"What?"

"I didn't stutter. Why do you want to learn how to fight so badly? Is it something your friend over there said?" he gestures in Zaid's direction with his chin. Zaid looks over as if he can hear our conversation, and he gives me the tiniest of smiles and waves at me. My heart flutters, happy to see he's not entirely furious with me, and I wave back, hand still clenched into a fist.

"No, it's not only that. I mean, yes. He did say that I don't know how to defend myself, and that stung," I start.

"Has he *seen* you shoot?" Alec asks, and pride wells in me at the validation.

"Yes, he has. But his argument was that a bow isn't best for every situation."

Alec rubs his chin.

"I suppose he's right," he says. "But I saw you swinging your bow at those bandits we ran into. I think you did just fine, all things considered."

It's strange, hearing the approval in his tone.

I step forward.

"That's exactly it, though. I did hit them with my bow, it's true. But I felt wildly out of control. If I can train, if I can get even a sliver of the confidence you have when you fight, I'd do better. I'd *feel* better. I want to be able to rely on myself."

Alec nods and sets his jaw, as if this all makes perfect sense to him.

"Then hit me. I know it'll hurt you too, but if you want to learn how to fight in the real world without someone else to help you, you're going to have to toughen up and take the hit. This is actually going to be nice, because then I don't have to hit a girl."

I interrupt him, stepping forward, swinging at his left bicep with my right fist. Lightning cracks in my knuckles as they impact with the hard muscle there. Pain erupts in my own left arm, and it pulsates in my right hand.

Alec gasps.

"Gah! Wow, you've got some power in those arms!" he exclaims.

I shake out my hand, hoping that the action will somehow ease some of the pain. Of course, it doesn't, but I continue to do so anyway.

"I asked if you were sure about this," I say defensively.

"Fates," he mutters. For a moment, we're both silent as he rubs his arm and I examine my knuckles. There's no sound around us but the whistle of the wind through the grass. "I thought you said you didn't know how to fight," Alec says.

"I don't."

"Could have fooled me," he grunts, massaging the spot on his arm while he looks at his own knuckles, which are already swelling. "Interesting," he whispers. "Where did you get strength like that?"

I raise my hands. "My bow, I suppose."

"Wow! Maybe I ought to give that thing another try," he says seriously.

"Should we keep going?" I ask, already returning to my previous posture. The soft mud shifts beneath my feet. My hand still hurts. But hitting him was thrilling, even with the pain I now feel; and his praise has my mind whirring. Maybe I do have a chance at becoming a capable fighter with some decent training.

Alec rubs his arm. "Well, I can teach you a few more things today, I suppose, but I'm definitely not going to let you hit me again. That's for sure."

I can't help my grin.

We spend the next half an hour or so going over different types of punches, accompanied with slow-motion practice for how to execute them. We practice my footing, both with a "sword" and without, and of course we go back to my breathing when Alec says I'm wound too tightly.

Finally, we've both had about as much practice as we can take for the day.

"I think that'll about do it for today," Alec says as he turns to head back to where we've rested today, to where Zaid now sits with his stacks of books, busy writing something. I shake my head.

"Wait. Uh, let's do something else?" I plead. Alec turns back to me and grins, and I immediately backtrack. "Not what I meant. Let's talk, or something."

"Ah, still feeling awkward about your lover boy?" he asks.

"He is not my lover," I say stubbornly, butterflies roiling in my stomach at the word.

I've been busying myself all day trying to learn how to fight, but in the back of my mind, I've been nervous about talking with Zaid after the whole scene earlier. I want to tell him everything, explain why I sent him away, but something tells me to keep this bond a secret for as long as I can. I've been so careful to hide any evidence thus far, and if I can keep Zaid from being suspicious, I need to. I want to be able to pull him aside and figure out what all this means for us, but I feel blocked, somehow, and worried about what Alec might think.

I hate that I worry about that.

"Right, right," Alec says, pulling me out of my downward spiral. He smirks, sitting back down in the grass we've trampled today. Then he lies down, leaning back and placing his hands behind his head. "I suppose interests change, don't they?"

21

I choose to ignore Alec's last remark, but I do join him, lying down on the ground beside him. The damp earth beneath my back calms me. My hair provides a sort of pillow as I turn my head to look at him. I'm close enough to make out the details of his face clearly, close enough that if I reached my hand out right now, I could touch his arm.

I let out a long sigh. "Let's talk about something else, please. Anything else."

Alec turns his body toward mine so he's now lying down on his side. The sunlight is fading now, and the yellow rays catch in his irises, making his eyes seem aglow.

"I have a question," he states softly.

"Ask away," I reply. I find myself feeling acutely aware of how comfortable I am right now, on the ground, in the presence of this person I only met such a short time ago.

"What encouraged you to learn how to shoot? You *clearly* don't like hurting people, and I'm not just talking about not wanting to hurt me because of the whole... it'll hurt you, too, thing."

A small smile crosses my face.

"I taught myself, shortly after I started working with my pappan. He mostly sets traps when he's on the road, but I thought it'd be more efficient if we could get our food this way instead. Plus, we've been tracked by larger animals a couple of times, and I wanted to learn how to protect myself... protect the crew, if I needed to."

I trail off for a moment as I reminisce in the memories of my pappan teaching me how to set traps, how to skin animals for food, how to cook them thoroughly by fire.

I remember seeing someone near SunSpar using a bow, and feeling breathless with excitement, then finding the materials to make my first few bows.

"Oh?" Alec asks.

"I once had a master visit my village, and my pappan arranged for him to observe my work. Near the end, he congratulated me and said he wanted to meet *my* master, and when I told him I'd learned on my own, he was stunned." The memory of that day still has me beaming with pride as I recall the look on the archery master's face.

"Rightfully so," Alec says. "With your aim, I never would have guessed you were self-taught."

Alec is quiet for a moment, and we just smile at each other. A woodpecker works at some far, far away tree, and the soft wind carries the faint sound to us. Aside from that, the world around us is silent. I never knew the grasslands would be so quiet.

I hope Zaid is finding the quiet helpful for his studies.

Alec speaks up again, drawing my attention back to him.

"You said a while back that you work with your pappan. When did that start, and why? Your mamman is on the Council, right? That's what Zaid said when he mentioned her being suspended. I thought family members of those on the Women's Council have an almost guaranteed position when they turn eighteen."

I take a deep breath. The air is beginning to grow colder, and it feels fresh and crisp in my lungs.

"It's not *required* of us to join the Women's Council by any means. You still have to be selected by the Council, but if you are a legacy, you very likely have a spot unless someone out there really doesn't like you. I started going with my pappan when I was almost eight years old.

"My mamman was expecting my younger sister, and she wasn't doing well. She'd lost several babies before and after me, and my mamman grew very distant, sometimes hostile toward me. My little sister Lilah was growing strangely, and my mamman was very sick. When it came close to when she was due to deliver Lilah, my pappan took me with him away from our village.

"He's never confirmed this – neither of my parents ever really talk about that time – but I think he took me away with him because he expected that my mamman, or my baby sister, wasn't going to make it."

"Why not stay close with them if he thought they would be lost?" Alec asks.

"He did it for me," I tell him. "So I wouldn't have to see her like that, so my heart wouldn't break as hard losing them. I didn't even really know if my mamman was with child at the time. I was so young, and with my mamman's history, they never told me when she was pregnant."

I stare into the sky as the weight of what I've said settles between us. Light, feathery pink clouds that freckle the sky drift lazily across it.

"I can't imagine," he says, so quietly that I almost don't hear it.

"Yeah," I say. "My pappan told me when I was young that I was a miracle, that my mamman wasn't supposed to be able to have children, and that she got so ill during her time with me that she couldn't leave her bed. I guess I've always assumed that the same was true for Lilah, except that my mamman was older, and Lilah had some problems growing inside my mamman's belly."

"Wow," Alec whispers.

I take another deep breath and raise my eyebrows. Thinking about my family, particularly Lilah and my mamman fills my stomach with worry. I hope they're alright. Even though my mamman and I haven't had the best relationship since I was very young, I still love her, still worry about everything Zaid told me about.

"But to answer your question, that's when, and why. After that, I kept going with him because I enjoyed it immensely. My mamman never really came back to me. Instead, her love and attention were focused on Lilah, so it was nice to escape with my pappan." From the corner of my vision, I can see Alec nod, and I turn back to face him. He picks at some of the long strands of grass that have bent beneath us. "What about you?" I ask. "What made you decide to be a mercenary?"

This question prompts a long whistle from Alec.

"Oh, the ever-insatiable desire to gain my pappan's approval," he replies. It's a light answer, spoken almost like a joke, but I can feel the weight behind his words.

"Oh?" I press when he says nothing more.

"I was a sickly infant. From the time I was born until I was about three years old, my parents were constantly worried about me. They took me to all sorts of healers and doctors, but nothing ever changed. This all would have been before you were born, if you're seventeen now."

"What was wrong with you?" I ask, leaning forward to listen more carefully.

"No one ever knew. I was just generally unhealthy, I suppose. Then one day, I was suddenly better. No one could explain it. But because I'd been sick before, I got a late start on a lot of things. It wasn't until I was almost four years old that I learned to walk on my own, another half a year before I could run, and so on. Because of my late development, my unhealthy infancy, and the mysterious injuries I'd always get, my pappan could never see me as anything but weak."

I sit up and look at him with wide eyes. I'm totally speechless. "Wow. I had no idea you went through that," I whisper.

He lets out a single dry, humorless laugh.

"That was the easy part. When my pappan couldn't see past my 'weakness,' he stopped paying me any mind, stopped coming around me. It was only my mamman who cared, and then she still fussed over me as if I were still sick."

Now I'm the one picking at the grass. Both of my parents have always loved me, even if my mamman had a tough time showing it. I have no idea how I'd have turned out if my pappan completely ignored me, despised me for something out of my control.

"So," Alec continues. "My pappan's distain and my mamman's fussing drove me to want to prove myself, prove that I was strong, that I *could* be strong. I worked hard. I trained. I exercised. My pappan is the Council Guard command officer, and I thought if I could only prove to him that I was strong enough to join the Guard, he'd feel inclined to look on me with approval, or at least regard me in some kind of way."

"Did you?" I ask. "Make the Guard?"

He gives me that smooth, confident half-smile.

"Of course I did."

"And? Did things get better with your pappan?"

The sky is now alight with deep reds and purples.

"Not in the slightest," Alec says. "If anything, seeing me every day only gave him cause to be embarrassed of me."

"Wow..." I whisper.

"Of course, I gave him plenty of reason to be embarrassed, once I discovered ale." Again, he says this in a lighthearted way, but his face is shadowed with a sadness I didn't think him capable of feeling. I, too, am filled with a deep sadness for him as he continues. "I was fifteen when he kicked me out onto the streets. I'd had the skills, the training. That's all I knew, so I put it to use doing odd jobs for people. Finding things, avenging people's petty qualms, and so on."

"I'm so sorry," I say, and reach forward, touching the back of his hand with my fingertips. He eyes our hands, then my face as I tell him, "When I was twelve, I went through a period of time where I felt this deep, inexplicable sorrow. I felt hopeless. I've always wondered what could have caused such a feeling to come from nowhere..." I trail off, searching his face for answers. "I wonder now if *your sadness* is what I was feeling."

As I say the words out loud, I'm certain they are true.

This thought has us both silent for several heartbeats, staring at each other with this newfound realization.

"Well," he says, feigning his usual confidence. "It's getting dark. We ought to go get lover boy and get moving. No time to waste."

He's on his feet in an instant, and I scramble to stand after him, brushing off my trousers and the lower part of my shirt.

"He is *not* my lover," I repeat with an angry tone, but my heart isn't in it. I don't know how I feel about Zaid at the moment. All I can think about is the conversation I've just had with Alec.

22

When we get back to our camp, Zaid has prepared supper without being asked. I haven't spoken to him much since he told me he has feelings for me, after bringing me news that my mamman has been forced to take a leave of absence from the Council and has been acting strangely and muttering things about leaving to the mountains to repay her debt. It's all just seemed overwhelming to me, and I haven't had much time alone to think things through to figure out how I feel. Now things will be even more difficult, I think, because he's upset that I told him off earlier.

I can tell by his frequent glances that he wants to talk, but I don't want to press him. Perhaps I'll wait until he's ready to come to me. At least that will give me time to think of some alternate reason for sending him away, so he didn't hurt Alec – and me – any more than he already had.

I suck in a deep breath that fills my chest and blow it out in a huff. We're traveling together; I'm going to have to talk to him at some point, and I may as well try and see how it goes. I decide to approach him.

"Hello Zaid," I say, swinging my hands nervously at my sides as though I'm a toddler afraid to ask for a treat.

Zaid regards me with his dark eyes wide, but the corners of his mouth turn up.

"Ah, want me around now, do you?" Zaid remarks.

The tension between us lightens, and I feel my shoulders and neck slightly relax.

"Yes, I suppose I do," I say, chewing at the inside of my lip. "I'm sorry for snapping at you earlier. It's not what you think."

"What is it, then?" Zaid asks. "To me, it looks like you chose Alec over me."

I resist the urge to roll my eyes at the dramatic wording of his comment. "I promise it wasn't that. I just didn't want you to hurt him, that's all..." I trail off. It's not technically a lie.

He stirs some kind of soup in a little pot that sits on the fire. It must be something he brought with him when he brought his horse, because neither Alec nor I had a pot with us. He takes a deep breath.

"I'm sorry I put my foot in my mouth. And bombarded you with information. And offended you when I said you needed protection. And I guess... I'm sorry for showing off back there. I wasn't going to hurt him much," he says. He keeps his eyes on the soup as he stirs. "But how I feel hasn't changed. I *know* you can take care of yourself. I've seen you in action. But I do think you should be more wary, and your skills with your bow only cover so many situations. Still, it wasn't my place to tell you that, and I shouldn't have been so aggressive with him back there. So, I apologize."

I grunt.

"Well, you were right. It never hurts to learn another skillset that will be useful in other situations. So, Alec is teaching me to fight, with my fists as well as with a sword, though he's having me start with that silly wooden one."

Zaid smiles.

"Yeah, I saw you guys training. Your form looks good, so he must know what he's doing. And... don't be too bothered by the wooden sword. Most of us start out that way. Better to be safe than sorry."

The soup splashes around within the pot as it boils, bubbles popping and sending tiny drops of scalding hot liquid over the edge. Although he only made the soup with a few ingredients – potatoes, carrots, and onions – it smells delicious, and my stomach grumbles at the scent.

"Right," I say, looking up to meet his gaze. "Thank you for that, and for making dinner... and for apologizing, too. I appreciate it, and I'm sorry if I've hurt your feelings in all this."

Zaid nods, giving me a tiny smile. "And hey, if you ever get tired of training under Alec, I'd be happy to teach you what I know."

"Right," I say, smiling back. "Trained by the Guard. I'll keep that in mind, thanks."

Alec approaches, already slinging both of his bags over his shoulder.

"Time to get moving," he says, looking past Zaid in the direction I assume we'll be traveling tonight.

"What about food?" Zaid asks. Having just cooked for all of us, I don't blame his begrudging tone.

"Pour it in a flask, and let's get going. We don't want to waste any time we have under cover of darkness."

Zaid turns to me, and I shrug. I reach down and roll up my blanket before securing it to my satchel and scooping up my bow and quiver.

Zaid hurries to get packed up as well, doing his best to pour the hot soup into three canteens. In his attempt to avoid being burned by the hot soup, Zaid flings his elbows out like a chicken attempting flight. I stamp out the fire, trying not to laugh.

"Remind me again why we can't travel during the day like normal people?" Zaid mutters.

"It's safer this way," Alec throws over his shoulder without looking back. "The more we travel at night, the less likely we are to be seen by people passing through. Trust me when I say the bandits out here are not to be taken lightly, and we can't risk the delay."

At this point, Alec is already several yards in front of us. Zaid screws the lids onto the canteens he's filled quickly and rushes to secure the still-hot pan to the outside of his own bag. He runs his hand over his horse's snout and gives her reins a tug to get her walking beside him.

"Right," Zaid says under his breath. "Safer." Then he raises his voice so Alec can hear him across the distance. "You know, Lane and I have traveled together a ton, and we've never once come across problems during the day."

Alec doesn't miss a beat.

"Have you ever trekked the grasslands?" he calls back.

"No, but..." Zaid begins.

"Then you have no idea what you're talking about," Alec snaps. Zaid and I jog to close the distance between us and Alec, and now we're merely a few feet behind him. "You have traveled in forests and deserts where nobody wants to hang around. You've likely traveled in groups, which overall makes you a more difficult target. The three of us, out here in the open like this –

that's just asking for trouble. We're not using any light, so tread carefully. The last thing we need is for one of you two to break an ankle."

We trek through the darkness for a handful of hours. All the while, Zaid tries to make conversation, and Alec makes a fool of him at every turn. I don't think Zaid realizes how much Alec is mocking him, because he keeps trying to talk with us every chance he gets.

Late, late into the night, Zaid's telling us about the different kind of training he had growing up, and how he'd consider being a mercenary if there was any real honor in the profession.

Alec responds with, "I'm sure you'd make a *lovely* mercenary. Sounds like you've got all the necessary traits. It's a shame we'll have to do without you. We could band together! Take the jobs by storm and split the profits!" he mocks.

"Alec," I snap at him, and through the darkness, I can barely see him smirk. I shake my head at him. There's no need for his rudeness.

Zaid doesn't seem to mind Alec's snarky retort. He opens his mouth to say something else, but I cut them both off, throwing my arms out and hitting them both in the stomach. My bag swings off my shoulder and the strap rolls down my arm, but I catch it quickly and pull it back up.

Zaid's horse snorts nervously. She jerks her head, pulling at the reins, and stamps her hooves.

Zaid stops talking, his jaw still slack. Alec, however, is instantly alert. His body tenses next to mine, and he narrows his eyes, looking out into the darkness, listening intently.

"What?" Zaid asks.

"Shh!" I whisper. "Listen. Do you hear that?"

In the distance, we hear yelping, howling. It sounds like a pack of animals, but there's something about the sound that runs my blood cold. Now Zaid hears it, too, and the three of us stand perfectly still, listening, waiting, trying to determine who or what the sound is coming from. Zaid does his best to comfort the restless horse at his side.

It isn't long before the howling intensifies, and soon it surrounds us. We can hear yipping and growling now, along with a dark laughter that contains no joy – only menace.

Alec gives a low grunt as his head whips from side to side, trying to see through the darkness. I'm unsure if he's acting this way because he recognizes these sounds or because they're new to him.

"We should have stayed quiet," he says in a low voice, throwing an irritated glance in Zaid's direction, and I take it he's come across whatever's making these sounds before.

"What?" Zaid asks, dumbfounded. "You're blaming this on me? I was the one who suggested we only travel during the day, remember?"

Zaid's horse whinnies as he struggles to hold onto her.

"Would you shut that thing up?" Alec spits.

"It's not her fault!" Zaid snaps.

Finally, the horse pulls out of Zaid's grip completely and races off. He reaches out to catch hold of the reins or the saddle – anything – but it's too late.

"Fates!" Zaid says. "Anya!" he calls after her quietly, uselessly. There's nothing he can do now; she's already raced away into the dark. I just pray that she'll be safe from whatever it is that's closing in around us.

"Alec," I say, dread caught in my throat, making my mouth dry, snagging at the words as they leave me. "What is it?"

But Alec remains silent as the laughter and howling grows ever louder. He draws his falchion in one hand and pulls the dagger from his belt with the other. Noticing this, Zaid draws his own sword and stands, ready to fight.

"Alec!" I whisper again. My heart is pounding in my ears. My palms are sweating. I've dropped my bag and stand with my bow drawn, ready to shoot. The moon is a mere sliver in the sky, and thick, puffy rainclouds have rolled in, blocking what light it has to offer. I squint, peering through the darkness, hoping I'll be able to see well enough to shoot. In darkness like this, I can usually rely on my ears, at least, but they're filled with the malicious sounds that come from all around us.

"They usually don't come out at night, unless they know where you're camping. They usually just attack travelers on the road in the daylight, where it's easy to see. It's not uncommon for them to venture out in the dark, if they sense there's something worth stealing."

"Bandits?" I ask, my voice just a little bit louder so he can hear me over the sounds that are now so close they're almost ear-piercing. With them this loud, I look around again, sure I'll be able to see someone or something nearby, but I see nothing. They've got to be right with us. Why can't I see them?

"Why don't we just offer up what we have?" Zaid suggests.

"What, like your horse?" Alec asks, and the comment hits *me* like a brick. I can only imagine how Zaid must feel. Still, he presses on.

"Surely, we're not that far from Helna. I think we could make it in a couple of days without our supplies. If loot is all they're after, we should just hand it over, so they'll be on their way."

Now five of them come into view, and I realize why I couldn't see them before. They're crouched down on their hands and feet in the tall grass. There has to be at least eight of them.

These are not like any people I've ever seen before. They're dressed from head to toe in black and gray terrycloth, crawling around on their fingers and the balls of their feet, backs arched, and buttocks raised into the air.

I feel like screaming and running, but I can't get my feet to move.

"Something tells me these aren't your run-of-the-mill bandits..." I say wearily, voice tight in my throat. I hold my bow steady, taking aim. I know I've got five arrows in my quiver, one nocked. I let the one loose, but the two bandits before me move in an inhuman fashion, jumping out of the way at the last second before my arrow can hit either of them. The arrow plunges into the ground, and one of the bandits scoops it up and yips excitedly. I immediately arm myself with another arrow.

"What in Fates' names are these things?" Zaid asks.

The three of us are back-to-back now as more bandits appear. There's a flash of bright lightning, and thunder immediately follows, rolling across the sky for several seconds. At its loudest point, the bandits yip and yell excitedly, and they use their legs and arms to propel them in every direction.

"Just people," Alec remarks through gritted teeth. "The bad kind."

Thunder claps again, resulting in yet another round of howling and yipping. These are *not* just people. Above us, the sky seems to split, and buckets of rain fall upon us all at once, soaking us clean through in seconds. The rain does nothing to discourage the strange and frightening behavior of the animalistic people who circle us ever closer. In fact, they seem to grow more excited, and energetic at this downpour.

At this point, if it weren't for the sound of the rain splashing in puddles all around us, I think I'd be able to hear my heartbeat over everything else. I'm not sure my heart has ever pounded so hard or so fast.

I draw my bowstring taut, but between their quick, unpredictable movements, the heavy rain that came out of nowhere, and the thick storm clouds ahead, I can't seem to hold a target. I don't want to waste any more of my arrows.

I need to do something, though, because as they come closer, the bandits begin to lunge at us. It's at this point that I come to a terrifying realization: They've got blades. Every one of them has a small, curved, and deadly-sharp blade secured to each of their palms.

Each time they lunge forward, they rip at us, throwing their hands through the air and slicing whatever they can reach. Because they've got us surrounded, there's nowhere for the three of us to go except backward until we bump into each other as we do our best to avoid being cut.

"Alec?" I ask, my throat tight with worry, voice strained.

"Think you can shoot them at all, Lane?" Zaid asks, his voice thick, as well.

"Um..." I start, trying and failing to hold my aim at any of them for long enough to send another arrow flying, but Alec interjects. He swings his sword and his dagger through the air as two rabid bandits lunge at him. He misses one, but the other cries out – a sharp, inhuman sound that chills me to the bone and makes my limbs tingle.

"She doesn't kill people," Alec says. I want to stop and stare at him for remembering, for mentioning it in a situation like this, when it's clear that I'm not going to have a choice.

"I think given our circumstances," Zaid replies, blocking an attack with his sword. "She might want to make an exception."

"It's not that I'm not trying!" I shout at both of them. "I only have so many arrows!"

Just as the sentence escapes my lips, one of these bizarre people lunges at me and swings. I think I've miraculously dodged it, but then my arm burns with an agony I haven't felt in a while. I clench my jaw and hold back a yell as Alec cries out. I want to turn to make sure he's alright, but I'm panicking. I pull my arrow farther back with excruciating effort that makes me want to scream. I grit my teeth so tightly that my jaw aches, and I let my arrow fly. It whistles through the air and makes a sickening *thud*, followed by another animalistic cry.

I've hit my mark, I think. Just four arrows left. Every rain drop that hits my arm, every splash of the mud around us, every movement I make sends jolts of pain through my arm and shoulder, but I don't have time to check my wound. Just as another bandit comes rushing in, I draw another arrow, pull back with another shockwave of pain, and send the arrow on its way. This time, I can see where the arrow has landed as lightning strikes above. For a moment, the world is illuminated with a bright flash of white light, and I can see that I've hit this bandit square in the eye. He stands, stunned, and tries to blink once despite the arrow sticking out of his eye socket. Black blood has already begun running down his face, and he drops with a splash.

I let out a little surprised yelp of my own and stumble backward into Zaid's sturdy back. He tumbles forward. He does his best to catch himself, but the ground has become a slippery trap, and he drops his sword and slides forward onto his hands and knees.

He scrambles for his blade in the mud, splashing madly as I shoot another arrow. Just two left.

Rainwater slicks all of our hair to our faces, so it's difficult for me to see what happens next, but I notice out of the corner of my eye that another bandit is rushing in, and I turn and send my second to last arrow into his chest.

By the time I look back to Zaid so I can try to help him up, he's doing his best to fight off a bone-skinny bandit with superhuman strength. The bandit has climbed up on top of Zaid, and he's doing his very best to get the thing off of him. I rush forward to do something – anything – to help, but I'm tackled to the ground by a bandit of my own.

23

I watch as Alec swings his sword, and in one clean swipe, the bandit that has attacked Zaid is missing a head, and dark blood pours over Zaid's face and clothing, only to be washed away in an instant by the pouring rain.

I can't see what happens next. Mud and rainwater pour into my eyes, nose, and mouth. Even in the struggle against the bandit that has me pinned down, blades cutting into my palms as I try to fight him off, I feel like I'm drowning.

I'm gasping for air. Even if I could think to cry out for Alec or Zaid to come to my rescue, I doubt I'd be able to get the words out, so I keep fighting, keep pushing back.

In one moment, the bandit kicks excitedly with his feet in a sort of jump, and I'm able to get my feet up onto his chest. I push with all my might, using a strength I've never known to launch him off of me. He flies backward a few feet and lands on his back, but he gets up faster than I do and shakes it off as though the force of my kick did nothing to him.

I feel my eyes bulge as I stare at him. I scramble backward, running my hands through the mud. Trampled blades of grass and rocks scrape against the cuts on my palms, and my arm is in searing pain, but it's all I can do to keep pulling myself backward as the bandit advances. He moves slowly this time, as if drawing pleasure from taunting me.

All at once, Zaid and Alec charge at the bandit advancing toward me, and just as it readies itself to pounce on me again, its arm is sliced clean through by the blade of Zaid's sword, and Alec drives his falchion into the bandit's stomach until the hilt is buried. He rips the sword back, sending that dark blood soaring through the air.

I'm finally able to find my feet again, and I nock my last arrow, sending it into the neck of another screaming bandit.

I grasp desperately for another arrow, hoping I miscounted, hoping maybe I'd find another, but my quiver sits empty on my back, so I grasp my bow just as I did with the bandits – friends, in comparison – who attacked us a lifetime ago.

But there's no need for another arrow, no need to wield my bow like a club. The eight who attacked us originally now lie dead at our feet, and the others who came late to the fight have now retreated, running quickly on all four limbs back into the tall grass and out of sight. We all stand perfectly still for several moments, waiting, listening, expecting that at any minute we will run into yet another wave of these atrocious beings.

When none come, though, I allow myself to release the breath I've been holding and turn to find my companions.

We're all panting and soaked through. The rain is still coming down as hard as ever, and I worry that we might not make it through the night if we can't find some shelter to address our wounds. I know mine are bleeding heavily, and I can't quite tell if it's from the blood loss or the overwhelming fight we just took part in, but I'm having trouble holding myself upright. My sense of balance seems to have been destroyed.

My head hurts, and although I don't remember hitting it, I'm sure I must have at some point during our attack.

And then, of course, I look at Alec and Zaid. Both of them look as awful as I feel, and I find I'm a bit relieved to see I'm not the only one who has taken a beating.

Zaid's got some nasty ribbon-like slices on his arms from where one of them got him when he was scrambling around for his sword. It's difficult to tell if he's got any other wounds through the darkness and the rain.

Just then lightning strikes and gives us a second of bright light. In it, I see that Alec is covered in blood. He's got a good-sized gash in his hairline above his forehead, right where mine seems to hurt the most. So perhaps *he* was the cause for this particular injury. His wounds become my own, and mine become his. Although this thought has been on my mind constantly since we met, it's still strange to see it in a full-fledged ambush like this.

Then another thought hits me: If that's what he looks like, my wounds must be as bad as they feel.

I breathe in deeply and walk a little closer to the two of them, reaching to grab one of our bags, which are sopping wet, trampled, and covered in mud.

"Are you alright?" Zaid asks, arms outstretched, offering to help me.

"I'm fine," I say as I bend to find my satchel in the pile of our filthy belongings. I lose my balance and, although it's already dark, the world begins to grow darker still as my vision fades at the edges. I grasp the thick strap of one of the bags, then Zaid's hand is on my injured arm, and that sends a jolt of awareness through me just long enough for me to struggle to right myself. Alec hisses and rolls his shoulder of the same injured arm.

"Looks like you're not," Zaid says in a soft, concerned tone. "We need to find shelter and get you cleaned up." Alec and I share a brief look, and Alec says what we're both thinking.

"Look around, Zaid. Where would you like to go? We won't be able to find any type of shelter for at least another few days."

"Well, we have to do something. We'll be dead of blood loss and exposure before dawn comes if we don't do something. Look at her." Zaid gestures to me. Although there's not a lot we can do in the rain and so far from shelter, my brain is whirring trying to think of a solution. I reach into the bag I'm holding – Alec's, I think – and feel around inside. When I find what I'm looking for, I pull it out.

I hold up Alec's blanket and assess it, trying to determine if it's usable. It's soaked through, and even though it's a lightweight blanket, it takes a great deal of effort to pull it all the way out of the bag. I think I can work with this, though, and I start to formulate a plan.

"Stop bickering," I say to both of them without removing my attention from the blanket in hand. The rain has lightened just a little bit, and I use the opportunity to twist the blanket, hoping I can get some of the water out. It takes everything I have to stay conscious as I work to wring it out. My arm is throbbing. My head is throbbing. But I shake it off as best I can.

"Alec, let me see your knife." I crouch down and dump out the contents of Alec's bag in the mud and put my hand out. Alec starts to argue, but I stop him. "I know, no one is allowed to touch your precious blades. But Zaid is right, and you're just going to have to make an exception for one minute," I snap.

Within seconds, the beautifully crafted knife is in my hand, and I get to work cutting his bag open.

"What are you doing?" asks Zaid.

"Do you want a shelter, or not?" I grunt through the effort and the pain. Exhaustion pulls at my body, and I don't know how long I'll be able to stay conscious. "We need to get something together, fast. I'm not going to stand out here with you both all night. Here. Zaid, take the blankets and wring them out. Alec, help me cut up these bags. We're going to try and layer up."

Without another word of argument, Alec shakes out the other bags, then takes his sword and uses the blade to work at the material. I take all of our longer weapons – my bow, Alec and Zaid's swords – and press them into the ground until they stay upright on their own. I hope this works.

Another bolt of lightning strikes, but this time, it's several seconds before we hear the crash of thunder, and even then, the sound is faded and far off. The storm must be moving away from our location. Still, it's almost an hour before rain eases to a drizzle.

By this time, we've fashioned a sort of tent by tying our blankets and bags together. The blankets go underneath, and the canvas bags on top to help shelter us from the water. Next, we crawl into the entrance, and I pray that we can be still enough that the fort will hold.

Once we are out of the direct impact from the rain, we use the fading lighting flashes to take stock of our injuries.

Zaid's forearms are covered in thin cuts, and he has a long – but seemingly superficial – cut on his shin.

Alec and I, of course, have the same series of wounds: One on the forehead, one painful gash on the chin, the thin yet deep slice to the triceps in our left arms, slashes in the palms. If Zaid notices the similarities between Alec's cuts and mine through the darkness and the rain, he says nothing about them. We do what we can to create bandages out of some belts and strips of canvas for now.

Then we settle in, the three of us huddling so much closer together than I would typically even consider. But in this moment, with the night stretching on ahead of us, the rain soaking us and chilling us to the bone, and the blood loss and exhaustion from the fight making me feel like I'll never be able to move my limbs again, I welcome the closeness.

Just as I begin fading off for the night, Alec shifts, bumping me accidentally with his shoulder. I grunt, and warm blood oozes out of my wounded arm.

I suck in a hiss of a breath, but I don't move.

"Oh, sorry," Alec says. "I was trying to adjust so I could see outside. I think it would be a good idea for one of us to be on Guard tonight. Just in case those *friendly* fellows decide to come back."

"That's probably a good idea," I croak. "You shouldn't do it all alone. If I feel like this, I know you're probably just as beat."

Alec nods. I can barely make out a hint of his smile in the darkness.

"Yeah, well, I've grown accustomed to experiences like this, though the rain definitely isn't helping much," he says. "But I'll gladly accept the help, and the company isn't so bad, either."

"I wish we could build a fire," I say, shivering. I don't remember ever feeling so cold in my entire life. I wonder if this is what a dead fish feels like on the inside. The thought makes me scrunch up my face, which pulls at the cuts on my chin and forehead. "Stupid rain."

Carefully, Alec raises his good arm above my head.

"Here. Come over here," he says softly. At first, I just look at him, and he chuckles, though the sound is weak. "Oh, come on. You're freezing. I won't try anything. I swear on my mamman's health."

I roll my eyes and let out a little sigh, but I do accept the invitation, and I scoot a little closer. Zaid snores from my other side, a deep, hefty sound with abrupt stops and starts that has Alec and me both laughing a little. At least he's getting a bit of rest. I hope he's sleeping well. Part of me feels guilty for sliding nearer to Alec with Zaid so close by, but Alec offered, and I wouldn't feel comfortable scooting closer to Zaid without his permission.

When I place my head in the crook of Alec's arm, I feel myself relaxing. I don't know how, but his body is still so warm, and it soothes some of the chill within me. I do my best to ignore the butterflies that make my stomach flip. I wonder if he feels that, too.

"Tell me something nice," I say through a big yawn.

"Something nice?" he asks, resting his chin on the top of my head. My chin aches as he does this, but it stops hurting so badly once he's stopped moving.

"Something warm," I reply, my voice soft.

"Well okay, then," he starts. His fingers trace warm little paths up and down my good arm. My wounded arm is nestled up against his side, and although it throbs and aches, the pressure helps. "When I was a kid, my mamman brought me to the market in Parth. She brought me there after meeting with the Women's Council member from that city. She said it was important for me to learn about the other cities we work with. I remember her walking me through the streets and looking at all the shops.

"She bought me this wooden toy sword and told me that, someday, I could join my pappan in his work if I wanted to. She stopped to talk with some of the merchants, and I wandered off to follow the smell of this *incredibly* scented sweet bread. I could hear her calling out for me all throughout the market, but I was so distracted by the smell that the sound was a million miles away.

"When she found me at the baker's sweet stand outside his shop, she pulled me into the warmest embrace I've ever received, and she was crying. She didn't chastise me; she wasn't even angry. She was just grateful I was safe. Any time I'm feeling particularly lonely, I remember that moment. I remember being so cared for. And the taste of that sweet bread she bought me afterward makes the memory so much sweeter."

"That's nice," I mutter. "You get lonely?"

Despite the cold and the pain, I find myself drifting off now that Alec's body heat has stopped my shivering.

I can just picture him raising his eyebrows as he gives my good arm a little squeeze.

"Oh, you'd be surprised," I hear him whisper.

"Who'd have thought?" I ask, fighting to keep myself awake. "Tell me something else. Why do you call your sword Rhetta?"

"All swords have names. I chose Rhetta for mine because she's a strong, sturdy beauty."

"Hmm," is all I can say in reply. Alec traces little circles on my arm with his thumb. The warmth of him is so comforting. Eventually, I can no longer keep my eyes open. Dawn should be upon us soon, and I hope we can wait out the rest of the night and find better conditions tomorrow. At least with the three of us in such a confined space, we should be able to conserve our body heat until the sun comes up.

As the rain slows to a drizzle, I drift off to sleep listening to Alec share more stories about places he's gone with his mamman, and I fall into dreams about being with my own family. Missing them makes my chest ache. I wonder how they're fairing, now. Do they miss me as I miss them?

I'm awoken by the sound of birds chirping overhead. In the early morning hours, the temperature dropped significantly, and I find myself cold and still extremely damp. My eyelids are heavy, and my entire body aches like nothing I've ever experienced. But I sit up slowly, doing my best to avoid pulling the shelter down on us, forgetting how low and poorly constructed it is.

The rain has stopped, and the smell of washed earth fills the air. The mud, the grass, even the scent of the sky is heightened, and if I wasn't so incredibly sore, I would stand up and dance in the smell.

But I can barely move. I don't think I'll be dancing anytime soon.

I take a few moments to try and warm up my limbs, turning my hands and feet in slow, painful circles. This helps a little bit. Then I start to stretch, and blood trickles out from the wound in my arm. It's hot against my tepid skin. I wipe it away in a panic, then try to adjust the bandages that have slid down my arm in my sleep.

Zaid wakes when he hears me grunting, and Alec adjusts in his sleep. I do my best to be quiet, but I've got one side of my bandage in my mouth as I try to untie the knot so I can rewrap it, and it's not going well.

Zaid sits up and rubs the sleep from his eyes.

"Hey," he starts. His voice is low, gruff. I've been with him when he's been tired before, but I've never heard his voice like this. I'm not sure if it's the poor sleep we all got last night, or just hearing his voice directly after he wakes up, but the sound is nice to hear. It makes me think I'm learning something about my companion that I didn't know before.

"Oh, sorry," I say with clenched teeth, still holding the cloth from my bandage in my mouth. I reach the hand from my right arm, my uninjured arm, up to my face to wipe away some frustrated tears. "I didn't mean to wake you up. I'm just trying to get this *damned*—"

I pull at the knot and grunt again. It's not even the pain that's the problem. It's the fact that every time I think I'm making progress, every time I think I'm holding it tightly enough that I can loosen the knot, the bandage slips.

"Fates!" I whisper. I feel like punching something.

"Here," he says. "I've got it." He sits up quickly and reaches over. I turn so I can face him a little better, and I drop the cloth from my mouth. He works at the knot, untying and retying it easily.

"Sorry I chewed that part," I say, embarrassed that I was just sitting here with that thing in my mouth, and now he's holding it.

"That's okay. I don't mind," he says.

Zaid refocuses, and in a moment, he's secured the knot.

He sits back a little bit, but I notice how close he sits to me, and my cheeks begin to burn a little bit.

"Crazy night we had last night, wasn't it?" I ask, if for no other reason than to distract myself from the warmth in my face. Zaid lets out a wry laugh.

"Oh, yeah. I think last night definitely qualifies as one of the strangest things I've ever experienced. I'm so glad our trade route doesn't come out this way. If ever it does, you can consider me sick." He runs a hand through his dark hair and smiles. The purple circles beneath his eyes only accentuate their deep, dark brown.

"Seriously," I say. "The sooner we get to Helna, the better. Did you *see* those people?" The hair on my arms and neck stands on end at the thought of how those bandits were running and jumping around on all four limbs like animals.

I'm shivering now, whether from the cold or from the fear I don't know. I pull my aching limbs closer to my body. My arm feels much better now that it's been tightly wrapped.

"If you're talking about those *things* crawling around, howling and driveling like a pack of wolves, I definitely saw them," he says.

His comment actually makes me smile, despite the shuddering that results from the image his description brings back up.

It was all so strange. Last night seems like a dream, and I'm so tired now that I start to laugh. As the laughter bubbles up, it warms me a little, so I keep laughing until I realize that Zaid is just staring at me.

"Sorry. I think I may be a little hysterical from... well, everything," I say, covering my mouth with my right hand. "I've never seen anything like that. I don't know what entices a person to crawl around with their backside in the air, but it's certainly not something that looked very comfortable to be doing."

Zaid returns my smile.

"Agreed. That's got to be *torture* for your back."

"I'm sorry about your horse, Zaid," I tell him, reaching out to touch his hand. He looks shocked at the touch, and he nods.

We allow the silence to settle in between us for a moment, both of our smiles beginning to fade.

"If you two are about to kiss, a little warning might be nice. Don't want to wake up to a cloud of steam in our sleeping area, you know." Alec's voice is also thick with sleep. He's had his arm draped over his face since I woke up, so I just assumed he's been sleeping this whole time. I wonder how much of that conversation he heard.

And the comment he's just made about me *kissing* Zaid... If I thought my face was warm before, it's on fire now.

Alec props himself up on his right elbow and looks around me. Thankfully, his messy hair hangs in front of his forehead, so at least that injury is hidden for now. I cover my chin with my hands.

"Just so you know, man, you've got your work cut out for you with this one," Alec says. "She's already declared more than once that you are *not* her lover."

"Alec!" I blurt, totally shocked. "Fates!"

He gives me a little wink, and I want nothing more than to reach over and deck him across the face. But my body hurts too much to move quickly enough, and smacking him would only result in me hurting myself, too. Instead, I bury my face in my hands and hope to disappear. I chance a small peek at Zaid, who grins.

"That's alright, Alec," Zaid chimes in. I whip my head around to look at him, eyes wide. "Your comments don't change a thing for me." He puts his hand gently on mine.

I wish again to disappear from this moment. From this field. From the entire universe. Anything to get away from this embarrassing experience.

I force myself to stand up despite the pain in my body.

"I'm going to check our supplies," I say to both of them, and to my surprise, both of them move as if they're going to come help me. "*Alone.*"

I shoot Alec a death glare and turn my back to them, yanking my bow from the ground. This forces our makeshift shelter to collapse on them both as I shuffle the small distance from our shelter to our pile of belongings.

It takes everything I have to close that short distance, and I have to shoo away a flock of birds that picks at what's left of our food. The fluttering of their wings echoes in the morning air as they fly away. I slowly get to my hands and knees. The mud squishes beneath me, and I adjust, trying to get as comfortable as possible before digging my hands into the pile.

I sort through everything that's left while Zaid and Alec work to make a fire in the wet field. All our clothing is soaked and mud-stained straight through, and much of it has been splashed with blood.

All the food I can salvage needs to be washed. Our bread has been soaked beyond saving, squished in the heat of our battle, and now picked apart by birds. We've got a small block of cheese that has been pushed into the mud with our potatoes, apples, and other assorted vegetables, but I think if we can find a way to wash them thoroughly, they should still be alright to eat. Once I've got things sorted out, I get up and drag myself over to our fort to get our blankets. I'll use them to pack up our things until we can get some more bags.

When I've packed everything back up, I leave our bags where we dumped everything out last night, grab a canteen of Alec's strongest ale, some sopping-wet gauze wrap, and a tiny travel-sewing kit that must be Alec's. I head back over to where the boys are still working to build a fire.

"There are some vegetables wrapped up in the green blanket. Zaid, do you think you could wash them with some water or ale from our canteens and throw something together for us to eat? Maybe keep trying the fire? I'll attend to Alec's arm and head, and then we'll get your cuts all patched up, too. Alright?"

Zaid nods and, without a word, gets moving.

I sit cross-legged in front of the pile of wet grass and material they were trying to use as kindling.

I gesture to the ground in front of me, and Alec plops down, looking proud of himself.

"Sweet of you to take care of me first," he starts, doing nothing to hide the smug grin on his face.

"I spent the entire night freezing and bleeding and aching, and I am *not* in the mood. Save your quips, or you can deal with these wounds on your own," I snap at him. Then, I lower my voice, so only he can hear. "I'm taking care of you first because I've got the same pains, and I know how they feel. Besides, I don't think it's a very good idea for us to go walking around with wounds that are obviously identical. At the very least, if they're dressed, no one will know just how similar they are, only that they happened in remotely the same area."

Alec raises his eyebrows and throws his hands up in surrender, but he says nothing for a while as I tend to his injuries. I start by cleaning the scrape on his forehead. It's not too bad, so once it's been cleaned and dried, I leave it alone.

I clean the injuries on his hands with the alcohol from his flask and wrap them. I'm pleased – for Alec's sake and my own – that the only injury that needs stitching is the slice in our arms. I take care to stitch the wound nice and tight. I'm not sure if our healing process is quite the same, but just in case, I do my best to ensure he'll have as little scarring as possible.

As I work, Zaid sets to cleaning potatoes with another flask of ale and begins chopping them. He mumbles something about going to look for drier kindling, and he wanders away.

It's only as I'm finishing up and he starts to work on my injuries that Alec speaks.

"I'm sorry about this morning. I shouldn't have said what I did," Alec says.

This apology takes me completely by surprise, and when I make eye contact with him, I can see that it's sincere.

"Thanks," I reply.

We fall silent again until Zaid wanders back to us.

"How far are we until we reach Helna?" he asks.

"Three days. Maybe longer, if our injuries from last night slow us down," Alec remarks in a somber tone.

"Well, we're going to need to find an alternate food source if it's going to take us that long. We can make what little we've got stretch one, maybe two days at most," Zaid says. "If my horse hadn't run off, we'd have a little more to go around, but..."

"But she's gone," I say. "I'm sorry, Zaid."

The three of us sit quietly as the serious nature of our situation really sinks in. Then, I get an idea.

"Alec, is there anything to hunt out here?"

"Rabbits, squirrels, lizards. Occasionally deer wander through, if you're lucky," Alec replies. I look over at the bodies of the bandits we killed last night.

"We should do something with those. They may have acted like animals... but they're still people," I say.

Because Zaid is the only one with two fully functioning arms, he pulls the bodies left over from last night's debacle into a pile. I collect my arrows from their corpses, doing what I can to avoid looking at them directly. Seeing them in the daylight only makes them more horrifying. Their skin is dark, grayish, and they're covered in long, twisted scars that make their faces and exposed bits of skin look otherworldly.

They're all so still, and despite the rain, the coppery scent of blood still hangs thick in the air above them.

Oh, Fates. I ended some of their lives.

I feel like vomiting.

The fear and guilt I feel at seeing them lying in a heap like this is almost too much. I'm glad to go hunting. At least I can put some distance between myself and those... things.

25

We travel as much as we can over the next couple of days. Our wounds are already healing nicely.

I'm able to shoot down small birds here and there that fly up from the cover of the grass, and we're finally able to cook them once the rain dries up at the end of the first day, but we've hardly had anything else to eat in days.

Finally, finally, the grasslands give way to winding stone-paved roads, and we begin to see little wooden huts with fires burning visibly from the windows in the distance.

"What are those?" I ask, mouth watering as if those huts are large, juicy steaks. Hunger has made us all a little delirious. "What are those things over there?"

My entire body begins to shake, and my wounds ache so deeply I feel as if I've broken my bones.

"That, sweetheart," Alec says. He's out of breath, and his voice is low with exhaustion. "Is the edge of the most beautiful city I've ever seen. *That* is Helna."

"Helna," Zaid says, chiming in just as deliriously. "Helna. Have you ever heard such a beautiful name in all of Maran? I'll bet they have all kinds of delicious, hearty foods in Helna. Quick! Let's pick up the pace!"

Zaid does pick up his pace, but Alec and I are too far gone to do much more than stare after him.

About an hour later, we are all officially within city limits, and I do feel much more hopeful.

"We're finally here," I say, breathless. "We're finally in Helna, can you believe it? What's the plan now, aside from food?"

Alec's face is serious. "I'm going to reach out to Rodrick's contact, see what new information we can gather as to my mamman's whereabouts."

"Right," I say, remembering our conversation with Rodrick back in Parth. All I want to do is eat and rest, but we have things to take care of, and we've already wasted enough time. "How do they know who your mamman is, or what information is important? Do they just watch everything?" I ask.

Alec nods. "Yes, to an extent. They watch for anything out of the ordinary, anything notable. Rodrick has countless eyes under his employ, and he sends word if anything pops up that he wants them to look for, specifically."

"Like your mamman," I say, starting to understand.

"Exactly."

The three of us meet up at a tavern outside of town and eat until our bellies are full and we're ready for sleep. Alec has already started asking around for his contact. When he sits back down with us, he grunts about his full stomach.

"Any news?" I ask.

"My informant will meet up with me first thing in the morning. I don't know what you two will be up to, but I've got no time to waste. In the morning, I'll stock up again on our provisions and get some new bags, and as soon as I get my information, I'm hitting the road again."

"Do you have much money left?" I find myself asking around a mouthful of food. "I think I still have a fair amount left over, if you need it."

One side of Alec's mouth tilts up in a smile.

"You keep what you have. You earned it. Give me the morning, sweetheart, and I'll make us enough for everything we need." His remark sounds so cocky, so I'm not surprised to hear Zaid give a snort before returning to his food. However, I've seen firsthand what Alec is talking about, and I believe him wholeheartedly. By lunchtime tomorrow, possibly sooner, he will have made himself a large sum of money playing Fates.

After we've sufficiently stuffed ourselves, I make my way to the counter to ask the young girl working there where we can find a room to stay in for the night.

The girl's got to be only thirteen or fourteen years of age. She barely looks at me as she greets me. All the while, her eyes wander back to our table in the corner, and my two companions.

"Miss?" I prompt when her attention lingers there. "Is there anywhere nearby we can stay?"

This seems to pull her out of her daze long enough to get me an answer. She shakes her head and blinks rapidly.

"Yes, my apologies. Helna's got a wide selection of inns to choose from. The most affordable," she pauses, looking me over, and I realize that I'm still covered in mud and blood, and my hair hasn't been washed in far too long. "Would be the Cat 'n' Mouse, just a few streets east of here. Just that way. You won't miss it —

it's got a big fat cat that always sits out at the front door, and the owner looks just the same." She covers her mouth and giggles.

"Thanks," I say, patting the countertop before turning to make my way back to my table.

"Miss?" she pipes up, tone polite.

I turn back around with my eyebrows raised.

"How did you come to travel with such companions? And two, at that?" she asks timidly.

When she sees my expression, the girl waves her hand in the air.

"I meant no offense! It's just... well... I want to travel as I get older – get out of Helna and see the rest of Maran. I've never even seen as far as the wood beyond the grass. You all came in so late in the night, or early in the morning as it is now." She gestures out the front window at the light that has begun pouring through the curtains, spilling out onto the tavern's wooden floors. "I just wanted to know how you came upon such capable, and um... attractive travel companions."

"Honestly?" I ask, thinking back on my journey so far. The girl nods eagerly, twirling her hair around her finger.

I think back to how I happened upon Alec, how I followed him because he felt familiar to me. I consider how I discovered that we're bound, and how I've been compelled to accompany him to ensure that he wouldn't get us both killed. I think about how Zaid found us on our way to Helna.

"I have no idea. To give you the short version, it just kind of happened. Fate, I suppose," I answer, though the words feel flat and foreign on my tongue.

This seems to dampen the girl's spirits a bit, and her shoulders droop.

"Oh, I hope fate is that kind to me, someday. If you're ever back this way, will you stop in and tell me how it all played out?" she asks.

"I promise," I say. We share a smile, and I look back at my two companions. "Well, I really should find that room. We've got a big day coming up, and the sun's already got a head start. Thank you for your service," I tell her.

The girl gives me a little nod.

"If you go to the Cat 'n' Mouse, tell them Juniper sent you. I'm always sending them guests, and I'll bet they give you a good rate."

"Thanks again," I say before returning to my table.

The Cat 'n' Mouse really is just a few streets away in the direction Juniper had pointed, and just as she mentioned, there really is a large, supremely fat cat curled up on the welcome mat outside the front door.

When we open the door, a little bell rings overhead, and a woman's raspy voice calls out from another room, "Oi! Be with you in a shake."

In just a moment, a short, round woman comes barreling in and squishes herself in behind the front desk.

"I'm Miss Kat. You lot look pretty sorry," she starts off, giving us a good long look, distain plainly written across her face. Whether it's from our filthy state or from the fact that I travel with two men, I'm not sure.

"Sorry to bother you so early, ma'am, but Juniper told me we could find some good rooms here," I say.

The woman nods curtly. "It'll be two rooms for you, then. One for you, one for the boys. That'll be six copper pieces a night.

Breakfast can be included for an extra two coppers total, but don't discuss your rate with anyone else, got it?"

Alec leans over the counter and gives the woman a charming smile, to which she actually smiles back, though the expression looks uncomfortable for her.

"Your hospitality is beyond generous. We wouldn't dream of taking it for granted," he says, voice smooth.

"Go on, then. Since it's already morning, I assume you'll be needing some rest. I'll send breakfast up around ten o'clock."

The three of us express our blur of thanks, and we head to our rooms.

Although I'm a little worried about Alec and Zaid being in the same room where I can't keep an eye on them, but I'm exhausted, and I would love the privacy my own room would offer.

"See you around ten, then?" I ask. They both nod.

Inside, the small room smells like lavender and sandalwood. The walls have been painted green and white, and the small space contains a bed with a thick green comforter, a small washtub, and a latrine. At the sight of the three amenities, I feel like crying. How long has it been since I used an actual latrine? Too long. How long has it been since I took a bath? The thought disturbs me so thoroughly that I immediately begin filling the tub. I spend probably too long cleaning myself up, washing and rewashing my hair and my body, taking extra care to clean the areas I've been wounded in over the last several weeks. I even take a moment to use the straight razor left on the edge of the tub to rid myself of some unwanted body hair.

When I'm finished and I towel off, I'm disturbed by how dark and filthy my bathwater is.

After tending to what's left of my wounds, I wrap myself in a soft, tan robe that hangs on the door, and I make my way to the bed. I lift the comforter, so deeply grateful for a cushioned, level place to sleep that tears well in my eyes.

I pull the soft covers all the way up to my chin, and before I know it, I'm fast asleep.

In what feels like a matter of moments, there's a heavy knocking on my door that pulls me out of whatever sweet dream I was having that has already faded from my memory. Groggier than I think I've ever been in my life, I drag myself out of bed and saunter over to the door. I pull it open to find Zaid and Alec standing on the other side.

They both look great – clean and neat, dressed in clothes that look borrowed. Alec hasn't shaved, but his facial hair has been trimmed to a soft, short stubble.

"What clothes we could salvage are being washed, courtesy of Miss Kat," Zaid says, holding out a dress that looks like it might be about my size.

"What's this?" I ask, trying to rub the sleep from my eyes.

"Something clean to wear," Alec says. His eyes dart down to my robe.

I snag the dress from Zaid's hand.

"Point taken. I'll wear it. Anything else?" I ask.

"Yes," Zaid says. "Miss Kat says that she will be sending breakfast up soon."

"Already?" I ask in disbelief. I just barely got to sleep. How is it so late in the morning already?

"After breakfast, I'm going into town to get some money, then collect some provisions. Then I'm going to see what information I can gather," Alec says. Alec gestures between Zaid and me. "You two need to decide what you're doing from here. Lane, would you like to come play Fates? You faired pretty well in Parth."

"I'd love to!" I say, remembering the high I felt from playing Fates for the first time. Between the two of us, if my luck still holds strong, we should be ready to move on in no time, with money to spare. "Let me get dressed now, and as soon as we've eaten breakfast, I'll go with you."

I hardly wait for them to answer before I close the door and immediately slip out of my robe and into the dress Miss Kat provided. Like everything else in this inn, the dress is a soft green. Its skirt flows just past my knees, and the loose-fitting sleeves go all the way down to my wrists. The bodice is form fitting, and I'm surprised by how well this randomly chosen dress fits me. I slip on my boots.

After breakfast, as Alec and Zaid are on their way out the door, I stop at the front desk.

"I see the dress fits nicely," Miss Kat says, giving a smug little smile.

"It fits very well; thank you so much for letting me borrow it. I will get it back to you as soon as I get my other clothes back."

The woman frowns.

"No need. The dress is yours. That blond hunk of yours bought it for you. He knew your size right off. Seems I judged you a little too harshly coming in with two men. It's clear the blond one is the one you go with. Give my apologies to your brother."

I open my mouth to retort, to tell her Zaid is not my brother, and that I'm not *with* Alec, but I find myself speechless. Alec has no responsibility for me, and he's stated many times that he doesn't care what I do. Why would he do this for me?

"Thank you, again, ma'am."

"You kids stay out of trouble," she says. "There are strange things afoot these days. The mountain to the north draws all sorts of folk that don't come back. Being so close to it, I'd say you're better off heading west, whatever your travels may be."

"I'll keep that in mind," I say as I leave the inn.

Helna's streets are all muddy cobblestone, and horses are everywhere: being ridden, being led, carrying supplies, and even just wandering the streets without anyone around to guide them.

Alec and I play Fates at a small tavern toward the middle of town, and Zaid watches us as we play.

By noon, we've earned enough money for some new clothes, some food, new bags, and I purchase a few more arrows to add to my quiver. I tell Alec that I'll go buy what we need so he can find some information regarding his mamman. Zaid comes with me. After we've gathered and purchased our provisions, I turn to Zaid.

"I need to stop at the postman's office. I want to send a letter home and tell my family that I made it safely to Helna. I want to check in and make sure they're doing alright."

When we find the nearest postal service, Zaid scrunches up his nose at the smell inside. The scent of bird is much stronger in this establishment than the one in Parth.

"Excuse me," I ask the patron, a twig-thin man with thin eyebrows that arch high up into his forehead. "I'd like to send a letter to Palandra, please."

"Your name wouldn't happen to be Lane, would it?" the man asks. He leans against the countertop.

"It is," I say, frowning. "Why do you ask?"

"Well, just the other day, I got a letter from Palandra. I don't get many letters from that area, see, so this one stuck in my mind. It's addressed to a Lane Shrayan. Let me see, I know I've put it somewhere around here. Give me one moment, and I'll find it for you."

The man rummages around beneath his desk for a few minutes before he finds the letter he was looking for. He stands abruptly, bumping his head on the underside of the desk before he's able to stand up all the way. He rubs the back of his head gingerly.

"Here it is, miss," he says. "Lane Shrayan, Palandra. Is this you?"

"That's me, thank you!" I take the letter from his outstretched hand, opening the envelope and unfolding the piece of parchment. My heart warms when I recognize my baby sister's handwriting. "It's from Lilah!" I exclaim, eyes filling with tears as I soak in all the words she has written for me.

Soon, however, a weight settles in my gut as I register the meaning of the words on the page.

"What is it?" Zaid asks, stooping to get a clear view of my face. He looks worried.

"My... um... my mamman is gone. According to my sister... she's been rambling for a while now about righting her wrongs, and the only way to do that was to see the witch. Lilah said she thought my mamman's ramblings were harmless, that she was just overstressed from Council business, but then she stopped eating, and now she's left altogether. My pappan is out on business for a month doing deliveries because we're away, and Lilah is home alone. She doesn't know exactly where my pappan is. My mamman was supposed to stay and take care of her. She's only nine. She can't be alone like that. I... I don't know what to do. I need to go after my mamman. But Lilah..."

I find myself trailing off, unable to even find the words to finish my sentence. What do I do? Zaid was right that things were off. Why didn't I take his words more seriously? I thought my pappan had hired someone new to help while I was gone... Why would he leave Lilah alone if my mamman was acting strangely?

It's only when Zaid reaches up to wipe tears from my face that I realize I'm actually crying. The postman stands awkwardly behind the desk, trying to look busy, but he's clearly drawn in by my reaction to the letter.

"Lane, it's going to be alright," Zaid says. "You go after your mamman. See this through. I'd have no idea of the first place to look for her, but it seems that you've got a pretty clear picture of what Lilah is talking about. I'll go home and look after your sister until your pappan returns."

"What?" I ask, eyes so full of tears I find it hard to see him clearly. I blink them away. "Why would you do that? Lilah isn't your responsibility. None of this is. Asking you to do that... would be so much."

Zaid takes my face in both his hands. His eyes are wide, totally sincere.

"Lane, how many times do I have to say this before you understand? I care for you. Deeply. Your happiness – your family – is important to me. Let me do this for you."

I'm completely stunned. Tingles spread throughout my limbs at his words, and I have no idea what to say. I wipe the stray tears from my face and brush my fingers across the backs of his hands, then pull him into a tight embrace.

"Thank you, Zaid," I whisper against his neck.

Zaid smiles and pulls back far enough to look at me. Then he leans forward, placing a small kiss on my nose that warms my entire body. His lips linger just a breath from mine, and in my gratitude, I start to lean forward, but the postman clears his throat to remind us that he's still with us, and the moment is gone. We pull away from each other, and I wipe another stray tear from my cheek.

"Oh. Um, thank you. Zaid. Thank you."

Zaid nods, and I can't help but think I see disappointment flash across his face.

"Let me find a horse. I'll be much faster that way, and I'll leave at first light tomorrow morning."

26

When I've written Lilah to let her know Zaid will be coming to look after her until we can get ahold of my pappan, and our preparations have been made, Alec, Zaid and I sit down to have one last meal together back at the same tavern we visited when we got to Helna last night.

Alec spoke to one of Rodrick's "eyes" who lives here in Helna. The man said that Alec's mamman had passed through not two weeks ago, headed to the swamp. By the time she'd reached Helna, according to the man, she'd become delirious, distant, and unresponsive. If she did respond to any inquiring minds, she repeated the same thing, over and over. Her son was in danger. She was worried about his health. She needed to pay her dues before the worst could happen.

When Alec pressed, his informant could say nothing more. Hearing all of this now sends icy chills down my spine, especially after reading my sister's letter that mentioned the way my mamman had been behaving when she went missing. Something about all of this seems wrong.

It all has to be connected somehow, and I feel it's no coincidence that Alec and I are bound if both of our mammans are experiencing the same phenomenon. I wonder if they could be bound somehow, as well.

I push my food away, appetite spoiled.

I chew nervously at my fingernails as Zaid and Alec discuss their plans for the morning. It isn't until Alec reaches up and grabs my hand, and Zaid looks at me with deep concern spelled across his face, that I realize I've bitten my nails down to the quick.

Embarrassed, I pull my hand from Alec's grip and set both hands in my lap beneath the table.

"Are you alright, Lane?" Zaid asks.

I shake off the distraction, feeling the weight of my braid bounce between my shoulder blades at the movement.

"I'm fine. Just preoccupied, sorry. The plan?" I redirect the conversation, hoping to get their concerned glances off of me.

Alec sighs.

"Zaid will be leaving on horseback at first light. Just as the two of you discussed, he'll set his course for Palandra and send a letter north as soon as he arrives. He'll also try to get in touch with your pappan's company to see where he went, and if he is able to contact him, he will. He'll send you updates until you return home, so long as you keep him aware of where you are headed."

At the reminder of the situation at home, my nerves return, and I pick at my jagged, chewed nails under the table.

"Right. Good," I say. I do my best to sit still, but it isn't long before my legs are bouncing.

Alec raises his eyebrows. I can't tell if he's noticed my shaking, or if he can feel how on edge I am through our bond, but thankfully, he doesn't mention it.

"You and I will continue north," he says. "I have a feeling that my mamman is not stopping to stay in the swamplands, but I have to check there. If she isn't there, or if I can find some other information, I will continue farther with you. We'll find your mamman too, Lane."

I nod, and I'm surprised by the tears I suddenly have to fight to keep them from falling.

"Thank you," I whisper.

Zaid pats my hand beneath the table, and at his touch, I'm reminded of the kiss he placed on my nose earlier, how I would have kissed him if the postman hadn't interrupted us. My already nervous stomach flips.

"I'll be right back," Zaid says, as he leaves the table to flag down a serving woman who seems to have forgotten our drinks.

I set my hands back on the table, gripping my spoon and tapping it against my palm.

Alec leans forward, placing the tips of his fingers against my bare forearms. The warmth of his touch is alarming, but it's also comforting, and it spreads to quiet the turmoil in my belly.

"This has to be connected," he whispers. "I can't possibly believe that both of our mammans are acting off and heading north out of coincidence. Not knowing what I know about us."

"I agree," I say, choking back the sob that rises in my throat when I hear I'm not alone in my thinking that something isn't right here. "There's just no way. We have to find them, Alec. Whatever is making them do the same things and act the same way can't be good."

When Zaid returns, he eyes Alec's hand on my arm, his fingers tracing warm little circles there, and Zaid slams the drinks he'd gathered down on the table, sending various liquids sloshing over the edges of our cups. He takes his seat beside me.

"I'm so glad you're headed home to check on Lilah, Zaid," I say, pulling my hands away from Alec's touch. "You have no idea what a relief it will be for me to know she's looked after. I don't know what possessed my mamman to leave her alone like that. She's only nine, for Fates' sake."

"Of course," Zaid replies, reaching out to brush a strand of loose hair out of my face, eyes still on Alec. "It's so important to have someone you trust. I'm just honored you've chosen me."

I frown at him and pull away gently. This touch feels different: It's missing the kindness it usually holds.

"Well, it was very nice of you to offer," I say.

"Ah, yes. This ever eager-to-help friend of ours," Alec remarks, staring right back at Zaid, cocky half-smile planted on his face.

"That's me," Zaid replies without missing a beat. "Lane can always rely on me."

Alec leans forward, placing his arms on the table, narrowing his eyes.

"I'm sure she can," Alec says. "And yet, I'll be the one seeing this journey through with her to its end. I will be the one to protect her."

Zaid has leaned forward, also, and the two men glare at each other, gritting their teeth and practically snarling at each other. I stare at them both with wide eyes for a beat, but then I shake my head as tension threatens to boil over within me.

"You're *both* being idiots," I say, slapping the table with both palms. The nearly healed cuts on my palms sting with the action, and Alec winces ever so slightly. "Clearly, the only person I should rely on is me, and I can take care of myself. You two better sort this out. Until then, I'm going for a walk. Don't follow me," I add.

I know I have to rely on Alec to some degree, at least to depend on him not getting hurt, but I don't need to mention that now. All I really need is to get away from these two fools and get some air. The sooner I can figure out how to break this bond and be on my own, the better. Then I will no longer have to worry about his profession putting me in danger.

"Lane, it's late. Allow me to escort you," Zaid suggests.

The two move to stand as I push back my chair and get up, but I put my hand out.

"Sort it out," I say.

I leave the tavern without looking back.

I wander the streets for a while before I find myself back at the Cat 'n' Mouse Inn. I stop into the café, a small kitchen with just a couple of white painted wooden tables. Miss Kat comes in and gives me a cross look.

"What can I get for you, girl?" she asks. Although her face is angry, her tone is soft. I sit up a little straighter. The last thing I want is to seem upset in front of the woman who has been hosting our stay.

"A water would be lovely, thank you," I tell her, sitting down in an empty chair.

"You got it." As she makes her way to the cupboards in the kitchen, she whistles to herself. She pours me a glass of water and returns to the table.

When she places the water in front of me, she leans forward, placing her elbows on the tabletop, which tilts slightly from the weight of her arms pressing down on it.

"Whatever's got you down..." she says. "Remember. There are few things in life worth getting truly upset over."

"Oh?" I ask. "Like what?"

She ponders this for a moment, pursing her lips.

"Burned food and death of a loved one is all I can think of. Everything else is rollable," she says.

"Rollable?"

She nods, her face serious.

"Yes, like this." She leans back, and as the table bounds back into its place, she rolls each of her shoulders dramatically, one at a time. "Anything else, you can let roll off your shoulders, just like this."

"Like this?" I ask, mimicking her motions.

She gives me a smile, and the expression looks foreign on her face.

"Exactly like that. Whatever it is, girl, let it roll."

I smile. Somehow, this near perfect stranger has lightened my mood exponentially.

"Thank you," I say.

She frowns at me and shakes her head.

"Don't know what you're thanking me for. It's only a glass of water." She winks. At that, she gives the wooden tabletop two hefty pats and leaves the kitchen to return to the front desk.

Let it roll. I suppose the tension that has sprouted between Zaid and Alec are not my problem. Even if they like to make my life miserable in the meantime, I suppose it should be fairly easy to ignore the issue.

I roll my shoulders as she showed me, and it really does help to relieve some of the tension that has accumulated there. I take a deep breath and let it out as I roll them again.

The situation with my sister, and the problem of my mamman going missing are far less "rollable," in my mind, but

Zaid will be heading home first thing in the morning to help watch over Lilah, and my mamman... well, I'll find her.

I swear it.

I finish up my water. I'm not sure where the boys are at this point, but I need a break from them, anyway.

I step out of the inn and breathe deeply the cool night air before making my way through the nearest side street. I don't really know where I'm going. I have no destination in mind, so I just wander around the streets, breathing and pushing myself forward, and trying to get myself to relax.

After several minutes of wandering aimlessly through the streets, I'm startled by a distinct feeling that I'm being watched. The hair on the nape of my neck stands on end, and my mind is on high alert, though when I peer through the darkness around me, nothing seems all that out of the ordinary. I shrug it off, but the feeling does nothing but persist and strengthen with each step I take.

I decide that it might be best to walk somewhere with a little more light to see by, but the streets at this time are all dark, nothing like the brightly lit streets and alleyways of Parth.

Still, the feeling doesn't go away.

Now as I pick up the pace, deciding that it's probably best if I just head back to the inn and go to bed, gooseflesh pricks up on my arms and legs. I keep looking all around me, but as far as I can tell, nobody looks very menacing. The few people that are out this time of night look like they're too preoccupied with minding their own business to even spare me a glance.

When I round the corner on my way back to the Cat 'n' Mouse, I've just started to try and force myself to calm down, telling myself audibly – albeit quietly – that no one is out to get me, and I'm just wound up from all the stress I've built up lately.

I'm so distracted by my own thoughts I don't even notice I've got company until a tall lanky man wearing clothes two or three sizes too big for him stumbles into me.

"Excuse me," I say to him. I can smell spirits on his breath, and I'm sure he's bumped into me on accident. I try to move around him, but he reaches out a cold, bony hand and grabs hold of my wrist.

"*Excuse me,*" I say, more harshly this time. I do my best to yank my hand from his grip, but as thin as his fingers are, they're strong, and I struggle against them. "Let me *go!*"

"What's a pretty gal like you doing out here in the dark?" he asks, words slurring together, the scent of ale so thick on his breath that I choke on the air between us. He pulls me closer, twisting the skin on my wrist painfully.

"Joe!" another man calls, fumbling around until he's reached us.

For a moment, my hopes are raised. I'm sure this man will help, that he'll encourage his friend to let me loose. But as he draws nearer, I can see he's in much the same state as his friend, and he smiles wickedly, a sickening grin that curls up too far at the edges.

"My, my, my, Joe. What have you found yourself? What is this pretty thing doing out here at night? Helna is a dangerous place for lovelies like this when the lights go out." This man runs a clammy hand across my cheek, and bile rises in my throat.

Chills spread like lightning down my back, and I recoil and spit in his face. This results in a heavy slap across my face.

I don't have a moment to think. I draw my leg back and bring it forward again, crashing the hard cap of my knee into the second man's groin. His face contorts as he drops to the ground, crying out. Joe, my original assailant, allows rage to flare up every feature of his face, and he lets my hand loose long enough to pull back his arm, threatening to strike.

Remembering Alec's remarks regarding the surprising power behind my punch, I pull my arm back, and, with as much force as I can muster, I swing. I know the exact moment my fist contacts Joe's face by two indicators. One, the *crack* and *squish* of his nose breaking. Two, the pain that erupts in my hand and shoots up my arm, radiating from my knuckles to my shoulder.

Joe is still reeling from my punch with his hands up to his face to try and quell the bleeding. I let out a pained gasp as I take the second or two that to rush forward and kick his friend – still lying on the ground – as hard as I can in the ribs.

The moment my foot makes contact, I feel them shift, one or two ribs sinking farther into the man's torso than they should. He cries out.

At this point, I'm out of breath, shaking. My mind is whirring. My heart pounds in my chest.

I don't allow myself a moment to rest, however, because while I'm fairly certain Joe's friend is down for good, I still have to deal with Joe himself. Although blood still gushes from his nose, he's regained most of his composure, and he lunges at me, both blood-soaked hands outstretched, fingers clenching and ready to grab me again. I duck as fast as I can, and he still manages to grab hold of me by the neck of my dress.

He yanks me backward, slamming me against the wall of one of the surrounding buildings. Even though he's clearly been drinking and his balance is off, I'm startled by the strength he has as he presses his body weight into me. He pushes his thumb into the wound on my left arm in his attempt to restrain me, and I cry out. The pain sends me reeling, and my head begins to pound. I feel dizzy. Nauseous. I writhe about beneath his grasp until I'm able to free myself, tearing my dress in the process.

The moment I can get behind him, I reach out and grab ahold of the man's shirt with both hands and use our momentum to spin him around in a half-circle, crashing him into the hard wooden wall of the building behind me.

I hear a sickening *thud* as Joe's head hits the wall, and the man falls limply to the alleyway floor. Though he groans, he does not get back up.

I backpedal until I'm several feet away from them, but I trip on the uneven stone and dirt street beneath my feet, and I fall backward, landing painfully on my backside.

The edges of my vision begin to blur, but I scramble to pull myself up. I have to get up before my attackers regain their drive. I have to get back to the inn. Thanks to the pain in my foot, my tailbone, and my hand, limping back to the inn is a much slower process than I need it to be.

When I finally reach the street that the inn sits on, I stumble into Alec and Zaid. Alec seems frantic, and I can tell by the way he walks that he's aware – at least in part – of what I've been through. Zaid clutches Alec's wrist, and Alec yanks it from his grasp.

"Let me go, you prick!" Alec says, holding his hand over his bloody nose. "I'm going to find—" he begins, but his sentence drops when he notices me with my arms wrapped around my torso and blood on my torn dress.

"Oh, Lane, I'm glad we caught you—" Zaid begins, but he also stops short when he registers my appearance. I'm filthy, hair in disarray, blood covering my dress, cheek already swelling from where the second man hit me. "Fates!" he gasps. "What happened?" He turns from me to Alec, then his eyes find me again.

Fates. If he was with Alec when this happened, it's only a matter of time until he starts to connect the dots now.

My two companions lead me into the inn and up the stairs to their room. Alec has a red welt already forming on his face. He rummages through one of his new and already repacked bags and returns with his medical kit.

"Have a seat," he says in a soft voice, and I obey without question. My entire body aches, and I want to get this man's blood off me *right now*. Now that the adrenaline has worn off, I feel completely exhausted.

As Alec works to clean me up, Zaid paces. I watch him carefully, waiting for him to bring up my bond with Alec. Right now, he's preoccupied with stopping the guys who hurt me.

"Who did this to you, Lane?" Zaid asks. "We must speak to the authorities. We... we've got to *do* something about this!"

"Good luck going to the authorities," Alec says, never taking his eyes off of me. His hands are gentle as they work to clean me up. "They're about as crass as they come. Helna falls under the order of the Women's Council, but just barely. They're a lot closer to bandits than just about anywhere you might have visited back west."

"Well, we have to do something," Zaid repeats. "I'll... I'll go talk to the front desk right now. See what they can do."

He gives me one more concerned glance, then he storms out of the room without another word. For a moment, Alec and I just sit in silence as he finishes washing the blood from my face and arms. He lifts my hand and examines my knuckles, comparing them to his, which are already swelling. My mind is whirring. What am I going to tell Zaid? Is there any way to play this off? Unlikely.

"You didn't hurt our hands like this when you hit me," he remarks with the tiniest hint of a smile playing on his lips.

"Well, I guess you just aren't as solid as the man who attacked me," I bite back, but I find myself starting to smile, too.

To this remark, Alec tilts his head and raises his eyebrows. Although his gaze still focuses on inspecting my hand, his smile widens, but then it quickly fades. He looks up at me.

"Lane," he starts, searching my face, still holding my wounded hand in his. "You know, I'm not one to tell people what they should or shouldn't do, but I wish you hadn't gone out by yourself. I... I should have been there with you."

I lean back. I'm startled by the softness of his tone, by the intensity and sincerity of his gaze. My heart begins to beat faster, this time not from fear.

"I didn't expect this to happen. I just needed some air. You and Zaid were making me crazy," I tell him.

"I get that, but you don't know Helna like I do. You've never been this far. And you could have been... Well, you could have been seriously hurt."

I wait, expecting him to follow up with something like "and that would have hurt me, as well," but he doesn't. He just sits there, looking at me sadly.

When Zaid returns, his face is red, and he grinds his teeth audibly.

"What good is it to provide a service to people if you can't give them any support in case of emergencies?" he asks, huffing. He finds his way to his bed and plants himself down. "This is outrageous."

"Zaid," I say, pulling my hand from Alec's grasp to face Zaid. "I'm okay, really. Any injuries I had tonight are minimal, see?" I hold my swollen hand up and wiggle my fingers. This still hurts, but much less than before. In my peripheral vision, I see

Alec wiggle his fingers, as well. "And trust me, I did not let those men go without a few injuries of their own. I'm…" I take a deep breath, sitting up a little straighter. "I really am okay. I won't go out again without one of you. Not here, anyway."

"What do we do?" Zaid asks, scooting forward on his bed. "I can't leave you now. It's too dangerous." I peek over at Alec, who clenches his jaw.

Fates, the last thing I need is for these two to start bickering again. I stand up.

"We stick to the plan," I say. "Zaid, I *need* you to go home. I can't go be with Lilah right now; I need to find my mamman. It's important that you go as soon as possible to watch out for her. No one is with her right now, you understand? If you truly care about my wellbeing, please go look after my sister."

Zaid stares at me with eyes so wide I fear he'll never blink again. His mouth opens and closes several times.

"What's going on between you two? I've noticed little injuries. Things I thought were coincidences. But I was with you tonight, Alec. You started bleeding out of nowhere, and you got up like you knew something was wrong. Look at the two of you." He gestures to the blood on both of our clothes, the swelling on our right hands.

I take a deep breath, share a look with Alec. There's no avoiding it, now.

"I'm not sure how to say this, Zaid," I start.

"Well, you'd better start talking," he says. "Or I'm not going anywhere." He folds his arms, emphasizing his statement.

"Lane and I are bound." Alec jumps in when I can't find the words to explain. "When I get hurt, so does she, and the other way around."

Zaid opens his mouth. Closes it again. "*How?*"

"We don't know," I say. "But we think it has something to do with our mammans disappearing."

"Both of your mammans are missing?" Zaid asks as Alec cleans himself up.

"Yes," I say. "Alec's ma' went missing first. That's why I came with him in the first place. To make sure he wasn't going to get me killed as he searched for his mamman."

Zaid nods, slowly.

"Then that day, back in Nerine, when you sent us home…" he trails off.

"That's when I pieced it all together."

"And the injuries you've always gotten? The ones the medic back home said were an illness?"

"Alec's," I say softly.

Zaid rubs his face with his hands.

When he doesn't say anything else, I prompt him again.

"I will be okay. Whatever happens, I know Alec wouldn't let me get badly hurt."

"How do you know that? Shared injuries aside, are you sure that will be enough? Where was he *tonight*?" Zaid asks.

"Where were *you*?" Alec snaps right back.

"Stop! I'm finished with this nonsense. I'm tired, and achy, and disgusting; and I'm going to bed. Zaid, I'm sorry we kept this from you. We're just trying to figure it out for ourselves, too. But I will be okay. You said so yourself, I'm not a child. I'll get by, and I need to make sure Lilah is alright. If I'm not up, please come and say goodbye before you leave."

I give them both one last conflicted look and head back to my room.

Although I'm exhausted from the night's events, and the drama of our conversation, I do feel as if a weight has been lifted. I could go right to bed and sleep for a week, but I take the time to draw myself a bath, knowing it's going to be my last chance in a while. Besides, although Alec cleaned the man's blood off my face and arms, I need to get the rest of it off.

I drop in some herbs I found up on a shelf above my bed when we arrived at the inn. Mint leaves and dried lavender, mostly. Then I climb in and let the water soothe my aching body as well as my temper.

As much as this trip has taught me about Zaid, and as close as we have gotten, I'll be glad to see him go tomorrow. I'll be glad to have him to take care of Lilah... but also glad because things were so much simpler before he joined us. I hope he can keep this new knowledge a secret, and I'm sure he wouldn't share it with anybody, but I take comfort in knowing from experience that nobody would believe him.

In the morning, I do awaken before Zaid has to leave. I find him just as he's about to knock on the door to my room. I'm happy to see that even after all the drama last night, his intentions really are to go back and protect my sister.

When I realize that, I walk straight up to him and give him a tight embrace. Against the hair that has grown to cover his ear, I whisper, "Thank you for doing this, Zaid. Thank you for everything. I know I can trust you with this."

Zaid squeezes me tightly, and whispers back, "I'm glad I know. I can't tell you how many times I've almost punched Alec in the face. Now I know not to do that. I'd never want to hurt you."

His comment makes me smile.

"Please write me as soon as you know she's okay. We're going north from here." I pull back and reach into the bag I have slung across my back. My hand still aches from last night, and my knuckles are bruised, but I don't think anything is broken. I pull out my map.

"Take this. Look it over. Compare it with the maps my pappan has in his office at home. If there are any small towns between here and the mountains, send your letter there. If not, send it here. I know I'll stop here on my way back home."

"I will," Zaid says. Then, he leans close. "Don't trust him, Lane. Listen to your instincts and trust only yourself. Bond aside, you should never trust a man who has only had to look after himself. You'll get the same outcome every time."

At that, he gives my left hand a gentle squeeze and leaves me to my thoughts. I watch the door to my room long after he's left the building.

It takes the rest of the afternoon to get out of Helna, and another day after that to cross out of the grasslands, over the bridge that connects Murkwater Lake to the Baskan Sea, and into Murkwater Swamp. All the while, things are tense between Alec and me. I think we're both so worried about our mammans that we're stuck in our own heads.

Finally, when we do talk, we discuss what his informant had told him. We discuss how strange it seems that Alec's mamman passed through Helna just over a week before we did, and she seemed dazed and didn't respond to anyone's questions, except to say that she needed to pay for the decisions she had made. Strangely similar to what my own mamman had been muttering on about before she disappeared.

"Still think I'm foolish for suggesting we go see that witch?" I say, raising an eyebrow at him. This is the first time since our time at the inn where things have felt somewhat relaxed between us.

As we work to make camp at the edge of the swamp, Alec huffs.

"Yeah, well, I like to *know* where I'm going before I head there. We don't know if this witch exists, or where she is located. How do you propose we find her? Unless you happen to have her marked with a big red X on one of those maps of yours."

"You know I don't," I say. I sigh, and we drop the subject. The fire burns brightly, and I join him, sitting beside it.

"Skewer?" he asks, holding out a stick with some meat and potato slices on it.

I take it without saying anything, take a bite, and chew as I stare into the fire.

"You know I wouldn't hurt you, right?" he asks.

I'm not sure if it's the flame flickering across his face, but his features seem to soften, the expression in his amber eyes genuine.

I fold my legs up around my side, holding my food up. Once I've swallowed, I say, "Sure, I know that. It makes sense. Hurting me would only be hurting yourself. That would be stupid."

Alec's body grows perfectly still. He says nothing, only chews the inside of his cheek and stares intensely at the fire.

"You seem mad," I venture carefully.

Alec grunts, and I give a frustrated gasp.

"What now?" I ask, irritated. What could he possibly have to be angry about?

"You're just... ugh," he grumbles.

"*Excuse me?*" I ask. "What is that supposed to mean? What did I do?"

He gives a one-shoulder shrug. "Nothing. If that's what you think, we'll leave it at that. We should turn in. Long day ahead of us tomorrow."

I'm left completely speechless, grappling for something to say. I don't know what he means by any of that. All I know is that I'm exhausted from our travels, and the idea of going to sleep – even on the hard ground – sounds wonderful.

I lay on my blanket facing Alec, who has turned away.

I want to throw something at him. Do something to get him to explain himself to me. But by the time I've worked through any reasonable things to say, it seems too late, and I doubt he'd answer me anyway.

Eventually, I drift off to sleep. All night I dream of Alec. In my dreams, he talks to me, but no words come out of his mouth. In my dreams, he gets farther and farther away, and then closer and closer until his nose presses against my own.

In the morning, I wake before the sun has risen completely, but it looks like Alec has been up for some time. He's packed everything but the blanket I'm lying on, and my bow, arrows, and satchel, that are never far from me.

"Good morning," Alec says. His tone is much more chipper than it was when we went to sleep last night, but there's still a flatness to it – or at least, I think I detect a flatness.

"Morning," I reply cautiously.

"You ready to get moving?" he asks, and I nod, already up and packing my belongings.

Now that the sun is coming up, I stare out across the horizon in awe. Way off in the distance, tall dark mountains with jagged, rocky ridges rise up into the sky. Below them, dark lines of trees frame their base. On my maps, that forest is labeled Darkwood. To the west a large lake stretches out for miles and miles, Murkwater, and to the east sits the landscape we'll be traveling in for the next week or two, at least: Miles of thick swamp with paths of dirt and mud and low-growing plants with thick, pungent, stagnant water.

"Careful, there," Alec says, reaching out to stop me just in time before I step into a rancid-smelling pool.

I let out a sigh of relief.

"Thanks. I only have one pair of boots, after all," I say.

"It's not that I'm worried about," Alec replies. His face is serious – eyebrows furrowed, mouth a straight line – as he leans forward and kicks a rock into the puddle. We only see it for a moment before it disappears into the cloudy water. "We've got no idea how deep any of these puddles are. Probably best to steer clear. Stay on the land we think we can trust."

I nod. "That's probably a smart idea."

I'm much more careful and conscientious of where I step moving forward. Small, raised portions of semi-dry land wind through the pools that are steadily increasing in size as we travel farther into the swamp.

The land areas are just wide enough for the two of us to walk abreast at their widest, and at their thinnest portions, we have to step one foot directly in front of the other and try to keep our balance, even though there's no telling in some areas whether the muddy land will hold or slide away beneath our feet.

Several times we're faced with having to scramble out from the water's edge after the land comes loose beneath us.

"Have you ever been this far out?" I ask, assuming that Alec has traveled all corners of Maran by now.

Alec adjusts his bags, moving them from one shoulder to the other.

"Not this far. I've been offered jobs this way, so I know what we're coming to, but I've never taken those ones."

"Why not?" I ask. Although we've spent almost the entire day in the swamp, I still breathe in shallow breaths, and each one nearly makes me gag from the stench that surrounds us. I've no idea what time it is, because since we entered this swampy wasteland, the sun has been shining distantly through a thick gray smog; and it doesn't seem at all like it's moved, though we've been walking for hours.

Alec lifts his chin in the direction we've been treading.

"See those trees way off in the distance? That forest is one that few people will venture into. Myself included."

"Why is that?" I ask.

Alec shakes his head. "Ghosts."

I let out a combination of a snort and a laugh, and I slap my hand over my mouth.

Alec raises his eyebrows at me, but his gaze remains on the ground at our feet. I turn mine back to focusing as well.

"Why do you *really* avoid that area?" I prompt, hoping he'll give me a serious answer.

"Ghosts," he says again, tone higher in pitch this time. I search what I can see of his face for a hint of a joke, but his expression remains solemn.

"Seriously?" I squeak. Of course, because I took my eyes off the ground in front of me, I slip again, causing mud to cover my shin and hip as I slide down into the pool to my right. Alec's arm reaches out in an instant, though, and he catches me. His bags slide down his arm, and he waves them loose to get a better grip on me. I gasp, but then I start to laugh because the pool only gets part of me covered in grime. When I gain my balance again, I'm only about knee-deep in the murky water. It's only when I try to wiggle free of the thick, slimy mud that engulfed my foot that I realize that the pool's depth isn't the problem.

My eyes widen in horror, and fear fills my body with a cold shock.

"Alec?" I ask, voice thick, the words catching in my throat. "Alec, I'm sinking."

"What?" he asks.

"I'm sinking!"

Panic grips me, and I clutch Alec's arms. I can tell by the stinging in my own forearms that I'm digging my fingernails into his skin, but I refuse to let go. I turn this way and that, but I can't seem to break free. The mud suctions onto me, and with every movement I make, I sink deeper into the swamp. Alec gets down on his knees, still grasping tightly to my arms.

"Stop moving!" he shouts, though I barely hear it through the *whoosh* of my heartbeat in my ears.

I can't see him past the mud that now covers everything thanks to my frantic splashing.

"Alec?" My breath struggles to come at all now, my chest is so tight, and the mud inches its way higher. It's up to my belly now, and I can no longer move my legs. I begin twisting my torso, trying to wriggle myself free.

"Lane." Alec's voice – calm and low – somehow cuts through my terror. "Lane, look at me. Stop moving. The faster you move, the faster you will sink."

I look into his warm brown eyes as he breathes deep, exaggerated breaths, trying to show me what to do. He raises his chin, keeping his eyes locked on mine.

"Come on," he says. "I've got you. I'm not letting go. Breathe."

I work to slow my breathing, try to match his inhales, and eventually, his exhales. As we breathe, my body relaxes, and Alec slides his hands up into my underarms. He grounds himself. Then, slowly, he begins to pull.

As my body slowly slides back up out of the mud, it takes everything I have not to kick and writhe to help him pull me out. But those words echo in my mind. *I've got you.* I cling to his arms. *I'm not letting go.* I use the strength of my own arms to pull myself up. *Breathe.* I keep inhaling and exhaling as deeply as I can, trying with everything in me to keep the muscles in the lower half of my body relaxed.

When Alec manages to pull me the rest of the way out, the mud makes a slurping sound as the swamp claims both of my boots. That's okay. At least I'm alive.

When he pulls me back up onto semi-solid ground, the two of us stand chest to chest. I don't know if his heart is pounding, but mine feels as though it will never slow again. We're silent, still clinging tightly to one another. Finally, Alec clears his throat.

"I never joke about ghosts... You should know that about me," he says, voice deep. His eyes search mine.

Although I begin to wonder why he hasn't let me go, why his warm, strong hands still grasp my upper arms, I don't move, suddenly terrified of putting any distance between us.

"Okay," I mutter. "I didn't realize."

His thumbs give my forearms a gentle squeeze, one thumb tracing the scar on my bicep. Then he lets me go, and I take a wobbly step backward.

I brush the muddy hair that's fallen out of my braid behind my ears, finally finding some sense of actual calm.

"So," I start, changing the subject as I peer into the fog around us. "Where are we going to make camp in this place?"

We don't make camp – not really, anyway. Instead, when we can find a piece of land that is large enough for both of us to stand side by side upon, we lay down both our blankets on top of each other and take shifts sleeping throughout the night.

We don't take shifts because we're worried about enemies catching us out here. We take shifts keeping watch because we don't want to roll into the horrible pools that creep in on either side of us.

Alec offers for me to rest first, but the thought of putting my head any closer to that foul smell has me reeling, so I ask him to try and sleep first. I doubt I'm going to get any sleep tonight, but I know I have to try and get used to it. I just need a little bit more time after being in the swamp water. We've got a while before we'll make it out of here, and I'm going to need some rest for the journey ahead.

Alec shifts for a bit, doing his best to rest this head comfortably while also trying to stay off his still swollen hand.

"Here," I say, sliding a bag filled with both of our clothing beneath his head as he lifts it up. "Better?" I ask.

He nods.

We pass several days this way: We tread carefully during the day, watching every step we take. At night, we take turns sleeping, clinging to one another so we don't fall in.

Finally, we spend our last night in the swamp. We've spent over a week trudging through a landscape that gives way beneath our feet, sleeping on damp blankets on ground that smells like rotten fish, though there's been no fish in this area for longer than humans have lived in Maran.

As things have progressed, we've gotten smellier, more restless, and continually more tense.

Now, however, as we pause at the edge of the dense, dark forest, strange things begin to happen.

Alec paces back and forth just inside the tree line – the first solid ground we've seen in over a week. He's been pacing for a good ten minutes now, and we're wasting precious fading daylight. Just inside the line where the trees have begun to grow, it appears already to be night within.

"What's going on with you?" I finally ask when it appears he's never going to stand still again. "We should keep going. We've got who knows how long until we reach our mammans. We can't waste any time. If you feel like moving, that's fine. The least you could do is move in the *right direction*."

I don't mean to sound so irritable with him, but I'm filthy and exhausted, and I'm ready to sleep somewhere that isn't sinking beneath me. To add to that, I can't get my mind off the fact that we don't really know quite where we're going at this point.

"Don't rush me, Lane. I'll go when I'm ready. I told you I don't mess with ghosts, and I wasn't joking," Alec says.

"You are the strongest fighter I've ever met," I say, waving my arms in the air. Every second we spend on this conversation, the sun sinks lower in the gray sky. "I'll bet there isn't an opponent in the world that you couldn't handle."

He frowns at me – a deep, unhappy expression that draws his mouth down in the corners. I've never seen him like this.

"I've never come across a *human* I couldn't handle. You can't fight a ghost!"

I throw my hands to my hips.

"Ghosts aren't real!"

"You can't know that, Lane!" he shouts.

I'm quiet for several moments. He can't be serious. I keep waiting for him to tell me he's been joking this whole time, but that confirmation never comes. Finally, I fold my arms and stamp my foot. I've wrapped my feet in cloth from one of Alec's shirts per his request, but the action still hurts a lot more than it would if I actually had shoes.

As calmly as possible, I say, "You know, every moment we waste out here is another moment our mammans could be in danger."

At that, I decide to just walk into the forest without him. Surely, if I just start moving, he'll be inclined to follow. I let out a deep sigh and head through the trees. I'm several paces in before I hear him shout.

"Fates! Wait up!" His footsteps crash through the soggy, dead foliage on the forest floor behind me.

28

Once it's completely dark, we decide to camp. Alec works to start the fire, a task that's proving to be much more difficult for him, for he pauses to listen to every sound we hear. I set myself busy clearing some of the foliage from our site, brushing it away with my feet. It isn't until I lay down my blanket that I hear the first strange, ominous sound: Something like a mix between a howl and a giggle, close enough that I think it's got to be just inside the trees, just outside of my line of sight.

"Did you hear that?" I ask, hating the quiver in my voice.

Alec's head snaps up.

"Hear what?" he asks, and I'm grateful that his tone also carries the same fear.

I listen for a minute, but I hear nothing more.

"I thought I heard..." I trail off, trying to find a description. What exactly *did* I hear? "Something..."

"Something like what?" Alec asks. He's back to working at the fire, but his head keeps lifting to listen. I shake my head and move to set his blanket down. The stench from the swamp is still thick on our blanket and our clothes.

"I'm not sure. I'm sorry," I start.

Just then, I hear it again. It seems much closer this time, but it's coming from a different direction than when I heard it before.

"That!" I hiss. My skin crawls. I'm not prepared to get into another fight. My mind flits back to our run-in with those animalistic bandits in the grasslands.

"Lane, stop it," Alec says. His voice is low, a warning. "That's not funny."

I want to tell him I'm not joking, that I really did hear something, but if he didn't hear it, perhaps I only imagined it. Maybe his paranoia about ghosts is getting to me, after all. I listen carefully, but I don't hear anything more.

"Sorry," I mutter. I sit down on my blanket, setting my bow beside me, keeping my quiver on my back. I pull out one of our drier loaves of bread.

Finally, Alec gets the fire started, and it flickers and threatens to blow out before finally growing large, but even at its full potential, the firelight is dim. The color of the flames – usually bright orange, yellow and blue – now take on a greenish-gray hue and burn much more dimly.

Alec lies on his own blanket, and I offer up half the loaf, but he just turns it down. He lies on his back with his hands folded beneath his head, but I can tell he's uneasy. His eyes flit from left to right, looking out.

Across the fire from him, I sit, watching him struggle. There's no way he's going to sleep tonight at this rate, so I gather up my things and lay them out beside him, between his body and the rest of the forest to that side.

Without a word, I curl up close to him and rest my head on his chest.

He stiffens for a moment, but then I feel his body relax, and he puts his arm around me.

"Thanks," he says, so quietly I almost don't catch it.

"I don't know what you're talking about," I say. I can't help smiling at his remark. "It's just cold on that side of the fire."

"Right," he replies. Within minutes, I hear the sound of his light snoring.

Although I try to stay awake, to keep watch, at some point, I fall asleep with the warmth of him beside me.

I have the strangest dreams. Dreams of Alec with twisted faces, dreams that my mamman is wandering through the forest in a white dress, and each time I get close to her, she disappears.

And so it continues for the next several days. The farther into the forest we venture, the darker our surroundings become until we can barely see if the sun is setting or rising, and with the darkness comes stranger instances. Things continue to grow more ominous.

Neither of us are sleeping well, and our sleeping close together has become a nightly occurrence. Sleeping close to Alec helps keep the nightmares away, or at least it helps keep them from escalating into frightful, unmanageable, unshakable things.

During the day, the urge to talk with him about our bond – about what he thinks will break our bond – and what this bond actually entails only gets stronger. Though the more time I spend with him, the more I get to know him, the more I think that breaking this bond may not be the urgent matter I originally thought it was.

One day, about a week into our trek through the woods, Alec and I begin to hear things synchronously, only the things we hear at the same time are nothing alike.

"Did you hear that?" Alec asks one morning, or at least I think it's morning because it's getting slightly lighter out.

"Yes," I say warily, peering out in the darkness, looking for wolves. That has to be the source of the sound I heard. I've never heard another animal snarl quite like that. It sounded as though it came from through the first few rows of trees to my left. "I don't want to fight wolves," I start, reaching for my bow. "They're too fast, and there's no telling if I've got enough arrows to take out a whole pack."

"What are you talking about?" he asks. "Wolves don't sound like that." His brown eyes are narrowed, on the lookout.

"No? Then what do you think it was?" I ask. Surely, it has to be wolves. I hear it again, and this time it comes from the right, as well.

"That laughter?" he asks. "I don't know if you've got wolves in Palandra, but I've come across wolves more than once. They don't laugh."

A deep, unsettling shock rattles stomach.

"That's not what I…" I start, but then I *do* hear the laughter. Deep and low and entirely joyless.

My heart freezes in my chest and my limbs go numb. I look to Alec, wide eyed and terrified, every hair on my arms and neck standing on end.

"What do we do?" I whisper, afraid that if I speak up, whatever made those awful sounds will catch us, if it isn't onto us already. I turn around frantically, searching the woods for any sign that someone – or something – is approaching us. The forest is dark, though, even though I'm sure it's early in the day. When I peer through the trees, I can't see much through the layer of dark fog surrounding us.

The laughter draws closer – comes right up behind us – but of course when we turn, we don't see anything there.

"Let me think," Alec whispers back. He's clutching the hilt of his sword, poised to strike if anything should jump out at us.

My memory goes back to those inhuman-like bandits that attacked us on our way to Helna. I remember their gray skin, the way they moved with ease on their hands and feet, blades strapped to their palms. I remember the wretched sounds they were making. I don't think I could handle another attack like that.

I'm in the process of gulping in air, trying my best to quell the cold fear I feel when the laughter sounds again. This time, it's joined by a shrill giggle.

Electricity bolts through my spine as I feel something icy and wet touch my hand.

I gasp as I whip around to see what it was that touched me, and I feel something press against my back.

"Alec, *run!*" I shout. Flooded by an overwhelming urge to flee, I take off in the direction we were headed. My panic-filled mind wishes briefly that the swamp hadn't claimed my boots. With only the cloth wrapped around my feet for protection, I'm all too aware of every rock and stick in my path, but I don't stop. I take only a quick peek behind me, but I can tell that Alec is also racing away from whatever had just made those sounds – whatever it was that touched me – with his bags slung across his back.

The laughs and giggles follow just as close behind us for some time, until suddenly, all the noises cease. I don't trust it at first, and we slow our pace to a walk to better listen to our surroundings; but after about an hour of hearing nothing more, I allow myself to relax a little bit. Maybe we were able to outrun whatever that was.

Although I hope this statement to be true, the way those sounds followed right behind us has me sure that whatever made those noises isn't something that can be simply outrun.

When we've calmed ourselves down, we decide to keep going. We're both too thoroughly spooked to want to talk. Honestly, I wouldn't know where to start, and the sooner we're out of these woods, the better.

We walk for another couple of hours until we come across a large, white-barked, leafless willow tree. On the path before us sit several more white trees, all without leaves, willowy branches dangling, waving back and forth as if in a light breeze, but I haven't felt any wind since we entered the forest, and I can't feel any now, either.

It's now quite dark out, and Alec and I decide to camp for the night. Alec wanders off in search of wood to start another strange, dim, and discolored fire while I sit down to care for my blistered, bleeding feet.

When I've cleaned my feet and re-wrapped them with cloth, I clear away a spot to make a fire and lay out our blankets beneath the big, white tree, close enough that we could use it to support our backs, as I'm sure we will take turns watching the forest tonight.

Soon, Alec returns with an armful of little branches. He lights a fire, and we eat mostly in silence, each of us stuck in our own thoughts.

Although we haven't heard anything strange for quite some time, Alec's face is still pallid, and I'm sure mine looks the same. When he joins me by the fire, he smiles, but the expression is small, wary. I lean back against the tree's trunk and look up into the lightless sky through the tree's bare branches.

"What time do you think it is?" I ask, wishing I could see a star, or a cloud, or something.

"In this place, Fates, who knows? Feels like it's been dusk for years," Alec says, tone tired and bitter.

"I'd love to be home right now," I tell him. Pulling my eyes away from the blackened sky, I look at him. His stubble has grown in thick now, and blond hairs about as long as my pinky nail cover his sharp jawline. He looks as tired as I feel, and although we're both beyond filthy, I lean in close and rest my head on his shoulder, hooking my arm through his.

"Warm bath, familiar bed..." I trail off, letting my imagination take me to a happy, safe, familiar place.

"I feel that," Alec says. "I'd love nothing more than to be back in Nerine taking jobs locally. I may do that from now on."

I raise my chin so I can get a good look at him.

"I thought you said you love to travel," I say, eyebrows raised.

"I do. I've been all over, and I've never experienced what we've been through on this journey. You seem to bring the worst kind of trouble," he says, brushing the back of his finger against my chin.

"What, you don't normally run into any trouble?" I ask. "I find that hard to believe."

Alec shrugs gently.

"I've run into trouble, for sure. Bandits, mostly. Crooks. Thugs who want to take my money. But that's about the extent of it, and that's every once in a while. Never in my life have I been through so much on one journey before, and never has it felt so ominous. It feels like the world is changing. Like I said, it must be you. You're bad luck." He nudges me with his elbow, and I push back.

Although I've never experienced Maran this far east, I have had the sense that things are changing, and not for the better. I recall what my mamman said on the day I left Palandra about things getting more dangerous throughout Maran.

"Well, I'll have you know that I have also had many travels in my day, and I have never run into so much trouble, either. So, it must be *you*," I say.

"Maybe it's the two of us together," he jokes, but then both of us fall silent, ruminating.

Maybe there is some truth to that.

"Perhaps you're right," I say quietly. "Maybe whatever is causing our shared injuries is bringing us bad luck."

I sigh. I haven't been so comfortable or felt so safe in weeks, and it's all thanks to my sitting so close to Alec. I've just begun to drift off to sleep when the strange things begin to happen again.

When I wake up, I don't know how long I've been asleep for, but Alec is no longer huddled close to me. Instead, he's sitting with his back unnaturally straight against the trunk of the tree as if he's trying to back away from something and has run into a barrier. His pale complexion is now almost transparent it's so colorless.

I sit up straight with a jolt and rub the sleep from my eyes. Alec looks truly terrified. I'm so shocked seeing him like this that it takes me a moment to find my voice.

"Alec?" I whisper to him, but he doesn't look at me. He barely registers that I'm awake. Instead, he stares forward, wide eyed, mouth open, bottom lip quivering. The fire has died down somewhat, and small shadows from the remaining flames dance upon his frightened features. "What is it?" I ask.

His jaw drops a little more, but he says nothing – just continues to stare straight forward. He shudders. I know I should turn and look, see what's going on, but something about the way he's acting has me cold to the core with fear. I'm not sure I want to see what has him so frightened.

Then, he speaks.

"Do you see that?" he asks. His voice is somewhere between a whine and a whisper, and it makes my stomach churn. I'm not sure if it's his expression that makes me so afraid, or if our bond goes deeper than we thought.

I hesitate.

"See what?" I pray he'll start laughing, tell me he's just messing with me. But his face remains deadly serious.

Very discreetly, he tilts his chin in the direction he's been staring.

Chills trickle down my spine, and I sit up straighter, trying to shake the feeling. Slowly, I turn, and I'm paralyzed by what I see.

Just inside the line of trees, barely illuminated by our dying firelight, stands a creature I've never seen before – something truly horrifying. Something with a body much like a human's, but naked. White, leathery skin hangs loosely on thin bones. Legs are bent, as if this thing sits in a crouch, and arms that seem too long drape low, knuckles dragging on the forest floor. The creature doesn't move. Instead, it sits, watching us. Its head, something like the skull of a sheep or a deer but much larger is tilted, staring back at us with eyes that, in the reflection of the firelight, seem to glow a dead blue.

The creature breathes deeply, and its entire body heaves with the movement.

"What... is that *thing*?" I ask. As slowly as I can manage without startling the creature, I scoot back until my spine is flat against the white tree's trunk. Alec's hand reaches to grab mine.

I find it impossible to draw my gaze away from this beast as it stares at us. Its head tilts to the other side, and for several minutes – what feels like an eternity – it just watches, staring at us with those glowing blue eyes, head tilting slowly from one side to the other and back again.

Finally, it shifts as if intending to move forward, dragging the hand that hangs on the end of one of those long arms through the dead leaves at its feet. I will my body to move, my arms to reach up for my bow, but I can't seem to get my muscles to respond.

The creature stops moving at the sound Alec makes as he draws his blade. In my stupor, I didn't even realize that he let go of my hand.

The sound of Alec's blade yanks me from my trance, and I find my senses once again. I jump to my feet and grab hold of my bow, then I nock an arrow and point my weapon at the creature. Its head snaps up, and it meets my eye, then it turns so quickly and flees into the forest that I don't even have a moment to shoot.

It's only at this point that I realize I've got a cold sweat covering every inch of my body, and my heart is pounding so fast that it aches in my chest. I venture a peek at Alec, who looks just as I feel. His hand grips the hilt of his sword so tightly that his knuckles are white, his fingers beneath them purple.

A sound like that of someone who has lost everything worth living for fills the night around us, so deep and full of sorrow that I feel as if I'll never be happy again. The sound is answered with another, and yet another farther off. If the source of this sound is that creature we just saw, then there are others, and they're communicating with each other.

"Still think ghosts don't exist?" Alec remarks. Although I would typically take these words as a joke, they are completely devoid of any humor.

I have no response for him. Any sarcastic comment I would normally have made to answer this question seems so ridiculous now. If that thing was a ghost, I hope I never see another ever again.

The sounds continue all through the night, ranging from those made of the deepest sorrows I could possibly imagine to something much more sinister, something that sounds so like the laughter we heard when we first entered this unusual forest. The voices range in distance, some sounding so close that we have to whip around just to be sure they aren't coming from right behind us. Others are so far off that they sound miles away. From time to time, Alec and I will see something creeping through the woods: a white figure dancing between the trees, only to disappear, or something dark and shadowy bouncing about in the treetops above us.

We spend the rest of the night with our backs pressed against that tree, squishing so closely together that we can't properly move, weapons drawn. It's only when that foggy, dim dawn light barely brightens our surroundings that we begin to relax. At this point, the majority of the sounds we've been hearing have faded away, and although I think we're both petrified of moving from this spot, we need to get out of this place, and the only way out is through. We need to get to the mountains.

29

We pack up our belongings and get away from those white trees as quickly as possible. As the day wears on, we're both quiet, each of us trapped in our own worries. We talk briefly in the afternoon, our conversation going something like this:

"Do you remember anything strange from last night?" Alec asks, almost in a daze.

"You mean seeing a ghost creature in our campsite, or staying up all night listening to those horrible sounds all around us?" I ask, tone bitter. "Or perhaps you mean being so afraid to close my eyes in case one of those things would come get us that I might never be able to sleep again? That kind of strange?"

Alec's shoulders droop. His eyes have dark circles beneath them, and I can tell he's just as exhausted as I am.

"Right. So that did happen," he says, tone defeated. "I've been so on edge since we entered this damned forest that I thought I was just losing it."

"I get that," I say. "Nothing like this has ever happened to me. I keep thinking it was a dream, as well. But I usually forget my dreams, and I can't get those things out of my head." Every time I close my eyes, the image of that thing right in front of us appears, fresh as it was the first time I saw it.

When we get moving again, I feel absolutely exhausted, as if I haven't slept in weeks. By the drooping of Alec's shoulders and the dragging of his boots, I know he feels the same way.

We know at this point that we're looking for a witch in the mountains, but we're not sure exactly the best path we need to take, or the exact location where we might find her. We don't even know exactly how long we'll be traveling this way before we reach the mountains.

The farther we venture into the forest, the denser the air becomes, and the more I feel like we're being watched.

After another day's travels, we've found ourselves in the thick of those same white trees spreading out in every direction. That feeling of having eyes on us, of something being horribly off, has gotten so strong that Alec and I do our best to make idle conversation just so we're not stuck with our own thoughts in the thick silence. Neither of us is eating anything – the stress of our environment has stolen our appetites.

"What's that?" I ask, squinting through the dim light that grows dimmer by the minute. We must be getting close to sundown.

"What's what?" Alec asks, following my gaze.

I point at what looks to be a manmade structure built between the trees ahead.

"That, over there. Is that a house?"

With some effort, Alec and I both pick up the pace, and although we got virtually no sleep last night, the two of us are soon racing toward the structure, energy somewhat renewed at the idea that we may not have to endure another night exposed in this Fates awful forest. Sure enough, the structure turns out to be a small, very old cottage.

"Let's have a look inside," Alec suggests, pushing the door open without knocking.

"Wait!" I say, suddenly skeptical. "What if someone lives here? If they live all the way out here, I'm not sure I want to go inside..."

Alec only peers behind us, eyebrows raised.

"I'd rather take my chances with a living person than face another night of... whatever it was we experienced last night."

So, we go inside.

The door creaks obnoxiously as it slowly opens, then the hinges give way to rust and decay, and the door drops, banging loudly against the floor, sending plumes of dust into the air. Clearly, the cottage hasn't been used in quite some time.

Alec does his best to put the door back into its place, if for no other reason than to shut the forest out.

"I wonder who lived here," I say, looking around, comforted by at the dusty state of this home. I find a box of matches on a hand-carved shelf and candles beside them. I light several candles, and the flame illuminates the room.

"I wonder who would *want* to live here," Alec says. He seems much more relaxed, and he reaches for one of his flasks to drink some ale, but it's long empty.

"Do you ever stop drinking?" I ask playfully.

Alec shrugs as he runs his hand over a cupboard door, gently opening it. Unsurprisingly, the cupboard is empty. I keep an eye on the door, sure someone will return any moment.

"I didn't drink last night," he says, and I swear I almost hear regret in his tone.

Alec makes his way into another room, and gathering some of the candles I've lit, I follow him into a bedroom, where he has found a small bed. He yanks off a thick comforter, which sends thick clouds of dust flying throughout the small space. I cough and wave my hand through the air, doing my best to clear some of the dust from the vicinity as Alec sits and gives me a huge grin.

"Found a comfortable place for us to sleep tonight."

I hesitate.

"We don't know who this bed belongs to..." I start.

Alec shakes his head. "Sweetheart, all that dust you were just coughing over means that nobody has been here in ages, and likely, no one will be returning anytime soon. Besides, if it's dust you're worried about, that comforter contained most of the dust, and we've been sleeping in the dirt for weeks now, anyway. What harm is a little bit of dust going to do?"

He makes a fair point, so I let out a small sigh and sit beside him.

"Hey Alec?" I ask. "Why are you so afraid of ghosts?" I lean over and place my candle on a little table that sits beside the bed. The flame dances from the motion, but it soon stands tall again.

"When I was a boy," Alec begins, leaning in to face me directly. "My grandmamman died."

"Oh, I'm sorry," I start, but he puts up his hand and makes a sour face.

"Don't be. She was a *horrible* woman. She was my pappan's mamman, and she hated children, me included. I think she was largely to blame for my pappan being unable to see past my weakness. She was sickly and thin and always angry, and when she died, I thought I would be relieved. Except, for weeks after we buried her, I saw her everywhere. She still looked so unpleasant and unhappy, but I always got the feeling that those emotions were now directed at me. She followed me everywhere."

"Fates, that would be terrifying," I say under my breath. Alec clenches his jaw.

"It was," he says, folding his hands in his lap.

"So, what happened?" I ask. "Does she still follow you?"

Alec ponders the question for a moment. "No. It lasted until I began my training to work with my pappan that she finally disappeared, though the feeling of being watched never went away until I became a mercenary, got out of town, started to drink."

I nod. Another reason he might drink so heavily if he thinks that doing so keeps his grandmamman's ghost away.

After another pause, Alec leans closer still.

"There's another reason I don't like ghosts," he says, voice low. My eyes search his face, which is startlingly open and sincere.

"What's that?" I ask, forcing myself to swallow. Against my will, my eyes keep flicking to his lips.

"I'm a killer," he says. "Taking a life is no small thing. If I've seen my grandmamman, if she somehow thought I had caused her death and could follow me that way, I'm sure the others whose lives I *am* responsible for taking are just as capable of haunting me the same way."

After all this time, his nonchalance around killing proves to be another mask.

"I had no idea," I say.

"That's the reason I never traveled this far north, once I heard about this place. If there was any place where those spirits could track me down, it'd be here."

I nod.

"I don't blame you for being afraid," I say, reaching out to take his hand in mine. "Especially after what you've been through. I never believed in ghosts myself, but after last night, I've changed my outlook. I can't wait to get out of this forest. The thought that we have to travel back through on our way home makes me sick. I'll be glad to have our mammans with us. Maybe the more people we have in our party, the less likely those things will be to come around again."

Alec gives me a soft, sincere smile. He lifts his hand to brush it against the now-healed scar on my forehead. His eyes search my face pensively.

"How strange it is, this connection," he says.

For the first time, I feel no walls between us, no masks or layers to hide who we are from each other.

"I know," I say, trying to ignore the heat of his hand on my face. "I'd love to know what bound us this way. Find out who else has experienced something like this."

Alec's smile spreads to his entire face, and he laughs quietly.

"What?" I ask, raising an eyebrow.

Mischief dances with the candlelight in his eyes.

"I've been wondering something different," he says, his hand opening, fingers brushing against my cheek, palm pressing against it.

"What's that?" I whisper, unable to make my voice any louder. My stomach flutters, and my heart isn't sure it remembers how to beat properly. Suddenly, it feels too warm in here, though I don't think there's been a fire in the hearth in a long, long time.

"I'm wondering..." he pauses for a moment. The look in his eyes is something I haven't seen from him before. Something intense, sincere. His fingers trail down to my jawline, brush against it on their way to my neck. They caress the back of my neck up into my hairline and find the tie I've used to keep my braid tight. He loosens it and runs his fingers carefully through my hair, letting it cascade down around my face and along my back. I shiver, though the heat in the room has only intensified.

I'm not sure what to do. I almost feel as though I need to jump up and run away, because I've never experienced anything like this. I've never been so close with a man before, never felt one's intense gaze fall so purposefully on me. Sure, I've seen men look at others this way, but I never thought I'd see it directed at me. Alec's eyes have me captivated, and I find myself frozen, unable to do anything at all but search his face.

Say something, fool, I prompt myself. Somehow, I find my voice, though it's so quiet I worry he won't hear me speak at all.

"You're wondering?"

I watch some conflict flash in those amber eyes, but he makes a decision and leans closer. His smile grows. His face is so close to mine now that I can feel the heat of his breath flutter against my chin. His fingers rest on the base of my neck.

"I wonder how else we're connected," he says, and for the briefest moment, his eyes flit to my lips before he leans in further still, brushing his lips against my cheek where his hand was just a moment ago. He plants a soft kiss there, and my body jumps at the sensation. I gasp. He doesn't retreat, though I'm sure he can feel my body tense. His free hand finds mine, and he interlocks our fingers as he moves to press his forehead against mine.

I'm breathing so rapidly I worry I might run out of oxygen. I close my eyes and feel our closeness, feel the warmth of his face.

"What..." I start, but that's all I get out. My insides are going wild. If this is the feeling people describe when they talk about having butterflies, they've got it all wrong. This is something different. More intense. It feels like... like bees, an entire colony of bees buzzing around in my chest, my stomach, spreading into my entire body.

"When you were hurt by those bandits," Alec says. "I felt as if it were happening to me. I felt your fear. And..." He places another kiss on my cheek, closer to my jaw. "I've been wondering for a while now," he says, pausing to kiss my neck just under my ear. I shiver again and squeeze his hand.

Somehow, without my knowledge, my other hand has found its way to his arm, and as I take a deep, quick breath, I slide my hand up to his shoulder: Something to tell him when my words won't work not to go anywhere. His lips trace lines lower on my neck before moving back up, brushing so gently against my lips that it tickles a little bit, and his breath hitches.

There it is again, that smile. This time my eyes are still closed, but I can feel his lips part for the smile. I can picture it in my mind, and the image in tandem with the feeling spreads warmth throughout my belly.

This is wild. I've never been kissed before, and I *never* thought I'd be kissing Alec, of all people. Sure, I've fantasized about it often enough with Zaid, and it almost happened at the postal service in Helna; but now I can't imagine being here, doing this with anyone else. Do I want this? With *Alec*?

"Um," I say, trying to clear the fog from my mind, though I stay close, unwilling to put any space between his lips and mine. I clear my throat. "Uh, wondering? You've been wondering what?"

My eyes open to meet his, which reflect the flickering candlelight. I want to lean back into him, feel the warmth of his face against mine. He looks the same as he always has, but in this light, he seems so... different.

"I've been wondering what else we can feel," he replies. The hand that rests on the base of my neck slides into my hairline as he pulls me even closer, finally pressing his lips to mine in a kiss like nothing I've ever imagined. His lips are soft, strong, gentle, though there's a pull in them that feels magnetic.

All I can think as this feeling – this closeness – explodes within me, is *finally*.

As I lean into his kiss I hear a little moan, and I'm surprised to find when he reciprocates with a moan of his own that the sound came from me. I've never made a sound like that before. I almost feel embarrassed, like I should apologize for sounding so strange, but it doesn't seem to matter. Alec deepens our kiss with one motion.

He pulls me closer, and the warmth that fills my belly ignites, turning into a fire like nothing I've ever felt.

I run my hands up his arms, feeling every curve of his muscle as I find his neck, tangle my fingers in his long, fine hair. Now it's his turn to react, and he does so by grunting, kissing me still deeper, pulling me up onto his lap.

I find my legs wrapping around his torso, and I want nothing more than to keep pressing against him until every part of my body is flush against his.

My breath comes in short, fast bursts, and my heart beats so fast that if I were able to think clearly in this moment, I might worry it's not functioning properly. But all I can think about is what I feel. All I can focus on is the need I have for him to kiss me more.

His hands explore my back, my hips, my shoulders, the top of my chest. They brush over my ribcage, and it's only when they find their way beneath my blouse that I pull back a little bit. His hand freezes, resting the warm tips of his fingers against the skin of my belly. My eyes widen, but I'm smiling. My mind is now whirring a million miles a second, but as Alec looks at me, I don't feel rushed. I feel nothing but desired.

"Is this okay?" he asks, wiggling his fingers just a little bit to indicate what he means. He's breathing just as fast as I am. Fates, as I look at him now, I wonder. Has he always been so beautiful? Is it the dim light of the candle? The fact that we have someplace safe to stay for once?

No. I should be honest with myself. It's the pull I've felt for him since the first time I saw him, just different. It's the reason I've felt such a strong need to defend him every time Zaid told me not to trust him. There's something here. I'm not sure if it's the connection that somehow binds us together or something else, but I would trust this man with my life.

"Um," I start again. Why do I keep saying that? I swear I have a working vocabulary, but the words don't come, and Alec starts to pull away. I feel his fingers move to leave my stomach, and I grab his elbow to hold his hand where it is. I nod, use the hand that's still up in his hair to pull him in for another kiss, and nod again as our foreheads and our noses press together. He smiles again. Fates, that smile.

Alec kisses me again, and I revel in the feeling of his hands spreading across my skin like wildfire. It isn't long before I remove my blouse, seeking more of that warmth of his flesh against mine. I work to remove his shirt, doing my best to ward off the thoughts that now flutter into my brain.

You must be crazy.

You don't do this.

You've never done this.

What are you doing?

Yet the desire to be closer with him is so much stronger, so much more prevalent than those fleeting thoughts, and I pull him closer still. I break my lips away from his and lean in to plant gentle kisses down his neck, across his collar bones. Every kiss I place echoes on my own skin in the same places. Now he pauses, and the groans that escape from deep within his chest only enhance the feeling.

I push back on his shoulders, lips still exploring his neck and chest, and he lays back onto the bed. His hands have found my hips, and the sensation makes my stomach flip. I let out a little laugh. I must be crazy, but no one has ever made me feel this way.

I'm not sure how long we spend entangled in each other's bodies, hands and kisses exploring everything, each sensation heightened by our bond.

Afterward, as we're lying in each other's arms, as our candle burns low and we work to catch our breath, I find myself so glad the thought crossed Alec's mind.

Alec lies on his back. One arm rests across his forehead, and the other holds me secure against his side. My head rests on his solid chest, and although we're both a little sweaty, and my face sticks to his skin just a little bit, I don't move. Instead, I curl up, one leg lifted up over his lower abdomen, listening to the *thump-thump-thump* of his heartbeat, letting myself experience every emotion that comes to me.

"Alec?" I say, voice soft and sleepy.

"Yes, sweetheart?" he replies, tracing his thumb over the scars on my arm.

The nickname makes me smile.

"When I found out about this bond, I wanted it gone. I thought being bound to someone else, especially someone with such a dangerous profession, was the worst thing for me."

Alec is quiet for a moment. His thumb stops its motion. "Oh?" he asks.

I start to drift off, but then I remember I have more to say.

"Alec?"

"Hmm?"

I yawn.

"I don't feel that way anymore."

Alec replies by placing a sweet, soft kiss on my forehead.

I don't know when I fall asleep, but this night is the first night where I've felt so comfortable, so safe, so completely and totally *not* worried, that I almost don't feel like myself. I wait for the bad dreams I've been having to resurface, but they never come. Instead, I fall into a deep sleep where my dreams that do come are long gone by the time I awake.

30

In the morning, I wake to the sound of Alec slipping his trousers on. I frown and rub the sleep from my eyes. I wish I could know what time it is, or how long I slept for.

Alec grins at me.

"Good morning," he says. He swaggers over and kisses me on the forehead. Suddenly, all memory of last night comes rushing back to me. My eyes grow wide again, and I cover my face with my hands.

"Last night didn't happen to just be a very vivid dream, did it?" I ask, and I realize I'm naked, covered only by an old bedsheet.

I'm suddenly so self-conscious that I don't know what to do. I find myself working my fingers through my dark hair, pulling it into a tight braid, just so I have something to keep me busy. As I do, I'm very careful to keep my body covered. Being exposed in the candlelight when emotions are high is one thing, but in daylight like this, even with the fog outside and the layers of dust on the windows, I'm certain I look much less appealing.

"Trust me," he says with that half-smile of his, pulling his shirt on over his head. "It really happened."

Oh, Fates. I sit up, clutching the sheet even tighter to my bare chest.

"Okay, then. Well, I suppose now we've tested your theory..." I start.

His theory was absolutely correct. Our bond goes much deeper than simply experiencing each other's injuries.

He smiles and sits beside me on the bed, putting his hand on my knee, and I melt into his touch.

But the moment is over too quickly as he moves to pull on his boots. I feel the need to say something, anything.

"I want you to know... I don't do this," I say, a blush coloring my cheeks.

"What, this?" he asks, gesturing to his feet. "Put your boots on? Sure, you do. I've seen you do it plenty of times. Though it looks a bit different now that you're wrapping your feet. But the principle is the same."

I frown at him, nodding at the bed beside me.

Alec pauses for a moment. "Never?"

I shake my head. "Never."

He seems to consider this for a second. "Not even—"

"Alec, never. I've never even been kissed before last night." At this, Alec raises his eyebrows, and I press on as my face heats. "I mean, I had a kiss on the cheek when I was twelve from a boy I thought I fancied, and Zaid kissed me on the nose back at the postal service in Helna, but I've *never* been kissed like that."

"Wait, Zaid kissed you?" he asks, a frown creasing the center of his forehead.

"On the nose," I repeat quickly. I'm not sure why I feel the need to defend myself, but Alec seems satisfied with my answer. He smiles again. I wish I could read his mind.

"I kind of suspected that might be the case," he says, half-smile spreading to a full grin. I wait for him to follow up with something more, but he doesn't.

Fates. Was I bad? Did I do it wrong?

"Have *you*?" I ask. Of course, I'm certain I already know the answer. With his charm, confidence, and muscular physique, I've seen women flock to him wherever he goes. I'm sure he's done... *that*... many times.

Alec looks at me warily. "Are you sure you want to talk about this? Now?" he asks.

I sit up straighter and nod. "Yes."

Cautiously, Alec answers my question. "Have I ever been in bed with a woman before? Yes. I have." He must notice my face fall, because he turns to look at me straight on, and he puts his hands in mine. "I have never experienced *that* with any of them."

Alec sets to work setting a fire beneath the stove – a task that is easier said than done, since the thing is ancient. As he works, I explore the little cottage, trying to find clues that might indicate who lived here, how long ago, and why they might have left, aside from the fact that the home is surrounded by woods that are actually haunted, of course.

At first, I only find the usual household items. Old wooden bowls, cups, plates, utensils. A very outdated latrine. A chest full of old clothes, and two pairs of boots – one for a man, and one for a woman, about my size. I put them on and lace them up. In the chest I also come across a stack of leatherbound books, pages well-worn and covered in dust. As I flip through the pages, I realize that these books are hand written. One is a ledger with a handful of names and birthdates written down.

Apparently, whoever lived here was a record keeper from the time when the founders of the Council decided to leave behind the patriarchal society they lived in before. I find myself feeling amazed and strangely reverent being in such a historical home. I always enjoyed my history lessons as a little girl, and to be standing in the place that was a part of that history fills me with a sense of pride.

Other books contain more of the same, and a couple of them appear to be journals, tales of their author's travels through the Baskin mountains. I don't have time enough now to read through all of these journals. The closer we get to the mountain, the more days that pass, the greater rush I feel to find my mamman. I can't explain it exactly, but I fear that if we don't reach her soon, it will be too late. It could just be the ominous feeling that seeps in around us from the woods, but every minute that I'm not moving forward or with Alec, I feel a deep sense of dread for what we'll find when we get there.

I flip to the last entry in one of the journals. On the last pages, the handwriting that has filled the books is scribbled, frantic, as though whoever was writing this was in a great hurry. The author mentions that his wife had gone back into the mountains, but rather than traveling over the rough terrain, she had decided to venture through the caverns below.

The man's wife had been gone for two weeks and had not returned. He was beginning to fret dreadfully. The last thing he wrote is that he wished she hadn't gone that way, for since the witch had led the settlers through the winding cave systems beneath the mountains, nobody ever seemed to return. He was unhappy to state that he was going to look for her. He didn't want to lose her like he had lost the rest of his family.

"Hey, look at this," I say, walking back into the kitchen area where Alec has fixed the stove and has almost finished cooking us breakfast.

"What's that?" he asks. He removes the soup he's made from the stove and places it onto the old wooden table. Steam and dust mingle and mix in the air above the tabletop.

"The people who lived here were travelers. Settlers from the original migration to Maran. The husband lost his entire family to the caves at the base of the mountain. The last thing he wrote was that he was going to look for his wife. I suppose that's why everything here is so covered with dust. He must have left in a hurry and never made it back."

"Huh," Alec says.

Voicing this probability makes me shudder.

"I think we should avoid those caves," I say, urgency filling my voice as I step closer, grasping the journal tightly in my hands. "We're so close. I don't want to chance us getting lost. The journal's author wrote of a way up the mountains, though he mentioned that the journey was arduous, the terrain unstable."

"Don't you think we should explore those caves? It seems that whatever is drawing people to the mountains could be in there," Alec says, but as he mentions the idea, both of us shake our heads. It doesn't feel right. The pull we feel that strengthens every step we take toward the mountain tells us that what we're looking for will be up.

"Got it. Avoid the caves, watch out for falling rocks," Alec says, sounding awfully chipper for discussing such a grim subject.

I frown at him.

"Why are you so happy?"

He grins in response.

"No reason," he says. He approaches me and puts his hand on my waist, then leans down and kisses me deeply. Every moment of last night seems to replay in my mind, and the memory melts away some of my foreboding.

My entire body seems to tingle at the thought, and I wonder if Alec can feel that, too.

Alec scoots an old chair out loudly and tests the weight of it with his foot before he sits.

I sit as well, and as he serves us food, I let my mind wander. I think of last night. Although I have never considered this mercenary to be someone I might want that kind of intimacy with, part of me feels that there was no better way for my first time to go. I trust Alec, and that trust goes deeper than just believing he wouldn't let me get hurt because he feels protective of me. But having that first time be with someone who can literally feel what I'm feeling? I've never heard of something so perfect. And it was... absolutely perfect. Even in this dusty old house on an ancient, creaking bed.

I sneak a peek in Alec's direction, wondering if he's thinking about it, too. I take a large spoonful of soup, burning the roof of my mouth, but I don't care. Anything to take my mind off of how awkward I feel. Am I supposed to act differently now? Are we going to kiss every time we see each other? How does anybody ever get anything done if they're kissing all the time? But the thought of kissing him has my mind betraying me again.

I feel Alec's eyes boring into me, and I fear I might drop my spoon as I rush to cover up my blushing face. I need to change the subject, quickly.

I clear my throat, doing my best to ignore the amused look on his face. He looks as if he can read my thoughts along with feeling what I'm feeling.

"Um. How long do you think it'll take us to get to the mountain?" I ask, praying that we can move on from this so my mind doesn't go in these circles until I'm old and gray.

Alec considers my question for a moment, slurping up a spoonful of his own soup.

"I don't know. A few days? Hopefully no more than a week. I'm starting to feel antsy taking so long. I've never taken so long on a job before, and the fact that it's my own mamman that I'm looking for... well, I feel the pressure."

I nod.

"Me too," I say. "I hope they're alright. I worry that with them both being so strange before they disappeared that something is wrong."

We eat for a while in silence, each of us pondering the situation our mammans may be in. I'm doing my best to stay hopeful, but I can't help fearing that by the time we reach them – *if* we reach them – something terrible will have already happened. They'll have moved on to another location and we'll be chasing them down forever, or... or they'll be dead.

I try to steer my thoughts in a more positive direction.

When we find them, they will be okay. We *will* be able to get them home safely without any more strange occurrences, without any more delays. Our families will be reunited. Everything will be alright.

I take a moment to sketch the cottage on my maps, and I leave the journals on the table. I know it's not a great idea to add weight for us to carry, so I'll leave the journals here and pick them up on our way home. The rich history within the pages is too tempting to leave behind for good.

It only takes us two more days to reach the foot of the mountain. When we do, we stand there, looking up at the rocks ahead of us.

The slope is steep, not quite steep enough that we won't be able to hike it, I don't think, but steep enough that we may have to use our hands as well in some sections.

Dark gray, jagged rock covers the entire mountainside, with trees that grow sparsely toward the bottom and closer together toward the top.

"So... did we decide on no caves?" Alec asks. His throat bobs as he swallows, still peering up at the heights we are going to have to scale.

"I don't know," I start, shocked when he takes my hand in his. In the cool morning air, his hand is soft and warm. That heat spreads in my belly again, and I can't help but smile at him, despite the feat ahead of us. "Do you want to become lost for all eternity?"

"That's a strange thing to be smiling about," he says, squeezing my hand.

"I was smiling about something else," I say, squeezing his right back. He shoots me a curious look, but his smile says he already knows.

31

We let the silence fall between us. When Alec speaks again, his cheerful tone is gone, and his face is solemn.

"Onward and upward?" he asks, and I nod.

I take a deep breath, adjust the bags over my shoulder and then my bow, making sure that everything is secure, and we set off, hiking at such an incline that within minutes, my calves are burning, and my breath comes in heavy, quick bursts.

The rocks are jagged indeed, and frail. The smaller ones crumble away beneath our hands and feet, so we're constantly scrambling.

It may be due to the intense focus we have on scaling the mountain, or the ominous air that hangs about Darkwood forest, but we see no animals, hear no birds.

"I can't believe how slick this rock is," I say, placing my hands just before me on the jagged gray stone to keep by balance as I adjust my footing for another step.

Alec hikes about a yard beneath me, and he only grunts in response to my comment as he, too, works to find the best place to set his feet.

A moment later, I think I've got my foot in a reliable position, but it slips as the rock breaks away beneath it. I catch my knee on a sharp edge of the rock, cutting through my trousers and scratching my skin, before tumbling backward. A strong, sturdy hand catches me by my lower back and halts my descent, and I look up at Alec, who now clings to the rock above me and holds me steadily close to him.

My breath catches in my chest, and it's only when I notice his knee is bleeding that I find my words.

"Oh, sorry," I mutter. I didn't consider how difficult it would be for us to hike up such a dangerous path if the risk of one of us being injured means that the other will be, as well.

When I first discovered this strange bond between the two of us was real, I wanted to do anything I could to keep him out of trouble to save my own skin. That drive is still present, but the urge to keep *him* from harm has tripled.

I run my thumb along the new scar on his bicep, the same scar that I incurred from the bandits weeks ago.

"Are you alright to continue?" he asks, and the question brings me back to myself. I back away from him, using my arms to scramble back onto my sore, blistered feet. I know he's experiencing the same pain. I try to be even more intentional with where I place my steps.

"Yes, let's keep going. The sooner we get up this mountainside, the better. I'll just be more careful moving forward," I say.

It's nearly impossible to make conversation as we hike. Both of us are breathless, sweating, ready to rest within the first couple of hours. When we manage to find a portion of the mountain that isn't as steep, we stop to drink from our canteens and give our burning muscles a brief moment of reprieve.

"How do you think we'll know when we reach the top if we've found their trail?" I ask, chewing the inside of my cheek nervously. I know we're headed in the direction all of Alec's informants have pointed us, but my maps don't show any detailed pieces of these mountains, and I worry this might have all been for naught if we get lost up here. The mountain range is vast – it's very possible we could simply miss them. "I think at this point, we're settled on investigating that witch idea. I don't have any others."

Alec clenches his jaw, but he looks at me with sincerity.

"Agreed," he says. "I hate to entertain the witch idea. It all seems so silly to me, but there are too many coincidences to ignore. Too many parallels between what our mammans have experienced, too much tied together between you and me. The legends I heard as a child – the same legend I'm sure you heard from Mathilda back in Nerine – all mentioned that the witch lived at the top of the mountains. So, we'll go there, and we'll see what we can see."

I let his words soak in. I think we've both felt for some time now that we're going in the right direction. Ever since we entered the forest at the base of the mountains, the pull has been stronger, and I think we're getting close.

"Earlier, when we were talking at breakfast," I start, hesitant to say what else is on my mind. Curiosity has been eating at me all morning, especially after my slide, after how I felt when he caught me and held me there. I feel drawn to him in an all new way, closer to him than ever before. But since last night, I've felt increasingly anxious that his experience wasn't the same as mine, that because he was my first, maybe I feel more strongly than he does. Or worse, I worry that he *knows* I feel this way and thinks less of me for it, somehow. I clear my throat and push forward. "When you said you've *been* with, um, a number of women..." I trail off. Am I brave enough to actually ask him the question that's been on my mind? I feel silly, but I need to know.

"What did you mean, exactly, by 'a number'?" I clear my throat again. I busy myself adjusting my bow across my back, taking another drink of water.

Alec only raises his eyebrows at me, small grin playing at the edge of his lips.

"Why do you ask?"

I want to sink into the rock below me and disappear, get lost in the cave system beneath the mountain. I swallow past the anxiety that threatens to close my throat. I take a deep breath, then I lean forward.

"Come on, Alec. Just answer the question, please."

Alec's smile almost goes away, and he pulls off his boot to shake out a couple of little pebbles. My own feet feel some relief when he puts his boot back on, grateful for the removal of those rocks. My skin crawls as I wait for him to answer.

"I don't know why you women care so much about these things," he says, and he looks at me in a way that says he expects me to drop it.

When I don't relent, when I don't change the subject, Alec's shoulders droop ever so slightly. He lets out a sigh and runs a hand through the length of his blond hair.

"Well, I don't know the exact number," he says slowly. "I've traveled a lot, and the company I kept... well, I kept a lot of company."

"Everywhere you went?" I ask. I really don't know why I'm asking, though, and my chest feels tight. Do I even want to know his answer to this question? Logically, I know I can't hold his past against him. I should just leave it alone. But I hang on every second of the time it takes for him to answer.

As we get walking again, Alec gives a one-shouldered shrug. We walk side by side for a moment as he considers my question.

"Not *everywhere*." He says it like a question. Lovely. So, it was often enough that it was *close* to everywhere he went.

I shouldn't have asked. I should drop the subject now, talk about something good, instead. I'm irritated with myself for bringing this up, and yet, I can't seem to let it go.

"How is that even possible?" I ask, shoving my canteen back into my satchel. "Did you care for any of them? At all?"

I already know the answer to the first question. I remember how charming he was with the server the first night we shared a room together, the one who basically begged him to go to bed with her after a glance.

Again, a little voice in my head tells me to stop pressing, that all I'm going to do is hurt us both. But I can't help it. Am I just one of his traveling bedmates? Am I just another of those women who fell for those amber eyes, that wit, that confident smile?

"Now, wait a minute," Alec raises his voice, turning to face me. He narrows his eyes at me. His shoulders draw back, his chin rises, and he clenches his fists. The action makes him slide a bit against the rock, but he catches himself quickly enough that he doesn't go tumbling. "That's not fair."

I can see the hurt in his eyes, see that I've struck a chord in him. Guilt pangs within me. I don't know what my problem is. After how close we've grown, I don't know why I'm asking questions that only cause trouble.

I grit my teeth as we come up on another steep incline covered in crumbling rocks.

"Sorry," I mumble. I'm not sure if he's heard me. I keep talking, trying to get him to understand how I'm feeling as I work to keep myself upright on the mountainside. "It's just... I really care for you. I don't want to be just one of the girls you bedded on your many adventures. I think... I think I need a minute."

I don't wait for his response. I straighten my belongings, so they're better secured on my back, and I climb ahead.

"Lane, wait," Alec says, climbing up the mountain after me. "You can't just say something like that and walk away."

I shake my head. "Just give me some time to think," I call back.

I know I'm going to see him again. We're going in the same direction. We have the same goal, the same destination. Eventually, I'm *going* to have to talk with him again.

But I'll deal with that later. Right now, I need some space.

I feel so silly. For telling him I care for him. For allowing myself to fall for him so deeply. It's all so new to me. What if he doesn't reciprocate these feelings?

I move fast climbing forward, throwing my muscles into overdrive as I work my way up the mountain. I don't care if I'm getting tired. In this moment, I do my best not to care that my muscles aching will cause Alec's to ache as well.

The tightness in my chest has only worsened, and I blame it for how hard I'm pushing my body to move forward, not the anxiety. I won't allow myself to feel that right now. I just focus on moving forward, and thankfully, Alec allows the distance between us to grow just enough that, it wouldn't take long to reach each other should either of us be injured.

After a couple of hours working to keep at a steady pace, I come to another area where the slope isn't quite as steep. I want to keep going, but I'm exhausted, and it's getting dark. It's been hours since I looked at Alec, though I know he's right behind me.

I can hear his grunting as he climbs to the area I've stopped in. I reach into my satchel and dig around for my flint. I light a small fire, roll out my blanket, and lie on my back to stare up at a starless sky.

The rock beneath my blanket is the hardest surface I think I've ever had to sleep on. Within moments, my shoulder blades are aching. I try adjusting, rolling onto my side, but every position yields the same results.

I close my eyes and listen to Alec moving around the fire, laying out his blanket and securing his bags.

Alec takes a long drink from one of his flasks, and I can smell the ale from where I'm camped.

I want to chastise him for drinking in such a dangerous terrain, but at least he's here, where I can see him, where I know he'll stay. I've positioned our camp so that we'll lie parallel with the slope, making it harder to roll down the mountain in our sleep. Still, I scoot a little closer, just in case. For now, despite the drink, he's safe. He'll sleep off the ale before we continue our trek tomorrow.

"Lane?" Alec asks, nudging my arm gently. "Lane, are you awake?"

I keep my eyes closed tightly and hope that he'll leave me alone for the night and let me think things through before we talk again. After letting out a dramatic, ale-scented sigh, Alec adjusts on his blanket and gets to bed.

I wake later in the night to the sound of lightning crashing. This seems to have woken Alec, as well, for he sits upright, looking startled. I don't know when it started raining, but after that crash of lightning, water pours from the sky onto us. It tumbles down the mountain, and in minutes, we're struggling to get our things packed up. The water has long since extinguished our fire.

"What should we do?" I ask Alec, all anger from earlier dissipated in the urgency of this rainstorm. My sopping wet hair whips my face in the furious winds as I rush to gather my bow and arrows, then my other belongings, doing my best to shield my maps from the rain.

Alec works to scoop everything he can manage to hold into his arms, then dumps it all into his bags.

"Should we go back down?" I shout through the rain.

"What, and waste all our progress?" he yells back at me. "No way. That will put us even further behind. You said so before – our mammans could be in trouble. There's no time to waste!"

"Well, it's clear we can't sleep here." I raise my arms to gesture at the water that rushes past our feet on its way down the mountain. "What do you suggest?"

I look down the mountain in the direction we came from. I don't want to go all the way back, especially since the decline is so steep, and it's so dark. Not to mention the added danger this fast-running water presents. I don't see that ending well. I also don't see us pointlessly holding our entire camp up all night or trying to go back to sleep in this wild weather.

"We keep moving forward, I suppose," Alec shouts. "The incline from here doesn't look too steep, and I think I saw some trees up there before the sun set. We might be able to find somewhere to shelter us from the storm."

Moving forward would be better than standing here holding everything.

Lightning flashes above us again, and once again, thunder follows, causing every hair on my body to stand on end.

A new fear arises in me, something that makes my skin tingle and my heart pause in its beating. We're on the side of a mostly barren mountain, with a wild storm all around us. We could be struck by lightning at any moment.

"Alec!" I yell, tone low, voice thick with fear. "We need to go. Now."

32

As if on cue, lightning flashes again, and once again, thunder follows right behind it. Alec seems to feel my urgency, and the two of us share a wide-eyed look of terror. As quickly as we can manage – despite struggling through the running water, slipping and sliding – we climb.

Several times as we make our way up, one of us or the other slips, scraping various parts of our bodies on the rough, jagged surface at our feet.

Still, we climb.

We keep going until we're gasping for air. The rain is coming down so hard at this point that trying for breath makes me feel as though I'm drowning, and my clothes are so drenched with rain that they weigh me down, slowing my progress.

The weight of my clothing is not the first thing on my mind, however. All I can think about is getting to those trees safely.

We don't talk. We don't do anything but focus as hard as we can on staying upright and getting to shelter.

We've just gotten past the first two or three trees that have grown through the rock when lightning and thunder crash almost simultaneously, and the rain comes down even harder. Thankfully, however, the trees grow more tightly together as we continue up, and we're grateful to have some kind of shelter.

Now, as we approach yet another rise in the slope, water falls in sheets, sliding down the mountain in thick streams that threaten to wash us away. We're grasping at anything we can hold. The combination of the rushing water and our grip crumbles many of the smaller rocks we try to hold onto. Now that we're high enough that we're surrounded by trees, we scramble for branches that might hold our weight.

Water continues to slide down the mountain. The first two waves push against us, but we're able to fight them back and remain standing. The third, however, catches us with such great force that Alec and I are lifted off our feet and sent tumbling. On the way, I can't tell if my injuries are Alec's or my own, but pain flares in my head, my elbow, my shin, and my hip. My arms and legs flail as I try desperately to find something to hold onto that will halt my descent. Finally, I crash into a tree. The force of the impact pushes sharp pain through my ribcage. I open my mouth to let out a scream, but my breath has been knocked loose, and the sound remains trapped in my throat.

Water rushes at my face, filling my nose and mouth, and all I can do is keep my head up as high as possible. I struggle for air and cling to the tree for dear life.

Finally, when I feel as though there's no way I'll be able to hold on any longer, the rain lightens – gradually at first, and then it stops altogether.

Fear strikes through my heart, flooding my body with a terrible cold that has nothing to do with the rain.

I can't see Alec.

Panic shoots through me, extending all the way to my fingertips. I try to call out, but each time I take a breath to try, the pain in my ribs silences me, and all I can do is croak.

"Alec?" I try again, and again, and again, until I'm used to the pain enough to push past it, to draw a deep enough breath that I can call out. I know that Alec, wherever he is, is in just as much pain as I am. Chances are that even if he can hear me, if he's conscious, he may not be able to respond.

I need to find him.

Slowly, I'm able to push off of the tree trunk enough to get moving, though each movement I make has me grinding my teeth against the pain.

"Alec?" I call out again. Without the rain, the night is back to being eerily quiet, save for the water dripping from the trees onto the hard rock below. Thankfully, my voice carries, echoing off the rock surfaces around me. I roll myself onto my stomach. In the process, I swear something in my ribcage gives. I wince and suck in a breath that makes the pain much worse. But I keep moving. Using my elbows and my upper body strength, I drag myself along the mountainside, over fallen branches and crumbled rocks.

"Here."

I almost don't hear the sound of Alec's voice, it's so hushed, so strained from his own pain. I pause my crawling to listen.

"Alec?"

"I'm here," he says softly. He's lying against a tree trunk of his own, clutching his stomach, arm pressed tightly against his ribcage.

I've never been filled with such joy as I am when I see his face in the pale moonlight that shimmers down through the tree branches and remaining rainclouds.

I work to pull myself over to where he sits, so relieved I found him that little laughs bubble up in my chest and cause us both to wince at the pain the laughter causes.

I put my hands on either side of his face, brushing away soaking strands of his blond hair. I press my forehead against his. I'm so grateful we're alive. I've never experienced rain like that before in my life, and I have no idea how we're going to make it up this mountain in our condition.

"You're okay?" Alec asks. His eyes are wide, his face pale.

"I think I might have broken a rib. But I can move. I'm alright," I assure him. He nods.

Alec looks me over, and the arm that isn't clutching his torso brushes lightly against the bottom left side of my ribcage, where I collided with the tree. I wince away from his touch, and he mutters a small apology.

"Do you think you can get up?" I ask him, though feeling the way I feel, I'm sure I already know the answer.

"I don't think so," he says. "Not long enough to hike, anyway. You?"

I close my eyes tightly. So much for making progress. All of my energy was spent finding Alec, and my adrenaline has officially worn off.

"I don't think I can," I croak. Tears sting in my eyes.

"Well," he says flatly after a while. "Looks like we're camping out tonight after all. I'm just grateful the rain has stopped. Let's regroup in the morning. Rest a bit for tonight, then we'll see if we can formulate a plan."

I give a solemn nod and move slowly so that I can lie against the tree. Now that the rain has stopped and my adrenaline has slowed, I realize I'm freezing. I wrap my arms tightly around myself, tucking my legs up into my chest and whimpering at the pain it causes me.

Alec gasps, but he puts his arm out and taps his chest gently. I just look at him, afraid to get close to him again when we haven't talked, haven't cleared the air from earlier.

He sighs, and the sigh is immediately followed by a rough cough, which has both of us groaning.

"Lane," Alec says through shallow breaths. "I understand you're upset, though I don't really understand why. All the women I've been with happened before you. But it's dark, and everything is wet, and the last thing we need is for you to grow ill on top of everything else."

Already I can feel myself drifting off into a strange, feverish sleep. If I don't get warm soon, I may not make it long. We should make a fire. That would be the best thing to do, but we're both exhausted, and everything is soaked. I grunt as I inch closer to him. I press my body against his, and my shivering immediately slows. The heat his body emits is intoxicating, and I soak it all in. I fall fast asleep with his arms around me, the two of us clinging to each other for warmth.

It's the strangest sleep I've ever had.

I sleep lightly enough to notice the two of us shiver throughout the night, but I sleep deeply enough that I can't get up or readjust. My dreams are filled with strange laughter and blurred images of a deep cave with carvings along the walls, old cages, black feathers, and the repeated image of the peak of a mountain.

Alec and I wake late in the morning. The sun is already high in the sky, and all signs of the rainstorm have dried away, with the exception of our still damp clothing and the sound of a small stream running somewhere nearby.

I push away from Alec's still sleeping body. His chest rises and falls in small, rapid movements as he breathes. I reach up to caress his face, and then I try to get up.

It's only when I sit up that I remember the horrible pain from yesterday as it returns with a vengeance. Alec winces in his sleep, and as I try to adjust and send another wave of pain coursing through me, Alec wakes, startled.

I try to stand. This act results in both of us gasping, and Alec puts his hand out and presses it against my leg.

"Woman!" he gasps.

"We need to keep moving," I tell him stubbornly.

"I agree with you. Can we pause for a moment, though? We went through hell last night, and we need to recuperate. We should proceed cautiously, take our time. We don't want to risk further damaging ourselves or falling further behind."

He's right. If we do keep moving right away, we need to be careful about it. Judging by the pain in my ribcage, I don't think we're going to be able to travel on foot for long, if at all.

"Fine," I pout. "What do you suggest?"

Alec leans forward.

"Let's rest here for the morning. See if we can find something to support our ribs so that moving doesn't hurt so damn badly."

I watch his face as he looks around for anything we might be able to wrap our ribs with. If we stay here, we're putting ourselves further behind, and we have no idea when we'll reach our mammans. Still, I don't have any better alternatives to offer.

I know there's no use in pushing ourselves too hard after such an injury.

"Alright, yes," I relent. "Let's get out of these wet clothes. I think the ones in our bags might be a little dryer."

Alec begins to smile, but I throw up my hand to stop him.

"Don't get any ideas," I tell him. "You're looking that way." Alec nods slowly, biting his tongue. We remove our wet clothing – except for our undermost layer, at my request.

After working at it for a while, Alec is able to start a fire beneath the tree, and I set all of our clothes nearby so they can dry out. Thanks to the still somewhat damp pine needles and leaves from the trees above us, our fire produces a thick, sweet-smelling smoke. I hold up our canteens, one of which still has some alcohol within.

"I'm dumping this," I say. "I think I heard a stream a little way off. I'm going to see if I can find some fresh water to replace this nonsense."

"Wait!" Alec begs, holding his hand out. "At least let me have some. For the pain."

His amber eyes look so innocent, so pleading.

I roll my eyes.

"Right. For the pain," I say. I carefully hand him a canteen, and he empties its contents into his mouth before passing it back to me.

"Thank you," he says, and I give him a curt nod.

"I'll be back. Try not to get into any more trouble while I'm gone, okay?" I say.

I turn and drag myself toward where I heard the sound of running water. Every movement I make aggravates of the sharp pain in my ribs. My breaths come in short, shallow gasps; but I keep moving, one canteen in each hand.

When I find the stream I fill our canteens with fresh, cool mountain runoff from the storm last night. The small stream bubbles down the mountainside, and the sound of its trickling instills in me a deep sense of calm, despite everything. I take a deep breath in, which is immediately rewarded with a staggering pain in my ribcage followed by a bought of excruciating cough. When the coughing subsides, I groan and do my best to breathe in more carefully. I place my hands in the cool stream, and the water refreshes and energizes my spirit.

Here in this little area, completely alone, I allow myself a moment to feel everything I've been holding back.

I think of my mamman, of how she disappeared, of what I know of her acting so strangely. I think about how afraid I've been that something has happened to her, especially since we reached Darkwood forest. Before, I felt like there was hope, that we would find our mammans and they would be fine; but something changed when we entered that forest, and I can't shake this feeling of dread.

I try to breathe out all the stress I've felt over wasting so much time. Being so close to where we think they might have gone, every minute that passes is present in my mind, a timer counting down.

I think of my sister, and although I'm not a devout worshiper of the Fates, I send a prayer to them that Zaid kept his word, that he got home safely, and that Lilah isn't home fending for herself.

I think of Zaid. I think of how kind he is to me, how expressly clear he's made his feelings, and I feel guilty that I've allowed myself to fall for Alec, when I wanted to be with Zaid for so long.

I think of Alec. That mercenary. I think of his cocky grin. His drinking habit. The carefree façade he wears for the world to see. I think of everything he's told me about his family, and his reasons for the path he's chosen. I think of our night together, and how our bond connects us more deeply than I ever imagined.

And then I allow the other thoughts to flood in all at once.

I worry that the way I feel may just be due to this bond we share, and that if I were to find a way to break it, I might not feel this way about him.

I worry that I'm feeling this way because Alec is the only person I've ever been this close with. If that's the case, that's almost worse – I've allowed myself to be swept up, and I gave a part of myself to him that I can never take back. I worry it meant nothing to him.

I feel foolish.

Fates, I feel so foolish.

And yet, despite how angry I am for insisting I join him on this wild adventure in the first place, I'm angrier still because the things I feel for him go beyond some physical attraction.

After some time spent at the stream, when I feel a little better about things, I center myself and work my way back to where Alec lays sleeping beneath the tree.

"We need to focus and find a way to get up this mountain. If you've got any ideas about how to make that happen, I'm listening," I say, waking him. I look around at our belongings. Then, taking my blanket in my hands, I tear it into two long strips. "Come here," I say, holding one strip wide open. "Let me wrap your ribs."

"I'm fine," Alec says, sitting up slowly. I roll my eyes.

"I'm dying over here, so I know you are not fine," I mutter. "Just let me wrap you."

Alec gives in and slowly scoots over.

He grinds his teeth as sit and wrap his ribs tightly. I can tell I've done the trick, because my own chest feels the pressure.

I finish it off with a tight knot and give him an awkward pat on the shoulder.

"Lane," Alec starts with a wary look on his face.

"Now you do me," I interrupt, holding the second strip out before him.

Alec and I spend the rest of the time it takes for him to wrap me up in silence. I don't want to discuss anything right now, so I welcome the quiet.

As Alec finishes with my ribs, he places a soft kiss on my cheek, and my body warms.

Having my ribs wrapped, I feel so much better. I feel so good, in fact, that I think I can make it back up to the flatter area where we were last night before the flood swept us downhill.

"Do you think you can keep going?" I ask him, moving my things carefully onto my back. I hardly wait for a reply before I stand, wobbly at first, but I steady myself soon enough.

"Sure," he says, following close behind me.

The hike back up to our spot from last night, even though it's only a few hundred feet from the tree that caught Alec, is a slow, arduous, and agonizing process. We spend the majority of the hike on our hands and knees, clutching at the sharp rocks to keep our balance and support our weight. Several of the rocks break apart and fall to pieces beneath our grasp, which makes the climb that much more difficult.

Then, of course, there's the tension that pulls like a rope tied between us, and how much I'd love for him to kiss me again. I press my hand to my cheek.

By the time we have reached our spot from last night, I'm utterly exhausted. My ribcage throbs. My muscles burn. My hair is beyond matted from the sweat and dirt that covers my body. Every little scrape and bruise feels as if it's beneath a magnifying glass. All I want to do is lie down and let sleep remove all memory of the last two days.

I've always loved to travel, and being out in the world is more comfortable for me than being in my own house. At this moment, though, I wish for home: for the comfort of my bed, for the quiet of my room, for the privacy of my latrine. I wish for my family.

Although we've only made back the progress we lost last night, we have to rest.

Alec busies himself right away making a fire, but I lie down directly on the flat rock and close my eyes. It takes me a minute to adjust so my ribs don't hurt quite so badly, but I'm so exhausted that I don't care about getting comfortable. All I want is to sleep, so hopefully tomorrow will bring easier travels our way.

"Lane?" Alec starts once the fire is lit, scooting himself close enough to me that his outer thigh presses against my hip. He peers over my shoulder, but I pretend to be asleep. I don't feel like talking now. Everything is complicated and jumbled up, and right now, I don't feel like sorting through it all.

Alec sighs, and the sound is truly sad. He leans in close so that his face is only inches from my ear. "You're allowed to be upset; I suppose. Just know... Bound or not, you are unlike any woman I've ever met."

He waits for a response, but several minutes pass by, and I do my best to slow my breathing and remain still. Though I'm not entirely certain what he means, his words send my gut fluttering, and my heart begins to beat faster.

When I don't respond, Alec gives me another gentle kiss on the cheek. The warmth that spreads through me from his kiss seems to ease some of the pain in my body.

"Rest well, sweetheart," he whispers.

He's called me by that moniker many times before, but it feels different now, and my heart flutters at the sound of it. I'm reminded of how I felt being in his embrace with those smiling lips against my own, the way he held me as though he thought he might lose me at any moment.

My stomach flips, and I press my hands tightly to my chest in order to keep my heart from beating its way out.

I fall asleep allowing myself to replay every moment of our night together, every sensation, every touch, every kiss, and replaying every word he just said over and over again.

33

In the morning, Alec wakes before I do, and I wonder if he's slept at all. He moves with much more ease today than he did yesterday, and that gives me the courage to attempt getting up.

I'm still incredibly sore, but with this wrap around my ribcage and a decent night's rest, I feel worlds better.

I even find myself smiling, which catches Alec's attention, and he raises his eyebrows at me, sending a smile of his own my way.

"Looks like someone had a good night," he says as he packs up our campsite, handing over a couple of turning carrots, which I immediately start nibbling on.

I want to tell him everything.

I want to tell him that I heard what he said last night about me being different. That I feel the same way about him. That there's a lot we're going to have to discuss about what we are to each other, and where this is going.

But I leave it be, for now. I don't feel that romance – or whatever future that may or may not be waiting for us ahead – is more important than finding our mammans. All our focus should be on the journey, on getting to them safely and quickly.

We stay quiet for a while as we get moving. Our pace is slow, but we are making progress, and things are already going much more smoothly than they did yesterday. Gray clouds fill the air and threaten rain, though, and I spend much of the day frowning at the sky.

When the first clap of thunder rolls in, I'm filled with a white-hot panic. I don't want to lose the progress we've made in another flash flood, but I also find myself shaking at the thought of the pain that would come from another tumble down the mountain.

My entire body aches just thinking about it. I don't realize I'm picking at my fingernails until Alec reaches out and takes my hand.

His eyes meet mine, and his lips turn up into an encouraging smile.

"Don't worry," he says, gently squeezing my hand. His hands are more calloused than usual, probably from all the efforts he made to support himself during yesterday's trek. "Now we know what storms can be like up here. And we've got time on our side. Let's do what we can to be prepared."

The trees grow much closer together up here than they did in the area where we were washed away before, and I consider our options. Reaching into one of our bags, I pull out two lengths of rope that Alec and I purchased on our shopping spree before we left Helna.

"Here, help me with this," I start, approaching a nearby pine tree. The tree is shorter than most in its vicinity, with wide branches that hang low enough that I can reach them.

Alec adjusts the bags on his shoulder and follows, stopping underneath the tree's large boughs.

We work to get all of our belongings secured up on a tree branch, including my bow, but Alec insists that he should keep his blades at his side, and I relent. After all, our luck has shown that anything could happen.

As the rain comes down around us, Alec and I sit huddled close together with our bodies against the tree trunk and tie ourselves to it. This way, come whatever water force there is, Alec and I will not be swept away again.

"Lane, I wanted to talk to you about before," Alec says. Although we're tied closely together, I lean forward so I can get a better look at his face. It's started getting dark out now, and the clouds above us make it even more difficult to see his facial expression.

I'm not sure I know what he's going to say. Throughout the day, I've gone back and forth about what I want. Even if he did mean what he said last night, "You're different" isn't exactly a profession of love. Even if he does love me – which feels a little silly to think about – he's still got his past, and his charm that would certainly get him the same amount of attention it always has. I'm not sure I'm enough to make him want to leave his options behind.

But I think I owe him some honesty, at least.

I put my hand against his chest.

"Alec, I heard what you said last night. About me... being different," I tell him.

Several emotions flash across his face. Relief, as the muscles in his jaw and brow relax. Then frustration as his teeth clench, making the sides of his jaw tighten and flex. Then his eyes widen and soften as they search my face.

He takes a deep breath.

"I didn't say you were different. I said you are unlike any woman I've met before," he says, his tone stern. "And I meant it. You're... stubborn. And crafty. Industrious. Amazing with that bow of yours. You're so serious, *all the time*. You plan. You worry. You don't kill. And intimate moments... well, they actually mean something to you. You may be surprised, but none of the women I've been with have made me feel that they just might mean something to me, too. My encounters with women have always been fun. You, Lane, have *not* always been fun."

I back away as much as I can with the rope tied around me. The rope presses on my injured rib, and I force myself to relax just a little bit.

"Lovely, thanks for clarifying," I grumble.

Alec's hands find my face and raise my chin so I make eye contact with him.

"No, Lane. You're missing my point. *You* are different. You make me feel like I can talk about my family. I have never shared my past with anyone. I don't know when you stopped annoying me and started impressing me, but I've never felt anything like this before. And the strange thing is, I felt this way long before you and I shared that night together."

I look up at him through tears that sting my eyes.

"It's whatever this thing is that binds us together. The reason we get the same injuries. The same reason we *feel* the same things," I tell him, though I'm still not sure. Those tears blur my vision, and I close my eyes before I can let them fall.

Alec's hands never leave my face.

"That may be, but it doesn't matter. Not to me," he says. "All that matters is that this connection I feel with you is something I've never had with anyone. For once in my life, I *want* to take things seriously. See where this goes. We've got to be bound for a reason, and I think we have an obligation to explore this together."

I'm quiet for a moment, and I blink back the tears that threaten to fall. It's all so complicated. Our bond, the moments we've shared together. I wonder if any of it actually holds any meaning. I don't believe in destiny. I never have. But there's got to be some reason that we've been bound this way, and he's right. We should figure it out together.

Alec draws in a shuttering breath.

"At the *very* least, Lane, I want you. I know I don't want to lose you, or this unique bond we share."

I don't know what to say. I allow the tears to fall as I grasp each of Alec's hands, which are still caressing either side of my face, and I lean forward. The rope pulls at my torso, but I don't care. I push my inhibitions aside and press my lips to his.

Although it hasn't been long since we shared our first kiss, it feels like it's been weeks, and the feeling that fills me when our lips meet is fresh, as though I'm feeling it for the very first time again. Warmth spreads through my body, and I feel as though I'm weightless. I no longer feel my injuries. I no longer feel anything except Alec beside me, his lips on mine.

"But wait," I say, pulling away just enough to whisper, a breath away from his face.

"Why wait?" he replies, dipping down to meet my lips again, and I put my fingers gently over his mouth.

"Are you *sure* you want this? You want... me?" I ask. I know that he says it's me that he wants, but he can't possibly guarantee that he *will* want me. If I'm going to let myself fall, I want it to be for something that will last.

Alec pulls himself away so he can get a clear view of my face. His brows furrow as he frowns.

"What?" he asks.

I shrug one shoulder. I feel embarrassed, like I shouldn't be asking, but that stubborn part of me has to ask.

"I don't want to do this if there's going to be anyone else," I tell him.

His hand finds my face again, and his thumb gently traces a scrape that has seems to have healed. His eyes search mine.

"Trust me," he says, voice catching in his throat. "There is no one else."

Those words are music to my ears, and they set my stomach aflutter again. But it's not that easy, and I need to let him know I'm serious.

"But what about later? When all this is settled, when we get to go home, what will we be then? How will we make it work?"

"Does it matter?" he asks, smiling. "We're in this now. Why ruin the experience with worries about what's to come?" But his smile fades, and I know he knows what I'm going to say before I open my mouth. "Right. You need a plan."

"That's right," I say. "I don't want to allow myself to get caught up with you if it's going to cause me heartbreak later. I... I don't think I could take it."

I can see him fighting himself as he formulates a response. The Alec I met back in Nerine would have made some joke about how this is why I've never been intimate with anyone before. Because I expect too much. The Alec I started this journey with would have said something about how I never let myself have any fun because my fear gets in the way.

This Alec, though, cares about whether or not he hurts my feelings. This one, for whatever reason, wants me. Wants to be genuine with me, even though he's genuine with no one. This Alec is allowing himself to be vulnerable with me.

"How about this, Lane?" he asks. "Let's get through this. Allow ourselves to see where this goes. Finish up this journey together, and we'll see how we both feel. Will you at least allow me that much time? Because I want this. I want you, Lane. Anyone else in comparison doesn't matter."

I raise my eyebrows at him.

"You say that *now*, when we're in the middle of nowhere, with no other prospects on the horizon. Do you know how you're going to feel when you have the opportunity to be with someone else?" I press.

Alec grumbles. He runs his hands through his hair and raises them, palms up.

"In all the time you've been with me, have I gone with another woman? Even at the start, when I could barely stand you. I've had offers, as you may recall. Have I taken the chance?"

I frown, remembering every woman I've seen who's been drawn in by his looks and charms.

"No, you haven't."

"Then how about *you* have a little faith in *me*?"

I stare at him for a moment, then I sigh. "Alright."

"Yeah?" he asks, grin lighting up his face.

"Yes."

He pulls me into a tight hug, sprinkling my neck, jaw, and cheek with excited little kisses. I'm startled to find that my ribs don't hurt anymore. My eyes widen, and he loosens his grip a little bit, noticing his lack of pain, as well.

Our bond may have *healed* our wounds.

I lean back and press against my ribcage where I was injured from the rainstorm. When neither of us experiences the rush of pain we were expecting, we alternate between exhausted laughter and frantic, excited kisses. This is huge!

I don't know how this works, but it seems as though our kissing may have healed our wounds. I try to think back to our time in the cottage together, our first kiss. I can't remember if we were injured at the time, or if I noticed anything healing unexpectedly.

When the storm has passed, Alec and I release ourselves from the tree we've tied ourselves to, and we continue the arduous journey up the mountain, pausing every now and again to entangle ourselves in each other's embrace and share deep, sweet kisses, exalting in the new discovery we've just made. Each time we do, any injuries we've obtained since the last kiss vanish almost instantly.

Three days later, we reach the top of the mountain. Up here the landscape flattens out exponentially, as if someone scraped away the mountain's peak.

Alec and I look at each other with raised eyebrows when we notice a well-worn gray brick entrance to an eerily dark cave across a dirt clearing from us. Even up here, although we see no clouds in the sky, there appears to be no direct sunlight. The entire area is flooded with a dim, gray light, coloring everything around us with the same gray hue. No animals scurry across our path, no insects chirp. All is still.

"That's... not suspicious at all," I say softly, running my thumb along the drawstring of my bow to quell my anxiety. This is it. This is where we'll find the witch. This is where we'll find our mammans. I'm sure of it. My heart beats fast in my chest, and my entire body jitters at the idea, but I have a hard time getting my feet to move. "We should probably go in there, huh?" I ask.

Alec nods, and he swallows. "I suppose we should."

As far as caves go, aside from the thick darkness inside, this one seems like any other. The darkness inside is not so surprising given the lack of light outside.

Still, something about the stillness and the quiet of this cave fills me with fear and doubt, and I fight the urge to turn around and go back down the mountain rather than take a single step inside.

But we've come all this way, and I'm not going home without my mamman.

I move one foot forward, then the other. Alec does the same, and soon we've crossed the clearing and now stand at the entrance. Alec takes my hand and intertwines his fingers with mine, and we venture inside.

The cave is so deeply dark inside that I can barely see, even just within the entrance. I start by groping the cave walls to find my way. I run my fingers against the moist, porous rock, but soon my finger comes across a broken piece of rock, thin and sharp as a razor.

I yank my hand back and instinctively put my finger in my mouth only to be met by the coppery taste of blood. Alec squeezes my other hand, which he's still holding, and I can feel his finger is now bleeding also.

"Sorry," I whisper, and my whisper echoes throughout the cave around us. Alec shrugs, then he pulls the hand he holds up to his lips and plants a small kiss on the back of it. "I have an idea..." I say. I pull at my shirtsleeve until it tears, and then I wrap the cloth around the fletching of one of my arrows. "Do you think you can start a fire?"

Part of me worries that starting a fire in here is a bad idea. It may will draw unwanted attention our way. I also don't want to waste any arrows in case I need them, but we need to be able to see where we're going. This is a totally unfamiliar area, and we know nothing about the infrastructure of these caves – if there are crevasses, or drop-offs, or any number of other things that could bring us harm.

"Of course," Alec says. He digs through his bag to find his flint, and after a few tries, he's able to catch the light, airy material aflame.

The cave lights up to reveal a passage on our left, and a wider entrance ahead of us.

"Which way do you think we should go?" I ask. I wish I had these caves marked on my maps, but as they are now, my maps useless to me. I quickly pull them out and mark down an approximation of where we are. I'll study more later, once we've returned our mammans home safely, but at least I've got a general idea of where we've gone.

Alec looks one way, then the other. "I can't say for sure," he mutters.

One of his hands holds mine, and the other holds our torch.

Although we decided to climb the mountain to avoid going through the caves beneath, I wonder if these caves connect, and one thought plays over and over in my mind: *People who entered the caves below never came back out.*

"I feel like maybe we should go that way," I tell him, feeling almost mesmerized, already stepping toward the wider path that stretches out before us. I don't know quite what we'll find, but something pulls me in that direction.

Alec seems to feel the pull, as well, so we start walking.

It's then that we hear a faint singing.

The sound seems to be coming from the wider path that we just chose to follow. The flickering torchlight illuminates small bits of the cave at a time. Unlike the outside of the mountain, which is covered in that same jagged gray rock, these caves are all a dark brown rock that seems incredibly solid, and bits of the jagged gray rock juts out from the cave walls often.

The cave is damp, and that soft tune echoes through the tunnels.

"What is that?" I ask, eyes wide.

"Ghosts?" Alec asks, his voice shaking. Chills run down my spine. I can go the rest of my life without another encounter with ghosts.

"Hopefully not," I reply. Unfortunately, I think we have to investigate. At least it's some sign that there's something in that direction. "Let's go."

Alec takes some pulling before he's able to get his feet moving again.

As we venture deeper into the cave, something glimmering catches my eye. Curious, I race up to see what it is. Writing has been carved into the cave walls. The carvings are old, and moss has grown in the lines that form the letters.

"Alec, bring the torch. Look at this," I say. I run my fingers over the mossy lettering and try to read the engraved passage as Alec brings the light closer.

Here lies the heart of a broken woman. A used woman. A mocked woman. Here is where we lay to rest her cares and weaknesses. From today forward, she will no longer fear men. She will no longer love them. She will no longer trust women. She will not allow herself to be torn apart, vulnerable, dragged through the streets, ever again. They called her a witch. So be it.

As I read, the singing we hear grows steadily louder, but now that I've started reading, I am so captivated that I just want to finish.

She is exiled, but they are to blame for the mess they will face. Lying men and greedy women who will do anything to obtain what they desire.

Here stands a woman proud, unafraid, and strong. She will carve her own way. She will bind herself in magic, in youth, she will revel in their downfall and watch as their world burns.

Reading this passage carved into the wall of the cave sends chills down my spine.

"Wow," I whisper. I feel as if I've touched history, read the change in mindset for someone broken. "Could this be the witch in the legend Mathilda told me?" I ask, looking up at Alec as if he could possibly have that information. "Do you think she has our mammans?"

Alec frowns at the inscription.

"Only one way to find out," he says.

A few more minutes of wandering through the darkness – following that singing as it grows louder and stronger – finally reveals a living area. The moment we turn the corner and enter the living space, the singing stops.

It really looks like someone is currently living here. There's a stove in a fireplace, a large bed with furs and feathers strung together on it, a chair, a table, and a large wall full of ancient looking cages.

The bars look to be made of both types of rock we've seen here on the mountain. The first rock is the same thick, brown, and sturdy rock that makes up the tunnels. This rock looks to have been used to shape the bars themselves, which are covered in the sharp, fragile gray stones that make up the mountainside.

Inside one of those old cages, my mamman stands with her back to us.

She's filthy, covered from head to toe in grime. Her golden hair is braided back, because no matter what, my mamman always tries to look her best. But it's clear she's been trapped in that cage for some time, and strands of her golden hair appear to have been pulled out. Her dress, once white and lacy is now tattered and brown, with only hints of the soft white material it was once constructed of.

Worst of all is her face. She looks a decade older. Wrinkles and tired lines trace the edges of her face, and beneath the grime she appears as if her very soul is exhausted, some light stolen from her eyes.

In the cage beside my mamman's stands another woman with long, beautiful golden blonde hair. Her face is also filthy, but hers has long lines cleared of the filth from tears streaking down her face. She wears what I imagine was once elegant, sea-blue blouse and matching trousers.

The two women hold hands through the bars of their cages. Their wrists have several big, dark purple bruises on them.

It's only when I croak out, "Mamman?" that their heads snap up, eyes finally landing on us.

"Oh, Alec!" Alec's mamman gasps. Her face lights up as she scrambles to the edge of the cage closest to us. That's when I notice the chains around their ankles, and the sores that cover their feet and ankles.

My mamman looks numb, almost bored.

"Julienne, we've been through this already. She's toying with us. Don't give her the satisfaction," she says flatly, wiping a stray tear from her face. "She's going to get more out of you if you keep getting your hopes up."

If Julienne hears my mamman, she doesn't respond. Instead, she busies herself pressing her body against the bars, reaching her hands out to Alec, who rushes to her side. He reaches his mamman in five long strides. His face is twisted with emotions. Joy. Relief. Love. Pain. Fear.

Alec's mamman clutches his hands with such desperation that her fingernails dig into his skin. My hands sting, and small scarlet lines appear across them. Alec frantically searches the bars for a lock, which he doesn't find.

I blink away the dazed feeling I have seeing them like this, and I chastise myself for just standing here. They need my help.

"Mamman, what *happened* to you? Is it the witch? The one from the stories?" I ask. At the sound of my actual voice – now that I can speak past that croak – my mamman's facial expression shifts from detached to horrified. Her eyes grow so wide that I think her skull must be expanding. All color drains from her face.

"Oh, Lane. It's really you..." she whispers. Then, "Get out." Her voice is low, gruff. There's an urgency in her tone I've never heard her use before. "Both of you. Get out. Now!"

I look toward Alec, hoping he can help me understand.

The conflicting emotions in Julienne's expression are evident. The relief of seeing her son again brightens her face with joy, but the same horror immediately follows.

I find my feet and rush to my mamman in her cage, but she scrambles back away from the bars, shaking her head so furiously that her braid whips her in the face.

"Mamman, we're here for you. We heard that you both were headed into the mountains, that you were acting—"

"Lane!" my mamman interrupts. "You and Alec need to leave. She can't see you. She'll lock you away, steal your youth..." She shudders. "When she comes back..."

"She?" I interrupt. "The witch?"

My mamman shows no surprise in my knowing of a witch, but she also doesn't really answer me. My mamman places her hand on her chest, choking back a sob. She waves her hands in the air, shooing me away. "Go! Go!"

"Not a chance," I say, gritting my teeth. I clutch the bars to her prison cell and press my face against them, trying to reach her. The jagged gray rocks leave tiny cuts on my cheeks. "We're here for *you*. There is no way we're leaving without you!"

Alec's mamman seems to get herself together, and she thrusts her arms all the way through the bars, grasping Alec's biceps with a pressure that makes my arms ache, and she shakes him.

"She's right. You need to go."

"No," Alec says firmly. He pulls away and searches the bars again for a lock we might be able to break. I do the same, but I can't even find a door. The bars go straight from cave floor to ceiling, and I have no idea how these two even got inside the cages in the first place. My mamman has turned away from me. She moves to the farthest corner of the cell, arms wrapped around her torso. Though her dress hangs loosely on her thin body, her shoulder blades are visible beneath the material. She rocks her body weight from one leg to the other, back and forth.

"How do we get you out of here?" I ask Alec's mamman.

A true look of horror freezes on Julienne's face, and her entire body begins to shake. At first I think she's looking at Alec that way, but I realize that she's looking behind him. I pivot on my heels.

I see a tall, extremely thin, proud-looking woman stands with a straight back just behind Alec. Her long, dark hair flows in straight curtains down to her thin waist. She has high cheekbones and wide lips like me. Crows' feet circle her eyes, and deep lines spread from her nose to the outer corners of her mouth.

A long, black-feathered gown sprawls out at the woman's feet and clings tightly to her bodice.

"It's a little late for that, don't you think?" The woman's voice has a musical, hypnotic quality to it, and I find myself mesmerized. Maybe she isn't as bad as I've imagined her to be. It's difficult to picture someone with such a soothing voice having much malintent.

"Excuse me, my... friend and I..." I gesture to Alec, and then to myself. "Have come a very long way looking for our mammans. Now that we're here, we would love to bring them home with us. Would you consider letting them go?"

The request sounds so strangely polite, given the fact that our mammans have been held in exit-less cages with chains around their feet. Still, that's how it the words come out of my mouth.

I glance over at Alec, who looks at me like I've lost my mind, but of course I'm improvising. I have no idea what to say or how to handle a witch. Up until a few months ago, I didn't even think witches might be real, and I was still skeptical that this witch was real until about five seconds ago. I definitely didn't practice what I would say.

This woman looks much less like the old hag I've envisioned. Perhaps she will be more reasonable than I thought she would. Perhaps for a price, there's a chance that she'll make a deal with us. That's her thing, isn't it? Making deals with people?

She raises both dark, thin eyebrows at me.

"No," she says, her voice silky smooth. "Your mammans owe a great debt to me, and they are mine until they've paid their dues."

Her words startle me. That's exactly what our mammans said over and over when they started acting strange and, ultimately, left home.

I'm not sure if Alec reacts because he recognizes this connection as I have, or if he's upset that she refuses to let them go, but he steps forward, hand on the hilt of his sheathed blade, preparing to strike.

The witch raises her hand, and with a flick of her wrist and a disinterested look in her eye, she whispers something I can't hear, and Alec freezes.

With eyes so dark they appear to be black, the witch glares at Alec, looking him up and down before turning her gaze to me.

"Why would I let them go if they owe themselves to me? That's simply bad business. They knew very well the consequences for making a deal with me, and they made the decision to proceed of their own volition," she says, matter-of-factly, as if we aren't talking about people's lives, but about something as mundane as perishable foods.

She actually shrugs her bony shoulders.

It takes me a moment to find my voice, and when I do, it's hoarse. I have a hard time getting the words out. I don't know if she's frozen me, too, or if I'm so shocked by this whole situation that I just don't know what to say.

I wiggle my fingers, and when I realize that I'm not frozen, I do find my voice.

"Perhaps I can offer you something in exchange," I say.

If the witch enjoys making deals, perhaps she'll consider taking something else.

"Lane, *no!*" my mamman shouts.

The witch flicks a furious look at my mamman, and her words catch in her throat. She gags. That horrible sound is followed by a pinched cry as one of her arms bends up behind her back until it pops. Julienne rushes against the bars that separate their cages and reaches out.

"No," she calls before turning to growl at the witch. "Marana, let her go! Stop!"

"Mamman!" I cry.

Alec makes a soft grunt as if he's trying to call out but can't open his mouth. The witch forces my attention back to her when she speaks.

"I have the two lives of noble, powerful women right here. What could you possibly have to offer in exchange?" she asks, raising her thin, dark eyebrows, finally looking at least vaguely intrigued.

But I haven't thought that far ahead. The plan, after all, has always been to find our mammans and bring them home. We never really considered what we would do if we found the witch holding them captive, because neither of us truly believed the witch was real – or at the very least, we didn't expect her to be so powerful after all this time. I silently scold myself for not considering this situation more seriously.

"Well…" I start, stepping forward, weaving my fingers together, bouncing them off of each other. I kick at the cave floor. I need to stall long enough that I can come up with a plan. Find something to barter with. This is my specialty – dealing with traders, discussing prices. "Maybe you could tell me *what* they owe you, and we can agree upon an alternate trade, instead."

The witch doesn't miss a beat. Everyone halts to listen to her response.

"They owe me their lives," the witch says nonchalantly, rolling her dark eyes.

I swallow past a lump in my throat.

Why didn't I expect that?

"They – what?" I ask.

This all sounds so ridiculous. What could they have bargained for that would cost them their *lives*?

The witch, who now looks bemused by my shock, smiles. Although it's not a horrible smile by any means, my blood runs cold.

"Let me tell you a tale," she starts, beginning to pace around the room. Alec's mamman speaks up now, her voice strained, an urgency in it that makes my body tense.

Alec is still frozen in place, and his eyes flick back and forth between me and the witch.

"They don't need to hear this!" Alec's mamman calls out. "They shouldn't have come here, and they were just leaving. Let them go!"

The witch gives her a sideways glance, and Alec's mamman makes a gurgling sound as if she's choking on her tongue.

"No, I think I'll wait to see how this goes. If you two women haven't told your children of the deal you made, their ignorance is on you." Now her attention turns back to me. "Years ago, two great friends made the journey to my home to ask me for a trade. One had a child who was chronically ill, and the other could have no children at all. Each time she grew with child, the baby in her belly would die before she could bare it life."

The witch's long gown drags on the floor behind her as she circles the room. I watch, standing so still that I'm painfully aware of my shallow breathing. I should be doing something, but I feel as if I can't move. My eyes flit to Alec, then to our mammans. I should be thinking up a plan. I try to force an idea to come to me, but the witch's story has captivated me, and I feel compelled to listen. I have so many questions.

Our mammans were friends?

What could possibly be worth trading your own life for?

If the witch intends to take our mammans' lives, why are they still alive?

The witch continues.

"It had been so terribly long since I'd had a trade." At this, she waves her hand through the air dramatically. "And I was *dreadfully* bored. So, I offered them a solution. I would grant the small child his health, and I would gift the other woman the ability to bear healthy children, as requested. Being the gracious goddess that I am, I even granted them both time, so that they could enjoy their gifts. But I was very clear. I told them that in time I would call to them, and they would be required to repay their debts, else their gifts would be revoked.

"I suppose she was already with child," Marana says, looking me over. "That was the first and only time I've ever made a deal with two women for the same purpose at the same time." The witch now fans out both hands, gesturing to the five of us.

"Here we are. What I didn't anticipate, however, is that their children would show up, as well. That is indeed an interesting twist."

Her amused smile returns, and she now circles me. She places a long fingernail beneath my chin and presses up just enough for me to feel it poke my skin. I keep my eyes on her until I hear Alec's voice. It seems he's found some way to unfreeze his tongue, at least.

"Leave her be, *witch*," he says, spitting out the last word as if it were poison in his mouth.

The witch snaps her head back to look at him, leaving her finger under my chin. Her lips curl into a wicked grin, nose and forehead crinkling to the point that she looks more animal than human.

"Who are you calling witch, *boy*?" she hisses back at him.

The way she addresses him, the hatred in her eyes, makes me worry so much more for Alec's safety than for my own.

"Stay out of this, Alec," I warn him.

But now her attention is on his face, and the look she's giving him makes me believe she could tear him limb from limb without ever lifting a finger.

"You *men*. Always interfering when it's *convenient* for you," the witch says. "Never acting out of love, only out of lust and self-interest. That is the curse you leave with the women who care for you."

I watch as his fingers curl ever so slightly, then his hand bends at the wrist, and he's actually able to grasp his sword. I don't know how he's managing to push past her magic, but from the bulging veins in his neck and the tightness I feel in my own muscles, I'm sure it's taking everything he's got. All the while, his eyes remain locked on the witch's. I feel the moment he breaks free of her spell, because I finally feel like I can move again.

In one quick motion, Alec is able to draw his blade and swings it at her, but she's too fast. She waves her hand abruptly and sends Alec flying across the cave, clashing painfully with the damp, rocky wall. I let out a cry as the air is knocked out of me, and Alec sucks in huge gasps of air.

Instead of falling, however, he adheres to the wall as if held in place by invisible chains.

The witch makes her way to him in smooth, serpentine paths. She takes her hand and runs it across his chest, pausing briefly over his heart. She digs her fingernails into his chest, and I grit my teeth against the pain.

"I had a man like you, once. Strong, capable. Charming. He used me, as he was lying with another. When I found out about the two of them, I tried to rise up, but I was weakened by the love I felt for him. I was sure he'd see sense, choose me, at the very least because the other woman he was involved with was married to our Patriarch. But he chose the other, and the two of them tortured me, mocked me, dragged me naked through the streets for all to see. Men like you aren't capable of love, or goodness, you see. So, I killed him, and his whore, too."

"You know nothing of me," Alec says through clenched teeth. Again, the witch looks amused, and she raises her eyebrows at him. "See this?" She wiggles her fingers against his chest, and Alec cries out in pain. I cry out, too.

Although her fingers are merely on the surface of his chest, they seem to reach much deeper than that, as if the magic in her fingertips is poison seeping through the skin. It feels as if she's gripping his – and my – heart. "*This* tells me everything I need to know."

From across the cave, the witch turns around, releasing Alec's chest from her grip, and the both of us suck in a deep, relieved breath. The witch's eyes fall on me again, and this time they seem almost too black, as though the whites of her eyes have been swallowed up, leaving only slivers of white in the corners.

"I'll make you a deal, girl," the witch purrs. "In exchange for your mammans, I will keep this foul mouthed, entitled pest. It's been ages since I've tortured a man." She looks him over. "He's strong, full of life. He'll last me so much longer than those two," she says, pointing over at the cages that hold our mammans. "Besides, I've drained quite a bit of youth from them already. This one here has so much more *vitality* left in him."

35

"Please, no!" I shout. I will my body to move. I reach for my bow and draw an arrow, but the witch merely looks at me, and my limbs go numb. My weapons drop to the floor with a disheartening *thud*. "There has to be something else you want, right? You said so yourself, men are no good, right?" I'm not even sure what I'm saying makes any sense, but I'm desperate.

The witch looks at me curiously.

"Not entirely true," she says, her dark grin widening. "They hold back, so ripping their screams from them is so much more pleasurable. Be honest, girl. I'll bet he drives you crazy, anyway. His mamman must have been eager to leave him behind when I called, and I know all too well his pappan wants nothing to do with him. He's a sellsword. A drunk. No one will bat an eye at his absence."

Her words strike Alec like a dagger. How could she possibly know Alec's insecurities just by touching his chest?

His wide, amber eyes glisten, and his mouth turns to a thin, straight line. His jaw sets, and I know he believes the witch's words to his core.

The witch turns back to Alec, fingers pointed at his chest once again, this time ready to strike. I'm filled with dread that she's powerful enough to rip out his heart right here in front of me. Never mind the fact that I would die, too. I have to stop her, for his sake. For mine. I can't watch her do this.

"*Wait!*" I scream, finally able to move again. I lunge forward. My heart feels like it's being crushed in my chest as I try to think of something, anything, that will get her to stop.

She pauses mid-thrust and eyes me.

"Of course, how silly of me. This is the part where you profess that you're *in love with him.* How pathetically predictable. I tire so of this plot; I've seen it far too many times." The witch shrugs, as if this is perfectly obvious information. "He'll only hurt you in the end." She sighs and returns her attention to Alec.

"Take me," I blurt. It isn't until the words have already escaped my lips that I realize what I've said.

In half a moment, all of my doubts surface.

What about my mamman? How will I ensure she gets home safely? How will I know the witch will go for it? If she does, what about my family? My sister? Zaid? What about the plans I had for my life? All of those would be gone.

Not to mention... I'm not sure what she intends to do if she takes my deal. Alec and I are still bound. Whatever tortures I face, he'll experience. But at least he'll be free, and since I'm not a man, I imagine she won't be as harsh with me. She's made her distain for men *very* clear.

Maybe he'll have a better chance this way.

None of it matters. If she'll agree to spare all three of them in exchange for me, if she will let Alec go, that's a deal I've got to make. Alec will ensure my mamman gets home safely – I know he will.

Mamman will take care of Pappan and Lilah. I pray to the Fates that Zaid will understand how grateful I am for what he has done for me, and that he will go on to make great changes in the world as he has planned to do.

If I stay here, the only person who will be disappointed that my plans didn't come to fruition will be me. I think I can live with that... if she allows me to live at all.

The witch shifts her weight as she waits for me to continue. She throws her hands to her hips.

"What?" she asks.

At least I've got her attention.

"I said," I tell her, raising my voice. I lift my chin and hold my head up high. "Take me. Let the others go."

The witch scoffs.

"What makes you think I'll trade their lives for yours?" she asks, and I'm just grateful I've given her some sort of pause.

"You don't want *him*," I say, pointing at Alec. "As you said, nobody would miss him, so what would taking him do, anyway? Spare you one annoyance? Give you a moment of entertainment? It's true – he's fit, and he's young. I'm fit as well, and I'm younger."

The witch turns her gaze back to Alec, then looks me over again. I take the opportunity to wrack my brain, hoping to try and make myself sound more appealing. I can hear my mamman trying to move behind me, and I can feel Alec's eyes boring into me, but I hold the witch's gaze steadily with mine.

"And more so," I say. "You said it yourself: He's a drunk. He has poisoned his body through with ale, but I haven't; I've barely touched the stuff. If you're looking for sustainable youth, take me."

I worry that asking her to agree to this, asking her to take my youth, will put Alec still in danger, but I comfort myself knowing that he will be far away from here, out of her reach. And if she's planning to use my youth up over time, then I have time to figure out how to break our bond, to keep him safe.

The witch listens impatiently to my case, and finally raises one dark eyebrow, lifting her hand to tap her lower lip with one long, pointed fingernail.

"Lane, don't!" Alec shouts from his spot on the wall through gritted teeth. Without looking at him, the witch makes a fist, and Alec cries out in pain. My body fills with a strange, nagging pain, as if every muscle is being strained. It's only when the witch relaxes her fist that the pain eases. It takes me a moment to catch my breath, but I do my best to stand straight.

I clench my fists.

"Interesting," she says, actually considering my offer.

I step forward, and with each breath I take I find more courage with which to steel myself, and I gain more confidence in my decision.

"You knew all those things about Alec when you touched him," I say. "Well, touch me. You'll never find another person with the determination I have to protect these people. I'm healthy, young, and strong; and I'd be happy to give that all to you. Just please, let them go." When the witch doesn't respond, I keep talking, trying to think of something I could say to make up her mind. "I read on the walls of your passageway that you were hurt, that you want to watch people pay for their mistakes. Well, these three are going to make the world better, so people like the ones who hurt you won't hurt anyone else. Each of them has a purpose."

I look at my mamman, who has tears streaming silently down her dirty face.

"My mamman is on the Women's Council, in a position she earned not from making some deal with you, but due to her own hard work and wisdom. She's a vital asset, and she cares so deeply for my younger sister, who I *know* will lead us into the future," I tell the witch, and as I say these words, I know them to be true.

I gesture to Alec's mamman.

"This woman here is just as important. She's working with the Women's Council to lead our continent toward prosperity. Without her, things are already falling into disarray. Think of the influence she – *you* – could have, now that she knows what you've been through."

The witch seems to mull this over, and I take her silence as a chance to argue for Alec's life. I look at him now, and tears fill my eyes. Although we're across the room, the connection we have through our eye contact makes me feel as if I'm in his arms.

"And Alec is a fighter. He's so much more than you know. He's kind, and positive, and so strong. He's got big things coming his way. He's going to help these women pave the way for greater, more widespread peace. He'll get them home safely." I know I've just contradicted my earlier statement, but I need to let Alec know she's wrong about him.

I hope he takes these words with him.

The witch raises her chin and looks down at me.

"And what about you?" she asks. "What will the world be missing if *you* were to stay?"

I'm certain she can see my doubts, my dreams and hopes, but I simply shrug.

"Nothing *they* couldn't live without. I'll leave some maps of the world unfinished. I'll leave an empty spot in my pappan's business. But *they* are going to make all the difference." I know there's more to this answer. I'll be leaving behind my sister, my family, the friends I have made. But I need to convince her that this is a trade worth making, and so far, she seems interested enough in the argument I've made for the sake of our continent. "I know it's a lot to ask, but if you care for the wellbeing of Maran at all, you'll let these three go."

"I've been around a long time," the witch starts, and she begins walking again as she speaks. "I've granted women with the ability to bear children. I've gifted them with fortune, intelligence, status, health... all the things that would make them more successful, more powerful, more fulfilled. Yet, I have never made a deal with someone whose intentions were not to improve their own situation or experience. You choosing to make this deal, even though I can see in your heart that it's a near impossible decision for you... well, I just haven't seen this before."

Nodding, I blink back tears and do my best to keep my head held high.

"Maran, you said?" the witch asks, her tone hinting at surprise.

Again, I nod.

Of all the things she knows, I find it strange that she's questioning the name of our continent.

"Interesting..." she says again, only this time, she follows it up with, "I thought I was long forgotten. It seems that after all this time, even my name is still sacred. Marana..." she says, coming to a halt in front of me, reaching out her long-fingered hand. "All right, girl. You have yourself a deal. You will stay, and your precious loved ones can go. *If* they leave quickly and swear on their lives and yours never to return."

Just as I open my mouth to agree to the witch's terms, Alec yells, "Lane, no!"

My mamman fights against her restraints, voice catching still in her throat, but it's clear she's trying to shout out to me as well.

It's too late.

I reach out and shake the witch's hand. Her fingers dig into my wrist, drawing blood that soaks up into her fingernails. I wince and watch as the blood she's absorbed fills her with a youthful glow, erasing the creases and wrinkles on her hands and face. She takes in a deep, sensual breath and smiles.

"I am not without mercy," she says, looking much younger and kinder. "I have been like you before. I will allow you a moment to say goodbye, but then they leave. Once I tell you it's time, I will not wait around for them to be prompted again."

"Thank you. Thank you so much," I say, nodding, choking back a sob.

Marana waves her hands with a bored expression on her newly youthful face, releasing our mammans from their painful holds and sending Alec plummeting to the floor. Marana backs away as Alec jumps to his feet, scrambling toward me. In another instant, Marana turns and closes her fists in my mamman's direction, and the bars that contained our mammans disappear. The two women rush to pull Alec and me into a tight embrace.

"Lane, *what have you done?*" Mamman asks, brushing loose strands of hair out of my face. Tears stream wildly down her face, and for the first time in my entire life, she looks truly afraid. For the first time in my life, she doesn't raise her chin in response to our situation. "You *cannot* go back on a deal with her. She will always find a way to get her dues."

Alec's mamman pulls him into a tight hug that knocks the breath out of him – and me – and checks his face and hands. At the same time, she notices the fingernail marks on his arm just above his wrist, where mine are. She doesn't say anything about it, though. I think at this point, she's simply grateful to see him again, grateful he's okay.

I take my mamman's shaking, too skinny hands in mine. She really does look tired, sickly, worn.

"I know," I tell her. "I meant what I said. I won't go back on this deal – not with your lives at stake. I'm staying here."

"No—" she insists, squeezing my hands so tightly that they ache.

"Mamman, this is my decision. Let me do this for you. You've done so much for me. Sacrificed so much. Fates, you made a deal with a witch, gave up your life even to bring me into this world. I won't forget that. But you can protect Lilah better than I can, and she needs you. Who else is going to teach her to contribute her best to the Women's Council? You know that's never been me."

"I cannot lose my child," my mamman says, pulling her hands away from mine so she can place them on my cheeks. She holds my face close to hers, and her eyes flit back and forth madly, as if she's trying to memorize my face in this single moment. Her thumbs trace my cheekbones, my nose, my jaw.

For the first time in years, I feel the depth of my mamman's love, and I cling to every second of it, trying to hold onto it so that when they leave, I'll have this to remember her by.

Alec and his mamman whisper quietly to each other as they embrace.

"I know it's hard, ma'," I tell my mamman. "Just think about what you have at home. Think about the child who still needs you so. The deal's already been struck, and you said it yourself – I can't go back. Go. You don't have much time."

Mamman nods. As much as I know she loves me, she's always been much closer with my sister, and I know my mamman is dying to get back to Lilah at home. Lilah is the more promising leader, too, and as my mamman is a member of the Women's Council who takes her work to heart, this knowledge can't be taken lightly.

My mamman looks to Julienne, and Julienne nods. She and my mamman both step aside, linking arms. Alec strides toward me. Dark circles form beneath his eyes from the shadow his deep frown casts upon his face.

"You shouldn't have done that," he says, his voice low.

I nod, swallowing past the urge to fall into his arms and sob. I reach out and take his hands, holding them tightly in mine, running my fingers across their surface.

"I suppose it's easier this way. Now we won't need to figure out how things will work between us," I reply, though the words feel flat, muted. I can't tell him what I truly feel. I can't tell him that I've never felt about anyone the way I feel about him. I can't tell him that the thought of not having him around every day makes me feel like my heart is going to implode. No, if I keep it casual, then maybe he'll be able to move on – to find peace out there in the world.

Alec closes the small remaining distance between us. I'm shocked by the tears that fill his amber eyes and gloss them over, falling freely onto his cheeks. He presses his forehead against mine, and when he speaks, his voice breaks.

"Don't do that," he says. "Not if you plan to stay here. Don't lie to me."

At his words, I find I can no longer hold back my own tears of. They spill over, trailing down my face in streams.

I close my eyes.

"Go, Alec. Please."

Across the room, Marana speaks.

"Your time is up. Your friends need to go now, or the deal is off, and I will keep all of you."

I find myself digging my fingers into Alec's forearms, pressing my forehead so hard against his that it hurts.

"No," I sob quietly. I just told him to leave, but I can't get myself to release him from my grip.

I don't want to let them go. I don't want to stay here with this woman who trades people's lives as if they're nothing. Alec holds onto me just as tightly.

Now both of us are crying, and I can't tell if the wetness on my cheeks is from my tears or his. Suddenly, he tenses in my arms, sliding one hand out of my grasp. This is it. He's going to say goodbye and leave with our mammans, and I'll never see him again.

My free hand runs up the back of his neck. I pull him in and press my lips to his, pouring into him all the desperation I feel. The wounds on our arms from my deal with the witch disappear as quickly as she made them.

That kiss says everything. In that instant Alec and I relive every moment, every touch, everything said and unsaid, every smile, every kiss since we met. We relive that single night we shared intimately together, and the fight that followed.

I pray that kiss tells him just how much he means to me – that foolish, happy-go-lucky mercenary with his love of ale and traveling, with his ridiculous charm.

"I said, that's enough," Marana says, raising her voice, which now turns hoarse and haggard. She flies at us, placing a long-nailed hand on Alec's shoulder. She opens her mouth as if to say something else, but Alec turns, letting me go.

Alec's free hand, the one he pulled away from me – which I hadn't realized had grasped his dagger – drives deep into the witch's ribcage.

Her dark eyes grow unnaturally wide as she registers what he's done.

Dark blood pools out around Alec's fingers, and Marana struggles to breathe, drawing in a harrowing, gurgling breath.

From somewhere deep within the mountain's cave system, an icy breeze rushes, whistling, into the witch's living space. It stings my skin and chills my very soul as it brushes past me. My entire body is filled with a cold that sends me shivering, and I suddenly feel a hollowness like nothing I've ever felt before.

The world feels frozen as I watch the life drain from this magical, ancient woman.

Marana's hand reaches up to Alec's face in a last-stitch effort to get him away from her. Her long fingernails rake down his jaw, and as small lines of blood trickle down onto his neck, the witch's eyes flutter closed. She gives a half-gasp and her body goes limp, held up only by the hilt of Alec's dagger and the strength of his arm.

Alec yanks his dagger free with a sickening squish, and the witch's body drops.

We watch in awe as her body ages instantly.

Her skin dries up and erodes completely, leaving bones that are accented by the black feathered gown that drapes over them.

I stare at her, unable to move my gaze from the body at our feet until Alec takes my hand again.

"Lane," my mamman says, rushing to embrace me.

I cling to Alec's hand and hug her back, though I'm still shocked speechless and shaking. With my free hand, I grasp at my mamman's filthy clothing. Her relieved sobs shake the two of us, and we hold each other for a long while.

Was I really going to let them leave without me? Was I so eager to deliver my fate to the witch?

I was.

Although I hadn't had any time to really process the weight of my decision, I'm flooded with relief that I get to go home with them, glad I won't have to spend another moment with that witch.

Thanks to Alec, this witch will never have the chance to break apart a family again. She will never make another deal.

This knowledge provides me some comfort, and I'm reminded of this deeply sad emptiness I now feel. My mamman backs away, and I give her a small smile.

"Alec, love," Julienne says, speaking softly, but with an urgency in her tone. "We really should be going. Ailene and I have been here for quite some time now, and we'd rather not stick around to see what happens next. We've got a long journey home."

Alec gives my hand another squeeze, and I sigh.

Finally, my attention turns to him and the scratches he's procured on his face.

Instinctively, my hand finds my own jaw, expecting to feel the same wound, touch the now cooling blood there.

All I feel is smooth, albeit filthy skin.

My eyes grow wide, and my heart begins to pound. I'm unsure if the somber expression on Alec's face is due to the wild moment that just ensued or if he, too, is aware of what I've just discovered. I fear he feels the emptiness, too.

Our bond has been broken.

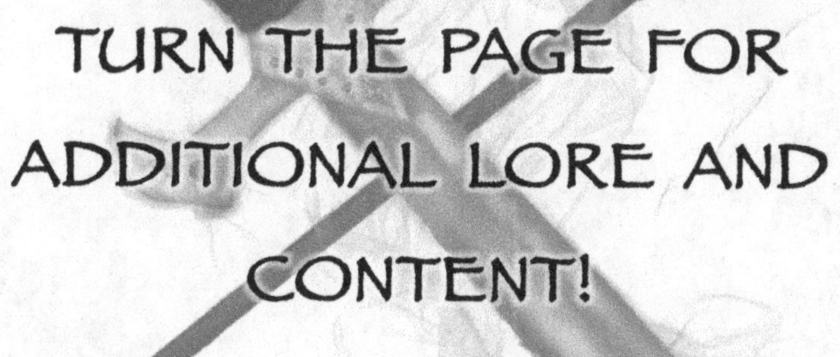

TURN THE PAGE FOR
ADDITIONAL LORE AND
CONTENT!

Excerpt from Women's Council: A History – Forging a New Path

The Patriarchy

Centuries ago, prior to the dawn of the Women's Council, the continent of Maran was unknown territory, and the continent we now refer to as the Nameless Country, was bustling and thriving. This continent was ruled by a Patriarchy, a ruthless group of men driven by their lust for women and desire for power. Women were merely tools, unable to make decisions for themselves or speak up against the wrongdoings of others. The Patriarchy set strict laws that applied to everyone but themselves, and the corruption that ensued bred chaos.

There were men outside the Patriarchy who were not blinded by such desires and greed. These men were also powerless against those who oppressed them, and they set an alliance with a small but determined group of women who wished for change.

Slowly, downtrodden citizens began meeting in the dead of night, whispering about a land beyond the mountains, a land where they might be safe from the ever-blooming madness that surrounded them and filled their waking moments with dread.

These whispers led to murmurs, murmurs to shouts. Soon enough, word had spread, and a movement began. Hundreds of people gathered, ready to make a better life for themselves. Many citizens stayed, blinded by the way of life they had known for so long, or afraid of the consequences they might face for leaving their world behind. Those that dared leave, however, collected what little belongings they could carry and began the long, arduous trek through the Baskan mountains.

Diary Entry of an Unnamed Settler

Our group travels slowly through the foot of the Baskan mountains. Winter is fast approaching, and our youth and elderly are taking ill. Some have already begun to perish. I fear if we do not find shelter soon, none of us will see spring.

The mountains are steep, their rocks jagged and fragile, difficult and unsafe for many of us to climb. If our people do not perish from exposure to the elements or starvation, many of us will likely face our doom at the mountain's mercy.

Anna, my beloved wife, has suggested that we turn back, face the penalty for our betrayals. But members of the Patriarchy are following us, and I fear facing those consequences will be far worse a fate than losing our lives here in the mountains. At least here, we're choosing our freedom, whatever it may cost us.

That is all I shall write for today. Light is dim, and I must tend to the ill. I overheard that our fearless leaders have found some caves for us to rest in. Perhaps these will keep us safe from the Patriarchy and the elements alike.

Untitled Document Retelling the Tale of Marana the Witch

Hundreds of years ago, quite some time before the migration southward and the settlement of Maran, Marana was a young, happy girl in love with a soldier. She had an innate magic, an old magic, that she practiced and played with and honed. The soldier she loved used her, however. Used her body and her heart. She found him one night in the arms of another woman, a friend of hers who was married to the Patriarch. She was heartbroken.

When she confronted the woman and asked why she had taken her love when the woman was already married, the woman scoffed. She said that the Patriarch could give her more than a soldier ever could, but her heart did not belong to him. Instead, she had found love and pleasure outside her marriage. The woman could have everything she wanted. She laughed at Marana, and Marana swore she would tell, for the Patriarch needed to know what the woman had done.

The woman was cruel, and she got to the Patriarch before Marana could. She spread rumors that Marana was ruining marriages, bewitching people's husbands. She was publicly humiliated by the people in her village. They stripped her, flogged her, dragged her through the streets. Meanwhile, the woman laughed. The Patriarch exiled Marana, tore her from her home and left her, bleeding and beaten, to find her own path somewhere else. She roamed the village outskirts for days.

She felt her heart blackening, as she could see no good in the people who had hurt her. She snuck back into her village one night, using her magic to take the lives of all those who had participated, everyone who had wronged her. Then, she snuck away into the night and found herself a new home in the Baskan mountains. There, she waited, until her story and her village were long forgotten, and others passed through the mountains seeking refuge from what would be known to later generations as the Nameless Country.

Retelling of the Legend of the Witch

For months, the group was lost inside the maze of tunnels. More died, and many considered resorting to eating their dead to survive, once the livestock had all been consumed. It was dark times. They prayed for an answer, for the Fates to help them. Finally, however, one day, a new face appeared in the crowd. An old woman appeared, someone who said she could help, that she knew the way out of these horrible tunnels. She offered to lead them to the other side of the mountain.

Each day, the woman appeared, mingled with the crowd. She seemed genuinely interested in getting to know the deepest desires of each person she spoke with as she led them through the tunnels. Each evening, she would disappear.

Finally, they made it out of the mountains. The group was so relieved. When the leaders asked what they could do to repay the debt they owed her for saving them, she couldn't think of anything they could possibly give her. Instead, she told them that, should she ever call on them, they would return to her.

Deeply grateful, the women named their new home after the woman.

After Maran's settlers had begun to build their new societies, particularly Grand Council Keep, Parth, Nerine, etc., and they began having children and settling into their new lives, Marana called for those initial founders – now older women themselves, and they left their daughters and sons behind to make the journey back. When they got there, they expected that Marana would need some kind of assistance, but she punished them all. Marana reminded them that they would need to pay their debts.

Those who had wished for their children to survive were either killed, or lost their children (now grown adults), in some horrible accident. Marana gained strength from those lives lost. From those who requested power, Marana kept them locked away in her cave, where she slowly drained their lifeforce. Marana regained some youth.

Over the following two generations, others would make the journey to see Marana, either looking for their loved ones or looking for some wish to be granted. Each time, Marana used her magic to bind them to her, so that when she made the call (when her own life force began draining), she would somehow take what they owed her.

Over time, fewer and fewer people went to see the witch, so she had fewer people to come back to feed her life force until she was nearly starved. Marana's name was only remembered as the name of their continent. Her story became merely a bedtime story that women told their children, then almost nothing at all.

Excerpt from The Structure and Creation of the Women's Council, Vol. 1

Purpose

After migrating away from Lithe, henceforth referred to as Nameless Country, the women who led the families and people who remained wanted to create a system that would focus on harboring peace. We have settled a new continent hoping to relinquish the hold the Patriarchy has had on our families.

Goals of the Women's Council

To build a society centered on peace and prosperity, where women will have a voice and a choice.

To provide support and relief to all parts of Maran.
> *The focus of the Women's Council is to give, not just seek power and status for ourselves.*

To solve problems and spread peace throughout the continent.
> *The Women's Council shall allow the cities of the continent space and support to develop their own cultures, while maintaining balance and peace.*
>> *The Patriarchy in the Nameless Country was so deeply intwined in everything that the people felt smammaned. They had to worship according to the Patriarchy's guidance. They had to follow strict laws. Every town developed in a similar way under the thumb of the Patriarchy. Creativity was stifled. Music had to be approved, or those who played unapproved music or expressed themselves in any way not deemed appropriate by the Patriarch would be made into an example. This example usually included public flogging, or even branding or a death sentence. Life in the Nameless Country was gray. In Maran, we will foster creativity and individualism.*

The Women's Council shall have the following structure:

Each city or village shall have one female representative. There shall be one Grand Countess.

The Grand Countess's job is to compile all the information brought in by the continent's representatives. She shall reside in Grand Council Keep for the duration of her assignment (this assignment is typically 10 years, unless unforeseen circumstances arise). The Grand Countess Councils with and guides the representatives in their support of each city.

The representatives shall speak for their city or village they represent. Each city shall have a smaller Council with varying numbers throughout Maran. The representatives are to take any information they gather from their own city Councils to Grand Council Keep at their quarterly meetings.

The Women's Council also has men who shall have supporting roles – accounting, trade management, and of course, military (though military focus shall be on protection, defense, and keeping the peace rather than conquest, invasion, or control).

Women's Council Motto
We do what we can today for a peaceful tomorrow.

Fates: Player's Guide

Nobody knows how old the game of Fates actually is, though people have been playing Fates since at least the settlement of Maran. The symbols on the dice depend on who made them. However, the symbols below are some you may come across as you play.

"The game is one part storytelling, one part strategy, and the rest luck."
— Alec Montrose, Bound

Pieces involved in playing Fates:
Four dice, each with unique symbols carved on them that together tell your story.

- **One black die (can be red): This represents your fate.**
  - -ӿ- means you die – if you die, your money goes to the storyteller.
  - ✳ means you prosper – you survive, and each player pays you.
  - -/- means you escape narrowly – you pay some money, either to the storyteller or to another player. If someone helped you, you pay that person.
  - - means your fate is unknown. Roll your fate again.
  - | | | means you share the wealth – money is split as evenly as possible amongst players (storyteller excluded). If this is your fate, you receive any remaining funds if money cannot be evenly distributed.

- **One tan die (can be white): This represents the situation.**
  - ✊ means someone helped you. In this case, if you escape narrowly, your money goes to that person.
  - ✊ ✊ means you help someone else. They may owe you money.
  - ◖ means someone has hurt you. Blood has been spilled. This often results in that player (or fictitious character – storyteller) taking your money.
  - ~ means an accident has occurred. Your money goes to the storyteller unless the Fates intervene.
  - ₒ means someone has robbed you. Your money goes to them.
  - ◌ means clean slate. Player's choice – reroll all dice, or roll chosen dice again. Limit one reroll unless entire dice set is rolled, and you roll another ◌ .

- o **One green die (usually green, can sometimes be a different color): This represents your journey**.
  - ■ ⚘ means you have been affected by the weather.
  - ■ ∿ means you have been affected by a creature.
  - ■ ⊚ means you have been affected by your environment (setting or situation).
  - ■ ♥ means you have been affected by matters of the heart.
  - ■ ♟ means you have been affected by another person. If playing with multiple players, they may help you, or you may be helped by a fictitious character. This decision is based on what other players have rolled on their turns, and on the storyteller's will.
  - ■ ♟ means the Fates have intervened. When the Fates intervene, your Fate is the opposite of what you rolled. {example: If you roll an -x- (your fate is death) and ♟ (the Fates intervene), you then ✳ (prosper – you earn money and live)}.

- o **One blue die: This represents your cost (how much money is given or taken in a turn).**
  - ■ This die is numbered either with numbers up to 6, or with even numbers only up to 12. In elite groups, these dice have also been known to be numbered in 5's.
  - ■ Cost starts low – tins. However, every five tins is equal to a copper, every five copper pieces is equal to one silver, and so on. Payment can be adjusted depending on the wealth of those playing. Lowest price is determined prior to starting. In higher class circles, payments start with silvers instead of tins, and go up to gold pieces, and even into precious jewels.

Setup: The game can be played with anywhere between two and five players at a time. More than five players takes too long and becomes too chaotic, so a soft limit was placed. There are a few ways to play with a group – and it's player's choice.

- o 1. Players team up. This increases the chances of players coming out with money for each person included.
- o 2. Players take turns. Dice is rolled for each person, and each player gets to hear his or her story as it plays out. This increases the chances of any one player coming away with the most money.

- o **The role of the storyteller:** The storyteller acts as a catalyst for every event, and although the symbols remain similar and tell the bones of a person's fate (what troubles they run into, whether they live or die, where their money goes), the story is the most integral part of the game. Having an experienced storyteller is what captivates most players and has them playing again and again.

To play: The storyteller holds in his or her hands the dice. Dice can be rolled one at a time, or simultaneously. Whatever the dice land on, that's the structure for the story. The storyteller orders the dice and tells the player of his fate. Storyteller orders the dice in whatever way best helps the flow of the story.

WANT TO SEE WHAT HAPPENS NEXT IN LANE AND ALEC'S JOURNEY?

Check back for Bound's sequel –

Severed, set to release in

March 2025!

Breyanna I.L. Evans is the author of several published works, including two children's stories, a poetry compilation, a novella, and three novels, with more on the way.

After graduating with her bachelor's degree in creative writing, Breyanna taught middle school and high school English. She now works as a reading intervention specialist and tutor mentor with the University of Utah Reading Clinic, hoping to help educators and struggling readers enhance their skills.

In her free time, Breyanna enjoys watching movies (fantasy or scary ones, mostly), painting, drawing, writing, reading, playing Dark Souls, and spending as much time as possible with her family.

Acknowledgements

I want to take this page space to thank everyone who helped in the development and creation of this book. Without all of you, this story would not have come to life so beautifully!

Thank you...

Danielle, my dev. editor, for the crucial early feedback you provided. Lane's motivations are so much stronger thanks to your support. Thank you for reminding me that my readers can't read my mind, and that the extra world building makes all the difference!

Zulie, for your willingness to talk with me and answer all of my "does this make sense?" type questions. Thank you also for always supporting my writing, and for your wonderful feedback and reviews!

Imogen, for reading and editing, for providing suggestions, and for asking questions! You are wonderful. Zaid is grateful for you, too!

Gilbert, thank you for your many phone calls. They seriously boosted my morale immensely. Thank you for geeking out with me. You're so sweet.

Brandon, for everything. For letting me talk endlessly about my books and ideas. For supporting me in every step of the process. For reading my work and providing me with critical feedback. For asking the hard questions. And for all your patience with me as I "just finish this scene" at 10 PM.

There are so many more people who have been an integral part of this process, I could fill a whole other book with my gratitude. You know who you are. Thank you for everything.

Acknowledgements

And now, to all the backers who supported this project's KickStarter, THANK YOU! Each and every one of you has made my dream for this book so much more attainable.

Gee Rothvoss

Gilbert James

Zulie Lockhart

Brandon Evans

Imogen James

Hanna James

Elivia Camper

Natalie

Максим Стоялов

Maran
Laden's Way
Maranee River
Keep
Siren's Way
Grand Council Keep
Nerine
Parth
Shale
Maranee Falls
Dunnen
Finnik
SunSpar
Palandra

Baskan Mountains
Baskan Desert
Darkwood
Maruaco Desert
Murkwater Lake
Murkwater Swamp
Bandit Camp
Nodon
Helna
Bandit Camp
Helnan Grasslands
Shradan
Flagua
Shradan Mines
N
W
E
S